Death Comes at Dawn

Book 2 of the Drum Series
The story of taming the west.

by

W.R. Benton

LOOSE CANNON ENTERPRISES
Paradise, CA

2016 Edition
ISBN 978-1-944476-19-9

www.loose-cannon.com

The Drum Series
by W.R. Benton

Silently Beats the Drum, Book 1

Death Comes at Dawn, Book 2

Green River, Book 3

Explore more than 30 other books, ebooks and audiobooks by this award winning and best selling author, at:
http://www.amazon.com/author/wrbenton

Dedications

To Nik, a special young man, full of love and energy, who loves his pap-pa.

To the memory of William Robert (W.R.) Patton, my grandfather, he was the type of strong and determined man who moved west and faced the dangers unflinchingly.

Table of Contents

"…that nothing's so sacred as honor and nothing's so loyal as love."
Wyatt Earp

"I had ambition not only to go farther than any man had ever been before, but as far as it was possible for a man to go."
Captain James Cook

"The future belongs to those who believe in the beauty of their dreams."
Eleanor Roosevelt

CHAPTER
1

J eb had just made camp and put on a pot of pinto beans on the fire, when he noticed he had visitors. For the last few hours he'd felt the nearness of someone, but was unsure who it might be. Since he was smack dab in the middle of Sioux country, he suspected it might be a group that didn't know him. He'd explained to old Moses, just the day before, how the Sioux were made up of many different bands, and while they were accepted in the group Buffalo Hump led, the other bands of Sioux had no such notions. *Then again,* he thought as he reached over and added a small log to his fire, *it might be Blackfoot.*

Near the fire, and tending to the horses, was Moses. The old black man was good with animals and it had quickly been decided, without a word spoken, he'd be responsible for the animals each time they camped. As he wiped a big roan down with dry grass, he spoke without turning his head and in a low voice, "They're out there. I saw one of 'em just a minute ago, and they're Sioux."

"Did ya know the man, Moses?" Jeb asked as he opened his palms and held them close to the fire to warm. While it was late fall, the really cold weather hadn't visited yet, though he knew it could come any day.

"Nope, that one I ain't never seen before." The old man replied, walked over to the fire where he quickly sat down and added, "So, what are we goin' to do now?"

Jeb thought for a couple of minutes, stood, and called out loudly in the Sioux tongue, *"Come, my friends, because it grows cold and I have a warm fire with food I will share with my Sioux brothers."*

Minutes passed slowly without any sounds and then a single young warrior walked into the open. He was a tall man for a Sioux, well over six feet tall, his eyes were as dark as coal, and his face was scarred from small pox. He didn't speak, nor did he threaten, he simply stood and watched the two men near the fire.

Seems to be just one of 'em, but why just one? I don't think I've ever seen just one warrior out alone, unless he's hunting. This feller is not wearing paint, so maybe he's a hunter, Jeb thought as he gave the warrior a big smile and said, *"Come, you can share my coffee and the warmth of my fire."*

As the warrior neared the fire, Jeb could see dried blood on his left shoulder and a fresh scalp on his belt. The scalp was that of another Indian, so Jeb kept his mouth shut as the man slowly walked toward him. Sitting on the ground by the fire, the brave suddenly spoke for the first time, *"I am called Many Horses and I am of the northern Sioux."*

"Ain't that the bunch that Crow Killer runs way up north?" Moses asked Jeb as he squatted by the fire and placed a large cast iron skillet on the hot coals.

"I think so, but I only met the man once and that was a long while back."

"Is your chief a big man named Crow Killer?" Moses asked the warrior as he glanced at the big man.

"Yes, the great Crow Killer is our war leader. Do you know of him?"

"I am called One Leg Standing by the Southern Sioux war chief, Buffalo Hump, and I am his son. I have heard my father speak often of the brave war chief Crow Killer, yet I have only spoken to him one time." Jeb replied as he pushed his hat back on his head so he could see the warrior better in the failing light.

If Many Horses was surprised that a white man was the son of Buffalo Hump he didn't show it, instead he spoke, *"I have been sent by Crow Killer to speak to Hump. I am to tell him of many things that have happened to my people."*

"Is your trail one of war or one of peace?" Jeb asked as he leaned forward and met the warrior's black and narrow eyes.

The brave hesitated for just a second or two and then said, *"Many white eyes have come to our lands. The buffalo are dying more each day by white men who take only the skins and leave the meat to rot in the sun to feed the vultures. These white men have guns that shoot many times and can kill from far away. I have been sent to Hump to see what can be done to stop the white man from killing our buffalo."*

"Shit," Moses suddenly said as he turned and met Jeb's eyes, "this is a fine mess. What's with the buffalo killin'?"

Jeb shook his head, met the old man's eyes and replied, "Moses, I told Hump years back a day would come when white men would be here in great numbers. I told 'em when they came, they'd outnumber the leaves on the trees. Now, I ain't sure, but I suspect there is a market for buffalo robes, since beaver pews have dropped off the market almost forty years ago. These white men are out to make an easy living."

"I don't foller ya none a-tall. Why would there be a need to kill buffalo? I mean, what in the world would a bunch of people back east need or want a buffalo skin fer?"

"Well, I ain't rightly sure Moses, but see, white people want this land and they'll eventually get it too. Back in the war I heard some officers talking once and a captain said the buffalo was the key to wiping the Injuns out. He said if the buffalo were killed off the Injuns would start to starve and a starving people would be easy to control. So, either a civilian market for buffalo robes has these white hunters out in force, or the government has created a market for the skins."

Moses looked confused for a minute, then reached up and as he scratched the left side of his face, he glanced at Jeb and said, "I don't understand. Either the people back east want these robes, or they don't. Right?"

Jeb gave a light laugh and replied, "No, it could be the government has made a market for the robes to kill off the Injuns food source. Now, I ain't sure about none of this, but I'd not put it past 'em to do just that. See, the government can get civilian leather tanners and such to ask for the robes and as they get the hides, why they'd even pay the companies a little bit to take the skins in. Then, the government finds a good way to use the hides so folks in the cities will want 'em. They'll try to keep the price lower than cow hides too. This stuff is all about supply and demand, don't ya see how it would work?"

"Kind of, but it's confusin' to my way of thinkin'. I mean, how can ya make somebody want somethin' they don't need?"

"Moses, the leather from a buffalo can be used to make anything cow leather can be used for, right? Ya could make bridles, saddles, shirts, shoes, belts, holsters, and the list goes on. Not to mention a buff robe is the warmest damn thing a feller or a woman can sleep under when the weather turns cold. No I suspect this wasn't just some hide man's idea and it scares the hell out of me. Don't you see, if they make the demand big enough, and keep the prices lower than regular leather goods, why, the days of the Injun will be over almost as fast as ya can snap your fingers."

Moses thought for a minute, raised his head and said, "Lordy Jeb, I see one hell of a war comin' then. I don't think fer one single minute these Injuns are a-gonna jus' quit bein' injuns without a fight. And, you

and me both know they ain't gonna stand by and scratch their asses as
the buffalo are all kilt off either."

And blood will flow to the point the Civil War will look small, Jeb
thought as he glanced quickly at the warrior by the fire.

Morning found Jeb and Moses riding beside the Sioux warrior
Many Horses as they moved east toward the village of Hump. While
the morning had dawned cloudy and the sound of distant thunder
could be heard, Jeb thought the majority of the storm would pass them
by to the north. Still, he pulled his old Union cavalry hat down low as
a light misting rain began to fall.

"Jeb?" Moses asked as he rode his bay up beside the one legged
white man a few hours later.

"What's on your mind Moses?"

"Do ya think we could talk to them folks in the gov'ment back east
and put a stop to the killin' of the buff's?"

Jeb gave a loud snort and replied, "Damn me if I know. But, all
things considered, I don't think they'd listen. Oh, they might sign a
treaty or two, but things wouldn't change in the end, not one iota. See,
once a market for something has been started and there is easy money
to be made, well, people will keep trying to make the money. I suspect
a treaty signed between the government and the Injuns wouldn't mean
shit to a bunch of buffalo hunters out to make a quick buck."

"Then we got us a bushel basket full of trouble comin' 'cause I
know there ain't no Injun out here that's gonna let the buffalo get killed
off without one hell of a fight. I mean, buffalo are their main food.
And, what're we gonna do when the brown stuff hits the fence? I mean,
which side will we be on?"

"I don't know, I honestly don't know."

The village of Hump was only a short distance away and it was
near noon when Jeb noticed the first member of the dog soldier clan
watching them as they drew near. As guards of the village, the dog soldiers protected The People as they went about everyday life and rarely
did someone approach the Sioux without notice. Jeb knew the man
watching them and suspected he'd let them ride into the village unques-
tioned. As the adopted son of Buffalo Hump, Jeb could come and go as
he pleased. And Moses was considered by The People to be a buffalo
God, so both of the men were able to relax as soon as the dog soldier
was seen.

Less than twenty minutes after first sighting the guard, Jeb and his
small group entered the village and rode to the lodge of Buffalo Hump.
As he dismounted, the young white man wondered what Hump would
do about the wasteful killing of the buffalo. The war chief was an intel-

ligent man, but one dedicated completely to the old ways. It was very likely a full blown war was about to erupt and that would place Jeb, Moses, and Faye between a rock and a hard place.

As the young boys took the horses away to the main herd, Jeb softly scratched on the leather flap that covered the doorway to Hump's lodge, and he heard a low command to enter.

The inside of the lodge was dim though it was well past the noon hour. A little fire burned in the center of the lodge and Hump was sitting by the dancing flames eating from a small wooden bowl. As his visitors entered his lodge, the old chief placed his bowl on the ground near his right foot and said, *"Welcome to my lodge, my son. First we will eat and then we will speak. It fills my heart with joy to see my son, One Leg Standing, has returned home to his people. And, I am also happy to see my friend Many Horses has honored me with a visit. Come, let us eat now and then we will speak."*

The meal was a simple hot soup filled with deer meat, roots, wild onions and some other vegetables Jeb didn't recognize, but he always figured if an Injun could eat it so could he. Kneeling beside the fire, Hump's wife added some meat skewered on green sticks and made sure they were leaning toward the hot coals to cook. Soon, in less than thirty minutes, the simple meal was finished.

"Now," Hump spoke as he leaned back against his wicker backrest, *"what is the purpose of a visit from my friend Many Horses."*

Over the next fifteen minutes or so, Many Horses explained in great detail what he knew of the white buffalo hunters. When he finished the lodge was deathly quiet as Hump considered what he had just learned. While his people too had noticed some butchered animals during the last year, there had not been many. *Could it be,* he thought, *that this is a thing that will not last long?* It could be some whites have need of robes only and already have much meat for the coming winter. They have the white man's buffalo, with the spotted skin and long horns, so maybe they fear the coming moons of deep cold.

Jeb and Moses eyed each other and as their eyes locked, both men were thinking of what Hump might say. While no large group of Indians had yet formed under the leadership of a single man, Hump was just the man to do the organizing if the need was there. *But,* thought Jeb as he felt a tightness deep in his gut, *if it comes to war and Hump is able to pull the various tribes together, the plains will run red with blood.*

"Return to Crow Killer and speak my words to him. I do not think this thing of killing the great one for hides is a thing that will last. Tell him that I think it is a small number of white men, less than three

hands, which need robes to fight off the deep cold of the coming months. Also, tell him, if the killing of our brother the buffalo continues with the coming of a new season, we will stop the white man." Hump spoke as he leaned forward from his backrest and met the eyes of Many Horses.

The younger Sioux warrior nodded in understanding and then replied, *"Your words I will carry back to Crow Killer. I will speak as you have spoken."*

Hump, indicated the conversation was finished by emptying his pipe. Many Horses stood and walked from the lodge.

"What now?" Moses asked later as they walked toward a lodge the Sioux kept for Jeb.

"We wait for now. I suspect the killing won't stop with the coming of spring, unless we're able to talk to them hide hunters and even then I think we'll be wastin' our time. Besides," Jeb said as he pulled the entrance flap to his lodge back, "I'm getting married in the morning, so I'm not going to worry about it all right now."

Moses had completely forgotten about Jeb's coming marriage to Speaks Much and with a big grin he asked, "Ya shore ya wanna jump broom with that gal?"

"Moses, what kind of talk is that from a man who's married? And, I happen to know ya and Yellow Leaf are very happy together."

"Yup, we're happy, so far, but marryin' up is a serious step. I think a feller should think on it fer a long spell, 'cause it ain't to be taken lightly."

Jeb laughed and replied, "Moses, I love the woman and she says she loves me. I've found a very beautiful woman and a smart one to boot, and to my way of thinkin' I'd be a damned fool not to marry her."

"Well, that could all be, but 'member that once a woman closes the trap on a man things are different from that point on. Ya'll no longer jus' have yer butt to take care of, but hers as well, and before long some youngsters too. It's serious business Jeb."

Jeb turned and grinned at his old friend as he said, "Ya know a man is less than a full man without a good woman in his life. I've never in my life, old friend, felt like I do about any woman like I do Speaks Much. Even Nancy, who turned her back on me a few years back I loved, but it was a shallow love, and not as deep as my love for Speaks."

"I hear ya, but still, don't take this marryin' as a little thing. It'll change yer life, mayhap make it better, but it is a hard thing at times, too. I'm sure ya and Speaks Much will be happy, only keep in mind ya always gotta work hard to make a marriage work. When I was a slave, well, times was different. After seein' my kids sold off and my wife took up the river, why I lost the will to live. It hurts a man when his wife is no longer there, 'cause he's only half full."

Jeb patted old Moses on his right shoulder and replied, "Moses, there ain't nobody going to sell off Speaks Much and if there are any children they'll be well taken care of."

Moses, who stood slowly shaking his head, finally said, "It don't gotta be a person that takes yer loved ones from ya, it can be God too. Death is jus' one way of losin' what matters most in a feller's life. Ya stay on yer toes and remember what I jus' told ya."

Jeb gave a mighty laugh, turned to Moses and said, "Aye, I'll remember Moses and I want to thank ya for being my friend."

"Yer a good man and the first white man I ever called friend. And, ya remember, if ya ever need me or somethin', jus' let me know. I'll always be around to help ya, son."

Jeb grinned and entered his lodge. He would be married to a white woman who had been taken in by The People when she was just a child. While she spoke passable English, and after talking with Jeb over the last year she had learned more, she still struggled at times to make herself fully understood. The love Jeb felt for Speaks was deep and he'd absolutely no second thoughts about his upcoming marriage. Soon they'd be riding side by side.

Over time he'd learned her white name was Betty, though it was only when they were alone and away from the Sioux that Jeb called her by that name. Of her last name she had no memory and both quickly agreed it didn't matter. All she could remember was her family had been headed out west in a wagon and were attacked by a large group of Blackfoot. It was only because she had been out picking wild flowers that she'd not died as well. After the killing of her family she'd wandered for almost a week on the open plains before a wolf of the Dog Soldiers spotted her hungry frame and brought her to The People. Less than six months later she was a full member of the tribe.

Laying down on his buffalo robe, Jeb was still thinking of the beautiful woman when he drifted off to sleep.

This morning just as the sun was coming up Jeb was married to Speaks Much.

As soon as the brief wedding ceremony was complete, Jeb and Betty were taken to a beautiful white lodge outside of the village. It was with great dignity and show that Jeb and Betty enter the lodge for their first night together as man and wife.

As soon as the leather flap covering the entrance dropped, Jeb pulled his new wife close, looked deeply into her brown eyes and said, "I love you Betty. I'm looking forward to a long life with ya, and a lodge full of children. Or, if ya want we can start a farm and live as a white farmer does."

Kissing him on the left cheek, Betty grinned and replied, "Jeb, we've no need to discuss the distant future on this day. Today I want only to love you and to be loved. Come, my husband, let us warm our robes."

Jeb kneeled in front of his new wife and grasped he hem of her long white deer skin dress. Slowly, so he could full appreciate her beauty, he pulled the dress up and over her head. It was not until the leather dress fell to the dirt at their feet that he took a good look at her wonderful body. *Many men would kill for a woman like this,* he thought as he pulled her close and kissed the side of her neck, feeling her shudder.

"Do you like what you have seen?" Betty teased as she kissed him.

CHAPTER
2

Four days later Jeb and Betty were tying their horses to a hitching post outside of Brown's trading post. The day was hot for that time of the year and Jeb could feel sweat running down his spine as he looked over at his wife, giving her a big grin. They'd decided some days before to go to the post and pick up some supplies they would need to make a home complete. Betty had also expressed a deep desire to pick up a few simple gingham dresses and other things a white woman would want to have. And Jeb, not worried about money since he still had gold coins he had taken from a white killer a little over a year ago, agreed on the trip.

The small brass bell mounted above the door gave a jingle as the two entered the store and stood by the door. Betty was instantly over-whelmed by the smells and sight of all of the goods she saw lining the aisles and stacked on shelves behind the counter. She could smell smoked meats, tobacco, leather, gun oil, and many other wonderful aromas. Though she was a white woman, the store was the first one she could remember being in.

"I'm sorry Jeb, but Injun women ain't allowed in the store. That ain't my say so, it comes from the company that stocks the store." A portly man said as he looked over the counter and noticed Betty.

"She ain't no Injun, she's white, Mister Brown, and she's my new wife. We had an emergency up in the hills and the Sioux were nice enough to loan hear a dress until we could get her a new one." Jeb lied as he made his way slowly to the counter.

"Well, hell, now that's a hoss of a different color, it surely is. Howdy do, my name is Brown, ma'am, and I run this place." He gave a big warm grin and then continued, "I got the best selection of stock this side of Saint Louis and my prices are lower than most."

"Well, let my wife pick out three dresses and some other clothing she needs. And, we also need five pounds of cured bacon, twenty pounds of pinto beans, four wool blankets, four gallons of whiskey, six pounds of Arbuckles coffee, three pounds of salt and add three pounds of black pepper. Oh, before I forget, add a pound of horehound candy and one pound of rock candy. How much will all of that cost me?" Jeb asked as he placed his hands on the glass display case in front of him.

"Well, you be using cash money on the barrow head, or credit?" the storekeeper asked as his eyes narrowed in thought and then he added, "So, you finally got married, huh?"

"Yep, I did Mister Brown." Jeb replied with a big smile and then continued, "Cash, I don't use credit if I can help it and ya should know that by now."

"The cost will be nigh on fifteen dollars Jeb, but I have to see what dresses she picks out before I can honestly say." The store clerk said as he added the items on a piece of brown paper on the counter top.

"Betty, ya get the dresses ya want and I think a sun bonnet would be good as well." Jeb spoke over his shoulder to his wife as he looked over the items in the display case.

"But, Jeb they are so expensive. Are you sure we can afford to get them?"

"Listen folks, I don't get much call fer women's pre-made dresses, so I can let ya have three fer the price of two. Hell, ya can't beat that now can ya?" The fat man smiled as he spoke and Jeb suspected by his tone that business had been slow, especially customers with cash.

Glancing at the big man, Jeb noticed he wore his wire-rimmed glasses perched low on his long and wide nose. His hair, what little remained, was long and his eyes had a friendly gleam to them. The young man expected Mister Brown was honest enough, and while his smile seemed warm and genuine, he appeared to either be worried about something or waiting for someone.

"How's business been?" Jeb asked as he picked up a wool horse blanket and looked it over.

"Fair, except for the buffalo hunters. They're a foul group and ya can smell 'em long before ya can see 'em. They carry the smell of death they do. With hides goin' fer five dollars apiece and a normal wagon load of hide numbering 'round a hundred or more, they make pretty good money."

Jeb lowered the horse blanket he'd been looking at and turned to speak to the man, "Hide hunters? Ya get a lot of 'em in here?"

"Only within the last year or so. There's a big call fer buffalo hides back east and I can sell every hide I can get my hands on." The big man spoke, gave a weak grin and then added, "But, I don't hold much to doin' it. Sooner or later the Injuns are gonna start raisin' hell over the killin' of them buffalo. Ya mark my words; we're in for a fight once they get wind of what's really goin' on."

At that point the little bell above the door sounded and two big men walked into the small store. Jeb didn't like the looks of either man, but he kept his mouth shut as they walked up to the counter.

"Give us a jug of whiskey." The bigger of the two men ordered as he pulled a gold coin from his right trouser pocket and placed in on the glass counter.

"Well, look over there Frank, we got us a squaw." The other man spoke and Jeb could feel his anger rise at the words.

Frank, the big man, turned and looked at his partner as he replied, "Leave her alone Wilcox. Ya should know by now any squaw around a tradin' post or fort will give ya the French pox. Hell, they're all a bunch of filthy bitches anyway."

Jeb moved to face the big man named Frank and said, "That woman is my wife. She is a white woman and you'll apologize to her right now."

Frank laughed, glanced over at Wilcox and said, "For a one legged sumbitch he's sure got nerve."

"I said ya'll apologize!" Jeb spoke brusquely.

The big man made a sudden move for his pistol, but before it could even clear leather there was the loud blast of a pistol shot, and dust flew from the middle of his chest as blood was blown out his back. The impact from the lead slug knocked him violently against the wall, where his body slowly slid down to the floor. The wall behind him had a bright red trail of blood dripping down.

"Go easy with that gun mister! I didn't say nothin' bad 'bout yer wife and I don't plan to either. I . . . jess thought she was an Injun, 'cause she's wearin'' them skins." Wilcox spoke as he raised both of his hands up and away from his pistol.

"Who in the hell are ya two?" Jeb asked as he turned to cover the man with his pistol. While the man seemed scared and he knew a scared man was often a dangerous man.

"We're buffalo hunters. We work fer a man called Laugherty, but I don't know his first name."

"Move over to yer partner there and check 'em out. Only do it slowly." Jeb ordered as he quickly glanced at Betty to make sure she was alright.

Wilcox moved to Frank's side, squatted and looked him over closely before he said, "He's dead as hell. I don't know yer name mister, but

Frank is Buffalo Watkin's kid brother. If I was ya, I'd fork and hoss and get the hell out of here while ya can. Now, I saw it all, and it was a fair fight, but I don't think that'll mean shit to Buffalo."

Jeb walked over to Wilcox and pulled the man's pistol from his holster. Turning, he handed it to Brown behind the counter as he said, "Mister Brown will keep yer gun until I leave and as far as yer man Buffalo goes, he can start the dance but he'll have to pay the band. Ya tell your boss that a Missouri boy named Jeb Patton killed his brother because he had a big mouth and insulted my wife. Not to mention he was a might slow at pulling his shootin' iron."

"Can I take his body now?" Wilcox asked as he glanced nervously at Jeb.

"Get his ass out of here. I didn't start this mess and ya damned well know it too. Ya just make sure Buffalo knows his brother brought it all on himself."

"I'll tell 'em, but it won't matter none though. He'll come for ya."

Jeb chuckled, put his pistol back in his holster, and then said, "Any time Wilcox, but let him know I live up in the mountains. Oh, and one more thing."

Wilcox slowly stood and asked, "What's that?"

"If I ever see you again, I'll kill ya on sight. Now, get his ass out of here and ya stay out until I'm gone. Iffen I was ya, I'd consider checkin' out the weather up around Montana way for a few years. Ya might live longer up there in the fresh air."

Twenty minutes later the goods were tied to the pack horse and Jeb scanned the area around the store for any movement, but he saw nothing. Mounting, the two of them rode from the trading post and headed west. Jeb wanted to make a few miles before dark and after killing the man named Frank he wanted his wife as far from the post as possible. For the remainder of the afternoon they rode at a mile after mile walk that placed them near a shallow slow moving stream near sundown. There were a few trees that lined a small meadow near the stream and Jeb decided it would make a good night camp.

As they stacked the goods they'd just purchased, constructed a lean-to over the supplies, and got a fire going, they made small talk.

"Jeb, why did that fight start back at the store? I know you had to kill the man because he went for his gun, but why did it turn ugly?"

The young man was confused at first and then he realized Betty didn't understand the ways of white people yet. Oh, she was white enough and she spoke English well, but she'd spent most of her life as a Sioux, so she thought like a Sioux. After thinking for a few minutes, he placed a small log on his fire, turned and said, "Betty, that man insulted ya when he called ya a filthy bitch. Any husband worth his salt wouldn't allow that sort of thing to be said about his wife."

"Jeb, they were just words and I'm but a woman."

"Maybe I ain't explaining this right. If ya were married to the chief of the village and another man spoke bad things about ya in front of your husband, what would happen?"

"My husband would stand up for me because of his position in the tribe and there would be a fight. A chief is a man of honor, to be respected, and so is his wife. But, Jeb, you are not a chief."

Jeb gave a light chuckle, smiled and said, "Betty among white men, all of them think they're a chief and they all ask for respect. Many of them don't get respect, so they demand it. Of those few men that have a sense of personal honor, dignity, and self-respect they don't need to demand it because it is freely given. I have always been a respected man, so when the man said bad things about ya, it was if he was sayin' them about me too. Do ya understand?"

"I think I understand it. I know you are a warrior and a man of honor, but do those men not know it?" Betty asked with a confused look in her eyes.

"Not out here they don't. See, out west a man can be what he claims to be and as long as he can do what he says he can, no questions will be asked. But, at times, strangers will come around and they ain't got no idea who they're talking to most of the time. I've known lawyers, bankers, and even university professors out here and by looking at them you'd never know what they'd once been. Those two men didn't know me or you, but they assumed ya were a squaw. I have found it's not smart to assume a damned thing out here because it can get you killed."

Suddenly, Betty turned her head toward the trail they had been on and as Jeb looked around he noticed the horses looking that way as well. Pulling his pistol, he said, "We have someone coming up our back trail. Ya get behind that log and don't move an inch. I'll see who might be bothering us on such a beautiful day."

Betty pulled her knife and the pistol Jeb had given her and moved behind the log. No sooner was she out of sight than he heard the hammer on her pistol lock back with a loud snap. Jeb moved away from the fire and into the trees on the right side of the campsite and wait for his visitors.

"Hallo the camp! Can we come in, we're friendly and in need of help." A male voice called from the trail a few minutes later.

"Who are ya and what kind of help do ya need?" Jeb yelled and quickly checked to make sure Betty was still behind the log.

"My name is Jefferson Jones and I have a woman with me that has a high fever."

"Come on in, but keep yer rifle up high in yer left hand. If ya so much as sneeze, I'll blow daylight through you. Do ya understand me?"

"I'll do it, but are you always this trusting?"

Jeb gave a low chuckle and then replied in a loud voice, "Yep, every damned time and that's why I've lived so long."

A few minutes later a big black man walked up to the fire, holding a scattergun in his left hand, and as he looked around he couldn't see a single soul. The man was well over six foot tall, maybe two hundred pounds and had the body of a blacksmith. Jeb, deciding the man was not out to harm him, stepped from the trees and made his way to the fire.

"Howdy do." The big man said as Jeb approached.

Jeb extended his right hand and as they shook, he could see his greeting had caught the man off guard. Giving a big smile, Jeb said, "Glad to meet ya Jefferson, my name is Jeb Patton."

"Mister Patton, my wife is in the back of our wagon and she has a very high fever. I know it ain't nothing that other people can catch or me and the kids would have it too. I'm scared to death she's gonna die on me."

Jeb, realizing the man was in need of serious help, called out, "Betty, come on out. We've a man here with a sick wife."

When Betty stood from behind the log, Jefferson gave a light laugh and said, "I can see she's of the trusting type too!"

"I will do what I can to help, but where is she?" Betty spoke as she neared the fire.

"She's in the wagon with a high fever. Do ya want to doctor her in the wagon or under our lean-to?" Jeb asked as he placed his pistol back in his holster.

"Bring her to the lean-to, that way I am closer to the fire if I need it."

Twenty minutes later the man's wife had been taken from the wagon and placed under Jeb's lean-to so Betty could tend to her. According to what Betty could tell the black woman was suffering from fever and diarrhea brought on by drinking bad water. Four little black kids between the ages of four and ten were sitting just outside the simple shelter watching Betty as she worked.

"Your wife has the healing touch, she surely has, and not many people do." Jefferson spoke as Jeb poured two cups of coffee and handed one to the man.

"Betty was raised by the Sioux and Injuns know how to treat things we don't even know about. While I don't always agree with what they do, it damned sure seems to work most of the time. Accordin' to Betty, yer wife has the bloody flux and bad water causes it."

"Jeb, why are you helping us? I mean you're a white man and from what I can tell from your accent, a Southern man as well." Jefferson asked after a few minutes of silence.

Jeb laughed, met Jefferson's eyes and then replied, "So, ya think I'm a plantation owner and don't like black folks? I've been around the tree a few times, Jefferson, and I judge no man by his color or religion."

At first Jefferson's eyes narrowed, but slowly a grin began to grow and he said, "No, not that at all. It's just hard to believe a white man would help us, especially one from the south."

"Jefferson," Jeb said as he placed his coffee cup down by his left foot, "I was a sergeant in the Confederate army during the war and I fought hard to protect our way of life, but I ain't never owned another person and I've never had the desire to either. I fought because a hundred thousand damned Yankee's invaded my country and to protect my states rights. Not once did I ever think I was fightin' to keep slavery alive in the Deep South, though that might have been what the big plantation owners had in mind durin' the war."

"I don't know about none of that. I only knew that when the war was over I was freed, but I had no job and couldn't find one. So, I heard about this small town out west that is made up mostly of freed slaves and I decided to come out this way." Jefferson spoke and then glanced over his shoulder to look at his wife.

"I have a good friend near here named Moses. Now me and him go back a ways and we've traveled many a mile together, but I think ya'll be surprised when you meet him because his skin is much darker than yours." Jeb spoke and then broke into a loud horse laugh.

"I'll be damned. You mean to tell me your friend's a black man?" Jefferson asked as he looked at Jeb with confusion in his dark eyes.

"Yep and there are other blacks around too. Now, Faye, we picked up along the trail and she's been with us every step of the way out west. She was married to a Sioux warrior, but he got killed last year on a raid against the Blackfoot. Let me tell ya, she's a pretty young woman with a good mind, but right now she is facin' hard times with a new baby and no husband."

At that point Betty walked up to the fire, poured herself a cup of the strong coffee and sat on the log near the fire. After a sip of the strong brew she said with a concerned voice, "The woman may die. I have seen this sickness before and it comes from drinking bad water. I have given her a drink made from the inner bark of a willow tree, but only time will tell if she'll make it, or cross over to the other side. She is passing too much blood and I cannot get it to stop."

"Oh, Lord God! She can't die! What in the world will me and my kids do?" Jefferson spoke, his tone filled with fear. When Jeb looked over at the man he could see the pain in his eyes.

"Jefferson, my wife didn't say she would die, she said she could die. If ya live out here long enough ya'll soon discover that there are other dangers besides Injuns. The water can kill ya, the animals can kill ya and the weather can for damned sure kill ya. This is a rough land we live in and one mistake is all it takes to end a life. Now, I suggest ya get yer kids and let's feed 'em some beans and bacon. Then, I want them to get to sleep early, because if your wife is better in the morning we need to be movin' on." As Jeb spoke he removed the lid from the cast iron pot the beans were simmering in and stirred them with a wooden spoon.

Hours later, as the fire cracked and popped and the flames danced wildly, Jeb was awakened by Betty's gentle touch on his right arm. Opening his eye's he could see her face in the dim firelight.

"The raven woman has journeyed to the other side. She no longer lives." Betty said as she shook her head.

CHAPTER
3

E arly the next morning the group gathered by a shallow grave Jeb had dug under a large oak tree. The wind was slight, but the sky was filled with low rain clouds, which seemed to add more gloom to an already disheartening day. The two oldest children of Jefferson's kept up a constant flow of tears as they cried for their dead mother, while the younger two simply looked on with big eyes unsure what was going on around them.

The sun briefly broke through the clouds as the small body of the woman was lowered into the grave. Jeb and Jefferson wrapped the dead woman in an old horse blanket and the two older children placed some wild flowers the early frost hadn't killed inside the cover with their mother. As soon as the grave was filled with soil and rocks placed on top to keep animals from digging up the body, a short prayer was said.

"Lord, please take care of my wife. Sara was a good woman, Lord, full of laughter and she was a good God fearing woman too. We're gonna miss her Lord, but she's in your hands now, so I'd appreciate if you'd let her know we love her. Ashes to ashes and dust to dust, Amen," Jefferson prayed in a weak cracking voice as both of his hands rested on a spade stuck in the soil near the foot of the grave.

Jeb placed a crude cross he'd made with his Bowie knife at the head of the grave and then put his hat back on his head. The group walked back to camp and Betty placed the leftover beans on the hot coals to warm up, as Jeb sliced some bacon and put the coffee pot on to boil. He thought of the black family and wondered what they'd do now with the mother dead.

"Ya given any thought to what ya'll do now?" Jeb asked as he looked at the grieving black man sitting by the fire.

"No, I really ain't thought much about it. I might still head to that town we was headed to, but I ain't sure. I don't really want to live in no town, 'cause it ain't a good place to rear kids. All that talk about a town was my wife's idea, not mine. What I might do is find a good spot of land and start a farm."

"Ya ever done much farmin'?"

Jefferson laughed and replied, "Jeb, when I was a slave I was a house slave. I didn't do much serious farming, but every slave had a small garden patch so they could always have more to eat. When I was only a boy the master had me learn how to blacksmith and I did that for a few years until he learned I had a good head for numbers and such."

"What happened after he found that out?" Jeb asked because he always found the past lives of the freed slaves to be interesting and none of the stories were ever the same.

"Well, Master Sidwell he taught me how to read, write and do my sums. Then, after I learned as much as I could, he made me the book-keeper for his place. Now, I not only know how to grow a family garden, but I also know how to manage a large place. If I can get some help, I could start a farm or a ranch."

"There's a lot of first-rate land out here, Jefferson, and good people like ya should be on it too. Yer only problem will be Injuns and they might not be a problem, if ya talk with 'em before ya settle down." Jeb spoke and then thought, *I'll bet old Hump would let this man have some land, if he gave him some gifts or such.*

Jefferson grew excited at the thought of owning a farm, grinned, and then asked, "Jeb, do you know any others of my kind out here?"

Jeb thought for a minute, pulled his hat off, ran his fingers through his hair, and then said, "Yep, I know of a few, like I said before. Moses, he lives with me most of the time, but he's usually with the Sioux durin' the summers. I'm sure he'd give ya hand, but keep in mind he's a real old man. He wouldn't be much use as a working hand, but he's a smart old coot and his mind alone would be a big help to ya. Faye, but I already told ya about her. There is also a younger man named Abe that lives way back in the mountains with his wife. I'm sure Abe would help ya put up a cabin and the outer buildings if ya want. He's a good man, as big as the mountain he lives on, and he has a voice that sounds like thunder."

"Well, that's all find and dandy, but what in the world am I going to do with my kids? It would be hard putting a cabin up, getting the first crops out, and watching them at the same time."

Jeb gave a low chuckle and replied, "Maybe not. I know a young woman that might do it, or if push comes to shove, and I'm sure my wife Betty would do it. Now, I'm sure both of them would do the job just long enough for ya to get a cabin made and then ya'll be on your own."

Jefferson thought for a few minutes without speaking and Jeb could hear the fire cracking during the silence. Finally, the man said, "Why would you do this for me and mine? I don't mean to be rude, but I've never had a white man do a thing for me, except beat me or keep me hungry. So, excuse me if I seem a bit on the uneasy side of all of this."

"Jefferson, out here yer color means little to most honest folks. Oh, they might not want to eat dinner with ya, or have ya visit their homes, but they'll respect ya if yer a man of honor. Keep yer word when ya give it, work hard, be honest and ya'll do well out here, even if yer blue. As far as me helping ya, well, I'll help any man that I feel wants to help himself. The west already has a lot of black folks out here and they're settling down and making homes, farms, and businesses. And, most of 'em are good folks too."

"Well, what now?" Jefferson said as he thought, *this is a good white man. I can't believe he'll help me get started and not want something from me. Maybe this move west was the best thing I could have done, but what else could I have done? I just thank the Lord I met this man instead of someone else.*

"I'll take you to see Abe and his wife. The trail will be rough, but we'll make it as long as ya take it slow and easy. The last thing we need is for ya to break down or lose some of yer stock." Jeb spoke, stood, and adjusted his gun belt as he added, "Jefferson, do ya have a gun?"

"I got that old scatter gun I put back in the wagon. I got me a pistol with a belt too, but I didn't think it'd be smart for a black man to walk around wearing a gun."

Jeb's eyes narrowed for a second, and then he stated, "Get the pistol and wear it at all times, except when you sleep, but even then keep in close. This is a rough land ya've come to Jefferson and ya'll need that gun a time or two in the future. As long as ya think long and hard before ya pull it, ya'll do fine."

Jefferson stood and walked off to his wagon. A few minutes later he returned wearing the pistol belt and Jeb noticed it held a new Colt. What surprised Jeb was the gun looked natural on the man, so he asked, "Ya know how to use that thing?"

Jefferson smiled, met Jeb's eyes and replied, "I can do the job, if need be."

We'll see my friend, it's only a matter of time, Jeb thought as he walked over and started breaking camp. Soon, the small camp was broken down and the gear loaded either on the pack horse or in Jefferson's wagon. Mounting, the small group headed north by west toward the cabin Abe had on the side of a large mountain.

The rain started a little after noon and while it was light, dark rolling clouds overhead promised to make the rest of the day a wet one. Betty dismounted and tied her horse to the black man's wagon and crawled inside to keep the children company. Soon the children were listening to Betty tell the story of a brave Sioux warrior as the wagon bounced and groaned over the rough trail. Jeb, like Jefferson, pulled his hat down lower and continued to move forward in the falling rain.

Near sundown the wagon suddenly quivered, the left rear wagon wheel gave a loud crack, and the wagon leaned far to the left side. Jefferson, an experienced man, immediately stopped the wagon and jumped from the seat. He was standing beside the wheel when Jeb rode up.

"What happened?" Jeb asked and suspected either the hub or a spoke had broken.

"Two spokes broke on the wheel. I should have checked them before we started the trip this morning, but with my wife's death I forgot." Jefferson replied as he knelt by the damaged wheel.

"Ya got a spare wheel?"

"Nope, I didn't have enough money to buy all the things I needed. I had to choose between a spare wagon tongue or a wheel, so you know which I took."

"Betty!" Jeb yelled as he dismounted and made his way to Jefferson.

The canvas at the rear of the wagon was pulled back and Betty's head poked out as she asked, "What do you need Jeb?"

"A wheel has broken on the wagon and I need for ya and the kids to get out and maybe get a camp set up over to the right, in those trees. If ya can do that, then Jefferson and I'll see what we can do about fixing this wheel."

After Betty and the four children left, Jeb looked the wheel over closely then asked, "I don't see how it can be fixed, do ya?"

"It don't look like it can be, not without some hardwood and more time than I have to do the job." Jefferson looked up at the sky and then continued, "I've some canvas tarp in the wagon, let's get it and make a shelter for the woman and kids. I don't think this rain is going to stop any time soon. Then, we'll fix this the only way we can do it and that's by making a skid. I could cut the ass off this wagon and make it a two wheeler, but I don't want to do that. How much further to where this feller Abe lives?"

"Not far, mayhap only three miles. I could go get him, but I know he ain't got no wheel and it would take time in this weather to get there and back." Jeb replied as he squatted and placed a wooden jack under the left rear of the wagon.

In less than thirty minutes a lean-to shelter was up, the kids were under it, and Betty was cooking a big pot of beans and smoked bacon. Later, when the beans were almost done, she'd put on a Dutch oven of cornbread. Betty loved to cook and though she'd lived most of her life with the Sioux, she had discovered she loved the taste of beans and they brought back faint memories of her earlier family. Maybe she'd been too young, or perhaps her mind had shut down, but she had no memory of the killing of her family. It was as if that complete day had been erased from her mind.

Jeb watched as the young man cut a thick and long pole from a nearby oak tree and trimmed it with his big knife. As he worked he said, "We'll lash this oak limb to the axle and make a drag. It can't be used for a long time or for real rough moving, but it'll last until we get to Abe's place. I've used a drag before and while I don't like to use them, because it's harder on the horses, it'll do in a pinch."

He's a smart man, Jeb thought as he watched the man use the big knife on the hard wood.

It was a little longer than an hour before the wagon was repaired. The drag was a crude looking affair, but Jeb suspected Jefferson knew what he was talking about. While Jeb had often driven wagons, carriages, or buggies, when he lived back east, he'd not used one at all since he'd come west. He owned little and wagons were slow and hard to use on rough mountain trails, so he usually had a pack horse instead.

Thunder crashed and lightning flashed long crooked reaching fingers of bright white on the dark horizon as the small group loaded in the wagon. As soon as the flap on the rear of the wagon canvas was lowered against the light rain the trip started once again.

While Jeb rode out in front to insure there would be no surprises or ambushes, he turned and glanced back at the man. He noticed Jefferson kept his shotgun beside him as he drove the tired team of four horses and his dark eyes were constantly scanning the country side. *That's a man who wants to stay alive,* Jeb thought with a low chuckle, *and he'll do well out here.*

It was near dark when the small group pulled up in front of Abe's house. Jeb dismounted and tied his tired horse to a hitching post and made his way to the front door. He glanced around and almost laughed at the shabby looking barn Abe had constructed and realized while it looked as if it would collapse any second, it was strong enough. *Funny,* he thought as he stepped up on the wooden porch, *it's not often I've ridden up here and not found Abe standing just outside the door with a gun in his hand. Then again, maybe I surprised him by coming while it's raining.*

Just as he was about to knock he heard a deep voice behind him say, "Who ya be and what do ya want?"

Turning, he saw Abe standing by the corner of the cabin with a Hawken rifle in his big hands. Smiling, Jeb said, "Abe, it's me and I brought ya some company."

The huge man walked forward, gave Jeb a big hug, and then asked, "Who'd ya bring? I hear'd ya was married, so did ya bring yer wife?"

Jeb laughed and then replied, "She's with us, but I got more than just my wife. I found a black family out on the plains and the wife died yesterday. I decided to bring 'em here until we can figure out what to do. The man wants to farm or ranch, but he's alone now and with no help. Hell, he's even got four youngsters to care for as well."

Abe gave a big grin and then said, "Jeb, ya bring them folks in and let's get some hot food in 'em. After we eat, us men folk can talk and see what is to be done. I will let no man, black, white, or red go hungry or wet on a day like this."

While the inside of the cabin was small, the group soon had a large meal of deer steaks, fried cabbage, and beans. More than once Abe proudly brought up the fact the vegetables came from his small garden behind his cabin.

After introductions were completed and Jefferson told his story, Abe pulled out his pipe and stuffed the bowl with tobacco. Lighting his pipe, he closed his eyes deep in thought and then said a few minutes later, "Jefferson, this land is rough. Now, I'll help ya get a cabin up before the snows and some out buildin's, but ya'll have to be a man who stays. If ya can stay and make a go of it, ya'll have a nice place in a few years. But, this land is hard on people who ain't tougher than it is."

"Abe, I don't expect an easy time of it. Hell, nothing in my life has ever been easy. What I crave and dream of is a place of my own with a few head of cows, some horses, and mayhap a garden. I think you'll find I'm a man who has made up my mind to make my dream come true." As Jefferson spoke, Jeb could see the determination in the man's eyes.

"I see you be carryin' guns—do ya know how to use 'em?" Abe asked as his eyebrows went up and his eyes grew larger.

"I can use them. I don't like to use them and so far I haven't had to fire a shot in anger. But, let me assure you Abe, I'll be able to defend me and mine."

Abe chuckled, slapped his right knee and then said through his laughter, "Now, where in the hell did a damned slave learn to shoot a pistol?"

Jefferson blushed slightly and then replied, "Abe, my old master ran a shootin' gallery in town on paydays and at fairs and what-not. I'd often run the booth and when I need to pull some customers in, why I did some fancy shooting."

"Yeah, right." Abe said as he shook his head and then quickly added, "You can bet yer black ass Jefferson, yer targets back in town weren't shootin' back. I want ya to remember one thing out here and remember it good, ya don't need to be the fastest man with a gun, you jess need to hit what yer shootin' at. Many men are quick on the draw, but piss poor shots."

Jefferson thought about what Abe had just told him, grinned and then said, "Abe, I'll remember that. Thanks for the suggestion. Now, do you know of any land around here I can use for my home?"

"I been thinkin' on that and down by the Little Piney River there is a nice stretch of land you could get from the Sioux. Hell, they don't ever go there and I'm sure old Hump would take some small things in trade for the land. If ya want, in the morning we can go and check it out." Abe spoke, and then leaned over and knocked the bowl of his empty pipe into the fire of his fireplace, looked over at Jeb and asked, "Ya got time to go with us?"

"I'll go. Betty and me are just travelin' right now and not really up to much. I think it would be good if she spent some time here with the women and kids. She's never been around any people but the Sioux, so the change will do her good."

"Fine, then at first light we'll head down to Little Piney and take a look see. Now, Jefferson, ya do some serious thinkin' on what out buildin's you'll need this winter, inventory yer supplies, and get organized. Winters out here are so cold even the bears wear coats!" As soon as Abe spoke, he broke into a loud laugh that echoed throughout he small cabin.

CHAPTER
4

Morning was cold, with a thin layer of frost on the ground, as the three men mounted and rode to the south. Abe told Jefferson the land he was going to show him would be warmer because it was on lower ground and not on the shady side of a mountain like his cabin was. Jeb watched the two black men as they rode side by side and talked. *They are so much alike,* he thought, *both are big and honest men. They're just the kind of men this land needs to bring law and order.*

Three hours after they left the cabin they were in a small meadow near a shallow running stream. Off to the north of the field were post oaks, cedars, and a few pines. Jeb noticed lots of game in the area and the soil was so dark it was almost black. Jefferson shook his head, glanced up at the sky, and then said, "Abe, this is a dream come true. I never in my life thought I would one day own land like this."

Abe chuckled, glanced over at Jeb and smiled, before he replied, "Hell, Jefferson, you don't own it yet. Ya gotta do some tradin' with old Hump and he's a wily one when it comes to tradin'. I suggest ya go to Brown's tradin' post and get some gee-gaws, powder, lead, and some of them wool blankets. I'll bet ya can get this place fer near nothin', but if ya ain't got the money, talk to Hump and make a deal. Ya'll find he's a fair man, but a firm one. Jes' remember though, if ya promise him somethin', ya'd better fer damn sure deliver when ya say ya will or have a good reason not to."

Jeb moved toward the two black men slowly and it was not until he walked by Abe he whispered, "Injuns."

Abe, not raising his head, spoke in a low voice to Jefferson, "Move slowly with me toward the trees and make no sudden moves."

No sooner had the two men turned to follow Jeb, the sound of a loud war cry was heard in the cool morning air. Abe broke into a run for the trees and as he glanced to his right he noticed Jefferson right beside him. Then, there came a noise, like a hand slapping leather, and Abe fell to the dirt with an arrow in his upper back. Jefferson stopped, pulled his pistol and cocked the hammer back, and then made his way to stand by the downed man.

"Get in them damned trees ya fool!" Abe screamed as he looked across the meadow and saw five Blackfoot braves riding straight for them.

"I don't think so. You're down and if I leave, they'll kill you." Jefferson replied and then knelt beside his new friend.

"Jefferson, ya gotta get in them trees. Those braves intend to run us both down and Jeb can only do so much by himself back there. Leave me, I'm done for."

Jefferson noticed the braves were near so he raised his right hand, and took aim at the nearest rider. The sound of his shot was loud in the still morning air, but he had the satisfaction of seeing this bullet knock the brave from the horse. He quickly swung his pistol to the left and then the right, firing both times. Abe was beside himself with awe as both braves were knocked from their horses and hit the ground hard. It was at that point both of the black men heard Jeb's rifle fire and the fourth brave was down as well.

As the fifth warrior kept coming and Jefferson fired once and immediately knew he'd missed. The fast charging brave had unnerved him and his shot went wide to the right. Before he could line his pistol up again, the brave rode by and as he leaned over he swung his war axe, striking Jefferson a glancing blow to his left arm. The wounded man screamed, turned, and shot the Indian's horse.

The animal fell with a scream of pain and started kicking violently in the loose dirt of the meadow. The brave jumped from his dying mount at the last second, ran toward Jefferson with deep hatred in his dark eyes and a razor sharp knife in his right hand. Jefferson, pulled the hammer back on his pistol, lined up the sights, and gently squeezed the trigger. The gun bucked lightly in his hand and he watched as the last heavy .44 caliber slug hit the red man in the middle of his chest, blowing blood and bones out of his back. He dropped as if he had been struck with an ax handle and lay unmoving.

No sooner had the brave dropped than Jeb came out of the woods and he was loading his Sharps rifle as he moved. He walked up to Jefferson and Abe shaking his head as he said, "Now, by God Jefferson, that was some shootin'!"

35

"Well," Abe spoke and then moaned in pain, "Ya'd better make sure them red skins are dead, or he might have to do some more."

Jeb told Jefferson to come with him and they checked the downed Blackfoot. The first four were as dead as hell with bullets in their chests, but the last one was still alive and singing his death song as they neared. Jeb pulled his pistol and calmly shot the man in the head, killing him instantly. Walking up to the dead brave, Jeb pulled his knife and lifted the man's head by his scalp lock. He placed the blade of the knife on the man's forehead and then completely circled the skull with the sharp blade. Grasping the front of the cut, Jeb pulled the skin up and then back removing the scalp. As the skin separated from the skull a loud sucking sound was heard and suddenly feeling movement beside him, he glanced over to see Jefferson on his knees puking.

"Well," Jeb said with a weak grin, "I don't suppose ya want them other scalps now do ya?"

Jefferson wiped his wet eyes with the back of his left hand, looked at Jeb and replied, "I've never seen such a thing done before in my life! Why on earth would you do that to another human being?"

Jeb gave a light chuckle, put the wet scalp on the sash he wore around his waist and said, "Counting coup son. The Injuns do it, the mountain men do it, and I do it. I know the first time ya see it done it's hard to take, but it is expected of a man."

"Ya mean I am expected to mutilate these men after killing them?"

"Nope, not mutilate," Abe spoke as he walked up, "but take their hair. The Sioux will respect ya more if ya have a Blackfoot scalp lock or two with ya when you talk to Hump."

"I'll try, but how many do I need?"

"Well," Abe gave a loud laugh, "how many of 'em did you kill?"

"Three I know for sure, but I can't scalp three men!"

Jeb placed his right hand on the big black man's shoulder, grinned, and said, "Come with me Jefferson and I'll show how it's done. After yer first one the other two will be easier."

Jefferson scalped the three braves, but a time or two he had to lean over and puke. It was not a task that he enjoyed doing, but by God he wanted this land and if the Sioux would be easier to deal with if he had Blackfoot scalps then he'd do it. Once the braves were scalped the two men returned to the woods where Abe had made a small fire.

"Abe let me see your back where that arrow hit." Jeb spoke as he walked up to the flickering flames of the fire.

"Give me a second and I'll get my shirt off." "Give me a second and I'll get my shirt off." Abe answered as he reached down, snapped the arrow shaft off leaving about 4 inches. He then pulled the buckskin shirt he was wearing up and then over his head.

"Jefferson, ya take your knife and put the blade in the fire. I want you to wait until its red hot before ya hand it to me." Jeb ordered as he moved toward Abe.

The arrow had gone in deep and Abe had lost a lot of blood. Jeb looked the injury over very closely and at one point even wiggled the shaft of the arrow to see if it was lodged in bone. Abe grunted as the shaft moved, but other than that he didn't make a sound.

Jeb walked to his horse and returned with a quart bottle of rye whiskey he always carried to help kill pain. Once he kneeled by Abe, he pulled the cork from the bottle and handed it him as he said, "Ya drink this. After ya finish about half of it I'll get that arrow out. Now, ya know I'm goin' to hurt you."

Abe gave a weak grin and said, "Yep, I've seen it done a time or two. Even had it done to me a couple of times before. Ya jes' make sure yer fast and do the job right the first time."

Five minutes later more than half of the rough whiskey was gone and Abe lay down on his chest in the dirt by the fire. Placing his right knee against the man's back, Jeb pulled and wiggled the shaft of the arrow until it worked free of the wound. As soon as the arrowhead pulled out the injury started bleeding freely. Jeb let the blood flow for about five minutes then glanced over at Jefferson and said, "Hand me that hot knife."

Jefferson handed the knife to Jeb, but he was totally confused and had no idea what was about to happen. Jeb, without even looking at Jefferson, quickly placed the red-hot flat of the blade against Abe's wound. A loud animal like scream came from Abe, his body jerked violently a few times as his flesh burned and melted under the searing blade. Jeb smoothed the flesh shut with the blade by weaving it to close the wound. When he removed the knife blade, Abe had passed out.

The smell of burnt flesh was strong in the air as Jefferson said, "I ain't never in my life seen that done before. I've heard of it being done, but by damn that was something to see. Will he live?"

"Hard to tell. Abe's a strong man and in good health, so unless it festers he'll live."

"What now? I mean, he can't travel like that, can he?"

Jeb gave a low chuckle, turned to Jefferson and replied, "We'll wait a couple of hours for him to rest and then we'll return to his cabin. Abe will be ridin' when we return too, because he's a strong and determined man. Out here, Jefferson, a man does what a man has to do. See, if we stay here too long other Blackfoot may come looking for their friends we killed. Abe knows the only real chance he has of livin' is to ride, so he'll ride."

"Do you think the Sioux will let me have this land?" Jefferson asked as he squatted by the small fire a few minutes later.

"Most likely. Humps a fair man and if ya give him some gifts, as well as make some promises ya know ya can keep, I think he'll let ya have it." Jeb said and walked to his horse, where he pulled a small pack from the animal. *Might as well have some coffee as we wait on Abe,* he thought as he made his way back to the small fire.

Jefferson looked into the fire for a minute or two and then asked, "What kind of promises do you mean?"

Jeb was placing the coffee pot on the fire when he replied, "Well, maybe ya'd give 'em part of your crops for a few years, or maybe share a cow now and then, but hell, I don't know. Just promise 'em something against lean times and Hump will see the wisdom in it."

"I could give 'em some crops. This soil is the richest I've ever seen in my life and I know it'll grow anything I plant. With the mountain behind me and the plains in front, why I'll bet even the winters will be mild."

Jeb laughed, slapped his left knee and said, "Bullshit. It'll get twenty below zero or more, the snow will be ass high to a tall Injun, and the wind will be hard enough to blow away anything not nailed down. Jefferson, the winters out here are killers and ya'd best always remember that too."

The sun was up and the frost was gone just a little after noon when the three men mounted up and moved toward Abe's cabin. Jefferson was amazed that the big man could ride after such an injury and treatment, but he kept his mouth shut. *It's a rough land I have come to,* he thought as he moved on his saddle to get comfortable, *but the men are tougher.*

About a mile from the cabin Jeb rode up beside Jefferson and asked, "Do ya have any money on you? I'm not askin' to be nosey."

"I've a few dollars, why?"

"I think it would be a good idea for us to see Abe home and then head down to Brown's trading post. Ya'll need some things when you speak to Hump and some things for yer cabin."

Jefferson thought for a minute and then asked, "What do I need for the cabin, I mean I brought most of what I'll need."

"First, you'll need a good rifle to back up that scattergun you have. A shotgun is okay for close in fightin' but ya'll need a rifle. Ya'll also need some ammunition for the rifle, some other things ya most likely don't have along. While I get Abe to bed and tell the women what is

38

going on, ya take a look at your wagon and decide what supplies ya might need. This ain't like back east where ya can just up and go to a store. Ya'd best get what ya'll need now for the coming winter months."

"I don't know if I've that much money. I only have a little more than forty dollars so do ya think he'd trade for two of my horses?"

Jeb chuckled, looked at Jefferson and replied, "Brown will trade for anything. He's a good and fair man, so I expect he will. Also, ya might talk to him about some credit at the post. Out here we often use credit against next year's furs, crops, or cattle to make our purchases. It's a different kind of land here, only ya have to make sure if ya promise to pay up at the end of the year ya do it. A man's word still means something here and many a man owns only his word. I have seen a lot of successful men out here start with only a handshake or by giving his word. It's all about honor Jefferson. And, besides, ya have three of them ponies from the dead Blackfoot ya can trade too."

As they pulled up in front of Abe's cabin the door opened and his wife ran out with a concerned look in her face. Jeb noticed she'd opened the door with a big Sharps rifle in her small hands, but seeing Abe sitting crooked on the bay she'd placed it against the door frame. A few minutes later the big man was inside the cabin and in a large feather bed. At that point, Betty looked his wounds over closely and immediately took charge of doctoring the man up. Jeb chuckled to himself as he watched the two women work together and he realized Abe was in excellent hands.

Explaining to Betty that he had to take Jefferson to the trading post, Jeb left the cabin and noticed the man coming from Abe's barn leading two fine looking horses. There was a big smile on his face and his eyes were dancing with excitement as he said, "Jeb, I have waited for something like this all of my life. I've always wanted to own a place I could call my own home. I will work hard and for the first time in my life, I am excited about having a real future."

Jeb looked at the man, pushed his hat back on his head and then replied, "Jefferson, ya'll have a place, but ya'll have to fight like hell to keep it and it won't be easy. I suspect Injuns will give ya a hard time, some worthless whites will try to steal ya blind, and just the weather alone will be a constant battle. Yep, ya'll have a place, but if ya want to keep it ya'll have to fight for it every day. Ya should do well at the tradin' post with five horses to trade. Keep one of the Injun ponies to ride back on, because they're better suited for out here."

Jefferson said, "I'm a free man now Jeb and I'll fight to the death to protect what I'll soon have. See, if a man has never had anything and he has no hopes of ever making his own decisions, well, he has no pride in what he does. So, don't ya see, he don't care much about what goes on around him good or bad. When I was a slave I worked hard for my master, but I gained absolutely nothing by my labor. All I did was to help him get richer and I saw not a penny for my hard work. But, now that I'll soon have my own place, I will make the decisions and what I do or don't do will impact me and mine. You'll find I'm a hard worker and I'll make do."

Jeb mounted his horse, looked over at Jefferson and said, "I'm sure ya'll do fine Jefferson. This land needs people like ya, though ya'll have a fight on yer hands makin' the place work. Only, from what I just heard, ya'll do, uh-huh, ya'll surely do."

CHAPTER
5

The small trading post was almost empty as Jeb and Jefferson rode in. The trip had taken two days and while the weather had been fair most of the time, the mornings were growing colder with each coming of a new sun. They dismounted in front of the store and tied their horses to the hitching post as Jeb glanced around the place. He wondered what sort of problems a black man would cause by coming to buy a few things. Jeb was well aware that many Southerners, just like himself, had moved west after the war. He also knew that some of them, even Yankees, had a deep and unforgiving hatred of all black folks. The last thing he or Jefferson needed was to have problems at the trading post.

As usual, the small brass bell above the door jingled softly as the two men entered the store. Brown was seated behind the counter working in his books and quickly looked up as they entered. The big man gave a big friendly grin when he saw Jeb, but his face turned confused when he noticed Jefferson.

"Howdy do, Jeb, who's yer friend?" Brown asked as he walked out from behind the counter and up to the two men.

"My name is Jefferson Jones and I am starting a place down by the Little Piney River and come to do some trading." Jefferson said as he extended his right hand, almost expecting the white man not to take it.

Brown quickly grasped Jefferson's hand and as they shook he said, "If yer with Jeb, yer a good man. We need good men out here Jefferson."

"He's got five really good horses outside Brown that he wants to trade. Now, I warned 'em that yer a shrewd horse trader and that ya'd most likely get the best end of the stick, but he brought 'em anyway." Jeb said and then broke out into a loud laugh.

"Well, we'll take a good look at them horses in a minute, but I've a suggestion for Jefferson and warnin' for you Jeb." Brown spoke, then looking as if he couldn't find the words he hesitated for a minute, but finally he continued with, "First and I don't mean no disrespect Jefferson, but be careful when ya come here. There's some men that come around here at times that, well, they don't care much fer anybody that ain't white. Second, Jeb, there was a tall lanky man in yesterday askin' about you. He wanted to know where ya lived, if ya came to the tradin' post very often, and askin' other such things about ya. While he claimed he was a good friend of yers from back in Missouri, I got my doubts. So, I didn't tell 'em shit."

Jeb thought for a minute and hoped it wasn't the law. Ever since he'd killed a man in a fair fight back in Missouri a few years past he'd wondered if the law was on his back trail. Realizing he had no idea who it could be, he asked, "Did he give a name or where he can be found?"

Brown met his eyes and quickly stated in a flat voice, "No, but he told me not to worry about it, because he'd find ya. Jeb, the way he said that made me think this feller is out to kill you."

"He'll find I take a bunch of killin' Brown. I don't start no messes, but I'll dance when the music starts. Next time ya see him, ya tell him that too. I'll not look for him and I won't avoid him. If he's out to kill me, he'd better do the job right the first time, 'cause he won't get no second chances."

"Well, let's go out and take look at them horses you got Jefferson. I'll give ya top dollar in trade for 'em and I promise you that." Brown spoke more to change the subject than for any other reason.

Two hours later the men were seated at one of the tables Brown had in the store sipping on a short glass of whiskey each. Usually men would eat or drink at the tables and the big man was making as much money off of his rough trader's whiskey as he was his trade goods. While he kept a pot beans on the stove, a slab of cornbread on the counter, and fresh meat in the root cellar, his food sales were usually poor. But that was mainly because Brown was a terrible cook. Whiskey was what most of the men wanted when they came in from the mountains, not his miserable grub.

"Alright, Jefferson, I'll give ya fifty dollars each for the horses in trade goods. That's two hundred and fifty dollars total. And, in the future I'll take any horses ya can round up for me. Now, I know for a fact there is a herd of 'em runnin' loose back in the canyons near the Little Piney River, so ya rustle 'em up and I'll buy 'em. I'll give you top dollar for each of 'em too!" Brown spoke with a grin as he looked over the top of his whiskey glass.

"Deal! Mister Brown, I need a hundred pounds of beans, another hundred of potatoes, five pounds of coffee, and a new Sharps rifle with ammunition. Also, throw in " Jefferson was interrupted by the jingle of the bell over the door as three rough and dirty looking men walked in.

Jeb looked the men over and what he saw he didn't like. One was short and fat, with long greasy brown hair, and his bulging right cheek held his chewing tobacco. The second one was of average size, but he was wearing an old Confederate gray uniform shirt, a faded Union blue cavalry hat, and his beard was filthy. The last man was tall, well over six feet and then some, had narrow eyes along with a long mustache that needed a serious trim. Jeb noticed the last man had a lit cigarette dangling from the right corner of his mouth. The three of them appeared to Jeb to be drifters from the war and without them saying a word he knew they were Southerners.

"Well, I'll be a sumbitch, we got us a black boy in here!" The short fat man said and then gave a loud chuckle.

"I think he's lost, don't ya know Frank." The man in the gray hat said and then grinned.

"Hell, Jim, since the war ended ain't none of them damned people know where to go or what to do no more. They're used to having a master tell things, 'cause they're too stupid to think on their own." The biggest of the three said as he broke out laughing and continued, "Mayhap we'll jes be his new masters!"

Jeb heard a chair slide with a loud groan from the table beside him and when he looked, Jefferson was standing. At that point, Brown mumbled something about having some supplies to inventory and quickly left for a back room. Jeb, suspecting a showdown was coming, slowly reached down and slipped the leather thong off the hammer of his pistol. Once he was ready, he stood beside Jefferson and faced the three men.

The fat one, called Frank by the other man, broke out laughing and said, "Ya gonna face me boy? Hell, I'll shoot ya and love every damned minute of it too."

"Yep, there's three of us, but only one of ya that count. Hell, this will be almost too easy!" Gray shirt said as he quickly glanced at his two friends beside him.

When the shooting starts, Jeb thought, *I'll take the biggest man out first. He's not a talker and I suspect he knows what he's doin'. Besides, the way he's carryin' that pistol means he knows which end is up. Of the three, he is the most dangerous one.*

"You *will* apologize to me." Jefferson said in a low flat voice as his right hand hovered right over his pistol.

"W . . . what did ya say?" The fat one spoke once more as he chuckled, "Ya want me to tell yer black ass I'm sorry? Ya'll be in hell before I ever apologize to the likes of ya!"

The man wearing the gray shirt made a quick move toward his pistol, but Jefferson pulled his with lightning like speed and before the other man had even cleared leather, the young black man had his pistol pointed at him and cocked, as he said, "Now, I don't want to have to kill none of you, but don't push me none *white* man."

"Sumbitch, did ya see 'em draw that shootin' iron?" The fat man spoke once more, but this time no laughter followed.

"Apologize to the man, Frank." The big quiet one of the group spoke in a low voice.

The big man turned his head and said, "Damn it John, I'll not say I'm sorry to any black man!"

John turned, looked Frank in the eyes and said, "Then you brace the man on your own. I called no one names and I want nothing to do with this. It was your big mouth and Jim's that caused this mess." As soon as he spoke, John moved to the other side of the small room, pulled out a chair, and sat down at a table, keeping his hands on the top.

"Well, if that's how it is, then I'm leavin' right now. Come on, Jim, let's get out of here." Frank said and turned toward the door.

As the two men started to leave, Jefferson holstered his pistol and started to sit down, when suddenly Jeb screamed a warning, "Don't sit!"

Two loud blasts filled the little room, followed almost immediately by a much louder blast from the right side of the room. One of the two men by the door was down and screaming, but the second one calmly pointed his pistol toward Jefferson, only to have two slugs hit him in the middle of the chest that knocked him back brutally against the door. One of the bullets had come from Jeb and the other from the black man.

"How'd you know they'd pull iron when they did?" Jefferson asked as he walked toward the downed men.

"It's the oldest trick in the book. All they wanted was for ya to holster yer gun and to be a little off guard." Jeb spoke as he neared the first man, the fat one named Frank. The man was still alive, but he'd not last the night. He'd taken a bullet in his belly and one in the side of his neck. The neck wound was bleeding like a stuck pig.

"I think my old scattergun did the neck job." Brown spoke as he walked up with his still smoking shotgun in his right hand and a big grin on his face.

"This other one is dead." Jefferson said as he knelt beside the man on the floor.

"Brown," Jeb said as he handed the trader two dollars, "this one here won't last the night. If ya'll put him up until he dies, then bury his sorry ass, I'll pay the bill for it. We'll be leavin' in the mornin', so I'll pay ya for the job now."

"That won't be necessary." John spoke from the table behind them and it was then that Jeb remembered the third man.

"And why not, Mister?" Brown asked as he blinked a couple of times and then looked at Jeb.

"I'll pay for both the doctorin' and the buryin'. I always knew Frank would die from his big mouth one day," the man suddenly broke out laughing and after a few seconds he added, "But I never thought it would be this way!"

"Ya goin' to start any trouble over this?" Jeb asked as he ejected his empty cartridges and reloaded.

"Nope. I'm a man of my word and I meant what I told those two before this all started. I want nothing more to do with this. Mister, I just fought for a lost cause for four long assed years and I've no hankerin' for any more fightin'. I don't run from trouble, but I damn sure don't start none, black man or not."

"Well, by damn, then let me buy ya a drink on the house!" Brown suddenly yelled and then smiled.

"First you'd better take care of your patient and get that body out of here." Jeb said with a grin.

Fifteen minutes later the small group was sitting at a table and John had joined them. Regardless of who he'd been riding with there was something about the man Jeb liked. He was a no nonsense type of man and also seemed to be the type of man that minded his own business. Jeb introduced all of them to the man named John.

"How did ya end up ridin' with those two?" Jeb asked as he lifted his whiskey glass and took a small sip of the amber colored liquid enjoying the way in burned this throat.

"I met 'em on the trail 'bout a week back. I'm heading to California and they suggested we ride together to make it safer. Last I heard they planned on going to Salt Lake or there abouts. So, I figured, well, even if I didn't like either of 'em very much, they'd add some protection for part of the trip." John spoke, threw back his drink, and then poured another one.

"Hell, now, ya slow down with my whiskey. I said the first drink was on the house, not the first bottle." Brown spoke as he watched the man pour the drink.

John reach inside his shirt pocket and pulled out two dollars. He placed the money on the table, grinned and said, "Now, don't worry about it."

"Ya got any idea why that Frank feller gave Jefferson a hard time?" Brown asked a question that Jeb thought everyone raised down south would know the answer to.

John laughed, lifted his glass and said, "He used to be an overseer on a big plantation back in Alabama, or so he claimed. I think when Jefferson pulled his pistol so fast he was fit to be tied. So, he decided to catch y'all off guard."

"What do we do with their horses and gear?" Brown asked as he poured himself another drink.

"Well, it don't matter none to me. I'd say give the horses to your man Jefferson here, since his shootin' did most of the killin', along with what gear they had. Hell, they didn't have much." John spoke, then turned to Jeb and said, "They were white trash and I suspect, Mister Patton, you know the kind of men I am talking about. Unlike most Southern men, they lacked a good upbringing and from what little I could see they were lazy, and no good. Hell, most nights I rode with 'em I slept with a loaded and cocked pistol under my blanket."

"I did that a lot during the war, but I ain't had to do it much since." Jeb spoke and then laughed.

"Is that were you lost the leg?" John asked and then gave a weak grin.

"Yep, small no name place on a hillside in Arkansas. I did hear ya say ya was in the war too, didn't I John?"

John laughed, poured another drink and replied, "Hell, weren't we all? Yep, I fought for the South, but I'm not sure why. I thought at first it was to protect our culture and way of life, and of course state's rights, but I'm not sure about all of that now. I think the whole she-bang was fought to keep our economy strong by using slave labor."

"You ever own any slaves?" Jefferson spoke for the first time.

John met the black man's eyes, nodded and replied as he raised his glass, "Yes I did, I'll not lie to you. I inherited 'em when my pa died and to tell ya the truth, I wasn't sure what to do with 'em. Mister Jones, I don't agree with slavery and I know that sounds strange comin' from a man who used to own slaves, but once I had 'em I was stuck with 'em.

I couldn't set 'em free, or my neighbors would have run me out of my own house, and I didn't want to keep 'em either."

Jefferson chuckled, pushed his hat back and pulled out the makings for a cigarette as he asked, "Well, what did you do about it then?"

John looked over his glass, grinned and replied, "I took the cowards way out I sold the place. And, a month later the war started on me and I went off to war. I was a captain when the war ended and I had me a few Mason jars full of Yankee greenbacks buried near my old place. Once the war was over I went back, pulled my money out of the ground, and took it to Saint Louis and put it all in a bank. I may have a pretty penny, gentlemen, but not on me."

Jeb thought for a few minutes, scratched the side of his face absent-mindedly, and then asked, "John, are ya interested in a business deal? I have a few dollars and I'm looking for someone who wants to maybe invest in a good man. Now, I can't claim I know a lot about the feller, but he's a good man with a gun, he thinks before he acts, and he's a hard worker. I'll bet if we put up, say about three hundred dollars a piece we could get him off to a good start. Now, it's important we help the man and not own any part of his business, so I guess it'd be a loan of sorts."

"You think this man is dependable?" John winked.

"I'd bet my life on him."

"How much interest will we charge him for the loan?"

"Well, the banks were chargin' six percent, but that was a few years back. Now, I suspect it will take at least three or four years before he'd be up and running good. So, I think about three or four percent a year would be fair. What ya say to that?"

John smiled, threw the remainder of his whiskey back, and replied, "Fine, Jeb, but who is this man?"

"Just some worthless man I know by the name of Jefferson Jones." Jeb said and then broke out in a loud laugh.

"Well, there ya go son!" Brown cried out and then slapped Jefferson on the back.

"Jeb, I don't know if I can take that much money. I mean what if it doesn't work out?" Jefferson looked around the table at each man as he spoke.

"Then we're out three hundred dollars apiece. Look, ya need the help and we want to invest in ya. Yer a good man and I trust ya, so what's the problem?"

"Oh, I don't know Jeb, but my God, six hundred dollars is more money than most folks make in three or four years and there are no guarantee's my farm will work."

John leaned forward and placed both of his elbows on the table and lowered his chin to his open palms. Grinning he said, "Jefferson, I'm going to say something and I'll only say it once. I was goin' to California, but I saw some sign of gold near here, so I'll head back east in the morning for some mining supplies. When I come back I'll bring my share of the money."

Jefferson thought for many long minutes, then finally he smiled, stuck out his hand and as John took it in his, he said, "Ok, I'll take it, but only as a loan. I thank you. John, what is your last name?"

John laughed and then said, "John Butler, recently of Macon, Georgia, and you'll do."

CHAPTER
6

The weather turned cold on the trip back to Abe's cabin while the wind whispered gently through the trees. By noon the snow started to fall and the wind was howling as the two men pulled the collars of their coats up, pushed their hats down, and cursed the weather. Mile after slow mile they continued to move, but finally it turned too rough to continue.

Due to the snow and the wind Jeb called out to be heard, "We need to hunt a hole! We can't continue in this!"

Jefferson didn't speak because of the winds, he nodded and raised his hands out from his side, with the palms up and open, as if asking, what now?

Jeb thought hard but he could not remember a cave or other natural shelter they could use near by. Usually he knew of some places, because he constantly scanned the country side looking for shelters to use in emergencies. *We've got to get out of this wind,* he thought as he beat his hands against his thighs to keep them warm, *or we'll freeze to death. The temperature has gone way down and I think this storm is a blizzard in the making.*

They were on the side of a tree covered mountain so Jeb pulled off into a thick group of pines and dismounted once out of the wind. The trees blocked the wind, but it was icy cold and a fire was needed. Jefferson constructed a lean-to while Jeb got a fire started, gathered up squaw wood from under the trees, and put a pot of coffee on to boil. By the time both men had their chores done a good six inches of snow covered the ground.

"Cold as hell out here." Jefferson spoke as he made his way to the fire, hunched down on his ankles, and held his open hands out to the heat of the dancing flames.

"We'll have a cold night, but we'll make out alright now. We're out of the wind, the fire is goin', and we have a shelter. Here in a few minutes I'll put on some beans and bacon, so we'll get a hot meal in us." Jeb spoke, rubbed the stump of his right leg and then glanced at the falling snow.

"A man could freeze to death out here in no time. Do you think it's snowing in the valleys as well?" The black man spoke and then picked up a small log and added it to the fire.

"Most likely. Winter has come a mite late this year, because by now it's usually pretty rough. I just hope it stops tonight so we can make a quick dash for home. We get caught up in these mountains and there'll be hell to pay. It might not clear for months and the passes can get over ten feet of snow in 'em."

"Lawdy, you don't think that will happen do you?"

"No, not really. Usually the first snow lasts a day or so, and then it melts away. Unless it's a strange storm, I suspect we'll be able to leave in the morning." Jeb pulled a big cast iron pot from his supplies, added some water and beans, and then placed it on the hot coals of the fire. In a couple of hours, the beans would be tender enough to eat and just before they were finished he'd add a few slices of salt pork to give them some flavor.

The snow stopped near midnight and though the temperature reminded low, Jeb knew the mountain passes would be open in the morning. He sat by the fire and looked up at the dark skies and wondered what the future would bring him, Jefferson, and his friends. The fire flickered in the background as Jeb wondered if Nancy was still with Caleb and if she was happy with her new life. While her rejection of him had been hard to take for a long time, he'd finally realized she simply loved another man. He was still thinking of his broken love when he fell asleep.

Dawn was chest-hurting cold and each time one of them spoke their breaths were clearly seen in the early morning air. Jeb rolled out from under his robe, quickly put his coat and hat on, and adjusted his gun belt. Like many old timers, the young man always slept with his gun close by, ready for instant use.

"Ya got any oil on the trigger or hammer of yer pistols?" Jeb asked as he blew life into a gray coal in the fire pit and Jefferson moved up beside him.

"Yep, oiled it good a couple of days back." Jefferson replied and wondered why Jeb would ask that question.

"Soon as some water gets to boilin' ya need to get as much oil off as ya can. Leave the oil in the barrel, but the hammer and trigger should have it removed. As cold as it is now, the oil will either slow yer action down or she'll freeze on you. That means when ya need to shoot, ya won't be able to do it." Jeb grinned, put some kindling on the fire, and watched flames eat at the dry wood as it snapped loudly in the morning air.

"You serious?"

"Uh-huh, I don't use much oil on my guns during cold weather. A few years back I had a man come into my camp and he tried to kill me. I pulled my pistol and the damned hammer was frozen in the down position, so I killed 'em with a knife. I had to put that gun by the fire to warm up enough to pull the hammer back so I could remove the oil." Jeb placed a small pot of water on the fire to boil and looked up at Jefferson as he continued, "I'm not teasin' ya either and ya'll see me clean my guns in a few minutes."

"Oh, I believe you, because it is that cold. I don't think I've ever seen weather like this. How cold do you think it is?" Jefferson asked as he squatted by the fire and placed the old coffee pot on to boil.

"Cold enough to split trees, but not so cold the bears have had to put their long underwear on yet." Jeb replied, gave a loud laugh, and met Jefferson's eyes.

Jefferson laughed and then said, "Horseshit. It's cold, but not cold enough to split trees yet. I'd guess it's about ten below zero."

They spent the better part of an hour cleaning all traces of gun oil from their weapons, loaded up their gear, and just as the sun broke through the gray clouds overhead they mounted their horses. The whole country side had turned into a white world of glistening and sparkling snow, and while it was beautiful, it made for a slow trip. The last thing either man wanted was for one of the horses to slip and break a leg. While they had a pack horse, a horse that had belonged to one of the men Jefferson had killed; they didn't want to be forced to leave any supplies behind due to an accident.

The day passed slowly and it was near dusk when they rode up to Abe's cabin. There was a gray tendril of smoke coming from the chimney and both of the men could smell food being cooked. After a day in the saddle with the weather as cold as it was, Jeb wanted a cup of hot strong coffee, then some food. He felt completely frozen and he realized Jefferson must have been about done in as well. It was with a stiff body that he dismounted, tied his horse to the hitching post, and walked into the cabin.

Betty ran to his side, gave him a big hug, as Clara sat in the corner grinning as she lowered her coffee cup and said, "Abe's still sleepin' but not fer much longer. I have to wake him up fer dinner in a minute or so."

Jeb could feel the pain starting in his hands and on his ears. He'd been out in the cold so long that he'd lost feeling in his exposed skin.

Betty, seeing his discomfort placed a large pot of water over the flames in the fireplace and said, "As soon as this water gets warm I want you and Jefferson to place your hands in the water. Now, it will pain you, but it will speed up the thawing out some. I learned it from the Sioux, but the key to it is the water can only be warm, not hot, and you are not to rub your hands at all. If you do you might injure the skin. Just keep the hands in the water until they feel normal. Your ears are red, but not white, so they'll be fine in a few minutes."

Both men made no sounds as they lowered their hands into the warm water, but Jeb knew that Jefferson was hurting as much as he was. Both hands felt as if they were on fire and it was well over ten minutes before Jeb pulled his hands from the water and gently dried them off with a towel. As soon as Jefferson was dried off they made their way to the table as Clara poured the both of them a cup of hot coffee.

"How's Abe?" Jefferson asked as he raised his cup and blew on the scalding coffee before he took a small sip.

"He's fine. It's hard to kill a tough old man like him. Abe's a man that, well, even hurt he'd be up doin' things jes' like it was all normal." Clara spoke and then a big grin lit up her face.

"Well, I'm going to need his help soon. I've enough supplies and such now that I can start on the cabin as soon as the Sioux say I can. Oh, that reminds me," Jefferson suddenly stood and quickly added, "I need to get my supplies off the horse and put our mounts in the barn. It's too cold for them to be out unprotected like that."

"Let me get my coat and I'll give you a hand." Jeb spoke and his chair made a loud scraping sound as he slid it back and stood.

"No, Jeb. There is no need for both of us to go out into this weather again. I'll do it and it won't take but a couple of minutes. You stay here and warm up, I'll be back directly." Jefferson spoke as he was slipping his coat on.

No sooner had the man opened the door to leave the cabin than a blast of cold arctic air chilled the small room. As the door closed, Clara walked over and stoked the fire up and added another log to the flickering and snapping flames. There came a noise from the rear room and the young woman made her way in that direction.

A few minutes later she returned and said, "Abe's awake and he wants to talk with ya, Jeb. Now I don't think ya should spend a lot of time in there, 'cause he's still pretty weak and needs some more rest."

Jeb stood, nodded in understanding, and made his way to the bedroom. As he entered the room he noticed Abe was covered with a thick patchwork quilt, had two pillows under his head, and was looking right at him. A lamp was turned down low beside the bed on a roughly made table. Jeb looked closely at Abe and could see beads of sweat on the man's face from the dim light of the lamp, but otherwise he looked comfortable enough.

"Ya hangin' tough?" Jeb asked as he walked to the side of the bed.

"Got me some fever, but that's purty normal for a wound like this. Clara says it ain't festerin' so I'll make it."

Jeb spent the next ten minutes explaining how Jefferson killed the men at the trading post, come into some money, and then asked, "Should we wait for ya to get better before we go and visit Hump?"

Abe shook his big black head and replied, "Nope. I don't see no need fer me to be up and about jes' so ya can see Hump. Besides, old Moses is with the Sioux and they respect the hell out of him, so it's likely they'll put Jefferson in the same category. I mean with 'em bein' black too."

"We'll leave in the mornin'. Abe, there's one more thing ya need to know about. Brown at the tradin' post told me a tall and lanky man's out lookin' for me. Ya keep yer eyes and ears open while we're gone. I've no idea who the man could be, but I'll bet ya my bottom dollar he's up to no good. If he'd been an honest man he would have given his name to Brown, so ya use some extra caution while I'm gone."

"Ya takin' Betty back wid ya?"

"Not sure that I will. She needs to be back with her Sioux family, but she might decide to stay here with yer wife. But, I can tell ya one thing, come spring I have to find me a place to make us a home. I've been thinking of settling about four miles down the Little Piney River from where Jefferson is going to build. Ya know the spot, where old Hatchet was rubbed out by the Blackfoot a couple of years back, in that big meadow."

"Good spot and good soil, it'll do. I'll be up and about by then. Ya leave Jefferson's kid's here with us and ya'll make better time. Once Hump gives 'em the land, then ya and him come on back here. Once ya bring 'em back, then ya and Betty can hustle back to them Sioux or to where ever ya want to go."

Jeb laughed, patted his friend on the right shoulder and replied, "I'll do that and I imagine we'll be gone less than a week. While it might be too late in the year for us to put a cabin up for Jefferson, I'd imagine he wants a clear claim to the land."

"He'll get it too. He's a good man Jeb and we need his type. It'll take 'em a season or two before he learns what he needs to stay alive, but he's got the bark on 'em."

Jeb walked toward the door, then suddenly turned and said, "Ya rest old friend. I'll be back soon and then we'll go huntin' us some elk."

"Waugh! Now yer talkin'." Abe spoke and then quickly grimaced in pain.

Morning was chilly, but it lacked the deep bone freezing cold of the past few days. A light frost on the ground glittered as long fingers of sunlight slowly reached out across the barnyard as they mounted. While Jeb could see his breath in the morning air, he suspected it would warm up after a few hours.

"Y'all don't worry 'bout a thing. I'll take good care of yer kids Jefferson, so ya jes' get a clear claim fer the land ya want." Clara spoke with a big smile as she met Jefferson's eyes.

"I know they're in excellent hands Clara and I thank you."

"Betty, take good care of Abe and we'll be back in about a week." Jeb said.

"Jeb, make sure you tell Hump that Abe is doing fine!" Betty yelled out as the two men pulled their horses around and headed north at a slow walk.

Jeb turned in his saddle, grinned and called back, "I'll tell 'em for ya. I'll see ya in no time!"

The first three days passed quickly and many miles were covered without incident. On the fourth day, as Jeb called for a long rest for the horses and a hot meal at midday, he realized he was close to the Sioux village. The wind was light and the temperature had gone up considerably since morning, so he'd enjoyed the ride through the mountain passes. During the ride, he'd watched the other man, evaluating him. Jefferson rode with his rifle out and in his right hand, resting it across his saddle. He was watchful and seemed to be adjusting to his new way of life very easily. *He's going to make good here, 'cause he's learning and he remembers what he's told,* Jeb thought as he dismounted and tied his horse to a low limb on a huge oak tree.

While the salt pork fried in the cast iron skillet, Jefferson asked as he sat on a large rock by the fire, "Jeb, have you given much thought to who it might be that's looking for you? I mean the man Brown brought up back at the store."

Jeb glanced at Jefferson and as he pulled his old briar pipe from his right shirt pocket he replied, "Well, I've no idea who it could be. See, I left Missouri before the war was over and I've been out here since. Before the war I did kill a man over a stolen horse, but nothin' came from it at the time. The law let me go free. Then again, it could be a member of my family or it might be a friend, but I've my doubts. Near as I can figure the man is up to no good and he'll find I'm able to meet him head on."

"Don't it worry you none to have someone on your back trail and not know who it is?"

Jeb laughed and said, "Jefferson, it's a rough life I live now and just stayin' alive takes all the energy I have. I won't run from the man, yet I won't go lookin' for him either. If he wants me bad enough, he'll find me. And once he finds me I'll find out who he is and what he wants. I learned a long time ago in the war not to worry about things I've no control over."

"Interesting view, but unusual."

The young white man laughed again and spoke as he lighted his pipe, "Well, hell, how many one legged men have ya seen out here to begin with? I'm an unusual man, but a fair one." Jeb turned the meat, placed another small log on the fire, and then said, "We should hurry and eat. I smell more bad weather coming."

Jefferson looked over head and saw not a cloud in the sky, but he knew Jeb had lived with the Sioux too long not have learned a few things he'd never know. *These damn Injuns know more about nature and such than a white man could learn in three life times,* he thought as he gave a grunt. He knew better than to even remotely question how he knew, because the odds where he had no idea and merely felt bad weather coming.

As soon as they had finished eating they mounted and moved down a narrow meandering trail on the side of the mountain. The weather remained clear for the first few miles, but Jeb noticed the temperature had gone down a little as they were eating. Dark gray threatening clouds that hadn't been there when they stopped to eat were now moving along the horizon to the west and he suspected more snow before morning. *If it all works out, we should be at Humps before dusk,* Jeb thought as he pulled his hat down a little lower on his head.

It was near dusk, as dark gray clouds rolled angrily overhead that Jeb spotted a lone mounted Sioux brave watching them from a slight rise on the rolling plains. The white man knew immediately the brave wanted to be seen and most likely he'd been trailing Jeb and Jefferson for hours. Nonetheless, they continued moving toward Humps winter village and ignored the lone wolf scout from the Dog Soldiers clan.

"Jeb, I ain't sure what I just saw, but I think it was an Injun," Jefferson said and then pulled the thong off of his pistol hammer.

"Easy, son, he's Sioux. Now, most new comers out here don't know a Sioux from an Oto, but the man won't harm us. I think I know 'em, but he's too far away for me to make out clearly. Besides, if he honestly thought we were a threat to the village he'd have killed us, or at least tried to do the job, long before now."

"I don't know if I like riding into a Sioux village or not. It takes a lot of guts." Jefferson spoke and then glanced around the open plains.

"Ya'll do fine. Just remember, if an Injun wants to kill ya it is likely ya'll never know it until ya wake up dead. They're good people, notional at times, but good people. I suspect he could see me, so he has an idea of who we are. As a matter of fact, if ya ever plan to relax on this trip, right now would be the best time to have at it. See, likely there are more than just that one out there and they're escortin' us to the village, so we're fairly safe."

"I'll be damned!" The young black man replied with his eyes wide as he glanced around rapidly, but he saw no one.

Jeb slapped his right thigh and with a chuckle replied, "I honestly hope not!"

Suddenly off to their right three Sioux braves appeared from a dry stream bed. They sat motionless and watched the two men for some minutes before one of them gave a loud war cry and rode his horse at top speed right for them. As Jeb looked up the other two were right behind the warrior and they were closing in fast.

"Don't touch a gun, those are Sioux. Right now they're playin' with us and we're safe. Easy now Jefferson." Jeb spoke in a low even voice.

About ten feet from Jeb's group, the Sioux pulled up short and a huge warrior spoke in surprisingly good English, "I see my brother One Leg Standing has returned with a Buffalo man. There will be much feasting and talk on this night."

"Hello, my friend Walks Like a Buffalo, it is good to see ya once more. I hope yer lodge is happy and yer belly full of meat." Jeb spoke and grinned at the big brave.

"Come, we will go to the village, eat and then talk. The old Raven One has been ill, but when I left he was up and walking around. He grows old and speaks often of crossing over to the other side, but all old ones speak of crossing. Do they not?"

So, Moses has been sick. Hell, I guess he must be eighty years old if he's a day and got 'em a wife half his age. I'm sure that alone would kill many an old man, Jeb thought with a chuckle as he looked at the warrior and replied, "Yes, the old one knows the day of crossing comes, so he will prepare to walk the long trail to the stars. Let us go to your village, eat, and then talk."

CHAPTER
7

The lodge was dim, though a small fire burned in the center, and Jeb could roughly make out each man, but the details on their faces were lost in the low light. Hump leaned over and silently added another log to the fire. As the flames ate at the wood and the light increased, Jeb noticed Moses was looking weak, but yet in fair shape. They'd been in the lodge for the better part of an hour with most of that time taken by smoking and then eating deer stew Hump's wife had prepared for her honored guests.

"You wish to farm the land by the cold river?" Hump asked in fair English as he turned to look at Jefferson.

"Yes, and when my crops come in I will share them with the Sioux. I hope to have some horses and cattle as well." Jefferson spoke and Moses translated for him, though Hump now understood a great deal of the white man's tongue. He just missed a few words here and there.

Hump sat quietly for a few minutes and then asked, "But, what if your plants do not grow? What if the grasshopper or hail destroys them?"

I have to answer this man honestly, Jefferson thought and then said, "I would give you a cow to make it up to you. Today I have many gifts I have brought for the mighty Sioux people and I wish to be your friend. I do not give these gifts because I fear you, but because I wish to be friends with the Sioux. I do not know what the future holds, only that I will pay for what I am given. I am known to be an honest man and I am a buffalo man, like Moses."

Moses didn't reply, but when Hump looked at him the old man nodded in agreement to the request.

"I have seen the scalps you have taken from the Blackfoot and I have heard the words of my son One Leg. I will give you this land you desire, as I know the men of the buffalo to be honest men and great warriors. For five seasons we will come in the moon of falling leaves and take what you have to offer the Sioux."

Jefferson could not help but grin and then he said, "I will keep my word to you."

"The land is yours as of this moment." Hump spoke and as far as Jefferson could tell, the conversation about the land was over.

"Tell me father, of the problem with the white hunters. I know Crow Killer sent Many Horses to speak to you, because I heard his words. Are the white men still killing the great one?" Jeb asked as he met Humps dark eyes.

"The white men still come and they are killing the buffalo. I would deny no hungry man meat, but they leave the meat and take only the skin. How can this be? Do they think the buffalo will last forever? Do they not worry of not having meat during the Moon of Hunger? I cannot understand why they do not take all our brother the buffalo can provide. Are white men such that they do not care of the future? Or, do they only need robes for the coming cold moons?"

Jeb thought for a few minutes, glanced at both Moses and Jefferson, before he said, "Hump, the hunters want only the skin of the buffalo. The skin is traded for the white man's money and a man can then buy what he wants. Each hide of a buffalo is worth much to the hunters and in a good week they can make enough to buy guns and many horses. They do not fear the coming cold season, because they will stay in the white man's village and drink the water of fire."

Hump didn't speak, but lowered his head and stared into the flickering flames of the small fire. Long minutes passed before he raised his head and looking straight ahead he spoke, "This cannot happen. The buffalo are sacred to my people. We will stop the white man from killing our brother, even if we have to kill every hunter we find. I will call a council of war and I will ask our elders to allow us to stop this killing of our food, for without the buffalo, there can be no People."

An hour later as Jefferson, Moses, and Jeb sat in front of the older black man's lodge, with the situation going around in each man's head. They all knew a fight between the hide hunters and the Sioux would bring the army, meaning an eventual death to the Sioux. There was no way the United States government would allow the hide hunters to be massacred and the hide harvest stopped, without a fight. And, it was the fight the Sioux couldn't hope to win in the end. Besides, Jeb reminded the other two men, a war might be just want the government wanted, so they would have an excuse to eliminate the Indians.

"Moses," Jeb asked as he stretched his one good leg out in front of him in the dirt, "what are ya goin' to do now? This will cause a big stink and ya bein' black ain't gonna help none if the lead starts to fly, and I think it will."

Moses gave a weak grin and asked, "Well, what do ya think I can do 'bout it? I ain't got no place to go, so I'm stuck heah for the comin' fight."

Jeb met his eyes, slowly shook his head, and then replied, "Ya can't stay here. If ya do, ya'll end up fightin' the army and that's a fight ya won't win. And, we both know if they catch a you ridin' with the Sioux they'll skin yer ass alive."

"Hell, what choice do I have? I ain't got no family 'round heah, 'cept fer Yeller Leaf and she's Sioux."

Jefferson had been quiet as the other two men talked, but suddenly he said, "Moses, I might have need of a good man who knows crops, horses and other critters. We could even build you and your wife a small cabin behind mine. I'd pay you at the end of each year, so you'd have some income. Let's say, oh, ten dollars a month. I know the average worker back east is getting fifteen, but I can't pay no more than that until I see how the money flows."

Moses gave a big grin and then asked, "Ya got any kids? I do love me some kids. I lost all of mine, way back when."

"I have four children Moses, two older ones and two little ones. What do you say, will you work for me?"

"I'm an old man Jefferson, not a young-un like ya are. I ache in the mornin's when I wake up and I'm slower than molasses bein' poured out of a bucket in the dead of winter mos' of the time. Iffen ya think ya need me, I'll go. But, it brings up 'nother problem."

Jeb pulled out his pipe and as he searched his shirt pocket for tobacco he asked, "What kind of problem?"

"Well, since Faye's husband was kilt by the Blackfoot a while back she's moved in with me. I guess I'm the closest thing to a family she's got, so I cain't jes' up and leave 'er."

Jeb laughed and replied, "Be like old times again Moses, me, ya and Faye!"

"Who's this woman Faye?" Jefferson asked as he looked at Moses.

Jeb spoke before Moses could, "She's a young black girl me and Moses picked up down in Arkansas a few years back. Hell, she can't be no more than eighteen and she's a looker too. She had a baby last year, but the boy died of a fever in January, I think it was. Her Husband was a big man with the Sioux, but he was killed 'bout six months back stealin' hosses from the Crow. She's had a hard time of it the last couple of years. I think I told ya about her the first day we met."

"Is she a hard worker?" Jefferson asked because while he didn't mind helping her, there would be no free rides.

"She'll pull 'er weight and then some, huh Jeb?" Moses stated and then gave a big toothless smile.

"She's a worker and always has been. And, the more I think on it, it might be best for you and her to get back with your own people for a spell. You've been with the Sioux for a couple of years and might go Injun on us any day now!" Jeb spoke and then laughed.

Moses stood and the other two men could hear his knees snap as he said, "Let me go and get her. We can talk to 'er 'bout it in person."

"Ya do that." Jeb said and then began packing his pipe bowl with tobacco.

Ten minutes later the old man returned with Faye by his side. She was dressed as a typical Sioux woman would have been, wearing a doe skin pull over dress, had a single strand of beads around her neck, and her long black hair was braided on both sides. Jeb noticed the birth of a child had made her previous childlike figure more mature and if anything the curves and bumps were much more accented. She was a very beautiful young woman.

Jefferson stood as Faye walked up and Jeb had to stifle a laugh, because he knew the young man had never expected a woman with Faye's looks to be with the Sioux. For a lack of anything better to say, Jeb finally said, "Faye, how'd ya like to ride with me and Moses again—like old times?"

Faye smiled, her eyes grew large, and she asked, "Ya mean it? I'd love to do that again, but where we be goin' this time?"

Moses sat down beside the fire, pushed his hat back and then said, "This feller here, Jefferson, he is offerin' us a place to live. We can work fer 'em and he'll pay us at the end of the year. He told me he'd even make us a cabin to live in."

"Is this true? Ya'll make a cabin fer us?" Faye asked as she glanced at Jefferson.

"I'd do that, but you'd have to earn your keep. Now, both Moses and Jeb say you're a good worker, so how about it? I got me four babies with no momma and I need some help taking care of them. I'll pay you, but it'll have to be like Moses said, at the end of the year. I'll have to sell my crops first."

Faye thought for a minute and her eyes remained on Jefferson. Finally, she smiled a warm smile and said, "I'll do it, but I ain't got much in the way of clothes, 'ceptin' these skins and such. I'll need some other things, but I don't know where to get 'em."

Jefferson smiled and then asked, "Can you sew? My wife had a sewing kit and lots of material, so if you can make your own clothes you're in good shape."

"What do you mean," Faye spoke as she looked quickly at Jeb, "yer wife *had*."

When Jefferson didn't answer, quickly Jeb said, "Faye, Jefferson was married until just a while back when his wife caught the bloody flux and died on 'em. She left 'em with four children and he needs help."

Faye lowered her eyes and as she kicked at the dirt at her feet she said in a low voice, "I'm sorry to hear 'bout yer wife. I'd be honored to help ya take care of yer kids, but that's all ya can expect. If yer lookin' fer live-in help, I ain't that kind a woman, but I imagine these two worthless men done told ya that. So, iffen I can share the cabin with Moses and still take care of yer kids, well, ya got a deal!"

Jefferson gave a small shout of joy, grinned and replied, "Faye, I'm glad you said yes. I only want help with my kids and I'm very happy I found a woman of color to take the job, too. To me it's important for my children to know who and what they are, but most importantly they need the right kind of person to teach 'em. I do thank you for takin' the job."

"Well, I ain't never had no school learnin's, so if yer lookin' fer a teacher ya got the wrong woman. I can only teach 'em what I know and that ain't much. I cain't read, cipher, or even sign my own name, but I know what's right and wrong. I can learn 'em how to be a good person, how to work hard, and how to live with honor, 'cause those things they don't teach in no book."

"Faye, take a seat, we need to discuss some other things too." Jeb said as he added two logs to the fire and then leaned back against a large rock. "Things are heating up with the whites and the Sioux. There are hide hunters out there killing the buffalo by the hundreds just for their skins. Hump has more or less said there will be a war over it if the whites don't stop. If ya go with us, well, at least ya'll be with yer own people, but things might turn nasty.

"Jeb," Faye spoke, met his eyes and said, "Since my husband died I ain't had nothin' but a hurt inside. I loved that man and when my little one died, I jes' 'bout give it all up. I thought it was hard when the Yan-kees hanged my pa, but losin' my whole family in less than a year al-most kilt me. Goin' with y'all might be jes' what dis hurtin' mind and body of mine needs to get better and heal."

Jeb could see the pain in her eyes as she spoke so he gave her a few minutes to calm down a little and said, "Alright then, Faye, we'll leave in the morning. We'll be traveling light, so ya can give away most of yer stuff and take what ya really need. As Jefferson said before, he'll build ya a place to stay and I'm sure ya'll not want for anythin' ya really need."

"I'll be ready by the time the rooster crows, but don't wait to hear one 'cause these Sioux ain't got none here abouts!" Faye spoke and then broke out laughing.

CHAPTER
8

Buffalo Watkins led his group with loud threats and an occasional ass kicking when it was called for. He was a huge man, well over two hundred and fifty pounds, long dirty black hair and beard of the same color, narrow eyes, and a quick temper. He smelled of death, because he was a professional killer. His first name was really Clyde, but since he'd started killing buffalo for hides he'd been given a new name by the hide buyer because of the large number of skins he usually brought in. Often on an average day he'd kill over forty buffalo and just the skinning of the shaggy beasts kept his crew of six busy until it got so dark they could no longer see. More often than not, he came to town with his three wagons overloaded and stacked high with the skins of his recent kills, and the wheels made deep ruts in the only road in town.

One day, a few weeks back he'd come to town with over three hundred hides in his wagons and he'd made over two thousand dollars for a week of work. After he'd paid his skinning crew his profits had amounted to over fifteen hundred, most of which he put in the town's only bank. Near as he could tell, though he could not count well or even read, he must have over ten thousand dollars in the bank for working that summer alone. Money only meant one thing to Buffalo Watkins, the ability to buy power, women, and good whiskey.

Buffalo walked into the town's only saloon and bellied up to the bar as he ordered a whiskey with a beer chaser. As he looked around the place he noticed it was almost empty and he quickly decided it was too early in the morning for most men.

"Barkeep," Buffalo spoke as he raised his shot of rye, "do ya know of any men in need of work?"

The bartender was a short and thin man, with long red hair, black garters around his shirt sleeves, and a slightly soiled apron around his waist. He glanced at Buffalo and smiled as he said, "Buffalo, I know of some men who need work, but few willing to work for hides. It's a dangerous job you have and not many are willing to take the risk. One day the Sioux, Blackfoot, or Comanche will find you out on the plains and that'll be the end of it."

Buffalo threw his rye back, wiped his mouth off with the back of his left hand and replied, "Aye, could be yer right 'bout that. I've had more than my fair share of luck when it comes to Injuns, but when they corner me they'll taste the kiss of my big sharps many times before I go under."

The bartender laughed, wiped off the bar with a dirty rag and then said, "I know, maybe, one man who needs to work bad enough that he might take the job. He lost all he owned in a fire a week back and then has absolutely nothing left to his name. As far as I know he has a good horse, guns, and the clothes he was wearin' when the fire started."

"He any damned good?"

"At what? He's a hard worker, excellent shot, and was an officer during the last war we had back east, or so I heard him tell. Just that reason alone makes me think he don't scare easily, so an Injun threat might not bother him much."

Buffalo thought for a minute then asked, "Which side was he on? Most of my boys, includin' me, are Southerners, so a Yankee mighten not work out worth a shit."

"South. He told me one night over a beer he was with the Second Missouri Calvary and a captain at the wars end. When the Yankees wanted all the soldiers from the south to take an oath of allegiance to the Union, well, he headed out this way for a spell instead."

Buffalo thought for a minute. If he had another good rifle shot he could buy three more wagons and start a much larger operation. There was big money to be made in hides, but at the rate he was killing the animals he could only stay out for about a week at a stretch. Usually by the end of a week his wagons were fully loaded and he was forced to return. Now, if he had two teams, two men could kill and the teams could keep the wagons coming and going from the small town. If nothing else, he could double his weekly number of hides and the cost of the extra wagons would not be great.

"Where can I find this man?" Buffalo asked as he looked over the rim of his beer glass at the bartender.

"He usually comes in just about now every mornin' to see if there is any work to be had. See, if anybody around here needs help they come in here first thing in the morning and see who wants to work. Lately there ain't been a soul in here and I'm starting to feel pretty sorry for the man."

"Well, I'll offer him a job and while the pay will be good, he'll damned sure earn every damned penny of it."

Just at that second the bat wing doors of the saloon swung open and a man of average height entered the saloon. His hair was blond, he was cleanly shaven, and though his clothing was old and worn, it was clean. Buffalo knew immediately it was the man they'd been talking about because he carried himself like a military officer.

As the man neared the bar, Buffalo saw his eyes were a pale endless blue and he had a slight grin on his lips as he asked, "Anyone been in needin' any help around heah?"

The bartender didn't reply, he simply pointed with his right thumb at the big man standing at the bar.

"Ya needin' some help mister? I lost everythin' I own in a cabin fire a while back and I'm lookin' for a few dollars to get me back on my feet again. I can ride, shoot, wrangle cows, feed pigs, cut wood, ya name a chore and I've done it."

Buffalo turned to face the man, smiled and then asked, "Ya ever shoot buffalo son? I need me 'nother gun."

The man grinned and replied, "Nope, I ain't never done that before, but I shot men and they're a lot smaller target. Are ya a hide hunter?"

Buffalo extended his right hand and said, "My name is Buffalo Watkins and I'm a buffalo hunter. I'll pay you ten percent of all the hides we trade or sale, as well as furnish the gun and ammo. I only use a Sharps rifle for kills and if yer a good shot, ya could make well over six hundred dollars in a couple of weeks or less."

As they shook hands, the man replied, "My name's Ben Bacher of late from the great state of Missouri. I'll take the job, but on one condition."

"What's that Ben?"

"I don't do no skinnin' at all. I saw all the blood and guts I ever want to see in the war. I'll shoot from sun up until the sun goes down, but I won't touch a knife."

"Fair enough. Now, some simple rules I have ya need to know about. No whiskey on the hunt, no causin' problems, and no playin' with the other men."

Ben laughed and asked, "Playin' with the other men? What in the hell does that mean?"

"I had me a good skinner a while back, but he liked men like most fellers like women. I caught him with one of 'em one night and I killed 'em both fer it. It goes 'gainst the Bible and I don't cotton to the idea a-tall. It jess ain't natural like."

Ben laughed once more, slapped the bar and asked, "Would it be possible for me to get a partial advance on my wages. I need a good meal, some better clothes, and some other gear."

Buffalo reached into his right trouser pocket and pulled out forty dollars in gold coin as he said, "Here's forty dollars. Ya get what ya need and I'll pick up ya a new Sharps, ammunition, and some other things ya'll need. The cost of the stuff I buy will come from yer first wages as well, but at least ya'll own 'em."

Ben took the money and slipped it into his pocket, grinned and asked, "Shall we have a drink to seal the deal then?"

Buffalo laughed, slammed his huge right hand on the bar and said, "By damn, that's a fine idea. Barkeeper, give us two whiskey's and two beers. I done found me another shooter and we're headed out in the mornin'. I'll meet ya for coffee and breakfast here at dawn. And, Ben?"

"Yup?"

"I'll take the cost of the drinks out of yer first week's wages."

"Now, for some reason Buffalo, I expected ya to say that." And Ben laughed.

The morning was raw cold with frost on the boardwalks of the small town and while Ben had been camped just outside of town in a group of post oaks, he'd eaten nothing in camp the night before, because he'd had no food. Instead of using the money from Buffalo for food, he'd bought some extra clothing and some other gear he knew he'd need out on the plains, figuring to eat the next day with what money he had left over. He'd ridden to town and was seated at a wobbly table in the saloon, which doubled as a restaurant in the early mornings. He was eating eggs and ham when Buffalo entered and yelled out for coffee.

"I got yer Sharps in the wagon and two thousand rounds of ammunition to go with it."

Ben looked around and noticed no one else had entered with the big man so he asked, "Where's yer skinnin' crew?"

Watkins laughed and said, "I never eat around them boys when I don't have to. They stink to high heaven and most of 'em take a bath only when it rains. They're in camp about a mile west of town and they'll do their eatin' there. When I come to town on business I stay in the hotel overnight."

"How many men do ya have?" Ben asked as he picked up his fork and started on the four eggs.

"I had six, but with the three new wagons I came into three more men late yesterday afternoon. According to my cook he has three more men due in by mid mornin' today, so that will give me twelve. Now, I ain't talked with none of 'em yet, but if they can skin, they'll do. I just don't want no drunks, funny boys, or lazy no goods on my hands. Me and ya do the shootin' and that's it."

Ben quickly finished his meal and stood as he said with a grin to Buffalo, "My breakfast and yer coffee are on ya. I paid for the drinks yesterday."

The big man chuckled, pulled out a dollar coin and dropped it on the table.

The six wagons creaked and groaned as they moved over the open plains, Ben glanced at the men he rode with. He trusted not a one of them, including his boss. Oh, they were honest enough to their own way of thinking, but greed was the main reason they were all hide hunters. If a man lived long enough, a hell of a lot of money could be made killing buffalo. At a time when most men would be lucky to make fifteen dollars a month working their asses off from dawn to dusk, a hide skinner usually made well over eighty dollars a week, if he could keep his hair until payday.

And, as Buffalo Watkins had said, the skinners all had a terrible smell of blood, guts, and unwashed bodies. When he'd first met the men at the small camp near town, Ben had fought down he urge to puke from the stench. He knew he'd get used to it, but at first it was overpowering.

The sun had finally come out from behind some low clouds and while it was late afternoon, the wind picked up and there was an icy tingle in the air. Ben suspected they were in for some heavy rain or maybe snow, if the dark clouds he'd been watching to the west moved toward them. His big bay moved at a slow walk and while most of the men were talking in low tones from where they sat on the wagons, Ben constantly scanned the countryside looking for threats. He might be new to the west, but one thing he'd learned in the war was a man could get killed in a second in rough country if he rode with his head up his ass. And, from what he'd heard, getting killed out on the plains was a lot easier than dying in the war because of the suddenness of the attacks.

Ben kicked his horse forward and rode up beside Buffalo Watkins. Turning slightly on his saddle the big man asked, "Somethin' on yer mind Ben?"

"Bad weather," Ben spoke and pointed off to the west toward the dark clouds as he continued, "and I wondered if ya thought of findin' a hole?"

"Yup, I been doin' me some thinkin' on it fer a spell now. I know of a small stream 'bout a mile up from heah that has some cotton wood trees around it. By pullin' some canvas from the wagons we can make some lean-to's fer some of the men. The rest can stay in the wagons."

"Sounds good. I hope the storm holds off until we have time to eat. I don't mind sittin' on my ass waitin' for a storm to pass, but I hate to go hungry as I wait."

"It won't happen Ben. Cookie, he's my cook, he cooked up some beans way before dawn this mornin' so we could have 'em fer dinner. He's a good man, fer a Nigger."

Ben felt his anger grow, but fought it down. The only problem was Ben was unsure how to address black folks himself. He'd heard 'em called all sorts of names, but none of 'em showed even the least bit of respect to a whole race of people, his people. No one could tell, nor had they ever, that Ben Bacher was a black man with white skin. Oh, he'd kept it secret, because times were rough even for a white man, especially since the war had ended and the blacks had been turned loose.

As he rode, Ben remembered his black mother's words to him when he was but a child, "Ben ya be the son of Marst Baldwin. He'll never admit to that fact, but he played with me many a time when I was young and in my prime. That's how ya got that white skin and only a little wave to yer hair, but yer legally as much a slave as I am. But, Ben, ya stay smart and Iffen ya get the chance ya pass yourself off as a white man. Ain't nobody gonna know, 'cept ya and me. Life is easier fer a white man Ben and ya remember that."

As soon as he was able, Ben had gone to town to pick up some things for Master Baldwin and never returned. He'd taken the last name of Bacher because he had read it on a sign over a lawyer's door and liked the sound of it. He'd been taught to read a little by some blacks on the plantation when he was still a kid, though if they'd been caught teaching him they would have been killed.

When the Civil War broke out, Ben had been living in the part of Missouri known as Little Dixie, and he decided to join the Northern Army. During the first days of the war he'd traveled to Saint Louis and joined up. He lied when he told Buffalo he'd fought for the Southern Cause, but Ben knew he had a Southern accent so the lie was easily believed. He hadn't lied when he said he'd been a captain. Thinking back, Ben knew he'd made the transition to being a white man very easily, but only due to his white skin and blond hair. He also knew deep down inside, he remained a man haunted by his hatred of slavery and the Southerners who had fought to preserve it.

Ben's thought was broken up by Buffalo's loud voice, "Hey, yer doin' some serious thinkin' there son. I don't think ya heard a word I said to ya for the last five minutes, did ya?"

Ben gave a shy smile and replied, "Buffalo, I was thinkin' on the war and what I saw. These wagons remind me of a battle I was in once, that's all."

Buffalo turned serious and said, "Son, all of us that fit that fight have us some bad memories. I've seen things most people wouldn't believe if I-un told 'em. But, what I said was the creek is comin' up, so why don't ya ride on a head and make sure its safe fer us to go there. Hell, if ya look over this next rise ya'll be able to see it."

An hour later the wagons were all in camp, wood had been gathered up, and a meal of beans, salt pork, and cornbread was warming on the coals. The old cook was as busy as a June bug in a barnyard full of hungry chickens as he constantly stirred his beans, added wood to the fire, and checked the bread in his old Dutch Oven. Finally, he put a huge pot of coffee on to boil so the men could have fresh coffee with their dinner.

The rain started to fall in big slow lazy drops as the last man got a tin plate filled with beans, along with a big thick slab of cornbread. Then they all moved to under the canvas shelters to eat. Ben, unable to stand the smell of the skinners, told Buffalo earlier he couldn't share a shelter with them. The big man laughed and told the new man he could share his shelter.

As Ben and Watkins ate, the rain started coming down harder and a popping sound could be heard as the big drops hit the tightly stretched canvas overhead. The material danced and moved with each gust of wind, but at least it was dry.

"When will we be at them buff's of yer-un?" Ben asked as he raised a spoon of beans to his lips.

"In the mornin'. But, we'll set up a campsite, get organized, then the day after tomorrow we'll start the killin'."

"Them big critters as dumb as I heard in town?"

"Not sure what you heard in town, but buffs are as 'bout as dumb as a box filled with rocks. I've had a stand where I've kilt over a hundred of 'em while they jess stood there lettin' me kill 'em."

"Why didn't they run on the first shot?" Ben asked, unsure if the big man was joking with him or not.

"Not sure. But, if the conditions are right, why a feller can kill and kill until his gun gets too hot to shoot anymore. I know, because I've done it." Buffalo spoke, shook his head and then quickly added, "They don't see too good, but they hear jess fine and they smell real good too. So, I don't think they know why a critter beside them falls and as long as they don't smell ya or hear ya move they won't go far."

"But, what about the noise? Don't the gunshot spook 'em a-tall?"

"Nope and it's my guess they hear the loud boom of the gun and jess think its thunder." Buffalo laughed and placed his empty plate down on the ground by his left foot.

Ben ate for a few more minutes in silence and thought of killing of a big dumb animal like that. *Hell,* he thought as he chewed his last spoon of beans, *it don't make no sense to kill a critter like that. Only, I need this job and the money. If I can get a couple of weeks work behind me, then I can move on up Montana way.*

As a false dawn was coming the next morning Ben rolled from his wool blankets and noticed the old Negro had a fire going and breakfast was cooking. He slowly put on his old hat and made his way to the fire.

"Howdy do, I'm Ben Bacher." He said as he squatted by the fire and placed his open palms near the dancing flames.

The old man looked at him, grinned and said, "Howdy, I'm called Cookie, but my real name is Franklin. Only, if ya wants to know the truth, I kind of like Cookie better."

"Fine, then Cookie it is." Ben liked the old black man and his honest smile right off.

"There is some coffee in the pot. The sow belly and biscuits will be done in 'bout ten more minutes, so ya'll have to wait fer any grub."

"I'm not that hungry. I've been havin' lean times of late and not eatin' like I should have been."

The old black man broke out in a low laugh and said, "Lean times and ain't got nothin' times, I know 'em both well. It was hard on me when Marst Link'um's army come through Georgia and freed me one day. Them Yanks told old Cookie he was free, but freedom don't put no food in a man's belly, give 'em a job, or a dry place to sleep. So, I moved out west and I been heah since."

"Ya like it out heah then?" Ben asked as he looked over at the old man as he turned some sow belly frying in a cast iron skillet.

"Beats da hell out of starvin' to death. But, I'll tell ya somethin' right now —one day out here on the plains there will be hell to pay. How long do ya 'spect these Injuns are gonna let us keep killin' off the buffalo like we are? Now, I ask ya that fer a reason. 'Cause sooner or later the shit is gonna hit the wall and when it does, some, if not all of us, are gonna die mister."

71

"Then why did ya come back out heah again?" Ben questioned as he gave a light chuckle under his breath.

Cookie gave a big toothless grin and replied, "Mister Bacher, to most of these white men I'm less dan an Injun, and all 'cause I'm black. In town, I'd be lucky to make two bits a day, sweepin' floors in a saloon and emptin' spittoons. At least out heah, danger's as it is, I can make me 'bout forty a week jess cookin'. See, I still got some of my self-respect left. I don't 'spect ya, a white man, to understand that."

"I can understand it easy enough Cookie and I respect ya fer it, but are ya much of a fighter if need be?"

"I've fit a time 'er two. Now why in Sam's hell would ya ask me a question like dat at a breakfast fire?"

"'Cause I jess saw three Sioux warriors peak over the rise to the west a few minutes ago. They road up over the rise, looked us over for a few minutes, and then turned away. I suspect at about full sunup we're gonna have a shit load of pissed off Sioux's ridin' this way."

The black cook;s eyes grew large and he said, "Yer jokin' with me or ya'd said somethin' when ya first saw them Injuns. Ain't ya?"

Ben didn't reply, but he stood, pulled his pistol and checked the cartridges as he made his way to the still sleeping Buffalo Watkins. Once under the hanging canvas he knelt and said in a voice just barely above a whisper, "Buffalo, I jess saw three Sioux. I suspect in a few minutes ya'll have to fight for any hides ya want to take on this trip. Now, the question is, from where do we do the fightin'?"

The big man quickly sat up, rubbed the sleep from his eyes and then asked, "Ya sure it was the Sioux? It might've been some other tribe and not them."

"I know the Sioux, because I've fought them a few times durin' the year I've been out heah. So, I'd suggest ya get yer men up and ready fer a fight. We'll have a chance as long as we make 'em think it'll cost 'em too much to kill us. See, they'll fight only as long as they don't lose too many men. We kill enough of 'em and they'll quit."

Watkins stood, adjusted his pistol belt, put his old hat on, and then bent down and picked up his Sharps rifle. He was just waking his men when the Sioux slowly rode over the rise and sat waiting in the early morning sun light.

CHAPTER
9

Jeb and his small group left the Sioux village an hour before dawn. While the morning was cold, the threat of rain from the day before had moved on and he expected a clear ride ahead of them. Faye had brought very little with her, just a few pots, pans and other things she'd need at the new place. Yellow Leaf and Moses were pulling a travois with most of their belongs tied securely on top and Jefferson joked that they must have been carrying gold, because of the deep ruts the poles left in the dirt.

The trip was easy and Jeb discovered he enjoyed traveling with his old friends. They laughed and talked until late each night of their trip through Arkansas and southern Missouri a few years back. Moses laughed as he brought up the talking chicken, as well as how Jeb had even been forced to steal clothes so he could enter his home state looking like a farmer instead of a Confederate sergeant. They'd shared so much and it looked as if there would soon be better times ahead for all of them.

It was early the third day after they had left the Sioux village that they entered the valley leading to Abe's cabin. Jeb squinted his eyes in the morning light to see better and he realized he could not make out the black man's cabin on the side of the mountain. The cabin should have been easily seen and it concerned him that it wasn't visible. Finally, he was able to make out a single thin finger of gray smoke reaching for the sky, but it seemed to be coming from the ground and not a chimney. Jeb realized immediately that something had happened.

"Y'all hold up. Something ain't right up ahead. I ain't sure what's happened, but there have been some problems." Jeb spoke as he pulled his rifle from its boot and then continued, "Jefferson, ya and the rest move over into those pines and wait for me to return."

"Do ya think they're okay?" Jefferson asked as he moved his horse up beside Jeb's.

Jeb looked at the man and he could see the fear in his eyes.

Unsure what he would find, but he knew some of them were likely to be dead, he replied, "I ain't sure yet. It could be the chimney caught fire, or a lamp was knocked over, but there has been a fire. Ya stay here, let me check it out, and I'll let ya know as soon as I'm sure it's safe for the rest of ya to come up. Right now ya move these folks back into them pines like I asked ya to do."

When he noticed the others moving toward the pine trees, Jeb cautiously started up the meandering trail to Abe's cabin. He was filled with deep, gut-eating fear for Betty and his friends, only he knew some of them could yet be alive. If there were survivors they would need some food, shelter, and maybe even some doctoring. He had no idea what had caused the fire, but the danger of a fire was a constant problem in the West with most homes made of logs and the chimney's made of wood as well. More than one family had perished in a late night fire.

As he entered the barnyard of Abe's place the first thing he saw was the body of the big black man hanging from a huge oak tree near where the barn used to stand. Jeb saw no need to check to see if his friend was alive, because his neck was bent at an awkward angle and Jeb knew his neck was broken. He noticed Clara lying in the dirt near where the cabin used to be and her dress was pulled up past her waist, so he knew she'd been raped before being killed. The top of her simple gingham dress was ripped and her left breast was exposed. Jeb dismounted, letting the reins to his horse dangle freely, and made his way to Clara's body. He removed his coat and covered her open unseeing eyes as well as her chest. He then lowered her dress to cover her legs.

As he stood in the barnyard he felt a great fear come over him as he wondered what had happened to Betty and Jefferson's children. He pulled and cocked his pistol, even though he realized the fire and killing had happened days before, and started looking for sign. He walked to the rear of the burnt cabin and heard a slight noise in the brush. Turning toward the sound he moved toward it, though he stopped when he recognized the sound of a pistol hammer being pulled back and locked into position.

"Who is in the brush? It's me Jeb." He called out, but he moved not an inch closer. He'd seen folks become unstable in the mind after a rough time and he didn't want to be killed by someone in that condition.

"Jeb? *Oh, Jeb!*" He heard Betty's voice and the bushes parted as she ran into his arms.

"Betty, did Jefferson's children make it out?" Jeb asked as he scanned the area, but he saw no sign of children.

Betty looked up at Jeb with tears in her eyes and replied, "All but the oldest one. He tried to fight the men who attacked us and they shot him. Jeb, it was horrible."

"I need to find those children Betty, are they near here?"

"I have them at a shelter I made back up the mountain aways, maybe a mile. I left them at the camp each day while I came here to wait for you to return."

"Let's go get those kids and then get right back. Jefferson, Moses, and Faye are in the valley waiting for me to check this place out. I dread like hell tellin' Jefferson his eldest is dead, but it can't be helped none."

As they moved through the rough and dense brush up the side of the mountain, Jeb was glad Betty had spent years with the Sioux. She had good woods sense and he knew the children were as safe as they could be under the circumstances. Wondering what had happened, he turned to his wife and asked, "Betty, what in the hell happened back there?"

"I'm not sure what happened. It was late and maybe the fourth night after you and Jefferson had left when we smelled smoke. I opened the door to go outside, thinking maybe the chimney had caught fire or a shingle, only as soon as the door opened two big men rushed in. They were a bit surprised when Abe killed 'em both with his shotgun, but there were others, too many of them. As soon as Abe's scatter-gun fired, three more men rushed in, dragged Abe out and strung him up in the big oak tree."

Jeb glanced at his wife and saw tears running down her cheeks as she spoke, but he knew sometimes crying was the best medicine. She wiped both her cheeks with the backs of her hands and then continued, "As soon as they took Abe out, Clara ran from the cabin with a pistol in her hand. She emptied the gun at the group and during the confusion I ran from the cabin with the kids. Jefferson's oldest had a knife in his right hand and when one of the men made a move toward him, the youngster stuck the man deep in the belly. Then I heard a shot, the boy was down, and he'd been hit in the head. I ran into the woods with the kids and we've been livin' off of berries, roots, and trapped rabbits now ever since."

Jeb stopped walking, took his wife in his arms and said in a gentle voice, "It's all fine now Betty. Ya and the kids are safe. We'll feed all of ya, let ya get some rest, and then we'll talk some more. But, just one more question Betty, did ya know any of the men who attacked you?"

"N...n...no, Jeb, but one of them, a tall skinny man, must have known you. I heard him yelling out your name as the horse ran out from under Abe when they hanged him. I also heard his name called out, but it meant nothing to me."

"What name did you hear him called Betty?"

"The name I heard was Crawford."

Jeb thought for a few minutes, removed his hat and ran his fingers through his hair before he said, "I know some Crawford's back home. But, I can't think of any reason they'd want to bother me. They were a strange bunch and we didn't have much to do with 'em."

"Jeb, he had such a hatred for you and I could hear it in his voice as he screamed your name. He's either been wronged by you or one of your family. But, this making war on kids and an injured man is not the way of a warrior; it is a coward's way."

"Uh-huh, that it is. Only, right now let's get those kids and take 'em to safety. Then I got me some skunks to trail."

Two hours later, back in the pines where Jeb had left his small group, Betty and the remaining children were sitting by the fire, each with a bowl of deer stew in their hands. Jefferson sat off to the side, mourning for his oldest child and every few minutes his body would shudder with grief.

"Moses, I want ya to take Betty, Faye, and the kids back to the Sioux with you. I don't like the idea much with a war mayhap comin' on, but they need protection and that's the best we got right now. After I take care of some skunks I'll come and get 'em."

"What 'bout Jefferson?" Faye asked as she placed a little more stew in a bowl for one of the children.

"He'll be alright with time. Right now he just needs to grieve over his child. Come noon I'll go back to the cabin and bury all of 'em. Once that's done, we'll be on our way."

"Jeb," Betty asked as her eyes met his, "how could that man hate you so much?

Jeb shook his head as he looked at the dancing flames of the fire and said, "I ain't got no idea, but ya can be damned sure, I'll find out. And, when I meet this Crawford one of us will die."

It was a little after noon when Jeb shoveled the last of the dirt on Clara's grave. Abe's had been filled first and then the young boy's. The white man felt a deep gut hurting pain as he buried Abe and his wife. While death came often and usually unannounced, Jeb was often shocked by the suddenness of it all. *Hell,* he thought as he stuck the shovel in the dirt by his right foot, *Abe, ya was jes alive a little over a week ago.*

His horse snorted and when Jeb glanced at the animal he saw Moses and the group coming up the trail. *Coming to say goodbye to friends and family,* he thought as he removed his hat and held it in both hands in front of his belt buckle.

Moses rode up, dismounted and said, "We come to see our friends off to the other side. Seems like at my age I'm startin' to say goodbye more often than I am hello."

"Mister Jones, would ya like to say a prayer?" Jeb asked, suspecting the man was hurting too deeply to do the job.

"No, I honestly don't think I can, but would you?" Jefferson spoke as he moved toward his son's grave and knelt.

Jeb waited a few minutes to allow each of them to gather around the three graves and then he said, "Lord, now ya know I don't talk to ya much. I don't usually ask ya for anything, but ya have three new folks up in heaven with ya right now and I'd like for ya to take 'em into yer arms and make 'em welcomed Lord. They're good people and I know they are missed here on earth. They lived hard lives God, each of them did, so give 'em the paradise they deserve. I want ya to pass on to all of 'em that we miss 'em, love 'em, and make sure ya tell 'em I won't stop until revenge is mine. This I ask in the name of Jesus Christ, our Lord and Savior, amen."

As his words were echoing in the cool mountain air Jeb put his hat on, moved toward his horse, and said, "Jefferson, let's ride."

It was three days later before Jeb found any sign of the men who'd killed Abe and it was more or less by accident. It was late afternoon when Jeb decided to camp along a narrow no named creek. The campsite was close to good water, wood for a fire, and he'd seen sign of game in the area. Once the campsite was established he'd gone hunting and it was less than a hundred yards from his campsite that he found his first sign of the men he was looking for.

He'd been walking along a thin game trail when he saw the setting sun reflecting off of something on the ground. Naturally curious, he walked over to see what it could be. As he neared the object he saw it was a small silver hand mirror that Sara, Jefferson's wife, had owned and her name was engraved on the back. He picked it up and placed it in his possibles bag. Jeb suspected the killers had found the mirror in Abe's cabin before the fire started. He began to circle the area and soon discovered where the men had camped. They'd been drinking hard and five empty whiskey bottles were found in the brush. He also noticed one of the horses had a nail hanging from a shoe and another one had a damaged shoe that left a strange mark in the soil. What confused Jeb was the fact it looked like the men had only left the campsite the day before and if so, why had they stuck round in the mountains? Had they been looking for Betty and the kids? Or, did they have some other reason?

He returned to the site and held up the small mirror for Jefferson to see. The young black man broke into tears.

Squatting by the fire he raised the small mirror in his right hand and asked, "This was Sara's mirror, wasn't it?"

"Yes," Jefferson spoke and then wiped his eyes with the back of his left hand before he continued, "my wife loved it and it was about the only thing she had worth anything. I could never give her much Jeb and she deserved much more."

Jeb thought for a minute and then replied, "Sara had ya, her kids, and a new life coming. None of us know when we wake up one day if it will be our last day, but if we thought about it too much it'd drive us crazy. Fevers, accidents, shootings, and other things can kill us in seconds. We need to enjoy life, love our families, and be ourselves because one day all of us will die."

"I . . . I know that Jeb," Jefferson said between sobs, "but it's hard to lose a woman you thought you'd spend the rest of your life with."

"Well, it happens and especially out here. Back east ya have the law to keep ya safe, doctors to keep ya strong, and stores to buy what ya need. Out here, hell, ya got to make due by yourself and without the things ya learned to depend on in the big cities. Ya need to remember that Jefferson, because from now on ya'll have to do things on yer own." As Jeb spoke he handed the silver mirror to his friend and felt the man's pain.

"Now, ya get dinner done while I continue hunting for some game. Put on a pot of beans, make some coffee, and gather some more wood for the fire."

"I'll do that Jeb, and thanks for bringing the mirror back, it's all I have left now."

"Not true, Jefferson, ya've got three little kids that depend on ya and ya've a chance at a new life most folks, black or white, would love to have. Ya can waller in yer grief, or get up off of yer ass and do what is expected of ya. Its yer choice, son." Jeb spoke harshly, stood, and then walked off in search of meat for dinner.

As he moved among the trees that ran beside the small stream Jeb thought of Jefferson and his family. The man had an opportunity that most folks would never have, especially a black man who'd spent most of his life as a slave. If he could get the death of his wife and eldest son behind him and move on, the odds were he'd have a very successful life, if he lived long enough. *What worries me the most is the fact he might miss something important if he has his mind on other things,* Jeb thought as he glanced down at a track left just a few minutes earlier by a deer, *and that could get me and him both killed.*

Jeb almost missed the deer when it suddenly stood from the spot where it'd bedded down and started bouncing away from him. He raised his rifle, lined up the sights, and squeezed the trigger, grinning as he saw the animal fall. He knew he'd have fresh meat for dinner for the next couple of days and jerky for many days after.

The evening past very slowly, with Jefferson sitting and staring into the fire more often than not as he listened to the crackle and pop of the burning wood. Jeb knew the man had some serious thinking to do so he allowed him to think without interrupting him. The young mountain man gave Jefferson the first watch mainly because he didn't think the black man was ready for sleep. Jeb, however, was asleep within seconds of placing his head on his saddle he used for a pillow.

It was just a little past midnight when Jeb felt a hand touch his left leg. He opened his eyes, saw Jefferson kneeling beside him and heard him say in a low whisper, "I have some movement near us, to the west side."

Rolling from his blanket, Jeb picked up his rifle, checked to make sure the thong was off his pistol hammer, and made his way into the shadows. He could see the light red eyes of the coals from the fire and he was surprised a few seconds later when he saw a long streak of lightning reach out across the horizon to the west. A few seconds later he heard the distant boom of thunder. *Damn me, that's the last thing we need, a storm. Hell, I have no idea who is out there and we got rain comin',* he thought as he scanned the area around him. He knew that just because the first movement Jefferson had noticed was to the west, the man or beast could have gone in just about any direction since then.

"Hello the camp!" A voice called out from the west side.

"I hear ya just fine! Who ya be and what do ya want?" Jeb replied and then moved about twenty feet to his left.

"Jeb Patton, I see yer still up to no good! Not very trusting are ya? This is Ty Fisher and I got an old man named Jarel Wade with me."

Jeb recognized the voice as soon as the man had said his name. While he knew Ty Fisher, he was hardly a good friend of his. They'd met a few years back, when Jeb had first come to the mountains, and Ty had learnt him a few things about beaver trapping. While the market for plews had quit by that time, Ty and a few of his type still remained in the mountains. He'd also met Jarel Wade in the past and he knew both men as good mountain men, tough as the mountains they lived in.

"Come on in Ty, before ya get yer backside wet!" Jeb called out, moved to the fire and added some kindling to red coals. He blew on one coal and the wood flared up as Ty and Jarel walked into the campsite. Jeb noticed both of the men were big, well over six feet tall and near two hundred pounds, with not an ounce of fat on either one of them. Both wore long hair and beards, and they looked enough alike to be brothers. As near as Jeb could figure, Ty must have been near sixty and Jarel was just a few years younger.

Squatting by the hungry fire, Ty gave a big grin and asked, "How ya been son? I ain't seen ya in a coon's age. Last I hear'd ya had a beautiful woman and a buffalo God livin' with ya."

Jeb grinned and replied, "The woman is named Faye and the buffalo God," at that point he broke out laughing, "should be back with the Sioux."

"Can ya believe the Sioux would make an old man a God? I hear he's a good man though, with lots of bark on 'em." Ty grinned and then continued, "Ya got any coffee? We're headed to either Brown's or Butterfield's to pick up some supplies before we go back in the mountains."

Jeb put the coffee pot back on coals, leaned back against a large rock and said, "Ty and Jarel, I got me one hell of a problem and I ain't sure how to skin the cat. But, first, let me introduce the man standin' behind y'all, his name is Jefferson."

Both of the mountain men looked over their shoulders and saw a big black man holding a rifle on them. Jarel broke out laughing and Ty soon joined in. As the laughter died down, Jarel said, "He's a good one that man is. Hell, I didn't even know he was behind us."

Ty grinned and his eyes reflected the flames of the fire as he said, "Ya'll do to walk the river with Jefferson. Not many men can get the drop on me, but old Jarel here is blind in one eye and he can't see out of the other. And, he's so deaf he can't hear a buffalo fart when he's standing right beside the shaggy beast."

All of the men were laughing as Jefferson neared the fire with his rifle still at the ready and asked, "Do you know these men Jeb?"

"Uh-huh, so ya can lower the rifle. But, ya did the right thing Jefferson, 'cause ya never know who'll try to enter our camp."

As soon as Jeb poured all of them a cup of coffee he explained what had happened. Many long minutes of silence followed before Jarel spoke, "I know this Crawford and he's a bad apple. A few years back he was suspected of robbing an Army payroll, but Ty discovered it was another man. While he might not have been involved in that robbery, there have been others and some back shootin' too. He's been suspected in a lot of different things, but none of it can be proved."

"I never met the man, but I've heard tell of 'em and none of what I heard was good," Ty added quickly as he raised his cup of coffee and took a small sip of the hot liquid. "They say he comes from the Missouri Ozark Mountains, but while he has an Ozark twang to his voice, he don't act like no mountain folk I ever met. He's got no honor and he'd kill his own momma fer a dollar, or so I heard."

"But why would he attack Abe and kill three people for no reason?" Jefferson asked as he moved closer to the fire in an attempt to avoid the chilly night air.

Ty spoke first and his words were full of anger as he spat them out, "I knew Abe well and he was one hell of a man, black or white. I ain't got no idea why Crawford would kill 'em, but mark my words, it don't make no never mind, because I'll kill the sumbitch on sight."

"Now, I don't know if it's true or not, but I heard a John Crawford rode for Quantrill and his bunch in the last war," Jarel spoke, pulled out his plug of chewing tobacco and cut off a big piece. "I also heard he hates blacks with such a passion that he's sworn to kill all of 'em he can find. I suspect, if he came from around where ya live Jeb, he might have heard tell ya were traveling with black folks. Then, when things got too hot for 'em in Missouri he came out west, got to thinkin' about a white man like ya runnin' with colored folks, and decided to pay ya a visit. But, hell, to be honest, I ain't really sure."

"What about going to the law?" Jefferson asked.

Jarel put the tobacco in his mouth, chewed a few times and spat in the dirt by his right foot before he said with narrow eyes, "Jefferson, they ain't no law out here and even if there was, ya black folks ain't got the same rights a white man has. I ain't never heard of a white man hangin' or going to prison for killing no black. Now, it ain't right, and we know that, but if ya want justice served ya'll have to see to it with yer own guns."

Jefferson's eyes constricted and he said in a flat voice, "Then by God, I'll see justice served. And, it'll be fast and final."

The small hairs on the back of Jeb's neck suddenly tingled and he felt an involuntary shudder go through his body.

CHAPTER
10

The mounted Sioux watched from the hill for many long and tense minutes as Buffalo Watkins and his men moved to defensive positions. Finally, three of the warriors made their way down the slope toward the white men, their horses at a walk.

"They want to parley, Buffalo. Why don't me and ya go out and see what they want. It might be we can avoid a fight here, if we handle this right." Ben spoke as he glanced at the big buffalo hunter.

Standing, Buffalo Watkins handed his Sharps rifle to Cookie, gave a weak grin and replied, "Alright let's go see what they want. Listen to me, all of ya. Don't fire unless they shoot first. If they want to talk then there is a slight chance we might get out of this still wearin' our hair."

The two men slowly made their way to the three mounted Sioux and when they were about ten feet from the horses they stopped. While neither of the white men spoke Sioux, Buffalo Watkins knew sign, so he asked the Sioux why they had come. For many long minutes the Sioux didn't respond and Buffalo began to think he might have used the wrong sign language.

Finally, a warrior wearing three long eagle feathers in his hair signed, *"Why are you on our land? We know you are the killer of our buffalo and you must leave. If you are still on Sioux land when the sun goes down this day you will all die."*

Ben knew enough sign to know what was being said was a warning and the situation didn't look good. He suspected Buffalo Watkins wouldn't leave and a fight was almost a sure thing. As far as he could tell, it was a fight the white men couldn't win, but Buffalo Watkins was a greedy man, so Ben felt more than just a slight tinge of fear.

"I understand." Watkins signed, turned and walked his horse back to camp.

Once back at the fire, the old Buffalo hunter called his men near and explained what was going on. What surprised Ben was when the man said, "We'll head back to town for a week and then come back out. By then the Sioux should be further south with the main buffalo herds and we can hunt up here without 'em botherin' us. If we stay, we'll have to fight and it's a fight we can't hope to win boys."

"Well, shit!" A tall thin man named Johnson spat out in anger as he began to gather up gear from around the campsite, "I ain't goin' to make no money this week!"

Cookie gave a loud laugh and replied, "Johnson, Iffen ya stay and fight these Sioux ya won't never make another penny durin' the rest of yer short life. Them boys ain't playin' and it's a dangerous thing yer talkin' 'bout, though ya don't realize jus' how lucky we are. Most of the time them Sioux jus' kill folks who piss 'em off."

Johnson looked as if he was going to say something, but hesitated. He slowly shook his head and finally said, "Awww, I guess yer right Cookie, but I got a family to support and this will hurt me some."

"I 'magine it will son, but if ya get killed, then what will happen to that family of yers? Jus' count yer blessin's and let's get the hell out of heah."

It was well after dark before the wagons pulled into town and all of the men except for the drivers and Cookie dismounted. Buffalo arranged for his new men to sleep in the livery stables, while he went to the saloon with Ben to discuss business. Cookie and the more experienced men driving the wagons would make camp a few miles north of town. Ben expected the big leader to be much madder than he was, and found it surprising that the man actually thought the whole situation was a bit funny.

"Well, what now?" Ben asked as they both bellied up to the bar and ordered a beer.

"We wait. Each year about this time the main buffalo herds head down south where it's a warmer winter. A few scattered herds will stay around here, but I didn't expect to do much real serious hide gatherin' 'til spring, though the hides are better quality right now." The big man spoke and then drained about half of his beer in one gulp. He wiped his mouth off with the back of his left hand and continued, "So, we'll go out next week, knock down a hundred or so of the beasts and come back here to winter."

Ben thought for a few seconds, and then he asked as he looked over his beer glass, "Ya ever run into them Sioux like that before?"

Buffalo Watkins laughed, turned to face Ben and then replied, "No, Ben, not in those numbers. Oh, I've ran into a small party of 'em at times, but not a large group like was out there this mornin'. I've been wonderin' why there was so many of them boys too, 'cause you usually don't ever see more than twenty of 'em at a time. And, if ya do, well, ya don't usually live long enough to discuss it later."

Ben met Watkins' eyes and said, "I think they're tired of the buffalo killin' and are going to put a stop to it if they can."

"I hope yer wrong son, 'cause I won't quit and neither will any of the men I know in the business. The pay is just too good for a man not to take hides. So, when we go out next time we'll be armed fer bear and I'll hire a few more men."

There suddenly came a voice from Ben's right, "Did I hear ya say ya was lookin' fer some men?"

Buffalo Watkins turned to face the man and when their eyes met he asked, "Ya always listenin' to other people's conversations? By God, I don't take kindly to that a-tall."

"Nope, I wasn't listenin' at all, but yer voice went up a few notches when ya said ya'd hire a few more men. I couldn't help but over hear ya then. I meant no offense, but me and my men are lookin' fer work." The man spoke and Ben noticed the man was tall, thin as a rail, dirty brown hair, and had hungry eyes. He suspected the hunger was not from a want of food, but of greed. Ben Bacher suspected the lanky man was a killer and a good man to shy away from for the most part.

"How many men ya got?" Watkin's asked and then ordered drinks for him and Ben.

"Ten men with me right now. I could have some more in a week or two."

"Ten would be enough, but I didn't catch yer name."

The tall man gave a grin, stuck out his hand and replied, "Crawford, John Crawford, recently of the great state of Arkansas."

Buffalo shook the man's hand, introduced Ben, and then asked, "How much ya charge me for ya and yer men to ride along in case of Injun problems when we take buff hides?"

"Twenty dollars a day, but we don't skin or kill buffalo." Crawford spoke and then grinned once more.

I don't trust any man that grins that damned much and his voice has a Missouri twang to it, not an Arkansas drawl, Ben thought as he watched Watkins considering the offer.

"I cain't go that high, but I can offer y'all fifteen a day and that's the best I can do. And, ya'll have to wait until we sell the hides a-fore I can even pay ya that." Buffalo Watkins spoke, leaned back against the bar and continued, "What do ya say to my offer?"

Crawford thought for a few minutes, then extended his hand once more and said, "Ok, it's a deal. But, if we run into Injuns, I'll call all of the shots. I'm an old military man from way back, so I know what I'm doin'. If you can live with that, why, we can do business."

The two men were still shaking hands as Watkins quickly replied, "Deal. I call the shots as we hunt and ya call the shots if we meet Injuns."

For some reason Ben didn't feel comfortable as Buffalo ordered three more beers from the bartender to celebrate the agreement. *I have a suspicion,* Ben thought as he glanced at the laughing Watkins, *this deal will cost ya more than a beer and fifteen dollars a day in the long run.*

A week later the group was back out on the plains. With six wagons and people Buffalo employed only a week before they had more than doubled in size. It was a group of nineteen men that moved westward in the light drizzling rain toward the first nights camp. Ben was uncomfortable and he knew at first glance the men who rode for Crawford were a hard bunch of killers. The minute he saw the men, Ben thought of raiders and partisans he had chased all over the state of Missouri during the war. He pulled Watkins aside the first morning while they were just outside of town and said as much to the old buffalo hunter.

Watkins had given a crooked grin and replied, "Hell, ya'll find a lot of rough men out in this country, Ben. If I was you, well, I'd jess be glad we've some fighters to go along on this trip. We could still run into them damned Sioux out on the plains."

"Ya might be right Buffalo, but keep yer eyes open. I wouldn't be surprised if this group tries to kill us once the wagons are full and then take yer hides into town as their own."

Buffalo Watkins laughed, placed his big right arm on Ben's shoulder and said, "Okay, I'll keep my eyes open and a gun near me at all times. But, I think yer barkin' up the wrong tree. I mean, hell, the man gave his word to protect us."

Ben met Buffalo's eyes and stated in a flat voice, "Yes, he gave his word, but how much do ya think that's worth? Mark my words, there will be trouble before all of this is said and done."

Watkins had laughed, turned, and walked to his horse. As soon as the big man mounted, the whole group moved toward the plains, leaving Ben with a deep feeling of apprehension as he rode along.

It was early the fourth day out when one of Buffalo's men returned from scouting that he announced a fair herd of buffalo where located a couple of miles to the west. Watkins had the camp broken down, the gear loaded, and in less than an hour they were moving once more. By ten that morning Watkins and Ben were on a slight rise looking down into a narrow valley filled with the big shaggy beasts.

Buffalo Watkins pointed with his right index finger off to the north and whispered, "Ya move off that way and take on that small group to the north. Don't shoot until ya hear me fire first. Iffen we're lucky we can get us a stand and kill a hundred or more between us. Jus' take yer time and kill one critter with one shot."

Ben nodded his understanding and backed from the rise slowly. Mounting his bay he moved out a fair distance to the east and then swung back toward the north. Less than thirty minutes later he had his smaller herd located. Leaving his horse in a slight depression in the otherwise flat terrain, he crawled forward until he was less than fifty yards from the big animals. Taking two old walnut ramrods, he stuck them in the ground so they crossed at the top making a crude X, he then tied the wood together where they met. Placing the heavy barrel of his sharps on the vee of the crossed ramrods he waited for Buffalo's first shot.

It was less than five minutes later when he heard the echo of Watkins' first shot, so he lined his sights up on the nearest animal, took a deep breath and slowly released it as he gently squeezed the trigger. The stillness of the morning air was shattered by the loud report of the big Sharps, but the animals seemed not to notice the noise at all. The buffalo Ben shot at took a few steps, shook its massive head, and suddenly went down on its front knees. Less than a second later the big beast fell to its right side, shuddered a few times, and then remained still. The other animals seemed to not notice the death and continued to feed.

Ben shot and killed more than twenty buffalo as the big animals stood in what the hide hunters had come to call a stand. The loud shots seemed to have no effect on the big shaggy critters and it wasn't until the smell of fresh blood became strong that they finally broke and moved away. At that point Ben stood, looked the killing field over closely, and realized he wasn't made out to be a hide man. He'd keep his end of the bargain until they went back to town, but he knew inside he wasn't cut out to kill buffalo.

For over an hour after his last kill, Ben heard Buffalo Watkins firing his rifle slowly but continuously. Finally, when the plains grew silent, he mounted and rode toward his boss. He had a feeling over a half a hundred of the big animals had been killed and he was right.

"I got forty of 'em, how many did you get?" Buffalo Watkins asked with a huge smile as Ben dismounted and off in the distance he spotted the six wagons nearing the slaughter.

"Twenty three and it took me twenty four shots."

"Fine shooting fer yer first time. Son, we just made close to four hundred dollars in less than a day! We have luck like this every day and we can head back to town in a week, sell what we got and then come back out! Hell, I'll bet we can make over four or five thousand, easy, if the hide prices keep a-goin' up."

The wagons broke off as they neared the slaughtered beasts, with two heading north to work on the animals Ben had killed. Scanning the country side, Ben noticed two of Crawford's men off in the distance. *Well,* he thought as he pulled his hat off and wiped the sweat from his brow, *at least they are doing what they're paid to do.*

It took the remainder of the day and part of the evening before all of the buffalo where skinned and loaded on the wagons. Back at camp Cookie had a big pot of pinto beans, cornbread, fried potatoes, and coffee waiting for the evening meal. Like all tired and hungry men, Buffalo's skinners spoke little as they ate, but Crawford's men joked and laughed about how easy it was to kill the big animals.

"They must be pretty dumb critters to jess stand there and let ya kill 'em like that. Why don't they run?" One of Crawford's men asked as he crumbled up some cornbread to his bean juice.

"Not much bothers a big animal like a buffalo, 'cept mayhap a grizzly or wolf now and then. Of course the Injun's hunt 'em, but they do it on horseback most of the time. So, as long as ya don't make any sudden moves ya can kill 'em in a stand like we did today." Buffalo spoke between spoons of beans.

"The noise from them big Sharps don't scare 'em none?" Another man asked from across the fire.

"Nope," Buffalo said as he wiped his mouth with the back of his left hand, "they must think it's thunder, 'cause it don't spook 'em none a-tall."

Crawford asked, "How many did ya kill today? All total, I mean."

With his face reflecting his pride Buffalo Watkin's said, "We got sixty-three and that's a good day's take!"

"Yep, that's a lot of critters. How much do you reckon they're worth?" Crawford asked as he picked up the coffee pot, refilled his cup.

"Well, hard to say, 'cause it depends on the market, but near four hundred dollars." Buffalo replied without thinking, but then paused, looked at Crawford and asked, "Why would you care?"

Crawford gave a low laugh and replied, "Just wonderin' is all. Hell, if I got to be out here it's nice to know what for!"

Ben noticed as soon as the laughter died down, Crawford grinned at a man sitting across the fire that started the conversation. The look he gave the man confirmed the suspicions that Ben felt all along. Sooner, or later, trouble would rear its ugly head and there would be a show down of sorts.

It was much later that night, after Ben completed his shift of guarding the horses and was having cup of warm coffee, when Cookie walked to the fire. The old man squatted beside the glowing coals and said, "I don't trust a one of them fellers 'ridin' with that Crawford feller."

Ben took a quick drink of his coffee, rubbed his tired eyes and replied, "Me neither Cookie. Ya'd best keep a gun handy and be prepared to use it in a second as near as I can tell."

The old man gave a low chuckle and stated, "Hells, bells, I always got my forty-four on me and I keep my sawed-off scattergun in the chuck box. And, ya can bet yer ass, both of 'em are loaded too. Oliest thing I cain't fig'er out is when the trouble will come."

"I suspect these fellers will let us load the wagons high and once we get close to town they'll start their move. These are lazy men, Cookie, and they'll let us do all of the work before they try to take the hides."

The old black man thought for a second, scratched the right side of his cheek, and said, "Well, if dey do try anything, I'll get me one of 'em fer shore. After what ya jess said the nearer we are to headin' back to town the closer my shotgun will be. And, once we start movin' back to town my old scattergun might jess become a permanent part of my right hand."

Ben laughed, stood on tired legs, and said, "I'm turnin' in now, but I figure it'll be days before any trouble comes, but when it does ya be ready for it."

Eight days later the wagons were stacked so high with buffalo hides they left three inch deep ruts in the soil as they moved. It was over dinner that night that the first hint of the problems to come became obvious to Ben.

"How many hides do ya think ya have now Buffalo?" Crawford asked as he bit into a piece of buffalo hump that had been grilled over the fire.

"Well, I ain't counted fer sure yet, but well over six hundred but mayhap closer to seven hundred. It's been a good hunt and I'm glad ya and yer men were around to protect us as we did the job too." Buffalo replied with a big grin on his face.

Crawford once again met the eyes of the man across the fire, gave a false smile and said, "Hell, that's better than four thousand dollars fer a little more than ten days of work. After ya pay me and my men off, ya'll still have a big chunk of change left."

"I figure my profits on the trip, after I pay your men and mine to be near three thousand dollars, but I'll have to buy more supplies to come back out in the spring."

"I don't think fifteen dollars a day is enough for my men, not after I've seen the money ya made." As Crawford spoke his eyes narrowed.

"I been thinkin' on that some too, and I agree with you John, so I'm gonna up your pay to twenty dollars a day. Hell, that's an even two hundred and after ya divided it up amongst yer ten men that's twenty dollars each. I know a lot of men who work a whole month fer less than a third of that, when they can find work that is. Even a good top hand on a ranch only gets thirty a month and found."

Crawford didn't say anything more, but once more his eyes met the eyes of the man across the flickering flames of the popping fire and Ben knew the problem would come to head within the next day or two.

CHAPTER
11

J eb and his small group had been on the move since way before
daylight. The four of them made excellent time and as they traveled
it was decided by the two old mountain men to get their supplies from
Butterfield's trading post. While both men liked Brown and he traded
fairly, they'd been using Butterfield's store for over forty years. Though
a very small town had grown up around Butterfield's trading post, it
wasn't much to look at. It was ten days after Ty and Jarel had walked
up to his fire that the one legged white man dismounted, tied his horse
to the hitching post, and entered the trading post with his friends.

"Well, now, I'll be damned Iffen it ain't ugly and uglier!" Butterfield yelled as he noticed the two old mountain men enter his store.

Ty gave loud laugh and then said, "Well, ugly must be Jarel and
uglier must be Jeb, 'cause I know ya ain't a-talkin' 'bout a handsome
feller like me!"

Butterfield was an old man now, well into his eighties, and while he
had turned the running of his trading post over to his grandson, he still
lived on the place. He'd once been a very big and powerful man, but
over the years his health had failed and he was now skinny, stooped
shouldered, and hard of hearing.

"Frank! Bring me out a bottle of my good rye!" The old trader
yelled over his shoulder to his grandson working behind the counter.

Soon the five of them were seated at the table, Jefferson had been
introduced, and the story of Abe's murder told. As he sipped on his
first rye, Butterfield didn't speak, but as he poured his second drink he
said, "Aye, I know this damned Crawford, and he's trash, he surely is.
He rode in here, oh, mayhap three years ago and didn't have shit to his
name. I fed 'em, gave 'em a small grub stake, and he stole my best
horse the next mornin' when he left. Now when I met 'em back then,

he was wearing a Confederate gray shirt and hat, 'long with some Union pants. He was alone in them days too, but a lazy no 'count like him will gather others jess like 'em before too long. And, ya can bet they're all out lookin' fer easy money."

"Ya ever hear him say what he did in the war back east?" Jarel asked as he leaned back in his chair with his whiskey held on his chest in both hands.

Butterfield chuckled and replied, "Yep, he was damned proud he'd rode with both Quantrill and some feller he called Bloody Bob, or some such nonsense."

Jeb grimaced with memories of the war and then said, "That must have been Bloody Bill Anderson and William Quantrill, Mister Butterfield. Both of them fellers led partisan groups for the South during the war. Some folks still consider 'em heroes but others think they were just a bunch of murderin' thieves."

Butterfield gave a dry grin and said, "Well, hard to say what they might have really been durin' the war, but if this sumbitch killed Abe we know what he is now, huh? By God, Abe was a good man!"

For the first time since they had entered the trading post Jefferson spoke, "Have you seen the man since that first time you helped him out?"

"Oh, once in a while he comes in and buys some beans and bacon, but he don't linger none, if that's what ya mean. I got no use fer the man a-tall and I told him to his face too. And, Jefferson, I'm sorry to hear yer son was killed along with my friends."

"How come you let him trade here if ya lost a horse to 'em?" Ty asked as he leaned forward and placed his elbows on the top of the table, holding his glass level with his chin.

"Shit," Butterfield spoke with a slight glint of humor in his old eyes, "like I started to say, he came back heah 'bout six months later and give me a hundred dollars for that critter. Now, it was only worth 'bout forty, so I had no complaints with the man after that. Besides, he stole it from my livery stables and he didn't leave me a foot in the bush, and while it made me mad as all hell, it didn't put me in no danger at the time."

"Was he alone when he come back?" Jarel asked.

"Nope, he had, oh, I'd say maybe four others ridin' with 'em."

"When was he here last?" Jefferson asked as he glanced at Ty Fisher.

"Well, I'd guess it was near a month ago or there abouts. My mind ain't what it used to be, so it is hard fer me to really say fer sure."

"Mister Butterfield, if he ain't getting his supplies from you, then where can he be buyin' 'em?" Jefferson asked as he placed his empty whiskey glass on the table and then waved off a second drink when Jarel raised the bottle.

"Only three places out heah he can get supplies, here, Brown's place, or that new town up north, what in the hell are they callin' that place now?"

"Coldcreek, I think, but it's had a few names over the last four years." Ty spoke as he grinned and continued, "Each new mayor changes the name it seems. Now, it ain't much to look at, maybe a hotel, saloon, livery and a few other small places, but it's got a pretty big store there."

"Why in the hell would a town be way out here?" Jefferson asked with a surprised look on his face.

"Railroad moved out this way and at one point the town was the end of the line. When the tracks moved on westward the town kind of died out for a spell, but now the government is buying buffalo hides as fast as they can load 'em on a train, so it's boomin' again." Jarel spoke as he stood and stretched his tired muscles.

"Well, that's where I think we should head to look for this Crawford feller. I don't think he's the kind of man who'd buy things at trading post prices, if he can dicker a bit in a town and save a sawbuck or three." Ty spoke, glanced around the table and then quickly added, "Not that your prices are high Butterfield, only yer a long way from a railroad and that gives the town not only a better supply of goods but it lowers the price a lot too."

"Yep, why I 'member back in '22 when all of my goods came in by pack horse from Saint Louie and they all cost me a pretty arm and leg then. Of course, back in them days I was the only place to trade at, so I had business all sewed up." Butterfield spoke as he stared into his half empty whiskey glass remembering the past.

Finally, Jeb asked, "Ya got any grub cooked up? I been eatin' what these two old mountain men call food and it's 'bout killed me."

Butterfield laughed and called out, "Frank!"

"Yes Grandpa?"

"Bring these men out some beef steaks and cook 'em black on the outside and bloody on the inside. Sling some fried taters, beans, and a big slab of cornbread on each plate."

"I still got some fried okra left over from lunch, so do ya want that on each plate too?"

"Hell, Frank, load them plates down good with whatever ya got and don't leave the kitchen 'til I tell ya to. These damned mountain men eat almost as much meat as a red skin does!"

After the meal the men were still seated at the table with Butterfield when the old man suddenly asked, "Jefferson, why is a man like ya out here? I mean out west."

Jefferson's eyes suddenly narrowed and he asked, "Ya mean a black?"

Butterfield, grinned, looked at Ty Fisher, and then said, "Ya come right to the point, don't you son? And, no, I didn't mean it that way, but to tell ya the truth, I was wonderin' 'bout that too. I know ya ain't no mountain man and ya won't ever be, 'cause them days are over. So, what brings ya out here is all I was wonderin'."

Jefferson relaxed, carefully formed his thoughts in his mind and replied, "Mister Butterfield, times are lean back east for black folks. The war freed all of us, but it ain't feeding any of us. It's hard for a white man to find work and all but impossible for a black man. I figure the future lays out here, out west. I just happen to be a man who wants a nice place to live, a small farm, and a little land of my own."

Butterfield laughed, slapped his right knee and said, "This man reminds me of old Ham, that was Moses' brother. Now, Ham, he was a smart man, Jefferson, only he didn't have yer smooth way with all of them big fancy words. And, as far as you bein' black, and ya used the word first not me, it don't matter much out this way what color yer ass is. Beckwourth, Hank, Ham, Moses, Abe, Nate Grisham, and old Black Bob were some of the finest men I've ever know'd and all but Beckwourth was a hell of a lot darker than you'll ever be. Son, some advice, ya can keep a-callin' yerself a black man and keep thinkin' yer still one, or ya can jess call yerself a man and be one."

Many minutes of long silence filled the room before Jeb finally changed the subject when he asked, "What ever happened to them two old fellers that raised ya Jarel?"

Jarel Wade gave a loud laugh and asked, "Do you mean old Teacher and Zee? Why them two have a big cabin up in the mountains and doin' very well. Both of 'em must be way over eighty or close to it, still work in a garden, have a few cows, and up until a year ago Zee was married to a Sioux woman. Only she took sick and died of a fever during a cold winter. They're like parents to me Jeb."

"I met 'em a few years ago, when I was trapping with Ty, and I liked 'em both a lot. But, ya know, I expected them two to die fightin' and not in retirement." Jeb spoke and then broke out laughing.

Jarel laughed and then replied, "Actually, I don't think either one of 'em ever expected to live to be thirty, much less to be the old buzzards they are. I love to listen to them battle with words, cuss, and carry on when they hit the whiskey. They're good men, Jeb, and both 'em still have a lot of bark on 'em, though it has worn thin in a few spots."

Ty pulled his pipe out, stuffed the bowl, and lighted it. After a few puffs to get it going well he spoke through a white cloud of smoke, "Fellers, let's get back to Crawford and the problems we got with the man."

Butterfield, just a little drunk, quickly added, "By God, now yer talkin', let's hang his ass like we did that big feller a few years back. Now what was that boys name? Ya might 'member, 'cause you brought 'em back after he killed all of them trappers fer their pelts, Ty."

Ty gave a hard look and replied, "Bull Singleton, and he cost the life of many a good man and woman before he went under."

"Well, let's catch this Crawford feller and string his ass up. They still ain't no law out heah and we all know he killed Abe, so we can give 'em a fast but fair trial and then lynch his ass." Butterfield spoke as he reached over for the bottle of rye.

"First things first, Butterfield. I suggest we all get a good night's sleep here, leave early in the mornin' and head up to Coldcreek. Once in town we can spread out and see what we can find." As Jeb spoke he absentmindedly rubbed the stump of his right leg and wondered what was to come.

Dawn broke very cold, with ice crystals in the air and the rough wooden front steps to the trading post covered with a thick frost. As Butterfield sat at the table nursing a bad hangover from the large amount of rye he had drunk the night before, the other men were giving their orders to Frank. Soon, a small mountain of goods were stacked on the counter and Jeb noticed, bacon, hams, tobacco, sugar, salt, pepper, and even some gee-gaws for Indians.

It was the gee-gaws that caught his attention and he spoke of it, "What's with the trinkets to trade with the Injun's for? I thought we were going to the town."

Ty Fisher laughed, pushed his hat back a mite, and then said, "Jarel and me don't ever move without something to trade to the Injuns. See, if push comes to shove, we might even enlist the help of some Injuns in findin' this Crawford feller."

Jeb thought on the comment for a second and it made sense to him. He'd been out west long enough to know very little happened in Indian country without them knowing about it. He knew, if needed, the gee-gaws could be used to gather the local gossip on what was going on out on the plains. *I wonder what Hump and the Sioux have found out about them hide takers?* He wondered as he picked up his much smaller pile of goods and placed each item in a canvas pack he used to transport it in. He'd found the oiled canvas kept his supplies dry and it made unloading a pack horse at the end of the day much easier.

"Did ya remember to pull me a jug of whiskey and a bottle of laudanum?" Jefferson asked, knowing the rough and raw trader's alcohol was all they had to kill pain with once a man was hurt. Laudanum was good for treating a serious injury, but it was habit forming.

"I put it on the counter there, on the right." Frank replied with a big grin as he pointed at the trader's whiskey and medicine.

Jeb liked the grandson of Butterfield and from what he'd heard from both Ty and Jarel he was a younger image of his grandpa. He was plump, had long brown hair and beard, clear green eyes, and a genuine smile, a rare thing among traders.

"Jefferson Jones?" Butterfield asked as he poured himself a half a glass of rye, or the hair of the dog, as the old mountain men called it. It was sure to cure the old man's upset stomach and end his retching from drinking too much the night before.

"Yes sir?" The black man asked as he turned toward the old man.

"If ya ever need a thing, ya come and see me son. I've been 'round black folk a long time and I've yet to meet one that was not a man of his word. As a matter of fact, if ya get that farm ya was tellin' me 'bout last night, I'll send Frank to Coldcreek to get the supplies ya'll need. I'm not sure they'd sell to a man of yer color, but they will to Frank."

At first Jefferson felt anger, but then he realized the old man's intentions were honest and his thinking might be right on the money. He'd not given the fact he would need things, or that he might have to buy them in a white town, any thought at all. He gave a big smile to Butterfield and replied, "I'll do that and I thank you kindly for the help sir."

Butterfield just chuckled and said, "I didn't think ya'd thought of all of that yet, not with the revenge on yer mind. Ya just go on about yer business, yer with three good men, and when ya need them supplies come and let me know."

Two hours later the four men were moving slowly over the open plains as a light, but cold, wind blew from the north. Jeb pulled his coat tightly around himself, pulled his hat down lower and glanced at Ty Fisher. Ty was riding beside Jeb and the weather didn't seem to bother him one iota.

Finally, Jeb asked, "Ain't ya cold at all Ty?"

"Little, but not compared to what I will be tonight. There's a northerner comin' son and the temperature could be fifty below zero by midnight. I suspect Jarel is leading us to a river about three or four more miles up the trail that has a nice grow of post oaks around it. We can get us some shelters up, a warm fire burning, and some stew in us in no time. Let's just hope the snow fall is slight and the weather is good enough for us to travel in the mornin'."

Jeb looked up at the dark gray clouds rolling overhead, realized they might be in for some rough weather, but he couldn't figure out how Ty could tell a severe snow storm was coming. While he could usually spot rough weather, he'd yet to be able to consistently call storms before they hit.

Jeb was still thinking about the weather two hours later when the wind started to howl, the snow was coming down in huge white flakes, and he sat under the canvas covering of his lean-to sipping a hot cup of coffee. Since the first day he'd met a mountain man, Jeb was never surprised by what they knew about the weather, animals, Injuns, or just people in general. *It's like they've become part critter themselves*, he thought as he leaned back against his saddle.

"I been doin' me some thinkin' on this Crawford feller. I think it would be best if me and Ty went in town together, then Jeb, and finally you Jefferson." Jarel spoke as he refilled the once emptied coffee pot.

"Me and you could act as if we want to join some buff huntin' team and look around the saloon a bit. Jeb, ya check out the livery stable, hotel, store and those sorts of places, while Jefferson needs to talk to any colored folks in town." Ty said and then added quickly, "And, Jefferson I doubt if anything happens in this town without yer people knowin' what's going on. But, remember, there won't be but a family or two in the whole town, so ya'll have to look hard to find 'em."

Jefferson laughed and replied, "From what y'all done told me, it's a small place to start with, but I'll find 'em if there are any in town at all."

"Well," Jarel spoke as he wrapped his buffalo robe around his shoulders, "all of ya get some rest and I'll stand guard. We'll be leaving an hour before first light."

CHAPTER
12

They were just one day out of town when they stopped for the night. The mules pulling the wagons were exhausted and ruts in the grasses, from the overloaded vehicles, were visible for miles behind the small group. Ben was concerned about the ruts, because any Indians that happened across the trail would be sure to follow and he knew after the warning given by the Sioux there would be hell to pay if the same group discovered them. He suspected there would be no warning this time, just a lightning fast attack that would leave most, if not all of the white men dead. At the same time, he expected Crawford and his men to make a move for the hides any day now, especially since they were so close to the town. Ben had slept poorly during the last few nights and his eyes burned from the lack of sleep as he'd worried about one attack or the other.

Cookie fixed a dinner of biscuits, buffalo steaks, fried potatoes, and the ever present coffee. As soon as the meal was finished and the dishes put away, the men not on guard duty gathered around the small camp-fire to talk.

It was the same each evening so Ben didn't give the situation much thought until John Crawford said over the rim of his steaming coffee cup, "Watkins, me and my men are takin' these hides the rest of the way. Ya can walk back to town and live, or fight us and die right where you sit."

"Well, now, Crawford, that's interesting. Ya think yer men can just up and take our hides from us without a fight?" Watkins asked in a flat voice as his eyes narrowed.

A few moments before dinner, Ben had loosened the thong on his pistol hammer and had been ready for trouble from the very start.

There came a loud scream from behind the chuck wagon and one of Crawford's men walked out reaching for something behind him. It was not until he fell that Ben saw a long butcher knife buried up to the handle between the man's shoulder blades. Almost immediately there came a loud blast from a shotgun from behind the wagon and he heard Cookie yell out, "Eat them lead beans ya sonsofbitches and I'll feed ya some mo'."

The man who usually sat across the fire from Crawford reached for his pistol, but Buffalo Watkins fired his pistol first and Ben saw the second button on the man's shirt disappear in a spurt of red blood. There followed four or five more shots, and all the while Ben kept his eyes locked on John Crawford, but the man never even blinked. Finally, after one more loud shot from the scatter gun it grew quiet.

"Ben, see what we got. I want to know how many men are killed or hurt, even his men." Watkins ordered as he continued to point his pistol at Crawford.

Ten minutes later Ben returned, squatted by the fire and poured himself a cup of coffee. Finally, he turned toward the ex-partisan and said, "You're a might shy on men to share yer pay with Mister Crawford. Ya got four dead, three seriously hurt, and one missing four fingers. Of yer three badly hurt fellers, well, I don't expect two of 'em to still be with us in the mornin'."

"How 'bout us Ben?" Buffalo asked as he glared at Crawford.

"One dead, Haines took a knife in the back while he was guarding the horses. I suspect he was the one they started the dance with. By the looks of the sign he never knew they were out to kill 'em until the job was done. Cookie cut his right finger a bit when he stabbed that first feller, but that's it."

Watkins looked at Crawford, slowly shook his head and then said, "Ya fellers always think ya can make money the easy way. Well, sometimes ya can and sometimes ya cain't. This time, ya cain't." Then, turning quickly to Ben he added, "Cut two horses for these three men. I want ya to let them keep one fully loaded pistol, one knife, and that's it. Then, as they ride off, me and ya will keep our Sharps rifles on their backs."

"Ya can't do that to us, that's the same as murder! Where do ya expect us to go?" Crawford screamed as he stood and Ben took the man's pistol from his belt.

"Where can you go?" Watkins asked and then laughed loudly as he said, "Why Mister John Crawford, ya can go straight to hell."

As soon as the three men had mounted and rode off, Watkins yelled, "Load it all up, we're riding through the night. We'll take it slow and easy for the mules, but I want to be long gone from here come sunup. There ain't no stoppin' until we hit the town."

It was mid-morning when the six heavy wagons entered the town of Coldcreek and Ben had never been so happy in his life to see a place. The wagons wheels creaked and groaned loudly as they neared the shipping center for the hides, located next to the railroad tracks. Buffalo Watkins dismounted, made his way inside and returned a few minutes later with a squirrelly looking thin man wearing gold rimmed glasses.

The two of them slowly circled the wagons and finally the squirrel said, "I'll get two of my men, grade and count the hides, then give you a price. But, if they all look as good as the ones I've seen so far you're looking at over seven thousand dollars."

"Holy shit!" Cookie blurted out from the top of his wagon seat.

"Well, get yer men. I'm staying right heah as ya do the task. Ben," Watkins said as he reached into his pocket and pulled out a gold eagle, "take the men over to the saloon and buy 'em some drinks. I'll come by directly and pay 'em all off fer the season."

"Alright fellers, ya heard the boss. Let's get over to the saloon and have a drink." Ben spoke and then laughed; more at the fact he'd cheated death than anything to do with being in a good humor.

He'd no sooner entered the saloon than he knew something was wrong. The place only had four men in it and it was too quiet. He bought a bucket of cold beer and took it outside for Cookie. While the black man might work for Watkins, he wasn't allowed in the saloon.

As he bellied up to the bar Ben asked the barkeeper, "What's goin' on around here? The town is quiet and this place is like a graveyard."

The bartender shook his head and replied, "Sioux. I guess ya took that job with Watkins and ya've been out on the plains, but we got us a regular war comin' with them red bastards."

"When did that start? Or, hell, why?" Ben asked as he pointed toward a bottle of rye on the bar.

As the barkeeper poured his drink, Ben heard the man say, "Near as we know, and it came by telegraph, the Sioux are pissed about the buffalo bein' killed off. They claim y'all are killin' the animals and just leavin' the meat to rot. But, I say, who gives a rat's ass what a bunch of filthy Sioux think."

Ben thought for a few minutes before he said, "We do leave the meat to rot and we just came in with six wagons stacked to hell and back with hides."

The barkeeper smiled and said, "So what? From what I hear there are millions of the big shaggy critters out there so what harm does six wagons loads of skins do to the head count."

"How many hide crews work out of here?"

"Hell, I don't know, maybe, uh, twenty or so, why?"

"And, how many towns out west are buying hides?"

"Near all of 'em from what I heard from the newspaper man, hell, there's good money to be made from hunting hides. All businesses make some money from the skinners and hunters, not to mention the money helps every town and city grow just a little more."

"Look, if there are, let's say twenty hunters in those crews here in town and they kill on an average what I killed out on the plains. And, I killed about forty a day, so that makes the daily killing average out to be around eight hundred buffalo a day, or over five thousand a week."

"So?"

"Do ya think the Sioux will allow over twenty thousand buffalo a month to be killed? And that's just from this small town."

The bartender thought for a few minutes as he rubbed a beer glass dry with a dirty rag, shook his head, and then said, "Nope, I think I see yer point. Only, shit, killin' the buffalo off don't hurt me none, now does it?"

Ben gave a dry laugh and replied, "It might if ya try to leave town."

At that point Buffalo Watkins entered the saloon, bellied up to the bar and ordered a rye with beer chaser. He gave Ben a big grin and said, "We made over seven thousand dollars. After I pay Cookie and the skinners, I'll give you your share. Near as I got it figured, ya earned a little over two thousand dollars for a few days of hard work. Now, as soon as spring comes along we'll head out again."

"Nope, I've had enough hide takin' Buffalo. I don't like the job and I was just looking for some movin' money when I met ya."

"Awww, come on Ben. Me and ya make one hell of a team! I'll tell ya what, ya go out once more and I'll split the profits fifty-fifty with ya."

Ben thought for a few minutes, remembered the Sioux were now at war, shook his head and said, "No thanks Buffalo. Yer a good man and ya have a good crew, but I'm not cut out to be no buffalo hunter."

Watkins pulled a wad of bills from his right trouser pocket and counted out twenty-one hundred dollars and handed the money to Ben. He gave a weak grin, stuck out his hand and said, "I'll miss ya son. Yer a good man Ben Bacher and if ya ever need work again ya come and see old Buffalo Watkins!"

As the two men shook hands, Ben replied, "I'll keep ya in mind, but don't wait on me. I've places to see and with this much money I might even head back to Missouri and buy me a farm."

At that point the bat-wing doors to the saloon swung open wide and two ancient mountain men walked in. They selected a table back by the wall so they could keep the door clearly in sight and ordered two beers. Ben noticed they talked with low voices and rarely did they look around the Saloon.

"Well, Ben, if ya change yer mind later just come by my room at the hotel." Watkins said, then turned toward his men and said, "Alright fellers follow me to my room and I'll see y'all get paid."

Ben felt filthy and knew he had the smell of death hanging on him. *I'll finish my beer, go to the hotel, and then have a bath and a good shave. No doubt about it, I'll have to throw these clothes away*, he thought as he gulped his beer down.

He had just started to turn from the bar when he heard a deep bass voice ask, "Ya at the bar, ya got a minute for an old mountain man? I'll even buy ya a beer!"

When Ben turned toward the voice he almost laughed, it came from one of the old mountain men sitting at the table, and he knew while both of the men were over the hill, they were still very dangerous men. He could see it very clearly in their eyes.

"I'll be over at the table, barkeep, so bring us three beers." Ben stated and made his way to the table.

"Have a sit down, young feller." The older looking of the two men said as Ben neared the table.

"Don't mind Iffen I do." Ben said as his chair made a loud screeching sound as it moved on the oak flooring under the table.

"Ya a buff hunter?" The younger man asked.

"Yep, was, but no more, because I quit today. And, I'm Ben Bacher."

There was a quick shaking of hands and then older man said, "I'm Ty Fisher and this young pup is Jarel Wade. We're lookin' fer a murderin' sumbitch named Crawford; know 'em?"

"Yep, I know the man. We had a run in with 'em out on the plains and ran his ass off. He went along on the trip to provide security against the Sioux, but once we had six wagons loaded high with hides and heading back to town he wanted to take the whole shebang."

Jarel snickered and said, "Well, at least he's smarter than most crooks, he let you do most of the work before he made his move."

"From what I heard from the barkeeper he's most likely dead by now. The beer slinger told me the Sioux were out looking for blood over the slaughter of the buffalo."

Ty met Ben's eyes and asked, "Is that why ya quit killing buffs, 'cause yer scared of the Sioux?"

Ben laughed and said, "No, I just don't really enjoy shooting any animal that just stands there and lets me have at 'em. But, while I ain't really scared of the Sioux, ya can bet yer ass I respect the hell out of 'em as fighters and only a fool would ignore 'em."

Ty grinned and replied, "Well, yer a smart man then. The Sioux can be some fierce fighters when they want to be and they've scared the shit out of me a time 'er two. All of 'em do have the hair of the bear on 'em, yep they surely do. Only a fool would say he has no fear or respect for the red man."

"Which way was Crawford movin' the last time ya saw 'em?" Jarel asked as he noticed the bartender bringing the beers toward the table.

Ben waited until the barkeeper left, and then he replied, "West and there were three of 'em and with only two horses. We made him leave three of his seriously wounded, but they all died before morning."

"That does happen to hurt people from time to time, but I don't suspect yer boys helped them along the way a mite, did they?" Jarel asked with a big grin.

"No, a few of the men wanted to jess kill 'em right off, but Buffalo Watkins he wouldn't let 'em do the job."

"Now, son, what in the hell is a Buffalo Watkins?" Ty asked as he raised his glass and blew the foam from the top.

"Big buffalo hunter. He's an excellent shot, overall a good man, though a bit on the wild and rough side."

"Hell, that sounds like ya when ya was a young pup Jarel!" Ty said and then broke out in a loud laugh.

"What are ya goin' to do now, Ben?" Jarel asked as he ignored Ty's comment.

"I ain't got no idea. I might just drift down Taos way for a spell, or over to Missouri."

Jarel spent the next ten minutes explaining how Crawford killed three black people, burned a home, and then disappeared. Hell, he'd seen enough killing in the Deep South. *But*, he thought as he met the eyes of both of the old mountain men, *I'll have to be invited to this dance.*

"So, with all of that said, how would ya like to help us skin a skunk?" Ty Fisher spoke as he pulled his pipe from his possibles bag and place it between his teeth.

"I'll come along. I have little use for a murderer." Ben replied and then leaned back in his chair as he held his beer glass in his left hand and rested it on his chest.

"But," Jarel said with a laugh, "first you need to find some serious soap, water, and new clothes, 'cause you're a bit ripe son."

"And" Ty was laughing as well when he added, "when a mountain man tells a man he needs a bath, well, ya can bet yer ass he needs it in the worstest way too!"

Two hours later Ben was in his room buckling on his gun belt after a bath, shave, and putting on some new clothes. While he felt better physically, his mind was worried over letting Crawford go when they had him. But, hell, the thought as he slipped the leather thong down over the hammer to his pistol, *we didn't know he did all them killings at the time. And, knowing Buffalo and the rest of the crew like I do, I suspect the only one that would have cared about people being killed would be Cookie.*

Ben placed his new hat on his head, adjusted his bandanna, and then left the room. He was to meet Ty and Jarel in the hotel lobby and it was one meeting he didn't want to miss. As far as he knew, the two old mountain men would ride through the flaming gates of hell to get their hands on John Crawford and when they did there would be a high price to pay.

In the lobby the two elderly mountain men should have felt way out of place, but they didn't. Jarel Wade had enough money saved to buy the place a couple of times over and Ty Fisher, while he lacked the funds, could have bought it on his word alone. Neither man seemed to notice the odd glances they received from the hotel's occupants as they passed by.

"Well, now, ya sure as all get out look and smell better!" Ty said as Ben came down the staircase toward the two men.

"I think the canvas pants and the work shirt will do better than the homespun ya was wearin' earlier. And, the new sheepskin coat is better than that thin thing ya had on in the saloon. Personal like, I don't care much fer the boots ya got on, but they'll do." Jarel stated as he looked the young man over closely.

Ben laughed and then asked with a big grin, "Do I smell any better after a bath and a shave?"

Ty slapped him on the back and replied, "Jus' like one of them French whores I met once down in New Orleans."

Jarel turned serious and said in a low voice, "Ben, ya'll find our travelin' partners a strange group. We got us a one legged man named Jeb Patton and a young man named Jefferson Jones. Now, if you don't like colored folks, ya speak up right now, because Jones is one of us and he's a part of this whole shebang."

"Uh, Jarel, ya forgot the other feller." Ty quickly added with a grin.

"Oh, yea, Jefferson picked up another black man named Cookie that was lookin' fer a job. Seems he used to work with the hide hunters too, but he quit." Jarel added, gave a crooked grin and added, "So, if yer a man that hates blacks, well, we're not the group for ya."

Ben laughed and thought, *if you only knew*, but said, "Nope, I ain't got no problems with any man's color, but I've had problems with some men of different colors. I don't like all black folks, but then again I don't like all white folks either. If a man will stand when trouble hits and is honest, then I'm likely to have no problems with him. Besides, Cookie I know and he has sand in his crawl."

"Well, come on out and let me introduce you to Jefferson and Patton then. I want to be on the trail in an hour. Once ya meet the boys, ya go pack yer gear, and then meet us at the livery." Ty spoke as he turned toward the door.

CHAPTER
13

M any miles away and out on the open plains, John Crawford was having a rough time surviving. Frank Young had been hit hard when the hide crew attacked and the man was still bleeding, though two days had passed. The other man, a ruthless killer by the name of Cy Light, was unharmed but absolutely scared to death. They'd seen the tracks of a large Sioux war party earlier that day and Light had counted the tracks of over one hundred ponies. They knew if the Indians caught them they were dead men and the three weren't easy men to scare. They'd spent the years of the Civil War riding together with both Quantrill and Bloody Bill Anderson, so they had years of experience of knowing when to be frightened and when not to be. Alone and deep in Sioux country, with just one hand gun and one knife, fear came easy to each of them.

"John, I think this horse me and Frank are riding is about done in ridin' double." Cy spoke as they made their way toward some trees growing beside a narrow stream in a small valley.

"Pull up in those trees down there and we'll see what we can do about it." Crawford replied, but deep in his mind he'd already decided.

Frank moaned in deep pain as the two men lowered him to a blanket spread out under a large oak tree. Crawford noticed the man's side was bleeding again and it didn't look good as far as he was concerned.

"Let me take a good look at your side and check the bleedin'." Crawford spoke as he pulled his sharp knife and kneeled beside the man.

"I . . . I'll be . . . alright in a few days. I jess need me some rest." The injured man managed to get out as he watched the eyes of Crawford closely, because he didn't trust the man.

Yeah, rest, and we're right in the middle of damned Sioux country, Crawford thought as he pulled Frank's shirt up enough to see the wound. The entry hole was about the size of a man's little finger while the exit was more than twice the size of a fat thumb. The injury had a bad bruise around it and both holes were still leaking blood.

"Frank, this ain't gonna work. Yer slowin' us down, the horse can't keep ridin' the two of ya, and I don't think even with rest ya'll survive."

"What do ..." Frank started to ask, but was cut short when he saw the knife in Crawford's hand fall with quick flash and felt the blade go deeply into his stomach and then slide up and under his rib cage.

Crawford quickly threw his left hand over Frank's mouth to muffle his screams and brought the bloody blade up and down twice more. Then, as the man's body trembled and quivered as death claimed him, Crawford ran the sharp blade swiftly over the man's throat. A fountain of blood quickly erupted; his heels drummed softly in the hard dirt and at last his body went limp. Frank Young had ridden his last trail.

Turning to face Cy, Crawford spoke, "He was dying anyway. The best I could do for him was to end the pain and make sure at least ya'll live. If the two of ya had kept ridin' that horse it would have eventually gone lame."

Cy didn't make eye contact with Crawford as he said, "Its best this way, if he was goin' to die anyways. Hell, I ain't got a scratch on me, so I deserve a chance to live." But, as soon as he had spoken he thought, *I'll never turn my back on ya when I'm hurt, ya sonofabitch, nor will I ever trust you again.*

"We'll rest here for a couple of hours. I know the horses need it and maybe we can find something to eat. Ya look fer some greens while I see if I can find any game in the area. Since we're close to water I might get lucky. Give me the pistol and I'll be right back" Crawford spoke as he cleaned his bloody knife off on the dead man's shirt and then stood with his hand out for their only real weapon.

It was just before noon when Crawford returned with two rear quarters of a deer he had shot about two miles from camp. The wind had picked up and the clouds had turned from infrequent puffs of thin cotton to a solid moving gray ceiling overhead. As he neared the campsite, he noticed no smoke from the campfire and small animal sounds that were usually so evident couldn't be heard. He lowered the meat to the grass and edged up to the spot where he'd left Cy Light.

Cy was lying in the grass, but Crawford was unable to determine if the man was injured, dead or sleeping. He decided to wait a few minutes and make sure no one else was around. The ex-partisan knew in a situation like this the first person to move was usually the first one to die. If Cy was asleep he'd be up and moving before long, if he was dead, well, he was dead. Crawford didn't really think the man was just injured because he heard no cries for help or moans that he knew so well of the wounded. *No, I'll wait and see what happens. If he's gone to sleep I'll kick his ass, but this don't look right to me for some reason,* he thought as he pulled the pistol and locked the hammer back.

Two hours later Cy still hadn't moved. Crawford made his way around the camp, making sure he was alone. It was not until he got to where he could see where the horses should have been that he knew he was too late. The mounts were both gone. Standing in the tall buffalo grass, Crawford cautiously made his way to the downed Cy Light.

The man had been shot full of arrows, scalped, and this belly opened up like a pig at a butchering. His unseeing eyes were open and not even the fly moving over the open left eye could make the dead man blink. Crawford knew immediately when he saw Cy's throat was cut the Sioux had done the job, because the cut throats were what all of the other tribes called them. After examining the arrow shafts and the moccasin tracks in the dirt near where the horses had been tied to a picket line, he knew the Sioux had done the killing.

While he didn't really care one way or the other about Cy Light's death, the fact he'd lost a man able to provide additional security, as well as the horses, bothered him a great deal. *Fine damned mess I'm in now. Miles from any town, by myself, and no horse,* he thought as he made his way to Frank Young. He'd found no weapons or anything of value on Lights body, but he knew Young had some matches and tobacco.

Frank's body had been scalped and mutilated just as Light's had been, except that Crawford had already cut the man's throat before he left to hunt. He sat in the grass near the dead man and thought, *the only reason them Sioux didn't come looking for me was the fact that we only had two horses. I guess after they found Young and Light, they must have figured they were alone out here. Nobody, white or red, would ever suspect three men to be riding two horses and that, Mister John Crawford, saved your worthless ass.*

The closest town was miles away, but Crawford started his slow walk as he kept to the lowest points on the plains as he moved north. As near as he could remember, he should be almost fifty miles from Omaha, and that would be a good two or three day walk, if he could stay alive long enough to get there. If he could only reach Omaha or Lincoln, he had money in both places and Crawford knew in just a few days he could have other men following him. There were always men out looking to make easy money and if he knew how to do anything, Crawford knew how to handle rough men.

He walked the rest of the day through and all of night. It was near dawn before he finally decided to stop and continue his move north that evening. He determined it would be safer for him to hide during the day and then move only after the sun had gone down. While traveling at night would make for much slower walking, he knew Indians rarely moved at night, so his biggest concern would be finding a good spot to hide during the day. What worried him the most was the fact a good hiding spot might look good at dawn, but not be so good once the sun was up. But, Crawford was a tough man, used to taking risks and chances, and he was unwavering in his strong desire to survive.

His first day hiding was long, dry, and he was hungry when he finally moved out from under a slight overhang he had discovered by a small stream. It was dusk, and though the sun had not gone completely down, a gray veil was covering the plains from horizon to horizon. In a few hours the moon would be out and Crawford knew walking would become easier at that point. He stretched his cramped and tired muscles, took a small sip from the stream, and started moving north using the stars as a guide.

It was near sunup when he spotted glowing red eyes in the distance and knew immediately it was coals from a dying campfire. The man moved forward on his belly and looked the campsite over closely. He spotted three horses and a mule, with two men stretched out in blankets near the fire, which meant the third man must be guarding the camp. At first Crawford planned to kill the camp guard with a knife and then simply shoot the other two men in their blankets, but changed his mind after he thought it over. *Hell*, he thought as he pulled the leather thong from his pistol hammer on his belt, *I might learn something if I talk to these fellers a little. I might even talk 'em into joining me, if I offer 'em enough money. No, I'll talk and see what happens. If they give me any shit I can always kill 'em later.*

Standing in the false dawn breaking in the east, Crawford called out, "Hello the camp! I'm a white man and I've had Injun trouble!"

A few moments of silence followed then he heard a yell in return, "Come on in, but keep yer rifle high and in yer left hand!"

"I ain't got no rifle, but when I come in both of my hands will be up high." Crawford replied and slowly made his way to the camp, scanning the countryside for the guard as he moved.

"That's far 'nough. Emmit, ya put some buffalo pies on the fire and let's see what we got here. Reed, ya move over to the left and keep him covered with your Sharps." The voice Crawford had heard earlier ordered from the dim gray light of early morning.

"My name is John Roland and my two partners were killed by the Sioux two days back. The Injuns got our guns, horses, and all of our supplies. Hell, I'm lucky to be alive."

"I'm Luke, the man by the fire is Emmit, and the feller with the big Sharps over there is Reed. How'd ya get away from them Sioux, 'cause that don't happen often."

Crawford told of how they'd been out hunting and continued his lie as he explained how one horse had broken a leg so they were forced to double up on one of the other mounts as they moved north. He explained that the only reason he could see the Sioux hadn't killed him was because the two men killed had been alone and with only two horses."

"Nope, I suspect that's not true. I'm willin' to bet ya a dollar against a plug nickel them Sioux knew ya were along with them other two fellers, but for some reason they didn't want to take the time to look fer ya. Yep, not a doubt about it in my mind, they knew about ya. I'm certain they picked up on yer tracks 'cause little escapes a warrior's eyes. I suspect they just didn't want to take the time to look fer ya." Luke spoke as he squatted and moved the buffalo chips around in the fire so they would burn better.

A sudden shiver went down Crawford's spine as he realized just how close to death he'd really come. He turned to Luke and asked, "You fellers heading out or in?"

"In, we've been out running messages fer the army in Omaha. Usually they only send one or two men, but with the Sioux raising hell like they are, well, ain't none of us go out with less than three fellers along."

"Do ya mind if I tag along with ya?"

Luke laughed, pointed at an old mule, and said, "It's not a problem, but ya'll have to ride that old Missouri mule, 'cause that's all we got left. We used him to carry the dispatches, mail, and supplies when we went out."

The man named Emmit moved over to the fire and started slicing salt pork into a large cast iron skillet. Crawford saw the man was of average size, had long brown hair, mustache of the same color, and quick eyes that spoke of his experience riding in Indian country. As he glanced at Reed he saw pretty much the same, except the man had blond hair and a full beard. Like Emmit, he was an experienced trail man as well.

"We'll eat a bite and then hit the trail. I've no desires to stay around out here any longer than I have to. The army ain't payin' me enough to seriously risk my hair." Luke spoke as he rolled up his blanket and grinned.

"When was the last time you et?" Emmit asked as he turned the pork with the tip of his big hunting knife.

Crawford, recently turned Roland, replied with a dry smile, "The day before yesterday I had dinner, but when the Injuns attacked yesterday they didn't leave a damned thing for me, except a little deer meat."

"I fig'ered as much. Damned red skins don't leave much when they pass through a camp, farm, or what-not," Emmit spoke and then continued as he pointed his knife tip at Crawford, "yer a lucky man, John Roland, 'cause not many survive when the Sioux are out in force."

Crawford felt his stomach rumble and heard it growl at the smell of the cooking meat. He'd been so scared as he moved toward Omaha and away from the Sioux that the last thing on his mind had been food, so now that he was reasonably safe, his hunger returned. He watched as Luke filled an old and beat-up blackened coffee pot with water, and then dropped a good healthy hand full of coffee grounds to the water. Reed walked to the fire, dropped a burlap bag, and then returned to his spot to guard the group. As Luke opened the bag, Crawford noticed it was filled with rock hard jerky and some stale biscuits.

While Luke pulled out four biscuits he handed a long sliver of jerky to Crawford and said, "Eat this slowly as breakfast cooks. There ain't nothin' worser than bein' hungry fer a spell and it makes a man feel a bit weak."

Crawford gave Luke the once over with his eyes and noticed the man was a big man, a little over six feet tall, maybe two hundred and fifty pounds, with black hair, a square jaw, and piercing dark brown eyes. John could see easily why Luke was the leader of this group, the man had an air of self-confidence and with just one look it was easy to see that the man knew the woods and plains better than some folks knew their kitchens. As he evaluated Luke, Crawford thought, *I'll ride to Omaha with these fellers. If they are on army business I don't want to kill 'em and then get the army involved, plus these three might be hard men to kill. The last thing I need is to pick up some lead or get the government after my ass fer some killin's.*

"Thanks, I appreciate the food." Crawford spoke and then asked, "How much further to Omaha, I kind of lost track the last couple of days."

"It's about a hard day's ride. If we travel hard and long enough today, we'll be there a little after dark. And, believe me, with all these

Sioux around we'll get in tonight. The only thing that could keep us from Omaha today would be if we run into some Injuns and have to hunt a hole to hide in fer a spell."

"Should be less Injuns the closer we get to the city, right?" Crawford asked as he tore off a large chunk of jerky.

"Maybe, but then again maybe not. If the Sioux want to ambush some army messengers or such they'll move in closer to the place. I can tell you one thing though, if ya want to still be alive when we do ride into Omaha, ya'd better be prepared to shoot in a second's notice to protect yer ass. We ain't really safe until we hit the middle of the damned town as far as I am concerned."

And, once we're in Omaha, I'll get some money from the bank, find a few men, and go back for my revenge against Buffalo Watkins. When I finish with his fat ass I'll go looking for Jeb Patton. If it's one thing I hate more than anything in this world, it's him, Crawford thought as he ran his right hand through his greasy hair and mechanically chewed his jerky.

It was well past sundown when the four men rode into Omaha and Reed was carrying a Sioux arrow in his upper back. After a quick breakfast that morning the group had broken camp and headed north with Emmit on point and Reed bringing up the rear. At the nooning, Reed had come forward and reported seeing some movement on their back trail, so Luke had decided to not make a run until they were closer to the town. He wanted their horses well rested in case they had to ride for their lives and it proved to be sound thinking, because about two miles outside of town they were suddenly ambushed and the group made a mad dash for safety.

Reed was bent forward over his saddle with a grip of steel on the saddle horn and his legs tight against the sides of his big roan. He might have been hurting, but the man knew it was nothing compared to how he'd hurt if the Sioux took his ass alive. It was only his years of living in the mountains and out on the open plains that saved his life, because a lesser man would have fallen or given up. The shaft of the arrow was completely through his body with the feathers visible in the upper left side of his back and the bloody arrowhead protruding from the upper left side of his chest. He'd been lucky and he knew it. The arrow had missed his lights and had come out more or less near his left arm socket.

"You!" Luke yelled at a cowboy sitting in front of the saloon, "Go and fetch me a sawbones and do it now!"

"I'll be right back!" The cowboy called out over his shoulder as he ran down the rough oak planking of the boardwalk.

"Let's get 'em off the hoss and on the bench there by the saloon." Emmit spoke as he dismounted and made his way to Reed's horse.

As they placed the injured man on the bench, he claimed he was well enough to sit up and refused to lie down. Luke had just cut the man's shirt off when a middle-aged man, wearing a brown derby hat, and carrying a black bag in his right hand rushed up. He knelt beside Reed, looked the wound over closely and then said, "He'll live, but I need for a couple of you men to bring him up to my office where I have more equipment and better light. His arm will be sore for a few days and it might be stiff for months, but it looks to me like the damage done was not great."

As Luke and Emmit helped Reed to his feet John Crawford said, "Fellers, thanks for the ride to Omaha. When ya get the time, ya two come by the saloon and I'll buy ya both a drink."

Luke looked over his right shoulder, grinned, and replied, "We might jes do that once we have Reed here looked at."

Crawford entered the saloon, walked up to the bar and ordered a double rye whiskey. As soon as his drink was brought to him he pulled out his last ten dollars. He knew come morning he'd draw more from the bank and the ten was more than enough money for the night. As he sipped his drink he asked the bartender, "What time does the bank open in the morning?"

The bartender was a big fat man, with huge arms, and long greasy brown hair. He gave Crawford a big tooth-gapped grin and replied, "Nine sharp and it closes at four on the dot. It's about the only thing in this whole damned town that is dependable, unless you count cowboys comin' in here to get drunked up on the first of each month."

Crawford laughed, ordered a beer, and then asked, "Ya got rooms to let here?"

"Yep, fifty cents a night and a bath is a dime."

"That's a single room right?"

"Yep, it sure is. Ya want to share a room it's a quarter a night."

Placing his money on the bar, Crawford said, "Take the price of the drinks, a bath, and two nights lodgin' from that. And, I want a single room."

The big man handed him a key along with his change and said, "Room 109, top of the stairs on the right, and the bathhouse is outback. Anything else you need?"

Crawford thought for a minute then replied, "Yup, send me up a bottle of rye and round me up a soiled dove for the night too. Send her up in a couple of hours. Any idea how much she'd charge?"

"Kattie is good and she's only a dollar a night, unless you want something special, then it's between you and her as far as the price goes. The rye is a dollar a quart."

"That's fine. In the mean time, I'll finish this rye, have me a hot bath, and change. Have the rye put in my room immediately and send the woman up in about two hours." Crawford spoke and then thought, *and by the end of the week I'll be looking for your ass Buffalo Watkins and when I find you one of us will die.* He quickly raised his whiskey, emptied the glass, and slapped it down on the bar top with a loud slap. He then turned and walked slowly toward his room.

CHAPTER
14

Jeb and his mixed group rode up to the small group of trees beside the small stream where Young and Light had been killed. Ty immediately saw Light's body in the grasses and warned the other men to come no closer until he checked it out. The old mountain man had two reasons for doing this; first he didn't know if the killers were still around, and second, he didn't want the tracks trampled on and the sign disturbed.

Thirty minutes later he mounted and rode back and said, "Sioux. They killed one man, another man was already dead before the attack, and a third man got away. Let's get over there and bury the poor bastards. From what I can tell, though, it was Crawford and his men."

Less than five minutes later both Cookie and Ben identified Young and Light, and the sign showed that Crawford must have escaped the killings. As soon as the two men were buried, Ben asked, "Ty, how did ya know Young wasn't killed by the Sioux?"

The old man chuckled and replied, "First, there was no sign of a fight at all. No arrows in 'em, no recent gunshot wounds, just stabs in his belly, and his throat was cut. Now, Iffen the Sioux had caught 'em alive, they would have taken him home to play with most likely. Also, by the lack of any sign of a fight, I'd say whoever killed the man, well, he trusted. His gunshot wound was old, because it was badly bruised and there were old cloth bandages wrapped on him."

"Couldn't the Sioux have snuck up on him, cut his throat then mutilate him like that?" Cookie asked with his eyes narrow with questions.

"Nope. See, a warrior could have cut his throat, and they for sure did mutilate him, but they had no reason to stab him in the belly like that. If a Sioux got 'em he would have cut his throat, but the sign I saw showed every warrior who approached him had walked right up to him, in clear view."

"So, he must have been dead when the Sioux arrived." Jeb spoke as he placed an armload of wood beside the dead fire.

"Yep," Ty said and then asked, "Jarel, ya read the sign the same way?"

"Pretty much the same, except I found some sign on the upper left shoulder where a knife blade was wiped clean and I ain't never seen a Sioux clean a knife on a dead man's shirt. As a matter of fact, they take pride in having a bloody knife blade."

Ty chuckled and spoke once more, "And, when I circled this place I found two quarters of deer meat back in the long grasses. There was a chunk cut out of one piece, but the rest was left, as if the man couldn't carry it all. What I think happened is, Crawford killed your man Young, then went hunting and got a deer. After he quartered it he could only carry two quarters, so when he returned to camp he found the Sioux had killed these men and took the horses. I saw tracks heading north, so I suspect he's walking to Omaha."

"How fur is this Omaha?" Cookie asked as he stoked the fire so he could fix dinner on the hot coals.

"Fifty miles and iffen he's lucky he'll make it. If he ain't lucky the Sioux will catch his ass and then he'll regret the day he was born." Jarel spoke as he pulled out a twist of chewing tobacco and cut off a large piece. After placing the tobacco in his mouth and chewing for a few minutes, he spat in the dirt by his left foot and continued, "And, so far this has been one lucky sonofabitch."

At that point a sharp crack of thunder was heard and when Jeb looked overhead he noticed clouds rolling. He had been so wrapped up in listening to what the two old mountain men could tell by reading the sign that he had failed to see the storm approaching and his lack of awareness scared him, because he knew it was a good way to die.

"We'd best get some shelters up and eat pretty dog-gone quickly if we can. It looks like a real ball buster of a storm comin' and in less than an hour or so." Ben spoke as he moved toward the supplies where the canvas had been placed.

Cookie placed a large kettle of leftover beans on the coals, made a pot of coffee, and pulled out some biscuits he had left from dinner the night before. The man gave a loud cackle and said, "I'm always ready to eat. These heah beans and bacon will be warmed up in 'bout ten minutes, the coffee will be done by then too, so dinner ain't no problem a-tall."

The men had three shelters up facing the small fire and, as soon as they'd completed the task, dinner was served. The weather, however, turned bad and the meal was eaten under the protective cover canvas provided as a hard rain beat a steady rhythm on the tightly stretched material. Occasionally bright white flashes of lightning would dance on the horizon, always followed a few seconds later by a loud crack of thunder. As Ben looked around at the other men, he noticed Ty Fisher leaning back against his pack with a book in his hands.

"Hell, ya a reader Ty?" Ben asked, somewhat confused that a rough old mountain man could read a real honest to God book.

"His nose is always stuck in a damned book!" Jarel Wade spurted out and then laughed.

Ty slowly looked up from his book and replied, "I always have been a reader Ben. I don't have no real school learnin's, not to speak of, but I ain't ignorant. Well, not like Jarel is anyway!"

The small group all laughed and then Ben asked, "What are ya reading?"

"A book by William Shakespeare called Hamlet, it's a tragedy."

Jeb gave a loud laugh, met Ty's eyes and said, "Ya mean to tell me, yer sittin' out here in the open plains in the middle of Sioux country, chasin' after a murderer, it's raining like a horse pissin' on a flat rock, and yer reading a book about a tragedy?"

Ty laughed, closed his book and said, "It's a good book about a young man named Hamlet who is asked by his father's ghost to avenge his death. Now, this boy's dead daddy had been a king, so it makes fer some interesting readin'."

Jefferson yelled out to be heard over the falling rain, "I read, but not no ghost and goblins stuff. Give me a good newspaper or a Mark Twain book any day."

Suddenly the downpour increased its tempo and all conversation stopped due to the noise of the falling rain. Ty went back to his book, Jarel whittled on a piece of pine he'd pulled from his coat pocket, Jefferson and Cookie went to sleep, and Jeb and Ben both stared at the falling rain thinking a lot about nothing.

Early the next morning the men were up and Cookie had a Dutch oven with biscuits cooking on the hot coals. The small group, minus Jeb who was guarding the camp, was gathered around the campfire enjoying a cup of coffee. The rain had completely stopped overnight, but there was a sharp bite in the wind and the temperature had dropped to the point the men could see their breaths. It would be a cold day to sit in a saddle for hours, except with the low temperature the mud had frozen and wouldn't slow the movement of the men.

"So, we just ride into Omaha and look for Crawford?" Jefferson asked as he poured a thick cup of oil, that Cookie called coffee, into his cup.

"No," Ty spoke, glanced over at Jarel and then continued, "I think a group our size would spook the 'possum. So, I been thinking maybe Jeb and Ben can ride in while the rest of us wait out of town a ways."

Jarel gave a loud laugh, slapped his right knee and said, "You jes' want to keep me from the saloons and out of trouble."

"No, not at all. Serious like, I mean, this Crawford is as dangerous as a cornered painter, we all know this and he'll notice any large group that rides in. If only two men go in, then he's not likely to notice it at all."

"Well, I knows I cain't go wid none of y'all. The man knows me and he'd spot me in a second." Cookie suddenly announced from the fire as he turned the salt pork with the point of his skinning knife.

"Cookie I don't think it would be smart to send either you or Jefferson into Omaha looking fer the man. No disrespect meant here, but as you said, Crawford already knows you. Now, if we can't find him the normal ways, then I'll send Jefferson in to contact the towns black folk. I'm sure they'll know if he's in town or not. Only, I suspect Jeb and Ben will find our man." Ty spoke as he made eye contact with the old cook.

Jefferson thought for a minute, pushed his hat back on his head, and then said, "I think you have a point there. I know no one in the town and while I could contact some other colored folks, I ain't so sure they'd trust me much either. Now, I'm sure I could get some information, but it might take me a spell, because nothing is more untrusting than a recently freed man. And, don't think that just because I'm black other black folks will take to me right off, because we ain't no different than white folks when it comes to trust."

Jarel stood, poured his coffee dregs into the fire, and said, "I'll go and relieve Jeb so he can eat. As soon as one of y'all eats come and spell me so I can have my breakfast. Then, we'll move off to the west a might, find a place for most of us to wait, and send Ben and Jeb into town."

The morning passed slowly and the ride was cold. Jeb's missing leg ached and as he rode he wondered about Crawford. It might be the man would recognize him, but he doubted it. He'd left for the war when he was just a kid of eighteen, been out west for a few years, and knew his physical appearance had changed a great deal, especially with his missing leg. As a youngster he hadn't weighed more than a hundred and thirty pounds soaking wet and in the war had even leaned him down to less than one ten. Except after coming out to the mountains he'd gained a lot of weight and none of it fat, by eating somewhat regular and working hard. The way he had it figured he was near a hundred and eighty pounds now and looked nothing like the split rail he'd been as a kid. Out west he'd done it all, built homes for friends, put up barns, cut wood for the trains, trapped, and just the life he lived alone put muscles on a man. *I may be missing a leg, but I'm in the best shape of my life*, he thought as he glanced around the countryside as he rode.

Jarel rode up beside Jeb and after a few minutes of silence said, "Jeb, me and Ty are going to head north and leave them two black fellers fer a spell. The way we got it figured is Crawford will most likely move west or north out of Omaha. I been thinkin' and I suspect he'll head north by west, hoping to get into the mountains."

Jeb thought for a few minutes, turned slightly in his saddle and replied, "That might be good thinkin'. We don't know much about Crawford and I suspect he'll soon gather up a bunch of rough riders and move on us. If we have a group west and one north we'll eventually cut his trail."

"Yep, that's jess what me and Ty figured too. If the man has money, or makes promises for easy money, he'll find men to ride with him. These saloons always have some fellers out to make money the easy way, so you can count on a few men bein' with 'em when he leaves."

"I was thinkin' on that. I like yer idea, so let's do 'er, but how will I find y'all?"

"We are near the southern part of the Platte River right now, so me and Ty will head north fer 'bout fifty miles above the town and then move over east closer to the Missouri River. But, keep in mind, we'll stay on this side of the Missouri. I got some Sioux friends up that way I can get to help us a might, if need be. I figured we can send Jefferson and Cookie out west, oh, mayhap the same distance and they can keep their eyes out. When yer done with yer business, jess ride north and we'll find ya, or our Sioux friends will."

"What about the two men out west?" Jeb asked wondering if maybe Jarel had a reason for sending the two black men out together.

Jarel gave a big grin and said, "Jeb, they're both good men, but I suspect your man Crawford will move north at first. I want our least experienced men on the west side of the town. I don't think either one of them men has enough bark on 'em, or experience, to face down Crawford and a bunch of cut throats. Then again, they might have to do the job, but I'd be surprised if it happened. We need our experienced fellers where Crawford is most likely to show up."

"Makes sense to me." Jeb said and the two men rode in silence for over an hour.

The Platte River was a good quarter of a mile wide and three inches deep, or so Jeb thought as he looked at the shallow and slow moving river. The land was flat, though a few trees lined the banks of the river and Jeb could see a whole lot of nothing in all directions as they paused for a few minutes on a slight incline just above the waterway. Ty had told him the water was not sweet, but a person could drink it if he was thirsty enough. At that moment Jeb was not thirsty or even hungry, he was just bone deep tired. The cold weather had made for a sore day in the saddle, just like he figured it would.

"We'll camp in the trees off to the right there," Ty spoke as he pointed with his right index finger, "and have dinner. Once we eat we'll rest the horses for an hour, then cross the river and sleep about a half mile inland. Come morning we'll all break up and move our own ways."

"Why the moving after we eat?" Jefferson asked as he turned slightly in his saddle to see Ty's eyes.

"Injun's mainly, but there are other reasons as well. How long you been out west Jefferson?"

"Not long and I'll be the first to admit I have a lot to learn. Only, we're pretty close to Omaha, or so I'd think, and you mean we're still not safe?"

Ty grinned, bit off a large chunk of his chewing tobacco, glanced at Jarel, and replied, "You'll do well out here if you know you have a lot to learn. See, as close as we are to the town there are a lot of movers comin' and goin' in and out. There are teamsters with wagons, individual riders, and even some small bunches like ours. Now, Jefferson, even the Injun's know that and they prey on those men as they travel on that rough road over there along side of the river. Any people movin' up or down that road would smell our fire or our food after it has been cooked. I think the Sioux move up and down that river a lot too, jess lookin' fer easy spoils. And, hell, that don't even count the bad assed white men that travel that road."

Jefferson looked embarrassed, lowered his head, and didn't speak. I should have thought of all of that, he thought.

Jarel rode up beside the black man and said, "Jefferson, if ya don't ask, you'll never know the answers. Now, what Ty told ya makes sense to ya now, because ya know the why, but before ya had no idea. Among friends, and ya remember this, there ain't no such thing as a dumb question. Hell, I'd rather you asked hunnert questions, if they teach ya something that will help keep us all alive."

Jefferson raised his head, met Jarel's eyes and replied, "I'll remember that Jarel and I do thank you for understanding. I knew about the smoke and food smells, but just thought we were too close to the town to worry about our safety."

Jarel laughed, patted Jefferson on the back and spoke, "Jefferson, not a man here didn't have to learn how to live out here. Now, me and Ty, since we're so damned old, we just have more experience at doin' it is all. You'll learn son, or else you'll die. And, one more thing to remember, ya ain't never safe out here, never. Not in the mountains, on the plains, in yer own home, or even in a hotel room. First time ya assume yer safe, well, you'll likely to end up a dead man. Now, let's get dinner on the fire."

As soon as the fire was started Cookie moved around the campsite preparing dinner. Ty had moved over by the road that ran parallel to the river to keep watch, while Jarel had moved out to the west. The old man hummed a song as he worked and Jeb watched the man with more than a little humor in his mind. Cookie seemed to always be in a good mood, knew his job, and could be depended on to do what was asked of him. Jeb wondered about the man's past.

"Cookie, you been out here long?" Jeb asked as the old man chopped up some chunks of salt pork to add to the beans.

"Nope, not that long. When the war ended, well, I couldn't find nothin' down in 'Bama, so I slowly moved up and out west. I worked fer a spell in Caintuck, some in Missouri, and then moved out to the plains."

"Must be hard for a man of color."

The old cook stopped working for a minute, as if he was in deep thought, then as he started chopping the meat once more he said, "Jeb, a man does what he has to do, or he ain't much of a man. Ya know, when I was a slave, I never had to make no decisions 'bout nothin'. A man, black or white, has to get off his ass and do fer his own self, 'cause ain't nobody gonna give him nothin'."

"But, now you're free."

"Yep, free to decide what to do, but that's 'bout it. Now, don't mistake my words heah, I'm glad I be free, but what I'm tryin' to say is, life is hard and fer a colored man it's twice as hard. But, a feller can only blame his skin color fer so long and then even he knows it's all a big ugly lie. I won't never be a slave 'gain, and I might not ever 'mount to much, but by God, I'll make the decisions along the way that make me the man I'll be."

Jeb thought for a few minutes, pulled off is hat and ran his fingers through his long hair before he said, "So, you're tellin' me that a man, no matter what his color, has the ability to be what he wants to be?"

Cookie dropped the meat into the cast iron pot, turned to look at Jeb and said, "That's what I mean. Freedom don't open no doors fer an easier life and in some ways it's made life harder on us slaves. But, jess' like you white fellers, a black man has to get off his rump and make a life. Hells bells, I could be back in town safe and sound, sweepin' the saloon, runnin' messages or what-not, but I'd not be the man I want to be. I want to live a life full of personal honor and be the man I can be."

"You're a man with pride Cookie and I suspect you'll do fine out here."

"Pride? I ain't real sure what that word means. I do know that I want to be a man I can be proud of when I'm old. One that can shave in the mornin' and not want to hide my eyes or cut my own damned throat over what I have done or didn't do."

Jeb didn't reply, but he knew how the old black man felt, because he felt the same way. A few minutes later Cookie went back to humming Rock of Ages as he placed the iron pot on the coals and then started fixing biscuits.

CHAPTER
15

Crawford entered his small room and was surprised at how nice it looked for a western town. While old, the furniture and decor were still in pretty good shape. His double bed had a firm mattress and there was even an old rug beside the bed. The room had been wallpapered in red and while he didn't really care for the color, at least it wasn't peeling or torn. *No,* he thought as he sat on the bed and pulled his boots off, *I've seen some sad places in my years, but this one will do.* He was tired and a few minutes later, after a quick smoke, he slipped his boots back on with a groan, and walked out of the room toward the bath house.

Once his bath was finished, Crawford pulled out his razor, and scraped off a weeks worth of whiskers. When he returned to his room a little later he noticed a bottle of rye on the dresser. Pulling the cork from the bottle, he poured two fingers of the amber liquid into a water glass that was next to the pitcher and quickly threw the drink back. He enjoyed the fire as it burned a trail down his throat to his belly. He had just refilled the glass when there was a light knock at his door.

He pulled his pistol, cocked it, and asked, "Who is it?"

"It's me, Kattie." A female voice from outside the door replied and then gave a low laugh.

Keeping his pistol ready in his right hand, Crawford slowly opened the door with his left, and was surprised at what he saw. Kattie was a very young woman and as far as he was concerned, she was a very beautiful woman. She had long blond hair, blue eyes, a big bust and a slender waist. Most of the soiled doves Crawford had known in the past had been well past their prime and had lost whatever looks they had ever had. He personally knew many whores in western towns that were thirty and looked sixty after a few years of being in the sportin' business.

"Ya gonna stand there a-gawkin' or invite me in, sugar?" Kattie asked and then broke out laughing once more.

"Uh, come on in. I was just surprised by your age is all." Crawford spoke as he opened the door wide for the whore.

"Well, I'm old enough, and I know a few tricks as well." Kattie spoke as she pointed to the bottle of rye and continued, "Mind if I have a drink?"

Crawford poured the woman a healthy amount of the rye in a glass, handed it to her, and then asked, "What's your normal fee?"

Kattie took a big gulp of the rye, wiped her mouth with the back of her left hand and said, "Dollar fer a quickie and three fer all night. If you want anything else, you jes' ask fer it. I will do anything you want if the money's right."

"You want to earn five dollars tonight?"

Kattie gave a deep lusty laugh and then said, "Sounds to me like you want the whole works."

Crawford moved over to the bed and sat down.

It was still an hour before daylight when Crawford awoke, rolled over and gave Kattie's right arm a hard squeeze. The woman moaned softly in her sleep and reached out for him. The only problem was the man was up and pulling his trousers up as her right hand searched the bed. Sitting on the edge of the bed, Crawford pulled his boots on, stood and buckled on his gun belt. He was hungry and suspected the restaurant down stairs was open, because in towns like this one the folks ate early.

"Where you goin'?" Kattie asked as she sat up and made no effort to cover her large breasts.

Crawford pulled five dollars out of his pocket and threw it on the bed. Grinning, he said, "I'm going fer some grub. If I'm still here tonight, you can earn five more. Like I said last night, you have a natural talent and a feller could learn to like keepin' you around."

Kattie smiled and replied, "I'll wait for you to eat and when you come back we can go another round, if you want to that is."

Feeling himself growing excited just at the thought, Crawford said, "Nope, not this morning, because I got me some important things to do. You get dressed and clear out for the day. Check back tonight, oh, around six and we'll see."

Kattie stood, knowing her body was almost perfect made a big show of dressing slowly, allowing the man to see the firmness of her body and to build up a strong desire for her once again. She knew if he was still in town that night she'd earn five more dollars the easy way. Finally, as her simple gingham dress fell over her shoulders she said, "I'll leave now at the same time you do. I'll be back tonight and if you're still here I'll show you a few other things I have in mind, if yer interested."

Crawford let out a laugh, placed his hands on his hips and replied, "Sure thing. I'll most likely be here and I'll think all day on what you jess' promised me. I thought we done it all last night."

As she walked by the man and opened the room door, Kattie glanced over her shoulder, gave a low lusty laugh and said, "We've jess' started sugar. Tonight you're in for the time of yer life, and that's a promise."

As soon as the woman left, Crawford could still smell her musky scent in the room and knew he wanted her once more. But, he had to eat, take care of getting a horse, and be at the bank as soon as it opened. He popped the cork on the rye, poured out a fingers worth into a glass and waited for his blood pressure to return to normal. As he sipped the drink, he wondered if Buffalo Watkins was looking for him and finally he decided it didn't matter much. Nonetheless, he knew when they finally met only one of them would walk away alive.

Breakfast was a simple affair of country ham, three eggs, fried taters, and piping hot biscuits and gravy. The hungry man washed it all down with four cups of scalding black coffee and even read the newspaper he had picked up at the front desk for three cents. The paper was a local edition and it was filled with stories about the railroad, a new granary, and on the front page some no named colonel had stated a war with the red man. The colonel's comments were humorous to Crawford as he read the military man's idiotic statements about how the Indian's would be beaten into the ground quickly. *Not without a lot of blood and a hell of a lot more time than you're thinking colonel*, he thought as he placed the paper on his table, dropped a dollar for the meal, and left the hotel.

At the livery stables he couldn't find a horse that he really wanted, but the man had a nice Appaloosa that he was willing to part with for forty dollars. The animal had a gray and black color and Crawford had learned years before to never ride an all white mount. He actually preferred dark colored horses, so he told the manager to keep the horse and said he would visit the bank and then return to pay him.

Entering the bank, he was not impressed with the place right off. The wooden floors had seen much use and were well worn, the windows were spotted and needed cleaning, and the teller was a skinny little squirrel in a barred cage. It looked nothing like it had a few years before when Crawford had made his deposit.

"Good mornin' suh, how may I assist you?" The squirrel asked and then gave a big grin, which showed his broken and discolored teeth.

"I wish to make a substantial withdrawal of eleven hundred dollars from the account of John Crawford."

The skinny man looked at Crawford, gave a twisted grin, and then asked, "Am I to assume you are Mister Crawford?"

Crawford reached into his shirt pocket and pulled out his bank book, which he slid over the counter so the squirrel in the cage could see it.

The man, who Crawford noticed was named Little by his nameplate off to the side, grinned and said, "I see you are one of our biggest depositors, uh, Mister Crawford. If you will give me a few minutes, I have to get the bank managers approval for such a large withdrawal."

"Son, you get whoever you want, but get my damned money. I ain't gonna spend all day in here just to get a little spendin' cash."

Ten minutes later, Crawford left the bank with eleven hundred dollars in his pocket. The bank manager had pissed him off, so he'd threatened to take all his money, which brought all kinds of apologies. *Hell, I might need this money anyway to get the men I need*, he thought as he walked back to the hotel. Once at the hotel he immediately placed eight hundred dollars in the safe, got a receipt, and walked over to the saloon. He considered leaving some of the money in his room, but he didn't trust Kattie not to come back and steal it, so he kept it in his coat pocket.

He entered the saloon, walked over to a table where he could see the main door clearly and sat down. He noticed a huge man of maybe three hundred pounds minding the bar. It was still fairly early morning yet, so he ordered a beer.

When the bartender brought his drink Crawford asked, "Know of any men around that need some work?"

The bartender, having been in the business a long time asked, "What kind of work? Most of the fellers who come in here already have jobs and those that don't ain't looking fer no hard work. Lazy bastards most of 'em."

Crawford laughed and replied, "Send 'em to me. I have a job I need done out west and I'll pay top dollar. Let 'em know, since its Injun country, they need to know how to use a gun."

"By God, that's fer damned sure, now that the Army has them red skins all heated up. I heard it was the buffalo hunters that started the mess, but the government has promised to clean it all up in a few days. And, of that I have my doubts. Hell, the army don't never finish nothin' quick like and I know, I was in it." The barkeeper spoke as he walked back behind his bar.

At that moment a young and rough looking man walked through the bat wing doors of the saloon and up to the bar. He glanced around the saloon a second, nodded at Crawford and simply said to the bartender, "Beer."

As the bartender poured the man a beer Crawford could hear them speaking in low tones. A few minutes later the young man walked up to Crawford's table and said, "I hear you're looking for men who know how to shoot."

Crawford looked the man over closely, because he didn't want to hire a drunk. The man was about six feet tall, long brown hair and beard, and his green eyes appeared sober and intelligent. His clothing was worn and while he needed a bath, he seemed to be just the type of man Crawford wanted. The man from Missouri realized it was the young man's clothing and filth that made him seem so rough and crude.

"I'm lookin' fer 'em. Can you shoot?"

"Yep, I was raised 'bout a hunnert miles west of here, right smack dab in the middle of Sioux country. I learnt to shoot as a young pup and I even speak some Sioux."

"Do you know of any other men that are looking for some easy money? I'll pay three dollars and day and even furnish the grub. The catch is, the work is out on the plains where the Sioux are. And, if you can bring me more men, I'll even pay you a dollar for every man that I take."

The young man thought for a minute then said, "I know of about ten other fellers that need work, but some of 'em cain't come into town right now. What if we meet 'em out of town a mile or so?"

"Sure, we'll do it in the mornin' or later on this evenin', but I ain't hiring 'em until I see 'em." Crawford spoke quickly and watched the man's eyes for any hint that he might be planning a trap. *He knows I have money, so I'll have to play this by ear and be careful*, he thought as he pushed a chair out from the table with his left foot and continued, "Sit and let's talk."

As the young man sat down at the table he said, "My name is Buck and I do thank you for the job. I was herdin' cows fer a spell, but lost the job as soon as they were sold off. This nickel I spent on this beer was my last penny."

Crawford didn't care a bit about the man or his past, all he wanted was killers. He suspected the young man was lazy and had lost his job, but he said nothing. Reaching into his pocket he pulled out two dollars and slid it over the top of the table toward Buck.

"Take this as part of your finder's fee for the men. I'm sure I'll take at least two of 'em and most likely all of 'em, and if so, well, you'll have more money after I see 'em."

"Why thank you kindly. I didn't catch your name Mister." The out of work cowboy said as he quickly plucked up the two coins.

"My name is Roland, John Roland. Buck, if you think you can do the job I'd like you to be my second in command of these men. You'll have to be tough to do the job, or so I think."

Buck gave a big grin, pushed his hat back and met Crawford's eyes as he replied, "I can do the job, but I'll expect more money. See, I know all of these men and most of 'em are wanted for small crimes and such, but nothin' serious. They know me and they all respect me."

Crawford gave a loud laugh and then asked, "Do they respect you because you haven't been caught yet?"

Buck laughed, nodded, and then added, "They need leadin' and as a group they'd be hard to beat, but man fer man they ain't worth a shit. They cain't think on their own is the main problem they have."

"We'll do the leadin' and your pay has just doubled. But, Buck?"

"Yep?"

"You try to double-cross me and you'll be the first one I kill. Do you understand that?"

The young man gave a loud gulp, nodded, and replied, "Mister Roland, I'll do the job fer ya and I'll do it the best I can. You can trust me and all of the other men."

Sure I can trust you, about as far as I can throw this table, Crawford thought, but he said, "Okay we have a deal. I'll meet you at sundown just north of town to go see this gang of yours. If things work out I want to be on the trail by sunup tomorrow so have the men ready to leave then."

The young cowboy gulped the rest of his beer, stood, and said, "We'll be there, north of town at dusk. The men will want part of their pay up front, jess' a few dollars. Can you swing that?"

"Each man will get twenty-one dollars in the morin', but they ain't comin' back to town here to spend a cent of it. If they spend it, it will be further down the road or after we finish the job. And, I want no hard drinkers on the trip."

"They ain't no drunks in the bunch, but they all like to relax now and then, by the way, you never told me what this job is Mister Roland." The cowboy placed his hands on the table top, leaned over, and grinned as he spoke.

"Why Buck, we are going to kill a man. A big man who has wronged me."

Turning and making his way for the door, the young cow poke spoke over his right shoulder, "Then I'll see you in the mornin' and we'll go kill this man. Hell, money is money, and it don't matter much to us how we get it."

As the bat-wing doors of the saloon swung closed as the cowboy left, Crawford thought, *that was easier than I thought. And, it looks like I'll get to spend a few more hours with Kattie this afternoon. I wonder if she'd be interested in goin' with us? Naw, that wouldn't work, hell, she'd take every penny them fellers will have on 'em and they'd end up owing her a fortune.* He gave a loud laugh which made the bartender glance over at him and shake his head.

CHAPTER
16

Jeb and his group ate and then moved about a mile west of the Platte River to spend the night in a small group of oak trees. While the weather was still cool at night, the clouds had turned a dark gray just before sunset. They all knew they might be in for another wet night, so Ty had the men construct some simple shelters using canvas to keep them dry, but he reminded them there would be no fire.

As they sat in the darkness, Ty said, "Come mornin' me and Jarel are pullin' out and headin' north. Jefferson, ya and Cookie move out west, 'bout fifty miles or so and settle in. Ya might have to go a little further out, dependin' on where ya find water, wood and other things you'll need, but keep it as close to fifty miles as you can. Ya two stay there until one of us comes and fetches y'all. Now, that might be a week or it might be a month. We'll divide the supplies in the mornin' and let ya two have most of 'em. Me and Jarel don't need much, so ya two can have most of what we got."

Jefferson gave a weak cough and then asked from the darkness, "Ya think we'll run into Sioux out there?"

Ty thought for a minute and then said, "You might, but Iffen ya do, don't start the dance. I suspect as long as they don't take ya fer buffalo hunters or soldiers you'll be safe 'nough. If you get the chance, tell them Sioux ya ride with One Leg Standing or ya know Walks Proudly, that's Jeb's and Jarel's Injun names. Hell, ya can even mention Moses if it'll help ya some and with ya two being black it jess' might keep yer asses alive. But, if things turn to hell and back, ya fight as hard as ya can, and then make a hard run fer Omaha."

"I think we should all get some sleep and move out in the mornin'. I'm afraid if this Crawford feller gets too much time he'll get organized pretty good. Once the man gets his shit together we'll play hell killin' 'em then." Jarel spoke for the first time that evening and everyone knew what the old mountain man said was true.

One by one all of the men except the horse guard rolled up in their blankets and were fast asleep. Jefferson had fallen asleep wondering what the future would bring him and his family, while Cookie had been worrying about running into the Sioux out west. Each of the men had been thinking of the future, except for Jeb, he'd been thinking of his past and wondering why Crawford hated him so much.

Morning was very cold and a light mist fell from a dark gray sky that seemed low enough overhead to touch. Cookie was the first one up and he muttered more than just a few curses as he gathered up his tinder and kindling, starting the fire. As soon as the flames were eating at the wood, the old man filled the coffee pot with water, dropped in a handful of fresh coffee grounds, and placed it on the flames. He glanced around the campsite, noticing a false dawn was just peaking over the small trees they had camped in. Long fingers of gray shadows reached out and covered most of the camp. The old man knew it would be a good thirty minutes or more before full daylight, because at the time, the whole cold camp was surrounded in darkness.

"Cold as a Yankee banker's heart out heah." Ty spoke as he moved over to the fire to warm up. After a few minutes he squatted beside the small fire.

Cookie hadn't responded to Ty because he had awakened in a foul mood. His rest had been poor due to a large pointed rock under his back. He'd even moved a couple of times, but the rock seemed to follow him, or else it had a passel full of bothers and sisters nearby. No matter where the man had picked to sleep after a few minutes he'd feel another rock in his back.

The black man pulled out a large slab of salt pork and shaved off a good three dozen slices into an old cast iron skillet. As he placed the skillet on the hot coals he'd scraped from the fire, he threw his head back and broke into his morning ritual of what almost sounded like the Battle Hymn of the Republic. "My eyes done seen the glory of the comin' of the Lawd; He be tramplin' out the vint-age where all dem grapes of his are stored; He done turned loose the fateful lightnin' of His big sharp sword; His truth is a-marchin' on."

As some of the yet sleepy men groaned and yelled at Cookie to quiet down, the old man gave a thunderous laugh, threw back his head once more, and continued even louder, "Glory! Glory! Hallelujah! Glory! Glory! Hallelujah! Glory! Glory! Hallelujah! His truth is a-marchin' on."

"Cookie! Shut the hell up! If there are any Injun's around they fer damned sure know where we be now!" Jarel spoke as he moved from under his canvas shelter to the side of the fire.

"Hell, Jarel, I was jes' funnin' y'all. I suspect we be safe 'nough now daylight is here and after all, there are six of us," Cookie said as he turned the cooking pork with the point of his knife and then started mixing his cornmeal to make cornbread. It seemed to the old man that while he hated to wake up in the mornings, his mood always changed after his mornin' song. As far as Cookie was concerned, the Battle Hymn of the Republic was a song of freedom and he sang it at the beginning of each day to remind himself he was a free man.

"Could be old man, but don't take nothin' fer granted out here. I don't mind Iffen ya sing or hum, but do it a little quieter next time." Jarel snapped back quickly and knew he sounded madder than he really was. Actually, he found Cookie to have a great sense of humor and Jarel knew laughter was important to any man who lived out west. A humorless man had few friends and most of them were loners, or so Jarel thought.

Ty had been sitting by the fire and laughing the whole time Cookie had been singing. He knew the old man was waking up the men and he was doing it in a way that most of them would find funny, once they were awake. Jefferson, Jeb, and Jarel walked off into the bushes to make their morning water, as Cookie continued to hum his song. Ty thought the old man reminded him of someone and it took him less than a minute to realize it was Zee.

Zee[1] was an old mountain man that rode with Teacher and they'd found Jarel out in a big blizzard when he was just a kid, in addition to being about dead. Well, once they had young Jarel they never turned him away and the youngster grew up with the two old men. Over the years, what they knew about staying alive had been passed on to the young boy and when he grew into a man, he was as tough as the mountains he lived in.

The small group gathered around the fire a few minutes later and made small talk as Cookie jumped around turning slices of pork, checking his cornbread, and pouring coffee for the men. Cookie knew he didn't have to do any of the things he was doing, but he honestly enjoyed feeding the others. Deep inside, the old black man had always wanted to own a restaurant where folks could come to eat a good solid

---

1   *Red Runs the Plains,* eBook by WR Benton

meal, but he doubted many white folks would want to eat a black man's cooking.

As soon as the meal was finished and gear loaded, the men broke up into their small groups, waved to each other, and then rode off into the falling mist.

The ride to Omaha was not as long as Jeb thought it might be, so he was surprised when two hours later they topped a small rise and could see the town below. He'd not been there but once and he'd not really cared much for the place at the time. The young man found the place too large, had too many people and everybody was in a hurry.

"It ain't much to look at, is it?" Ben asked as he turned in his saddle and pulled out the makings of a cigarette from his shirt pocket.

Jeb leaned forward, rested both of his hands on the pommel, and replied, "Too many people for me to like much. But, she's grown a might since the last time I was here. Seems as it the whole town is growing toward the hills and away from the river."

"I know what you mean about a lot of people. I've found big cities make me uncomfortable and to tell ya the truth, I feel safer out on the plains with the Sioux on the war path than I do in most towns." Ben replied and then lit his smoke.

"Well, let's go get a hotel room, clean up a bit, and then go skunk huntin'. But, we'll take no action against the man until we see what he's doin'." Jeb spoke and then kicked his horse gently in the ribs and moved down the slope toward Omaha.

The town of Omaha was choking with activity as the two tired and dirty men rode down the main street at a slow walk. Teamsters yelled at their mules, wagon wheels creaked and moaned as they moved through the town, and horses lined both sides of the main street tied to hitching posts. Jeb pulled up in front of a hotel called the Western Inn and dismounted. As soon as Ben joined him the two men kicked as much mud from their boots as they could and entered the building.

The ever present brass bell jingled as the two men entered the lobby and made their way to the front desk. The man behind the counter was a short and fat man with a bald head. Jeb noticed right off the man was on the high side of sixty if he was a day old and his eyes were squinting as if he once wore glasses and was forced to be without them.

"How much are yer rooms?" Jeb asked as he glanced down at his boot and noticed mud near the toes.

"Singles are a dollar a night, a double is a dollar fifty, but two of ya can share it." The man spoke and then he gave a big grin.

"Well, give us the double. Now, how about a bath and some grub?"

"The bath will cost you both a dime and the food is available either here at the hotel or down the street at the Blue Goose. Now, I'd suggest the hotel restaurant, because the prices are discounted for guests by ten percent. And, the cook is my wife and she started cooking long before you was even born."

"Where is this bath house?" Ben asked as he started unbuttoning his coat due to the heat in the hotel.

"Out back and I can take the money for both the room and baths right here. You'll just need to show your room key to the boy out there and he'll take care of you. So, a double room for one night and two baths is one dollar and seventy cents."

Jeb slapped a double eagle on the counter, grinned and said, "Take out fer two nights, a bottle of rye whiskey, and tonight's bath. Keep the rest in case we decide to stay longer, but give me a receipt."

The old man smiled and replied as he wrote out the receipt, "Sure, I can do that. Now, if either of you boys need anything just let me know."

Ben had been fairly quiet, but he'd been thinking. He suddenly asked, "Ya got a guest here by the name of John Crawford? He's a good friend of my families and I heard he might be in town."

The old man pulled out his ledger, scanned two or three pages, looked up and replied, "Nope, ain't nobody here by the name of Crawford. I got me a bunch of John's but no John Crawford. And, before I forget, one of you needs to sign the ledger too."

Jeb picked up the pen and pulled the ledger around so he could sign it. He took his sweet time and looked at the names above his entry. He didn't see any name even close to Crawford so he asked, "This friend of Ben's is a tall man, maybe six foot six, and as thin as a rail split six ways. Seen any one that looks like that staying here?"

The old man shook his head and said, "Nope, no tall and skinny fellers here at all. Then again, he might have stayed at one of the other places in town. If I see the man, do you want me to tell him you're looking for him?"

Ben nodded his head and replied with a big smile, "Tell 'em his old buddy Ben Moreland is in town and I've a message from his ma. But, make sure ya tell 'em that everything is alright, she jess wants him to pick up some things on his way home. I got the list in my shirt pocket."

The clerk picked up two brass keys and handed them to the men as he responded, "I'll do that. If he asks, should I tell him what room you're in?"

Jeb had just turned to walk away so he said over his shoulder, "Naw, we want to surprise him, because he ain't seen us in years. But, it's worth five dollars to ya if ya'll let us know as soon as ya've talked to 'em or seen 'em."

"Sure, I can do that."

The room was small but clean, with one small window overlooking the main street. After placing their gear in a far corner, both men sat on the edge of the bed and took off their boots. No sooner had Jeb leaned back on the bed than a soft knock was heard at the door. Both men pulled their pistols and the sound of the hammers cocking back was loud in the small room.

"Who is it?" Ben asked as he moved toward the door.

"My name is Abraham and I work for the hotel. Y'all ordered a bottle of rye whiskey?" A deep male voice spoke from the other side of the door.

Ben opened the door to notice a small black man holding a bottle of rye in his left hand. When he noticed the pistol in Ben's hand the man chuckled and said as he handed the bottle, "Yer a man who has been 'round I see. I jess brought ya the drink and ya'll find I'm little threat to anybody."

Ben pulled out a dime, handed it to the man and said, "Thanks for the bottle. And, Abraham, ya did say your name was Abraham, did ya not?"

"Yep, it sure is. Can I do somethin' else fer ya suh?"

"Abraham, ask around town and see if a feller has been looking for men to ride with 'em. Now, I want ya to do this without drawin' any attention to yerself or gettin' into any trouble. If ya can find out what I want to know, I'll see yer well taken care of."

The man smiled a knowing smile and replied, "If there is a man lookin' fer men to ride with 'em I'll know by mornin' most likely. Then again, Iffen he's already got some men and left I might not learn much."

"Ya jes' do yer best and let me know as soon as ya find out anything." Ben closed the door, grinned at Jeb, and said, "Ya might be surprised how much folks in this town know. I don't think a dog can pass wind in this town without them knowing when it happened and the color of the dog."

Two hours later, after they'd both had a hot bath, a quick shave, and a shot of rye, they walked from the hotel room onto the streets of Omaha. The first two stops were at livery stables, but neither owner remembered seeing a man like Crawford. Also, three hotels on the main street hadn't seen the man and a check of the saloons didn't turn anything up either. Feeling frustrated Jeb returned to the hotel. *I'll think on this a spell and then come back out, right now I'm just wastin' my time*, he thought as he walked along the crowded street.

As he entered the lobby the clerk called him over to the desk and said, "Mister Patton, I think I have some news for you."

"What kind of news?"

"Well," the old man said as he met Jeb's eyes, "Maybe nothin', but I had a man who used to come in once in a while and sweep the place up. He's jess a cowboy that's out of work and I think he did the job mainly for beer money. Anyways, this morning when he came in he said it was his last day. He said he had a job with a man that was lookin' for fellers to ride with 'em for a spell. The cowboys name is Buck, but I don't know his last name."

"Did he mention a name or anything else?"

"Nope, nothin' else."

"Where can we find this cowboy?" Ben asked as he moved closer to the desk.

"Not sure 'bout that neither. He was sleepin' over at Lighton's livery stables, but I ain't sure if he's still there or not."

"Thanks, and take five dollars out of the eagle I gave ya and keep it. Ya've earned yer money. Oh, and send yer feller Abraham up in a few minutes, I might have some errands for him to run for us, if that's alright with ya."

"That would be fine and that's why Abe works here, to take care of our guests. I'll have him up to yer room directly."

Ten minutes later the man was in the room, sitting on the only chair, and listening to Jeb as he said, "Abe, take a look around for the cowboy that works here at times sweepin'. I think the clerk said his name was Buck and he usually sleeps over at Lighton's Stables."

Abe rolled his eyes, grinned and said, "Hell, we all know Buck. Yep, he's at Lighton's and has been since he came to town. He works a bit here and there, so Lighton lets him sleep in the place for free. Bucks lazy and no account, but he's jess a kid as far as I'm concerned."

"Well, I need ya to do two things for me then. First, make sure Buck is still in town and plannin' on still sleepin' at the stables, then see if ya can find out anything about him riding with a man."

Abe laughed and said, "Me and Buck get along fine. I'll know in five minutes if he's ridin' with anyone, because Buck has a big mouth. He'll brag that he has a new job and he'll want me to know all 'bout it too."

Jeb pulled two dollar coins out of his pocket, handed them to Abe and stated, "If you find out what I need to know, there will be five more dollars for ya later."

Abe grinned, stood and as he made his way toward the door, Jeb heard the man mutter, "This is Abe's lucky day! I got me two dollars and five more on the way! Yep, it's my lucky day."

CHAPTER
17

Jefferson rode in silence beside Cookie and had a very uncomfortable feeling. The cool falling mist from earlier in the day had quit, but the dark threatening clouds still rolled and tumbled over head, promising another wet day. For the last two hours the big black man had the feeling he was being watched, or at least followed. He stopped each time when they rode over a small rise on the plains and glanced behind them, but he saw nothing.

Finally, after the feeling got very strong, Jefferson turned to Cookie and said, "I got me a feeling we're a-bein' watched, but I ain't seen no-body."

"I got the same feelin', only I don't think it's Injun's or they would have made themselves known by now. Hell, I've had this feelin' ever since we left the others this mornin'."

Jefferson glanced around once more, only the open plains revealed nothing that alarmed him. Turning slightly in his saddle he pulled up and said, "Let's make an early camp for lunch and see if anyone comes up to us."

Cookie gave a low cackle and then replied, "Sure, but don't expect company to jess ride up and say howdy do. Usually out heah if a feller is trailin' somebody he's usually up to no good or needs help."

"Well, I don't like this feelin' and I ain't the kind of man that runs from trouble. If it's trouble they want, I'll give 'em a belly full."

Over the next rise they sighted a small narrow stream that ran beside some trees, so the two men soon had a noon campsite established and some beans heating up in a cast iron pot. Cookie was frying some bacon when they heard a shout, "Howdy the camp! I'm a white man and in need of help."

"Come on in, but keep both of yer hands up over yer head, or I'll shoot." Jefferson said as he moved over beside a large log and quickly dropped behind it. He lay down and pointed his rifle toward where he had heard the voice. Cookie moved over into the trees and covered their rear in case it was a trap.

Many long minutes passed before the two black men saw a lone man walk from over the rise with his right arm over his head and the other hanging loosely from his side. As the man neared, Jefferson noticed blood dripping from the hanging arm and the man appeared to stumble as he walked.

When the man was about twenty feet from his log, Jefferson yelled out, "That's close enough. Now, who are ya?"

The man was pale and obviously seriously injured so it took a few seconds before he managed to stammer out, "Names Lewis and I am a dis . . . dispatch rider fer the army. I need . . . some doctorin'."

"Move over by the fire and sit down. If ya got a gun, drop in on the ground before ya move to the fire. And, keep yer hands were I can see at all times, or I'll drill ya right through yer breadbasket." Jefferson ordered as he watched the man closely.

The man dropped two pistols from his belt, a knife, and then a small hidden gun like the type gamblers usually carried. He moved like a drunken man to the fire side and then collapsed in the grass.

"Cookie, ya move over here by the log and keep me covered, but check behind ya at times. I'll go check that feller out and see what kind of conditions he's in. He don't look too good from what I could see."

As soon as the older man was behind the log, Jefferson moved forward with his pistol cocked and ready in his right hand. He left his rifle with Cookie back at the log.

The black man moved to the fire and squatted beside the fallen white man. He could see immediately that Lewis had taken a bullet to his left shoulder and from what he could tell the wound was bleeding freely. What concerned Jefferson was that the white man was dressed in the blue wool uniform of the army and wore the two yellow stripes of a corporal on his arms.

"What are you doing out here alone with the Sioux all pissed off?" Jefferson asked as he holstered his pistol and pulled his knife.

As he cut the wounded man's shirt so he could see the injury, Lewis spoke, "I wasn't alone when I started this trip. Me and Private Mooney were ridin' dispatches . . . fer the army. The Sioux ambushed us about five miles back and killed Mooney first thing. My hoss was hit, but kept movin' until just over that rise."

Jefferson raised his head and glanced around, expecting the Sioux to be on the rise watching him, but he saw nothing. Looking back down at Lewis is asked, "Them Sioux still on yer ass?"

"I don't think so. There . . . was only four of 'em and I know me and Mooney downed two of 'em for keeps and hurt one of 'em bad."

Lifting his head, Jefferson called out, "Cookie come on in, our visitor is with the army."

As Jefferson looked the wound over he realized he knew little or next to nothing about treating serious injuries. He turned his head as Cookie neared and asked, "You know much about doctoring up bullet holes?"

Cookie laughed and replied, "Hell son, I can do the job almost as good as I can cook a pan of biscuits. What ya got there anyways?"

"Shoulder wound and it looks like the shoulder blade was shattered by the bullet. He's lost a lot of blood, so I don't know if he'll make it or not."

Cookie moved over to the injured man, knelt, and looked the injury over closely before he said, "Yep, his shoulder blade is busted up a mite and he's lost a lot of blood, but he's got a good chance. I've seen all kinds of hurts heal, 'cept those shot in the belly. Long as this man don't fester, he'll live."

"I'll get that bottle of whiskey and you can start to work on 'em." The younger man spoke, stood, and then walked off toward the supplies.

"How bad . . . is it?" Lewis asked between clinched teeth.

"Ya'll be hurtin' fer a spell, but ya'll live, unless them Sioux decide to come back after yer ass. Then we'll all be in a world of trouble."

"Wh . . . why would two black . . . men . . . help me?"

Cookie laughed, looked at Lewis and then replied, "I was jess' askin' my own self the same damn question. To be honest with ya, ya need help and the God Lord sent ya to us, so we'll do the best we can."

An hour later Lewis was wrapped up and sleeping beside the fire. His face looked feverish, beads of sweat ran down his face, and his breathing was a little irregular. The rain had quit, but the temperature remained cool.

"What we do now?" Cookie asked as he poured some coffee into his cup.

"I've been studying on that for the last hour. I think the first thing I need to do is to go to his horse and his gear. If he was carrying army dispatches, we'll need to fetch them as well."

"Dispatches? What's that?"

"Papers and such the army sends out to other army folks. They got orders and letters and such in 'em."

"Look here, Jefferson, this whole thang is turnin' into a big mess. What're we gonna do with a hurt army man and the Sioux out lookin' fer blood. Ya know, jes' like I do, if dem Injuns find this man with us we're dead as hell."

Angry, Jefferson snapped out at the older man, "Hell, Cookie, what was I supposed to do, let the man bleed to death?"

"Nope, I didn't say none of that. But, now we gotta get this man and his letters to the army before we can move on west. I ain't so shore this is a good thing, but the Lord gave it to us, so we'll handle 'er as best as we can."

The younger man thought for a moment and then replied, "Well, we'll let him sleep today, but come sunup his ass will be on a horse, even if I gotta tie him to it. I think we're a little less than ten miles from Omaha, so we'll take 'em there in the mornin' and turn him over to the army."

Cookie shrugged his shoulders, grinned and said, "Ain't no other choice, but I think we should move in a couple of hours. If them bucks that got away go back and get some help we could be dead by mornin'."

Jefferson thought for a few minutes, then stood and said, "You've a good point there Cookie. I'll go get his gear. And, exactly two hours from now we pull out."

While Jefferson was gone the old men sat by the fire listening to the injured man breathe. Cookie was no fool and he had a serious itch to mount and ride off at that moment, but he knew he wouldn't. He was a man of personal honor and, though he was a bit scared of the situation they were in, he'd die before he ran.

Jefferson soon returned and unloaded the white man's gear from his horse placing it with theirs. He walked over to the fire, squatted on his heels and said, "Must be ten thousand dollars in this man's saddle bag and it is all wrapped up in paper that is stamped as army payroll. Oh, there were a good dozen letters and such too, but the money is what caught my attention."

"Ya know if this man dies we could keep that money and nobody would ever know." Cookie said with a twisted grin on his face and twinkle in his dark eyes.

"Yep, somebody would know."

The old man's grin disappeared and he asked in a serious voice, "Now who in the world would know about it?"

"Me and you. I know ya was teasing me, but this kind of money would tempt a lot of men Cookie, even some good men. And, to be honest, I thought about keeping it, but I can't do that."

Cookie laughed and said, "Jefferson, yer a good man and an honest one too. Let's hurry and eat, then get the hell outta here."

Two hours later, Lewis was tied to the mule. They'd been forced to leave some supplies behind, but the two black men figured they could pick them up on the way back out. Jefferson had tied Lewis' arms around the horse's neck and his feet under the animal's belly. After checking the injured man once more the small group turned to the east and started moving as quickly as they safely could. The animals were kept at a fast walk for the better part of two hours. Finally, late in the day, they rode over a slight rise and saw the town of Omaha near the Missouri River.

Entering the town, Cookie led the small group to the sheriff's office and as he was tying his horse to the hitching post he said, "A couple years back I spent the night here, fer raisin' hell when I was drinkin'. I hope this old boy don't 'member me."

Jefferson dismounted and as he was checking on Lewis he replied with a laugh, "I wouldn't worry much about that right now, Cookie. I suspect the army will be pretty happy to get this money back and they'll take care of any problems you might have."

Stepping up on the boardwalk Cookie chuckled and said, "Ya might be right 'bout that, fer sure."

Less than five minutes after Cookie entered the Sheriff's office, the door opened and a short fat man wearing a star stepped outside. He looked Jefferson over closely, saw the injured man on the horse, and asked, "Where'd ya find this feller?"

Jefferson quickly explained what had happened and he noticed a puzzled look on the old lawman's face, so he asked, "Is something wrong marshal?"

The man met his eyes and quickly replied, "By God, I'd say so. I got a telegram from a small post about a hun'ert miles west of here that said an army payroll was taken and all the troopers killed. Now, ya come ridin' in here with a soldier boy tied to a horse, and I'll be damned if I know what is goin' on. The telegraph said there were no survivors of the attack, but a little over ten thousand dollars was missin'. Happened, oh, a week back maybe."

Jefferson was quiet for a few minutes as the sheriff sent his deputy to get a doctor, but then he finally said, "We have just about that much money. The man had it in his saddlebags. Like I said, he told us he was a dispatch rider, so I assumed the money was army money."

141

"Well, I doubt if this boy is a real soldier, so if he ain't ya two got ya's a sizable reward comin'. The army is offerin' five hundred dollars for the safe return of the payroll and 'nother two hundred for information about the robbers. As soon as the old sawbones looks this man over, I'll go through some wanted posters I got and see if I can place his face on one." The fat sheriff spoke, placed both of his hands on his hips and then continued, "Who would have thought two shiftless blacks would ride in here this mornin' with the army's money with 'em? Now I've seen it all."

Cookie just laughed, but the way the white man said 'shiftless blacks' pissed Jefferson off, so he said, "Sheriff, *blacks* can be honest men too."

The fat man looked surprised, grinned, offered h is hand and said, "Son, I didn't mean no disrespect, but since y'all are free men now, I ain't sure what in the hell to call ya's. I called ya shiftless because most of y'all don't have a steady job these days. However, I am glad ya brought this hombre in though, because it saved me a few days in a wet saddle."

As the two men shook hands Jefferson replied, "Just call me by my name and thing's will be fine. That old fart standing by your door is Cookie."

At that point the doctor arrived and they slowly lowered Lewis to the mud beside the horse. The physician quickly looked him over, grinned, and then asked, "Who doctored this man up?"

Cookie stuck his chest way out and replied, "Why I did. I did a pretty good job of 'er too, didn't I?"

The doctor laughed, shook his head, and then said, "Overall you did an excellent job, but one of his ribs is shattered and it could have moved, and punctured a lung. That ride could have killed him."

"Hell, I knew that. But, the Sioux are a mite pissed right now." Cook spoke and then let out a slight chuckle, because he'd known no such thing.

"Doc, don't spend a lot of time on this boy. I got me a sneakin' feelin' he'll stretch a hemp rope in a few weeks." The sheriff spoke as he turned and made his way back toward his office door.

"Sheriff Main, it doesn't matter if you hang him later or not. I'll do the best I can to keep him alive until you place a rope around his neck."

The sheriff stopped, just as he was about to open his door, turned and replied, "John, I know ya will, but it might be a damned waste of time and effort. I just remembered seein' this man's face on a poster. Ya do yer job and I'll do mine."

Cookie, wanting to defuse the anger he could feel between the two men, asked, "When will we find out 'bout that reward money?"

The sheriff laughed, pulled his old hat off, and then said, "Give me a couple of hours to make sure this man is wanted, wire the army, and then see what they say."

"We can't wait that long Sheriff. We are moving out west on some business, would it be possible to find out about the reward on our way back to town, say in a couple of weeks?" Jefferson asked as he glanced at Cookie.

"Son, the army moves about as fast as a snail's ass and that's on a good day. Hell, it might be a week before they bother to answer me, but sure, check back later. If the reward is given to the two of ya the bank will have the authorization to pay. But, don't be upset if the army ain't said much when ya return. The Lord and the United States Army both work in mysterious ways." As soon as he'd spoken the sheriff laughed, opened the door to his office and walked inside, leaving Cookie and Jefferson to watch the doctor along with some other men move the injured Lewis.

"Mount up Cookie; we got a lot of miles to make up." Jefferson spoke as he walked to his horse, mounted, and started a slow walk from town.

CHAPTER
18

Jarel and Ty had stopped in Omaha earlier, just long enough to pick up a few supplies, and that was on the outskirts north of the town. The two crusty old mountain men didn't need much to survive, but as they'd aged they had grown very fond of coffee, tobacco, and a shot of whiskey on cold winter evenings. Less than ten minutes after leaving the store they were once more on the trail heading almost due north.

As they rode, the earlier mist turned into a very light snow and the temperature dropped quickly. They pulled their hats down lower to cover their faces, wrapped their blankets around themselves tighter, and kept moving. Weather never bothered Ty much, though he hated to ride very far in hot weather, because he hated the feeling of sweat running down his back to the crack of his ass. Jarel was just the opposite; he disliked riding in hard rains and more than once in the past he'd break out into a line of heavy cursing, all because he was wet.

"Where ya want to stop fer the day?" Jarel asked as he dropped back and rode beside the mountain man a few hours out of town.

Ty considered the question for a minute and then replied, "Hell, it don't matter much to me, but let's try to cover at least ten more miles or so. I don't mind the cold much; only this snow might get rough."

Jarel glanced overhead at the gray sky, checked the horizons slowly, and then said, "I don't like the look west of us, could mean more snow. Little early in the year fer a ball buster of a storm, but it could happen. Let's find a spot after a few more miles and hole up and see what happens. Way I got it figured is Crawford is still in Omaha."

"Maybe he is still in town and then again maybe he ain't, hard to say 'bout a man like him. Only thing I am sure of is if he heads our way we'll know it. Hard to hide a large group of men and I'm sure he'll have ten or more ridin' with 'em."

Jarel gave a low chuckle and then asked in a serious voice, "Ty, does it ever bother ya to be growin' old?"

Ty laughed, slapped his right thigh and then said, "Nope, not at all. What bothers me is living long enough to continue to grow old, 'cause it seems like everybody wants to kill me lately. Ya know, honest like, I never really expected to live to be thirty, much less the age I am now. So many others we've known have gone under."

"Uh-huh," Jarel spoke softy and then added, "they surely have. Hatch has gone under, Deerhead, Abe, and most of the men we started out with are all gone. Seems to me the only ones left, besides us, is Butterfield, Zee and Teacher."

"Well, hell, Zee and Teacher are both a million years old and too damned mean to die. I don't think God wants either of 'em and the devil is scared of 'em." Ty said and then broke out laughing.

"Good point there!" Jarel replied and then added, "I'll scout on out a bit and see how things look up ahead."

By the time Jarel was out of sight, Ty was thinking about his past. He'd never married like Jarel had and wondered if his life might have been different if he had. He suspected he wouldn't have married a white woman, because they were too controlling as far as he was concerned. *She'd have me raisin' chickens and cows, splittin' firewood, and goin' to church each Sunday,* he thought as he glanced around the countryside.

Less than two hours later he rode into a small group of trees and saw Jarel sitting by a small fire. Ty hadn't noticed the smoke, but that didn't surprise him, because Jarel knew how to survive out on the plains and in the mountains. As he dismounted he noticed a canvas lean-to had been constructed and wood had been placed in the very back to keep it dry.

"Snowin' harder now, only I still don't suspect no real ass kickin' storm." Jarel said as Ty approached the fire and squatted by the flickering flames.

"Naw, couple inches would be my guess and it'll be gone by noon tomorrow."

"What do ya want fer dinner? We got bacon and beans or beans and bacon."

Ty chuckled and replied, "Let's have bacon and beans, we had beans and bacon last night. If this weather ever dries out a might I'll get us some fresh meat. But, we'd play hell finding any game with this bad weather comin' on. Gonna be some cold doin's by mornin'."

Jarel placed a big cast iron pot on the flames, turned to Ty and said, "Waugh! Ty, we've both seen lean times before, when a man was lucky to have a little pemmican! Beans and sow belly ain't my favorite food, but it'll keep a man movin' 'til he can make fresh meat."

"That it will old coon."

The remainder of the day was spent caring for the horses, repairing worn gear, and sleeping in the shelter. The wind picked up and as it howled it caused the canvas cover to snap and pop to the point Jarel was afraid it might actually blow off. Because of the wind and snow, both of the old mountain men were reading as the sky grew steadily darker and neither noticed the movement around them. As Ty would recall later, it was a pilgrim thing to be doin', even if the weather was bad.

A little after midnight, the wind died down, but the snow was still falling in a lazy way that let the flakes twist and turn slowly as they dropped from the dark sky. Ty was sitting under a large pine tree, near the horses, when he saw a very slight movement on the other side of camp. Melting back into the darkness of the small trees, he made his way to where Jarel was sleeping. Touching the old mountain man on the right ankle, he watched as Jarel's eye's opened, he listened for a moment, and then rolled into the darkness taking his rifle with him. Ty moved back into the trees.

Nothing was seen or heard until about two hours before daylight, when a thickly accented voice called out in English, "Walks Proudly, are you well?"

"Many Horses, is that you out there in the darkness?" Jarel yelled in return as he recognized the Sioux warriors poor English.

"I wish to speak to Walks Proudly. Will you share the warmth of your fire?" The brave yelled back in the Sioux tongue.

"Come Many Horses, we will sit by the fire and talk." As soon as Jarel spoke, he moved toward the fire pit and knelt. Using his flint and steal, along with a char rag and some pine pitch he soon had a small fire burning. As soon as the flames were eating at the wood, he placed the coffee pot on the flames.

The brave walked to the flames, turned and gave the call of a night owl, and they were joined by ten other Sioux warriors. As soon as the braves were seated around the fire, Ty walked up and squatted by the dancing flames.

"So, my brother, what brings you out in cold weather?" Jarel asked as he leaned over and repositioned the coffee pot to keep the handle from getting too hot.

"We are looking for a large group of white men. We saw their tracks in the mud one sun back, but lost them in the storm today just before darkness fell."

Ty gave a low chuckle and then said, "And, you thought we might be them?"

Many Horses gave a slight grin, shrugged his shoulders, and replied, "We saw the light from your fire last night and decided to wait until dawn to see if you were the ones we hunted."

Jarel thought for a moment as he poured coffee into three cups, and asked, "Why do you hunt these white men? They could be the army."

Many Horses shook his head and said, "No, they are not the white man's long knives, because they do not ride in straight lines like the soldiers. They move all over the land, as if they have no worries or as if there was no danger. I thought they might be the hunters of tatanka, but they do not have a wagon."

Those riders could be Crawford and his group, Jarel thought as he looked at the muscular warrior and replied, "I think it is Wa ku ta, or as the white men would say, the one who shoots often. He is a killer of men and he is of little honor."

The warrior did not speak as he thought on Jarel's words, but finally he said, "There would be little respect in killing a man with no honor. I do not understand why he is on the land of the Sioux."

Ty gave a low chuckle, looked at the warrior and stated, "He's lookin' fer a white man named Buffalo, and I think he wants to kill him. But, Many Horses, do not take this white man lightly, he is a killer. He killed the big raven man and his raven wife who lived on the west side of Baldy Mountain, as well as a small buffalo boy child. This man is called Crawford."

"I knew the big raven man, whose name I cannot say because it might anger his spirit, was a man of great strength and honor. Was he killed in a great fight with the weak one?"

"No, the weak one hanged the raven man from a tree."

"Aiiieee, that is not a good way to die. Did the weak one not know that the spirit of the buffalo man cannot be free if he died the hanging death?"

Jarel gave a flat chuckle, met Ty's eyes and then said quickly, "He cares not of another man's spirit, Many Horses. He did not kill the raven man in battle, as a Sioux warrior would do, instead he used many men to capture him and then hanged him."

"So, the weak one knew of the raven man's great strength and did not kill him with his own hands? He must have feared his courage and strength."

"No, Many Horse," Ty spoke as he slowly stood, "he killed the raven man because of his black color and for no other reason."

The brave was quiet for a long time but finally he spoke once more, "I have killed white men, but they are my enemies. I did not count coup on them or kill them only because they were white. I kill them to keep them from my lands, to protect The People, and to enter into battle with them is a great honor. This hanging death is the way a coward would kill a true man."

Jarel met the warrior's eyes and said flatly, "And, that, Many Horses is why we search for the weak one."

"So, Walks Proudly, you walk the trail of revenge for the raven man and that is a good thing to do in memory of your friend."

"Yes, we will kill the weak one and when we do he will die slowly and without honor."

Once again the brave was silent as he thought. Finally he spoke once again, "This trail you ride, is it a trail that Wakantanka wants you to walk alone?"

"No, the Great Spirit has not sent me a sign that I am to walk this trail alone, only that it must be done."

The brave leaned over, added a small log to the fire, glanced quickly at this braves and then said, "It is a good thing you do. My warriors and I wish to ride by your side. As man with the strength and honor, the raven man had should be avenged, and we will ride the trail with you."

Jarel simply said, "Then, let the Sioux ride by my side, I am greatly honored. Let this be so."

The Sioux warrior looked over at his braves and then said, "Pis ko, you and Tagu' will leave at first light and look for the sign of the white men. Once you have found it, return to us. But, for now, let us sleep and rest, because the rising sun will bring much traveling."

An hour later, as the braves slept by the small fire, Jarel looked over at Ty and grinned as he said, "Night Hawk and Old Buffalo are the best trackers of the whole damned Sioux nation, as far as I am concerned. The minute I heard Many Horses tell them to leave at first light, I knew he was serious about helping us."

"Yep, I hunted with Night Hawk and with his sharp eyes, his name is appropriate!" Ty said with a crooked grin on his face. As soon as he spoke he glanced up at the gently falling snow and knew it would soon stop.

"Ya think this group is Crawford?" Jarel asked.

"Has to be, Jarel, 'cause the hide hunters are all in town for the winter. I don't think ya'd catch them boys out until the weather clears and the buffalo move back up this way. Right now most of the big herds are way down south. Then again, I might be wrong and it's an-

148

other group of men, but ya can bet yer ass the group is made up of white men."

"That's the way I figure it all too and 'sides, Many Horses said there were no wagon tracks."

"Well. . ." Ty started to speak, when Jarel heard a sound that sounded like a flat hand slapping a thick log and saw his friend knocked to the ground with a Blackfoot arrow in his upper left shoulder. Ty quickly reached up, broke the shaft to the arrow, and picked up his rifle.

Horrendous war cries broke the morning stillness as Blackfoot warriors suddenly ran into the campsite from all directions. Jarel was surprised to see the men rapidly appear in the falling snow and visibility was difficult at best. Ty raised his Hawken rifle, sighted in on a huge brave, squeeze the trigger, and had the satisfaction of seeing his man go down. Throwing his rifle to the ground, he pulled his two pistols and started placing his shots at the Blackfoot braves.

Jarel raised his rifle, but was struck hard from behind and fell to the ground with a warrior on his back. Pulling a pistol from his belt, he twisted his gun hand around and pulled the trigger. He felt blood and gore spray onto his legs and then felt the Blackfoot fall from him. Rolling, he glanced around and saw a brave moving toward Ty. Jarel didn't have time to aim, so he pointed his pistol at the brave and jerked the trigger two times. He was surprised when dust flew from the center of Indian's chest with the first shot and then the man's head exploded like an over ripe melon with the second. Everywhere he looked, the Blackfoot and Sioux were locked in combat to the death. Blood flowed, screams of pain and victory were heard, and the noises of battle were loud to his ears. Then, as quickly as it had started, the Blackfoot were gone.

Jarel felt blood running down his face and reaching up he discovered at some point in the fight he'd taken a glancing blow to the head. Ty was moving around, checking to make sure the dead Blackfoot were really dead. The Sioux seemed to have lost more than half of their small group, but the old mountain man had no idea how many were dead or just injured.

Suddenly a horrifying scream filled the air, followed by a loud choking sound. Ty looked over at Jarel, wiped his bloody knife on a Blackfoot warriors legging and said, "He was just wounded and playin' 'possum, but he ain't no more."

It took almost ten minutes to walk around the camp and determine the extent of the damage done by the Blackfoot. Many Horses had taken a knife wound to his left arm, six of his men had been killed, and only one of the remaining four was uninjured. The only positive aspect was none of them were injured seriously.

"Jarel, can ya come over and take a look at this arrow in my shoulder?" Ty asked as he sat down beside the fire.

The mountain man made his way to Ty, pulled the man's shirt off, and gave the wound a solemn evaluation before he said, "It ain't in deep, so I can cut 'er out."

"Well, have at 'er son."

Jarel heated the blade of his skinning knife for a few minutes, waved it in the air to cook it down and then cut a circle around the arrowhead. Grasping the broken shaft with his right hand, the old man pulled steadily and was satisfied as the shaft with the arrowhead still attached came from the wound. Ty gave one small grunt of pain. A shudder went through his whole body and Jarel could see beads of sweat on his friend's face. The younger man made his way to the supplies, picked up a small keg of whiskey and poured a full cup for Ty. He returned to the injured man's side and handed him the cup filled with the strong amber colored liquid. It burned like the flames of hell as it went down.

Unexpectedly, from behind him, there came a fearsome scream and Jarel knew the Sioux were giving their victory screams as they scalped and mutilated the dead Blackfoot. He'd seen the Sioux mutilate often following a battle and unlike the white men he knew, the warriors mutilated to keep their enemies from fighting them on the other side after they died. They didn't mutilate to be cruel or animal like, but to prevent fighting the dead warrior again in the hereafter. It made sense to Jarel, when viewed from an Indian's perspective.

Ty and Jarel soon scalped the men they had killed, but neither of the white men mutilated the dead. The Sioux understood, because both of the white men had said years before, they could take hair, they couldn't mutilate the dead. They'd both told the Sioux the Maker of All Things told them to take scalps, but not to cut their dead enemies. The Indians never questioned it again.

An hour after sunup the survivors of the Blackfoot attack sat around the fire eating a breakfast of jerky and coffee. Most of the men were silent, but the Sioux were generally very quiet when away from the village anyway.

Finally, Jarel asked, "What do we do now Many Horses?"

"We will do as we spoke of doing. Night Hawk is uninjured and he can still find the white men. Old Buffalo still lives, but he cannot ride the long journey it could take to find the weak one. Night Hawk will go and return when he has found the ones we seek. But, we must move to another place as soon as we have eaten. The Blackfoot will return to this place."

Ty wondered where the warrior planned to move and not have the Blackfoot follow. The old mountain man knew the Blackfoot to be excellent trackers and untiring enemies when they got on a man's back trail, so he asked, "Many Horses, where are we to move the Blackfoot cannot find us?"

"The stream behind these trees is where we will ride for a few miles. We will head down stream so the mud from our horses cannot be seen, unless they get on our trail early in the day. I know of a small cave, maybe a half a day's ride from here, we can find shelter in. The Blackfoot may know of it as well, but if they chose to fight us there they will lose many men and their squaws will grieve for days. I do not think they will attack the cave."

Jarel stood, started picking up their gear as he said, "Well, let's get a move on, I never have liked havin' Bug's Boys on my ass. They ain't quitters and I suspect we're in for a rough time of it, even if things go well."

A few harsh commands were given in Sioux and Night Hawk mounted his horse and rode away. The remainder of the small group gathered up their gear, loaded the ponies, mounted and started moving south, down the shallow stream.

CHAPTER
19

"I'll be a sumbitch!" Ben screamed as he paced the floor in the small hotel room. Jeb was gathering up their gear and placing it on the bed as his friend vented his anger. The old black man, Abraham, had returned a few minutes earlier and said that Buck was no longer staying at the stables. Old man Lighton informed him that, 'Buck done quit and left town this afternoon.' If the situation hadn't been so serious, Jeb would have laughed at his friend and his insane behavior. The one legged man considered most anger to be a complete waste of time and while he did get mad at times, it was rare and he never got upset over something he had absolutely no control over. And, the fact that Buck had left, well, Jeb felt they had absolute no control over at all, so why get pissed?

Finally, as Jeb laid his Yankee canteen on the bed, he turned and said in a flat voice, "Ben, that's 'bout enough. I can understand yer anger, but it ain't gonna change a damned thing. What we need to be doin', instead of bein' in this room listenin' to ya cuss, is to try to find out where Buck disappeared."

Ben had been ready to loosen another string of cussing when he met Jeb's eyes for a second, lowered his head, and then replied, "Yep, yer right. I get so damned mad over things sometimes I feel like I'm about to bust a gut. Ya figure we can track that Buck feller?"

"Well, I think I might be able to track 'em. Abraham said Buck was ridin' an old black mare with new shoes, so the tracks will be fresh and sharp. New shoes always leave a nice clean mark. Also, if you re-member, the old man said Lighton saw Buck ride out of town and the cowpoke was headed north. Now, get yer gear and let's ride, we're wastin' daylight."

As Ben started placing some items they'd purchased at the store that afternoon in his packs, he turned and said, "I'll bet he'll meet up with some other fellers too, or at least with Crawford. If Crawford has a large group of men with him they'll leave tracks a baby could follow."

Jeb grinned, slapped Ben on the back, and said, "Let's get on the trail, now that you're clear headed again."

The two men rode out of town at a walk and less than a half of a mile later Jeb spotted the crisp and clean tracks of Buck's mare. Dismounting and walking over to the tracks, Jeb squatted and memorized the track. Growing up hunting in the Missouri Ozarks, then the long years of the war, and his time out west allowed the man to become very good at memorizing tracks of all sorts of critters, including man. As he mounted, he said with a sly grin, "I got the boy now. Once I get the feel for a track, I don't ever forget the look of the critter that made 'em. I'm like an old coon dawg on a trail."

Ben laughed and replied, "Go get 'em Blue!"

Jeb gave a low coon dog moaning howl and chuckled as they rode north. Both of them were aware of potential ambush sites, but neither expected Buck knew anyone was behind him, so they were relaxed. Most likely Buck would feel he was safe and sound with either his friends or Crawford. *Fellers just don't realize out here*, Jeb thought as he rode with the gentle sway of his big bay, *that the minute ya leave town yer fair game to others who might have a hankerin' to kill ya, so only a fool would not watch his back trail.*

Three hours after leaving Omaha, the two men pulled off to the side of the road and moved into a group of oak trees. Ben dismounted, ran a picket line from one tree to another and tied both horses. Jeb unforked his horse, cursed the aching of his right leg under the strain of his peg leg, and pulled a small pack from behind his saddle.

"Get a fire going and dinner started, while I gather some wood, water, and care for the hosses." Jeb spoke as he pulled his canteen from the pommel of his saddle.

Ben's eyes grew large, his mouth flew open and he asked, "Fire? Jeb, have ya lost yer damned mind? We start a fire and those men will see it."

Jeb gave a wide crooked grin and relied, "I doubt it, since they're miles behind us. And besides if they ride up on us and we don't have a fire, they'll suspect we're up to no good."

Ben grinned back and said, "Behind us? I never saw a soul and now yer tellin' me they are behind us?"

Jeb's mouth grew tight and his eyes narrowed as he spoke, "I spotted where Buck left the main road about four or five miles back. A larger group of riders left the road at the same spot, but earlier today. He's there and so are about ten other riders, so we'll watch our asses from now on out."

"I'll be damned. Ya saw all of that and didn't say a word to me? How come?"

"No need to say anything, 'cause we ain't goin' to do nothin', yet. Ben, they're on the north side of town, so it makes sense to me come leavin' time they'll head north," Jeb said as he met Ben's eyes and then continued, "so we'll let 'em come to us."

"Think they'll come by in the mornin'?"

Jeb chucked, pulled his old hat off and said, "Ben, do I look like one of them fortune tellers they got at a county fair? Hell, I can't see the future even a little bit. I ain't got no idea when they'll ride, but I'm sure it'll be in a day or two. A big group of men like that don't usually stay in one place very long, because they don't have much patience."

"So, we jess wait?" Ben asked as he pulled the makin's of a fire together and pulled out a wooden match.

"Yep, unless ya have a better idea."

Ben laughed and replied, "Hell, I ain't even sure where I'm at, except north of Omaha. I'll be the first to admit, I don't know my butt from a gopher hole out here, so I'll leave the decision makin' up to ya. Ya listen to me and we'll end up in Tucson or Santa Fe."

Jeb smiled and then spoke, "Ain't them two places down in Texas, near Little Rock?"

Both men laughed a few minutes and then things returned to normal as Jeb moved off to find some water for the night.

A few miles south of Jeb and Ben, Buck was sitting beside a large fire and enjoying a plate of ham and beans. The food was the first good meal he'd had in over a week, because he'd used his limited income to buy a beer or three each night after work. Each day he'd usually pick up some bread at the bakery, a can of peaches or pears, and save the rest of his change for beer. While not a drunk, Buck did enjoy a beer or two each evening in the saloon and while he didn't realize it, it was the talking and being around other people he enjoyed more than the beer.

Taking a bite of the beans, Buck turned toward Shorty McWilliams and asked, "These fellers all ready to ride when Crawford gets here?"

Shorty McWilliams was a tall man, well over six feet and six inches, and near two hundred and forty pounds, thus his nickname. His hair was sandy in color and his square unshaven jaw gave him a rough appearance. His teeth were even and snow white, his eyes were a deep green, and he was filled with spitefulness. Rumors had been going around that Shorty's family had been killed by the Sioux a few years back and that was why the man was so mean and worthless. He was a small time crook, cattle rustler, and on the dodge from lawmen from most of the west. Shorty spat his tobacco juice into the flames of the fire, turned to look at Buck and replied, "They'll ride. But, I want to know a little more about this heah job we signed up fer."

Buck laughed and said, "We're to help Crawford kill a man that wronged him."

"Shit," Shorty spoke and spat brown juice once more before he asked, "what kind of man needs hep killin' another man? This Crawford don't sound like he has any balls at all, or he'd brace the feller he wants killed himself."

"Look," Buck spoke as he wiped his mouth off with the back of his left hand, "fer what he's payin' us, I don't mind goin' along fer the ride. I mean, after all, to kill one man is simple, so the money will be easy."

Shorty didn't answer right off, but he was thinking. Finally, a few minutes later he said, "Somethin' ain't right 'bout all of this. I don't think this jasper yer man Crawford wants to kill will die easy. Nope, sounds to me like the man he's after might not be easy to put down a-tall. Hell, Buck, why else would he need so damned many men?"

"Shorty, we'll all sit in the rocks, on a hill, or hide in the trees. When the man he wants killed rides by we'll blow his ass off his saddle. Easy job, easy money."

"Maybe we will and then maybe we won't. This feller Crawford is after must be a real hard man to kill and he knows it too. I'm tellin' ya right now, if I don't feel good about the job when we see this feller we're to kill, I'm backin' out."

"Ya turnin' coward on me Shorty?"

Shorty thought about pulling iron and killing Buck right where he sat, but instead he controlled his temper and said, "Nope, I ain't scared of no man, but I don't like the feel of this whole shebang. Besides, how do we know it's just one man we'll have to kill? This feller might be surrounded by a big group of fellers."

Buck thought over what Shorty had just said and realized he didn't know if the victim would be alone or not, and that made him think. *Hell,* Buck thought, *I never thought to ask him that question. It could be that feller has a bunch of men ridin' with 'em too. That could be why Crawford needs all of these men. If that's the case, I ain't sure I wanna be part of this either.* But, instead of discussing the situation with Shorty, Buck replied as he pointed toward the road with his right index finger, "Here he comes now, ya can ask 'em."

Crawford was relaxed in the saddle as he rode, because he'd spent most of the afternoon enjoying Kattie's lovely charms, and she'd been very good. His mood was cheery and his body was relaxed after spending a couple of days with the young and talented whore. Of course, the rest and good food hadn't hurt him a bit either.

Pulling up beside the picket line, Crawford dismounted and tied his horse to the rope. He approached the fire, grinned, and squatted as he asked, "Where are the guards?"

Buck and Shorty exchanged shocked looks and then Buck asked, "What guards?"

Crawford's eyes narrowed and spoke in a flat voice, "Buck, from now on, we'll have guards posted all the time. I mean any time we stop, I want at least one man guarding us."

Shorty gave a low chuckled, glanced at Buck and stated, "That's bullshit and ya know it, too. Why in the hell do we need guards jess outside of Omaha?"

"Because I said so, and I run this outfit. If ya don't like it, leave." Crawford felt his temper rising.

Shorty stood, turned, and started to walk away, but as he did so he spoke just above a whisper, "Sumbitch thinks he can run these boys like the damned army does."

"Hey, ya got something to say to me, ya say it to my face! Don't be mumbling behind my back." Crawford yelled as he slowly stood and pulled the thong off of his pistol hammer.

Shorty turned and as he did his right hand quickly reached for the forty-four he wore low on his right side, but he didn't even clear leather. Crawford's gun barked once, then twice, in less than a second it seemed to Buck. The young cowboy noticed two dark holes you could cover with a silver dollar suddenly appear in the center of Shorty's chest.

The big man was hit and hit hard, but he was not an easy man to kill. He kept trying to raise the pistol he felt in his right hand, but his body refused to obey his thoughts. Finally, with all the effort he could bring forth, the gun raised about six inches and he squeezed the trigger. The injured man was surprised when he saw dust fly from near his right foot. Shorty never felt the third slug that struck him between the eyes and he was dead before he hit the ground beside the fire.

Buck stood and moved over to check Shorty. He only needed a slight glance to see the man was as dead as he'd ever get. The last bullet had torn the back of his head off and while the body still twitched, the smell as his bowels emptied told the young cattle hand that Shorty was beyond help. Buck turned and glared at Crawford.

"Son, he started to pull on me first. I didn't start his mess and I rarely do, but I always finish what I start. Now, ya got somethin' ya want to say?" Crawford spoke as he pushed his pistol back into his holster.

"No..no..it was a fair fight. But, ya didn't have to kill 'em."

"Buck, understand somethin' and keep it to mind, I *never* shoot to injure a man. If I shoot at a body, I always shoot to kill. I've seen too many injured men come back and kill the other man."

Buck shook his head, shrugged his shoulders, and then asked, "What now?"

"Have some of the men drag his ass away from the fire. Dead bodies always spoil my food and I'm hungry. And, Buck?"

"Yes, suh?"

"Remember what I said in the saloon about killin' ya first?"

Buck met Crawford's eyes and replied, "Yep, I remember it."

Crawford laughed, looked at the young cowboy and said, "Well, I guess now you'll be the second one I kill, huh?"

CHAPTER

20

As the two men rode westward, Cookie was deep in thought. He'd spent enough time out west to know better, but he was thinking about the reward money and what he could do with his share. He knew that much cash at once might be more money than he'd ever see again, so he'd have to use it wisely and not waste a penny of it. He was thinking hard when Jefferson dropped back beside him and said, "Cookie, I ain't sure what you're thinking on, but you better start paying attention to where we're at and what's around us. This ain't the best time in the world for you to be lost in thought."

The older black man grinned and replied, "Yep, yer right on the money with that comment. I know'd better, but I got to thinkin' 'bout what I could do with the reward."

"If you don't pull your head out of your rear," Jefferson said with a dry laugh, "you'll not have to worry about it."

Cookie lowered his eyes and quickly replied, "I'm sorry. I jess ain't never had much money and, well, I need to do somethin' special with my share."

Jefferson knew how the old man felt, because he felt that way himself a lot of times. It was hard for a man to make much real cash money and any man without some cash money was facing some serious problems. He gave Cookie a big grin and said, "Look, wait until we get to camp, then dream all you want. Right now, though, I need you to help me keep an eye open as we ride. You been out here long enough to know we've both got to keep our eyes open as we travel."

"I hear ya son and it won't happen again. Let's ride."

Later that night as they sat around a small campfire hidden back in some dense brush, Jefferson poured himself a cup of hot coffee as he asked, "So, what was all that day dreamin' you was doin' earlier today about?"

Cookie stretched his legs out in the dirt, pushed his hat back on his head and said, "I think I'm gonna start me a eatin' place, if we get that reward money from the army."

"Well," Jefferson started speaking as he lowered the pot back to the flames, "that's good to hear. Hell, it ain't likely you'll starve to death then, huh?"

Cookie laughed, looked at Jefferson and said, "Nope, not likely. But, I ain't shore how to go 'bout this business idea I got in my head."

Jefferson thought for a moment, lowered his cup to the dirt by his right foot and asked, "You worried about feeding white folks?"

"Yep, I am. I don't think they'd eat at a black man's place, do you?"

"What I'd do, if I was you is one of two things. We both know you could move to a town full of blacks, but hell they ain't got any real money right now. Or, get you an honest white man to go into business with you. And, let me tell you right now, I'm sure Jeb, Jarel or even Ty would be more than happy to go into business with you." Jefferson spoke and then gave a quick laugh.

Cookies eyes lit up, he gave a big grin and said, "Okay, so I do that, but where do I start a business?"

Jefferson laughed once more and replied, "I ain't sure about the where part, but it has to be in a town or city. You go someplace else and you'll have no customers."

"I fig'ered as much. I don't care much fer Omaha at all, so that place is out. Kansas City ain't bad, or mayhap Independence, 'cause I like both of them places."

"Have you ever given it any thought to maybe headin' further out west, maybe to California?"

Cookie chuckled lightly and said, "Nope and I don't wanna go way out there either. I don't speak no Mexican and I'm too damned old to be movin' that far."

Suddenly, Jefferson froze and with a lowered voice said, "Cookie, I think we have Indians."

"God almighty, where?"

"I just spotted some movement a minute ago over by the horses. Stay relaxed until we see what they want, maybe we can talk our way out of this."

Cookie, frightened, stood and instantly Jefferson heard the older man scream and noticed him fall backward. As he glanced at the old black man he saw an arrow sticking in his upper right arm. His eyes were huge with fright and his lower lip was quivering.

It was then that the younger black man noticed dark shapes moving from the shadows toward his fire. It only took him one glance to see it was the Sioux. Jefferson didn't move, but remained seated by the fire as a large group of Sioux warriors quickly surrounded them. He'd heard enough talk from white men to know any sudden movements he made right then could well be his last. So, as he looked at the Sioux, he attempted to determine who the leader was.

Many long and tense minutes followed without a word spoken by anyone around the fire. But, finally a young warrior asked heavily accented English, "Why you on land of Sioux?"

Jefferson noticed his heart was beating fast and his hands felt sweaty, but he swallowed his fear to reply, "I've been sent by One Speaks and Walks Proudly."

There was a quick exchange of Sioux among the braves and then the young warrior spoke once more, "One Speaks is not known by the Sioux. We know only One Who Speaks."

Jefferson gulped loudly and instantly replied, "That is the man. He is the son of Buffalo Hump, a Sioux chief."

The brave nodded, knowing Jeb very well and then asked, "Why has The One Who Speaks sent you into the land of the Sioux?"

"We are seeking a man. We are looking for a white killer of my raven people."

"The Sioux have no killer of your people."

"I was sent west and told to wait for The One Who Speaks and Walks Proudly."

There was a quick exchange of words among the braves and then the young warrior spoke, "Come. We will return to our village and let Hump decide what must be done."

Jefferson helped the injured Cookie to stand and then asked, "Can I care for my friend before we leave?"

"Yes, work your medicine on him, but hurry, because we are not alone in this darkness of night."

The injury to Cookie was slight and Jefferson was relieved when he noticed the arrow had only struck the muscles in this upper arm. The arrow had passed all the way through, but the younger black man knew the injury would heal in less than a week, unless it festered. Cookie was quickly bandaged, given a tin cup of whiskey for the pain, and mounted, within thirty minutes of Jefferson's conversation with the warrior.

The night passed slowly with the Sioux constantly moving north, except for a few very short periods of rest for the horses. While the weather was nippy, the heat of the horse between his legs kept the younger black man warm and he was sure it was the same for Cookie. It was during a break near dawn that Jefferson gave the older man another cup filled with the rough traders whiskey and said, "We're two lucky men Cookie. We met up with Hump's group of warriors and not some other band. If it had been the Crow, Pawnee, or Comanche, we'd most likely be dead right now."

Cookie gave a dry laugh and said, "Hells, bells, son, I hurt bad 'nough as it is. But, the way I got it fig'ered, yer right 'bout us bein' lucky it was Hump's warriors. these Injuns is a rough bunch and they don't care what color a feller is. Only, why did these fellers shoot me, do ya think?"

"You moved too quickly and they didn't know if you were goin' for a gun or not. That's why Jarel warned us to always move slowly around Injuns when ya first meet up with 'em. Near as I can figure they live a dangerous life and can't afford to take no risks at all. They shot you to protect themselves, don't ya see?"

The older black man thought for a few seconds and then grinned in the poor moonlight as he replied, "Oh, I sees it now, but at the time I was a bit corn-fused, as my ole daddy used to say all the time."

Seeing the Sioux warriors mounting, Jefferson said, "Let's mount up and get moving. I suspect these warriors are worried about something and they don't like being out here no more than we do. You'll be fine in a few days, but Cookie?"

The old man had just placed his foot in his stirrup and replied, "Huh?" as he mounted.

"The next time, and there will be a next time, we see Injuns, don't move . . . not even an inch."

Cookie gave a low chuckle and moved his horse slowly toward the moving Sioux.

As dawn was reaching out with fingers of yellow light from the mountains to the east and the clouds overhead turned a bright orange, the group of Sioux and two black men entered the village. The group rode their horses to the teepee of Hump. Once in front of the chief's lodge, the warrior who spoke English dismounted and made his way to the buckskin flap that covered the entrance. Jefferson noticed the man scratched it softly and cleared his throat.

Almost instantly the door flap was thrown open and out stepped Buffalo Hump, the leader of the Sioux. He glanced around and then asked, "Why does Long Horn visit my lodge as the sun is born?"

The brave quickly explained what had happened and the old chief didn't say a word until the younger man quit speaking. Then, he met Jefferson's eyes as he said in passable English, "Come, we will eat and talk." But, as soon as he had spoken he turned to Long Horn and said in Sioux, "Awaken the old buffalo man and bring him to my lodge. Things might be said that I must clearly understand and he will know the words of the white man. There might be words spoken I will not know."

Hump, Jefferson, and Cookie entered the lodge and were quickly seated around a small fire. Hump's wife was not in the lodge and Cookie felt his fear rising, until the younger man touched his left knee and said in a low voice, "Don't be scared, I know this man. I just got some land from him, so we're among friends."

For over five minutes not a word was spoken in the lodge. Just as Jefferson was about to speak Moses entered the lodge and sat on the old chief's right. A couple of more minutes passed as Hump thought out his questions and then he turned to Moses and said, "Tell these raven men I am honored to have them visit me, but why are they on Sioux Land? The young raven I know, because I gave him the land by the cold river, but he was not found near his new land."

"Howdy boys, I'm Moses. I know ya Jefferson, but who's yer friend here?"

"He's Cookie and he rides with Jeb and his bunch after Crawford."

"Yep, I 'member that sumbitch, he kilt Abe. So, yer out lookin' fer 'em then?"

"Kind of. See, Jeb wasn't sure if Crawford went north or west, so he sent Jarel and Ty up north, me and Cookie out west, as him and Ben rode into Omaha."

"Hell, it sounds like Jeb's got a whole army wid 'em now, huh?"

"Enough of us to do the job, if we can find the man."

Moses turned to Hump and explained to the chief what was said. Hump understood most of what had been said, but he was confused over why they were looking for a white man. The old black man quickly explained about Abe's death and how Crawford was the killer.

The chief didn't speak for a second or two and then said, "I knew this raven man who was killed and he was a man of great honor. At one time we, the Sioux, wanted to kill the one we speak of, but this was not allowed to happen. He, the one who has passed over, was a man of The People and will be missed in our hearts. I can see why these two were on our lands, but no one has seen a lone white man. If one had been seen he would have been killed and I would know who carried his scalp."

Jefferson met Moses' eyes as he explained the old chief's words, and then he asked, "Moses, are we free here or captives?"

Moses gave a dry laugh and then replied, "Both."

Cookie, confused, spoke for the first time in the lodge as he asked, "Now what in the hell does that mean?"

Moses faced the man, his eyes grew narrow, and he replied, "Cookie, there is a war brewin' up of the likes ya ain't likely to ever see again. Oh, yer both free men, but only a fool would leave this village now."

Hump leaned near Moses and asked the old man in a low voice what had been said. After he heard the words from Moses he met Cookie's eyes and spoke, *"The Sioux people and the white eyes do not agree on the taking of the hides."*

"What did he say Moses?"

"There is trouble comin' over the takin' of buffalo hides. Hump here jess said that the Sioux and Whites don't agree over what should be done."

"So," Jefferson spoke as he leaned back on his elbows to get more comfortable, "where does that leave us Moses?"

A grave expression came over the old mans face as he said slowly, "Right smack dab in the middle of the damnest war ya might ever see young pup. Yup, we're all caught right in the middle."

CHAPTER
21

Jeb and Ben enjoyed a quiet but cold evening, with little talk between the two of them, because both were thinking of Crawford and the situation to come. Beyond any doubt they'd find the man, but it was the unknown aspect of the future that concerned them. So many unexpected things could happen and it worried them a great deal. Finally, Jeb asked, "You ready to start the dance?"

Ben thought for a second and then replied, "Yep, I think so. My biggest concern is how many men he'll have with 'em."

"Yep, I been thinkin' on that as well. Ya know, if it was just him it'd be easy, but if he has all those hombres with 'em, we'll have to find a way to get him aside."

"Yup, and a man like him won't want to be alone long unless he's in a room someplace."

Jeb gave a low chuckle, leaned back against a log, and said, "It ain't likely he'll be alone much, if at all. If he's movin' after somebody, and I suspect he is, then he'll stay with the men he's ridin' with most of the time. The way I figure this is he's either after Buffalo Watkins, or my ass. He's made it very clear that he don't like neither of us much. Now, I ain't sure what he's got on me, or why he killed Abe, but I know for damned sure he has reason to kill Buffalo."

"Ya figure he killed Abe out of the blue? I don't think that's what happened, especially after he was askin' about ya at the tradin' post and all."

"Nope, he planned Abe's killin', but for the life of me I don't see why he did it. But, it might be like Ty Fisher told me, Crawford just don't like black folks. Plus, he had to know Abe was my friend, so mayhap he thought by killing him, I'd come for 'em."

"Well, if that's what he thought, it worked."

Jeb gave a slight chuckle and replied, "It worked, but maybe too well. See, once he killed Abe and the rest, he sealed his doom. None of us will quit now until Crawford is hanged or rubbed out. "Ben," the one legged man's eyes narrowed to just slits as he continued, "Crawford is livin' on borrowed time. If I don't get his ass, Ty, Jarel, or one of the others will."

Ben thought about Jeb's words for a minute and then asked, "So, how do we handle this?"

Jeb smiled and replied, "Not sure yet. When they pass by we'll get on their back trail and see what happens. If we follow 'em long enough, well, somethin' at some point will happen that will give us our chance. We'll just have to be patient and not crowd the man. Odds are he has a bunch of no-goods ridin' with 'em. Ya know the kind, so they'll probably never suspect they're bein' followed. A big group of fellers always develop a false sense of security when they ride, as if their large numbers will protect 'em."

"Won't their numbers alone keep us off their asses?"

"No, not at all, and at some point we'll start to whittle their numbers down a mite, but most likely we'll wait until Ty and the rest join us before we open the dance. I ain't no coward, but I ain't no fool either and it'll take more than the two of us to take on this group."

"Well, it makes sense to me, what ya've said so far. I'll leave the plannin' up to ya, because all I know is cavalry tactics and such from the war."

Jeb chuckled and as he rearranged the wood in the fire he said, "Ben, ya'll be a good help to us then. I spent the war, most of four years, in the infantry, and I've done a lot of fightin' up close and personal like. But, don't forget we have two old mountain men along with over forty years of experience each fightin' Injun's, renegade white men, and every kind of critter you can imagine. No, what Crawford should really fear is Ty Fisher and Jarel Wade, 'cause those two won't play with man or give him an even break—they'll just kill 'em."

Miles away, as Jeb and Ben sat in the cold air discussing John Crawford, Buffalo Watkins was drinking whiskey in a saloon in Coldcreek. He usually had two drinks each evening and then returned to his room for a good night's sleep. He was half finished with his first drink and considering his money. Earlier in the day the bank had informed him that his money had grown to the point he no longer needed to hunt, but Buffalo, while not really a greedy man, wanted just a few more dollars before he put his Sharps away for good. The bank teller had shown Buffalo in his bankbook where he had twelve thousand dollars in his account. While not really able to visualize that much money, he knew it was enough for him to buy a farm, livestock, and hire help to run it. The only factor bothering the big man was that he felt the amount should be rounded out to fifteen thousand. He was a man who liked nice even numbers and he felt twelve thousand was an uneven number. Watkins figured one more week on the plains and he'd quit for good.

He had just raised his whiskey glass to his lips when he heard a voice speak from behind him, "Buffalo, I been lookin' fer ya."

Watkins recognized the voice and sipped his drink before he replied, "Well, ya found me Wilcox and I ain't gonna hire you back. I ain't putting up with yer drinkin' no more."

Wilcox gave a weak laugh and then said, "Hell, I ain't lookin' fer a job. I'm the head skinner for Laugherty now and workin' out of Omaha. Anyhoo, I wanted to let ya know yer younger brother, Frank was killed a few weeks back at Brown's tradin' post."

Buffalo Watkins didn't speak for a minute, but then he turned and asked, "Who did the killin'?"

Seeing the deep anger in the big man's eyes, the weak grin on Wilcox's face faded quickly and he replied, "A big one legged man with a Southern accent. Now, I have to say, Buffalo, it was a fair fight. Yer brother, well, he was jess a tad too slow that day."

"What's the name of this one legged man, Wilcox?" As soon as he spoke, Buffalo threw down the remaining whiskey in his glass, slapped his empty glass down on the bar with a loud bang, turned to the bartender and indicated he wanted another double shot of rye.

"He said his name was Patton, Jeb Patton. But, Buffalo, Frank insulted the man's wife and, hell, nobody will take that kind of talk from another man."

Buffalo picked up his refilled glass, took a deep drink of the whiskey, and replied, "Frank always had a big damned mouth. And, I figured it'd get his ass killed one day, but I cain't let his killin' go unavenged. Like it says in the Good Book, an eye fer an eye and a tooth fer a tooth."

Wilcox gave a dry snicker and said, "Well, ya might have yer hands full when ya try to kill this Patton feller, 'cause I don't think he'll kill easy like. Buffalo, there was a no nonsense air 'bout 'em that scared the shit right out of me."

"And, speakin' of ya, where were ya when Frank was killed?" Buffalo glared at Wilcox as he asked the question and the smaller man felt his gut tighten.

"Right beside 'em Buffalo, and let me tell ya right now, he might have jess one leg, but this Patton is as fast as greased lightnin' with a pistol. Hell, ya know Frank was quick, but he never even cleared leather."

"And, ya, I suspect didn't do a damned thing, did ya?"

Wilcox lowered his eyes and replied, "No, Buffalo, there wasn't a thing I could do. Ya know I ain't no quick draw artist. 'Sides Patton already had his pistol out and Frank was on the floor as dead as last year's Christmas turkey in seconds. I ain't no coward, but my momma didn't raise no fool."

"Ya said ya ain't lookin' for no work right now? Hell, it's the wrong time of the year for takin' hides, so I know ya ain't got a job."

"I got a few bucks to see me through winter, then it's back to the plains. I made good money workin' in Omaha last summer."

Buffalo called the bartender over and ordered another drink for himself and a beer for Wilcox. As soon as the drinks were delivered he spoke, "Let's go to the table on the far wall. I want to talk with ya for a few minutes. And, Wilcox, when ya want another beer you jess tell the bartender. I'll buy ya a few tonight as we talk."

A few minutes later the two men were seated at a roughly made table with one leg shorter than the others, which made it wobble as soon as it was touched by either man. Ignoring the table, Buffalo Watkins turned to Wilcox and said, "Ya get a good look at this Patton feller?"

"Hell yes and I talked to the man too."

"What's he look like?"

"Average kind of feller I'd say, 'cept for the missin' leg. Brown hair, wore it long, green eyes, and maybe a hundred and eighty pounds. He's tall though, six feet or more."

"Beard?"

"Yep, he wore one and it's the same color as his hair, but trimmed neat like. He was dressed like many fellers out here that was in the war back east. He had canvas jeans on, buckskin shirt, and an old Union cavalry hat on, ya know the dark blues one, but it didn't have no hat band or nothin' on it."

"You said Frank insulted his wife? Now, why in Sam's hell would he do that?"

"Well," Wilcox started speaking, but then realizing he had a beer in his hand took a big gulp, wiped his mouth off with the back of his right hand, and continued, "Patton's wife was a white woman, but at first

167

Frank thought she was a squaw. I thought she was too, 'cause she was wearing a squaw's clothes. You know buckskins."

Buffalo sipped his whiskey, looked over his glass at Wilcox and asked, "Where's this one legged sumbitch at now?"

"Well, I ain't real sure 'bout that. He said he was a Missouri boy, born and bred, but I remember him a-sayin' he lived up in the mountains. Hell, he cain't be no mountain man, them days are long gone."

Buffalo didn't respond. He sipped his whiskey and when his glass was empty he ordered another round for them. Finally, after thinking on the situation for a long time, Buffalo asked, "Ya want to earn some extra money?"

Wilcox, had just taken a big drink of his beer, choked for a minute or two, turned to face Buffalo Watkins and replied, "Not if the job's what I think ya have in mind."

"I'm gonna kill this man Patton."

"I ain't interested in the job, Buffalo. He told me if he ever saw me again he'd kill my ass on sight and I believe the man."

Watkins let out a loud laugh and replied, "Yer scared of a one legged man?"

Wilcox looked deep into the bigger man's eyes and said, "Buffalo, I wouldn't face that Patton feller for any amount of money on this earth, and he could have no legs and I'd still not take the job. I saw something in his eyes that told me he's a man of his word and I'll not take the risk of facin' 'em again."

"Okay, ya hide from 'em if ya want, but I'm goin' after 'em in the mornin'. Now, if ya ride along, I'll pay ya five hundred dollars just to point 'em out to me. And, ya don't have to do a damned thing after that. What do ya say to my offer?"

Wilcox sipped his beer and gave the offer some serious thought before he replied a few minutes later, "Alright, I'll ride with ya, but I won't go near the man. Buffalo, if you'd seen the smooth way he pulled that gun and the speed he did it, well, ya'd not want to see it again. And, I warn ya, ya draw on him and yer a dead man."

"I won't brace him with a gun. No, not with a gun. This is one man I want to kill with my hands or with a knife. I want him to suffer and know his death is comin'. Frank wasn't much of a man and like I said he had a big mouth, but by God he was family."

"Buffalo, where ya gonna start? Them mountains are big and high and he could be on any of 'em."

"We ain't gonna look for him, ya fool, we'll let him come to us. Now, didn't ya say he was at Brown's tradin' post when the killin' took place?"

"Yup, that's where we was at. Ya'd just fired me and Frank was at the tradin' post pickin' up some supplies fer Laugherty."

"I figured he went on a long ass drinkin' spell after huntin' season quit, hell, I never suspected he'd been kilt. But, it don't pay no never mind, we'll ride to Brown's in the mornin' and camp nearby. Sooner or later this Patton feller will come back and when he does, I'll have a go at 'em. Nobody kills a Watkins and gets away with it." Buffalo gulped the remainder of his rye, stood and said, "Be ready to ride at first light at the livery."

Morning was wet, with the wind howling, as the two men rode. Dawn was attempting to break through the thick clouds over head, but to Wilcox it looked as if the sun would never come out, so he pulled his thick buffalo robe tighter around his shoulders. Long hours passed without a single word being spoken by either man. Part of the silence was due to them moving through Indian country but the real reason was both men were deep in thought. Buffalo Watkins was thinking of his revenge and Wilcox was worried about what would happen if Patton saw him again. He had absolutely no doubts the man would kill him.

It was near dark as the two wet men pulled up into a bunch of oak trees beside a shallow stream and made a hasty camp. Within twenty minutes a shelter was up, a small fire was burning, and the mounts cared for. Both men sat under the canvas shelter as the rain beat with a steady rhythm on the tight material overhead.

Finally, Buffalo reached into his pack and pulled out two long strips of jerky and handed one to Wilcox, as he asked, "Ya tired?"

"Not much. I'm mainly wet and I hate ridin' in the rain. Why'd ya ask?"

"Well, we're in Sioux country, so it'd be smart to stand guard over the place as we travel."

Wilcox gave a loud laugh and replied, "Hell fire, Buffalo, ain't nothin' out in this weather, 'cept fer ducks."

"I said we'll stand guard." The big man's eyes reflected his anger. Buffalo Watkins didn't like his orders questioned by anyone.

"Okay, if ya want me to guard, then I'll guard, but if ya ask me, I don't think we'll have any problems tonight."

"I didn't ask you. From now on out we stand guard every night until we get to the tradin' post. And, I'll warn ya right now, fall asleep on guard duty I'll personally cut yer damned throat. Do ya understand me?"

Shit, thought Wilcox, *if Buffalo here don't end up killin' me, Patton will. What in the hell have I got myself into here?*

169

It was over coffee the next morning by a small fire, when a large group of Sioux rode over a slight rise and sat watching the two white men in the trees below. Buffalo noticed the Indians right off and he warned Wilcox in a low voice, "Sioux, but for God's sakes man, don't try to fight 'em. There are at least twenty of 'em and I don't like the looks of this."

Wilcox, his eyes large in fear, glanced at the mounted braves and quickly pulled his pistol as he screamed, "These red bastards ain't takin' me 'live to skin and gut like a pig!"

At the sight of his pistol clearing his holster the leader of the Sioux gave a bloodcurdling war cry and charged his horse at the camp.

"Damn it Wilcox!" Buffalo screamed as he moved over behind a log and pulled his big Sharps up to his shoulder. While the braves were still off a long distance, the big white man started calmly squeezing the trigger. His first shot knocked a brave from his horse, as did his second and third shot. The big .45/70 lead slug doing terrible damage as it struck flesh and bone.

Wilcox, knowing if they could make the attack too costly for the Sioux they might survive, gave a loud laugh from behind the log and screamed, "By God, that'll learn 'em."

"Shoot and shut the hell up Wilcox or we'll both be dead in a minute or two! We have to turn the charge from us or they'll overrun us!"

Wilcox rose slightly, sighted in a brave, but then suddenly screamed as an arrow pierced his left shoulder. "I'm hit!" He yelled as he dropped back down behind the safety of the log without firing.

Buffalo didn't even glance at the man as he continued shooting at the Sioux, but he did say, "Wilcox, if you don't start shootin' son, we're both dead, arrow or no arrow."

Wilcox broke the shaft of the arrow, raised once more and as soon as he'd fired his Sharps he noticed one brave less in the group. It was at that point the attackers broke hard to the right and circled back around to the top of the hill.

Watkins watched the warriors as they met at the top of the hill and he finally saw the war leader. Raising his Sharps once again, he adjusted the Creedmore sights for the distance and wind, and then took a deep breath. As he slowly released the air from his lungs, he very gently squeezed the hair trigger on is big buffalo rifle.

The Sioux, who must have thought they were a safe distance away, were surprised to hear the loud boom of the Sharps, but even more surprised when Crow Killer was knocked violently from the back of his horse. Two braves immediately dismounted and ran to the man, but there was little they could do for him. The big lead slug from the big bore rifle had struck the chief in the middle of his chest and half of his back was blown away. Crow Killer was dead. Seeing the rapid losses from the attack and now the death of their leader, the Sioux quickly called the attack off and placing the dead man over his horse they started back for the village. All knew their medicine was bad this day and decided the cost of killing the two white men was too high.

Ten minutes after the Sioux left, Buffalo stood from behind the log and grinned as he said, "They don't like the taste of lead them boys don't. Now, Wilcox, get over by the fire so I can patch ya up. As soon as I'm done we're moving on, because I got a man to kill."

CHAPTER

22

Ty and Jarel rode beside the Sioux warriors for the remainder of the night, but about two hours after dawn they reached the cave. It was near the Missouri River and the small stream they had moved down emptied into the larger tributary less than a half a mile away. As they left the stream, one of the warriors remained behind to cover the trail as well as he could. Though the snow was still falling lightly, the brave made every effort to hide where they had left the stream.

It was not until they were inside the cave that Ty spoke for the first time since they'd left their camp, "So, ya figure the riders they saw sign of might be Crawford?"

Jarel removed his hat and placed it on his bed roll as he replied, "Yep, I think it is, but it's hard to tell really."

Ty thought about the odds it could be Crawford and then said, "Well, as soon as we get these Blackfoot off of our asses we'll take a look-see. Ya ain't gettin' me out movin' now with Bug's boys stirred up good like they are."

"It is good we have bad weather coming." Night Hawk spoke from near the fire.

Jarel and Ty both looked out of the cave and noticed large white flakes of snow falling harder and heard the gusts of the wind. Both of the men knew since it had snowed lightly all night their tracks would soon be completely covered. Exchanging glances, both men smiled and then Ty said, "Now, this is a real stroke of luck. Them Blackfoot won't come out a-lookin' fer us now, 'cause it would all be a waste of their time. They might be good trackers, but nobody can track a body after snow covers the tracks and they damned well know it too." And, turning to Many Horses, Ty asked, "So, my friend, what do we do now?"

The warrior, his eyes gleaming, said, "We will wait for one sun, then we will find those white men who are riding on the lands of the Sioux. This white man who is without honor must not be allowed soil the sacred land of our ancestors."

As the brave spoke, Jarel felt an uncontrolled shudder run down his spine.

Two days later the small group was moving over the plains as they searched for the whites. It was near noon, as the group stopped to rest the horses and eat a light meal, when Night Hawk gave the call of a robin and walked to the fire leading his tired horse. The warrior tied his mount to the picket line, walked to the fire and squatted by its warmth. While most of the snow had melted, there were still patches of white scattered on the ground and the temperature was well below freezing.

"I have seen the white eyes." The brave spoke as he placed a large piece of buffalo meat on a stick and placed it near the fire to cook.

"How many hands of white men?" Many Horses asked as he met the brave's eyes.

"Two hands and one finger."

"Are they near?" Ty asked as he moved to the fire and sat in the dirt beside the warrior.

"Less than half of a sun."

"Shit!" Jarel exclaimed as he quickly glanced at Ty, "That's only half a day's ridin'."

"Who are these white men and are they ready to do battle?" Many Horses asked.

"All are young men and they have many guns and horses. They are men who can be killed in a short battle of maybe less than four hands of heartbeats. I have seen them and they are lazy. I counted one finger of them guarding and he was sleeping. I could have taken his life, only I was sent to find the white eyes, not to fight them. I waited, knowing in my heart there will come another time to count coup."

Jarel, remembering that Ben and Jeb were to follow Crawford and his men if they left Omaha asked the tired warrior, "Did you see sign of One Who Speaks?"

"I have seen the One Who Speaks and shared the warmth of his fire last night. He is with a man with hair the color of the rising sun. He is well and also follows the man without honor."

Jarel grinned and turning to Ty he said, "It looks like both Ben and Jeb still have their topknots."

"And, did the One Who Speaks give you any words to speak?" Ty asked as he pulled out a hard piece of jerky from inside his possibles bag and tore off a piece of the dried meat.

"His words to me were for us to join him in his attack on the one without honor. He is less than a short ride from here, in some trees near this same river. So, we must hurry if we will meet him this day. The snow will make the travel hard and the wind will cut like a cold knife, but this must be done."

Standing, Ty gave a big crooked grin, adjusted his pistol belt and replied, "Let's ride then, the day ain't gettin' no younger."

The going was slow, with the wind strong and blowing snow making visibility very difficult. More than once Night Hawk had to dismount and get his bearings before moving forward once more, but move forward they did, though it took much longer than they had expected.

Finally, after four hours in the saddle, Ty turned to Jarel and yelled to be heard above the harsh wind, "Jarel, we have to find some shelter! This wind is too strong and I'm starting to get frosting on my face and hands."

Jarel turned slightly in his saddle, cupped his hands around his mouth and yelled back, "Just a bit more! Night Hawk says we are near!"

"He'd better hurry, or I'm pulling out and huntin' my ass a hole! This is dangerous weather and not to be taken lightly!"

Many Horses, hearing the conversation and understanding most of the English words rode up beside Ty and said in Sioux, "Over the next hill and we will be with The One Who Speaks. Just a bit more my friend and you will be warm once more."

True to his words, as they topped the next hill, Ty could see a small fire burning down in the oak trees. While there was no smoke, the bright color of the fire was quickly noticed.

Nearing the camp, not a soul was seen, but at the last minute he heard a voice command in English, "That'll be close 'nough!"

Recognizing Jeb's voice, Ty called out loudly to be heard over the wind, "Jeb, it's us, Ty Fisher and Jarel Wade!"

174

Jeb stepped out from behind a tree, gave a big grin and screamed to be understood, "Come to the fire! It's too cold to be talkin' out heah in the wind. Move deeper into the trees and to our camp."

The small group of three Sioux warriors and two white men quickly dismounted, tied their tired mounts to a picket line, removed packs and saddle bags and moved to the warmth of the fire. The cold was numbing and all of the men were shaking as they stood by the dancing flames of the fire.

"Pull out yer cups and get some hot coffee in ya. I got some whiskey to take away the chill, if ya want some." Jeb spoke as he added two more logs to the fire, knowing the men were about frozen.

"I'll pass on the whiskey, 'cause it ain't safe to be drinkin' out heah with Crawford near, but I'll damned shore have some hot coffee." Ty spoke as he opened his possibles bag and pulled out an old beat up tin cup. Holding the cup with trembling hands, he gave a big grin as Jeb poured the coffee.

Soon, the whole group was sitting around the fire and discussing Crawford and his group of men.

"Me and Ben been on their backsides since they left Omaha. I ain't sure where the boys headed, but he seems to be waiting fer something or unsure where to go. First they moved out west a ways, then they cut back east real sudden like and camped just a few hours east of here. From what I can tell, he's meanderin' like a damn river."

Jarel thought for a moment and then said, "Nope, he's lookin' fer somebody. He might be out to meet somebody, but I don't think so. He has enough men to do whatever he has in mind, and me, well, I think he's after either you or Buffalo Watkins. From what Cookie told us he has a reason to want to see Buffalo dead and he fer damned sure ain't lost no love fer ya a-tall, Jeb."

Jeb, stretched out by the fire on his buffalo robe, gave a loud laugh and replied, "Well, he'll soon have all of me he wants." And, then his eyes constricted and his expression took on a grave look as he continued, "He killed Abe and that man was a better man than Crawford could ever be in two lifetimes."

"Waugh! That's fer damned sure Jeb!" Ty spoke and then turned to face Many Horses as he asked, "What do we do now my friend?"

The leader of the Sioux thought quickly, "Let Night Hawk warm by the fire and eat. Once he has rested he will visit the white men and see if things are still as they were. I think it would be good to have one of you that speak the white tongue to go with him. You can listen and Hawk can count coup on the guard." Then smiling the warrior added,

"It is time we let the white eyes know they are not welcome on Sioux land."

The four white men all wanted to go, but Jeb knew his peg leg would slow him down and Ben knew he lacked the experience, so after the two of them explained their thoughts, Ty said, "Let Jarel here go along. He's got good feet when he's near the camp of an enemy and he's a might younger than me. Of all of us, I suspect he'd do the best job."

"But first," Many Horses spoke, "let us eat, drink of your coffee, and rest. When the night is half finished, Night Hawk and Walks Proudly will visit the camp of the one without honor."

Hours later, after a big meal of buffalo stew with cornbread, and pots of scalding thick coffee, Jarel Wade and Night Hawk were positioned in a thick group of oak trees watching the big group of white men. Both men had slept for a few hours and were well rested for the job they'd come to do.

"They still only have one guard, near the horses. Do you see him?" Hawk signed as he grinned at Jarel.

"Yes, only one. I do not see the one I seek, the man without honor." Jarel signed back and returned the braves grin.

"It is too hard to see with the low fire and robes cover most of the sleeping men. Let me silence the guard forever, run off the horses, and you stay to cover me."

"Good. You move slowly and do not rush this. If anyone moves, I will shoot them dead." Jarel signed once more and then started checking the loads on his weapons.

When he turned to look at Hawk again the man had already disappeared into the inkiness of the dark night. *It always scares me the way them boys can move so quiet like that,* Jarel thought as he gave a quiet chuckle.

Night Hawk approached the sleeping guard and pulled his sharp knife as he neared the man. From what he could see in the light, the white man was young, but he was walking a warrior's path, so death could visit at any time. The young white man never heard the Sioux brave and the first and last hint of danger was when the keen edge of the big skinning knife slid quickly over his exposed throat. Hawk held the jerking man as his life's blood spurted from his slit throat, and it was not until the man voided his bowels and quit kicking his heels into the snow that he released him. He removed the man's scalp and tucked it into his sash.

Moving quickly to the picket line, Night Hawk moved down the rows of horses and cut each animal loose. It was as he neared the last horse, a big bay, that the horse gave a loud nicker over the foreign smell of the brave. Instantly there came a shot from inside the camp and Hawk felt the impact of the bullet strike him in the left leg. The force of the bullet striking threw him to the ground, where he quickly moved into the brush that surrounded the camp.

Jarel had seen a lone white man suddenly stand, aim his pistol at where the guard had been and then heard the shot. He had no idea where Night Hawk was, but he suspected the brave was safe enough, so he raised his rifle and put a bullet into the back of the standing man. Jarel grinned as he saw the man knocked down hard by the slug hitting him and he lay unmoving beside the dying fire.

At that point all hell broke loose as someone screamed, "Get them damned horses! Get to the horses!"

In a matter of seconds, men were jumping up and pulling weapons, but no one moved in the direction of the scattering horse herd. Instead, most of the men stood in the middle of the camp unmoving. Jarel lined his sights up on the biggest man in the group and smiled as he watched the man go down as the slug took him in the center of his chest. Jarel stood, and moving like the wind, ran to the agreed upon meeting place, but an hour later Hawk had still not returned.

Jarel, figuring the warrior had been hurt, knew better than to return to look for him at that moment. If the brave was able to move, he'd head to where they were to meet, if he wasn't able to move, he'd hole up some place and wait. The mountain man quickly decided to wait until later in the day and hope the whites would relax enough so he could look for Hawk.

It was a bit after noon, when an injured Night Hawk neared the spot he was to meet Jarel. His leg was stiff and pained him a great deal, but if he wanted to live he had to keep moving. As he stumbled along he saw a slight movement to his left and as he turned he saw it was Walks Proudly.

"Hell, son, you took long enough. I can see you're injured, did the bullet strike the bone?" Jarel said as he quickly moved to the man's side.

"No, it did not hit the bone, but there was heavy bleeding at first."

Jarel looked down at the leg and noticed it was still bleeding a little, but Hawk had bandaged the wound using some pieces of buckskin from his shirt. Since they were still close to the white camp, a fire could not be made, so Jarel pulled the wounded brave under the lower limbs of a huge pine. As soon as the warrior was on the ground, the mountain man removed the bandage, gave a low grunt, and reached into his possibles bag. He removed some cotton cloth, a salve made of salt, bacon grease, whiskey, and coal oil, and started working on Night Hawk. It took him over five minutes to remove pieces of dirt and grasses from the injury, but in less than fifteen minutes the Sioux warrior was re-bandaged. Jarel noticed beads of sweat on the man's face and he knew the wound had to hurt like hell. Hawk hadn't even moaned once during the doctoring.

"Yer a lucky man, Night Hawk, the bullet only made a path through the meat of your leg."

"Of this I must thank the Great Spirit. If it had hit the bone I would not have been able to move at all."

"Well, you'll be fine in a week, unless bad spirits enter the bullet hole and cause it to fester on ya."

"Of evil spirits I do not worry. I have my medicine pouch and I have been wounded many times in the past and yet I live."

Jarel gave a low chuckle at the Indian's belief in his medicine and he started to speak when he suddenly heard a white voice call out, "Buck, ya find any sign of them horses?"

"No, but ya keep yer damned voice down. Hell, Conway, who knows where them damned Injuns are and here ya are, shootin' off yer big mouth loud like this."

The man called Conway didn't speak for a few minutes when abruptly he called out once more, "I see blood over heah. I see a lot of blood."

"Keep yer damned voiced down ya fool! I'll be there in a minute and take me a look see. Ya stay there." Buck replied as he moved toward the one called Conway.

Signing to Hawk, Jarel said, "I must kill these white men. They will follow the blood and find us here. I will move off to the right and then make my attack."

Night Hawk pulled his rifle up, checked the load and replied in sign, "Go my brother and I will cover your back."

The wind had picked up once more and that helped cover the small noises Jarel made as he left the tree and started circling the white voices. His first goal was to see how many men were involved. He had only heard two voices, but that didn't mean there weren't others that hadn't spoken at all. Finally, after checking the area, he saw only two white men. Jarel suspected the group had sent out a number of men as couples to try to recover the spooked horses. The two men he saw standing in a small clearing had one old mare and it was being held by a tall lanky young man who was bent over studying the ground.

"Yep, whoever it is they've been hit pretty deep."

"Ya think it's an Injun, Buck?"

"Yep, I see a moccasin track heah, and it looks to be a Sioux design too." As soon as Buck spoke he raised his head and took a good look around and then added, "He must be holed up around heah. Let's flush his ass, kill 'em, and get back to the camp. I suspect nearly all of the boys are back by now and will have most of the horses."

Jarel stepped from the brush he had been hiding in and said, "I think yer killin' days are 'bout over boys."

Buck and Conway were both shocked at seeing a white man suddenly materialize from the woods, but Buck recovered first and asked, "Ya lookin' fer Injun's too?"

"Nope," Jarel spoke slowly and was glad his injury from the Blackfoot attack didn't bother him much, because he knew a fight was coming, "lookin' to peel me some polecats."

Confused, Conway asked, "What in the hell ya talkin' 'bout old man? Hell, ya cain't peel nothin', yer too damned old."

"The two of you listen to me. I'm after a man named Crawford and I 'spect ya boys work for 'em. If ya work for him, then yer two skunks I'm gonna skin. And, I can still do the job, old man or not."

Buck gazed into Jarel's eyes and then slowly raised his hands as he said, "Looky here mister, I don't want nothin' to do with none of this. All I know is I took a job with Crawford to hunt a man that wronged 'em. I didn't sign on to be anything else, hell, none of the boys did."

Jarel thought for a few seconds and then asked, "Who's yer boss lookin' fer?"

"A big feller that goes by the name of Buffalo Watkins. Seems this Watkins feller screwed Crawford over and the man wants revenge."

"Okay, let's say I believe ya, what are ya doin' out here now?"

"Sioux ran our horses off last night, killed two of our men and badly wounded another one."

Jarel gave a loud laugh and said, "Yep that was me and Night Hawk."

Buck, looking confused asked, "Now why would ya, a white man, and a Injun run our horses off and kill our men?"

"Buck, I think that is the name I hear'd ya called a few minutes ago, yer boss is a cold blooded killer. He killed a very good friend of mine a while back and I don't take kindly to that. Now, ya and Conway have a choice. Ya can leave and never come back, or pull yer guns."

With a speed that surprised Jarel, Conway suddenly pulled his pistol and fired before the old mountain man realized what was happening. Jarel felt the bullet take him low in the left side, but he raised his rifle and jerked the trigger, and watched as the bullet struck the man on the right side of his head. Conway was knocked to the ground where he lay twitching and jerking. Jarel swung his rifle toward Buck and saw the deep fear in the other man's eyes as he attempted to fire before the old mountain man could. He didn't do the job and was struck about an inch above his belt buckle by two bullets, one from Jarel and the other from Night Hawk. The impact of the bullet knocked the thin cowboy around and down. Buck landed on his face and noticed as he breathed that he didn't feel any pain. But, try as he might, he was unable to lift his pistol. Suddenly, a gray veil covered his eyes and quickly turned black.

Jarel checked both of Crawford's men and found them dead, or so he thought. He raised the side of his buckskin shirt and noticed a shallow furrow plowed in his side from the shot by Conway. He made his way to the tree, gave Hawk a big grin and said, "Let us leave. I have a feeling the white men are down to just one hand of men that can still fight."

"First we must bandage your wound, Walks Proudly, so others that follow cannot see the blood we have lost in our battle with the white eyes. And then, we will return to our camp and tell the others of our honor in this battle. It is a great day to fight the white men who killed the buffalo man."

CHAPTER
23

"Look, we're leaving . . . Buck or no Buck. Him and Conway been gone all day. I suspect they either ran away or they ain't comin' back. We've got enough horses for those that are still able to ride, so let's move." Crawford ordered as he sat by the fire and sipped his coffee.

"But, it ain't like Buck to not come back. Hell, if he wanted to quit he would have told ya to yer face." An ugly looking young man of medium size spoke from the other side of the fire.

"Maybe, I don't know 'em that well, but we are leavin' as soon as I finish my coffee. If they are still comin' they can trail us and catch up later. I don't want to stay around here with the Sioux on the prowl."

"What about the wounded man?" A short plump man named Holly asked from beside the ugly one.

"If he can ride bring 'em, if not leave 'em."

"Ya cain't leave a man just because he's wounded and can't ride!" Holly almost shouted.

Crawford grinned, stood and emptied his cup into the fire as he replied, "Of course I can and I will. Now, get loaded up and let's get going. We've wasted enough time today."

"Look," Holly said as he stood and walked up to Crawford, "it'll be dark in a couple of hours, why don't we "

Crawford struck the man hard in the mouth with the flat of his hand and the force of the blow sent Holly to the ground. Standing over the man, Crawford yelled, "I don't want to hear another word from ya!" and glancing around at the other four men he lowered his voice and said, "Mount up. If you're wounded and able to mount ya can come along, if not, stay here and take yer chances."

Two hours later, four men rode across the plains.

While Jarel thought Buck dead, following the attack, he'd been very much alive. He'd taken both bullets in his belly and though he knew his injury was fatal, he prayed he might yet pull through. The pain from the injury was a coming and going thing, which seemed to claw at his guts one minute and then vanish the next. His real hurting and pain started when he was found by a wandering band of Blackfoot not soon after Crawford and the rest had ridden off.

The Blackfoot quickly hanged the man from the limb of a huge oak tree by his ankles and then opened him up like a deer. Long purplish rolls of intestines fell to the ground under him and the braves laughed at his screams of pain and fear. After slicing long thing strips of flesh from his arms, legs, and rear, they built a small fire under his head and once again laughed as he twisted and turned to avoid the heat and kisses of the hot blaze. Soon, bored with playing with the white man, the warriors added more logs to the fire, and danced around him giving loud war cries as his brain cooked in the dancing flames of the fire. When the Blackfoot rode off two hours later, even the man's mother wouldn't have recognized his blackened and disemboweled remains. And a deep sickening sweet smell of burnt human flesh filled the night air.

Forty miles and two days later, Crawford topped a slight rise and noticed a train moving westward on the horizon. He grinned, looked over at Holly and said, "Here comes our ride boys."

Holly, who had grown to hate Crawford, spat a long brown stream of tobacco juice from his mouth and said, "We cain't ride on that train, hell, it'll be gone by the time we get to the tracks."

Crawford shook his head slowly and replied, "Holly, does yer momma know she raised an idiot for a son?"

Holly was unsure what the man meant, so he kept his mouth shut.

Watching the smoke from the train a few minutes, Crawford raised his right leg and placed it over his saddle. He pulled out the makings of a smoke and as he rolled his cigarette he thought of the train and how it was his way out. He'd seen no sign of Buffalo Watkins, or of Jeb Patton, so he decided the night before to ride north and see if the railroad had laid tracks this far west yet. He now saw that they had.

"How come they . . . . why they . . . why they got . . . got a train way the hell out heah?" The ugly man, who Crawford had learned was named Lee, asked as he rode up beside the others. Lee had a bad stutter when he was excited that bothered Crawford.

"Hides, son. See, them buffalo hides bring top dollar back east, so the tracks are there to move the skins. I know a hide hunter that made thousands of dollars in less than two weeks huntin' those shaggy assed things." John Crawford explained, but left out the fact that it was Buffalo Watkins, who they had been looking for.

"Sh . . . sh . . . shit!" Lee managed to stuffer out and then add, "Th . . . th . . . that's a lot of mon . . . mon . . . money."

The men laughed and Crawford replied, "Yep, it is, but only if ya live long enough to get to spend it. With the Sioux out in force now and on the war path, only a fool would be out huntin' buffalo. And, besides, most of the buffalo are way down south now and all the hide crews are wintered up in some town."

"Well," Holly spoke, "ya never did tell us where we was headin'. Are we still goin' there?"

Crawford gave the question some serious thought, turned in his saddle and looked at Holly as he took a long drag on his smoke. Finally, he said, "Nope. Too many Injuns between here and Coldcreek."

"What're we goin' to do now?" Holly asked.

"Meet the next train and flag it down. Then we'll load our horses onto a car and ride to the next town. Once there I'll pay ya boys off and we'll go our separate ways. How does that sound?"

"Damn . . . g . . . good t . . . t . . . to me." Lee spoke once again, "I'll buy me a wo . . . wo . . . woman with my share."

All the men laughed.

Gently kicking his horse into a slow walk, Crawford started moving toward the tracks. He hung back a little and as the three men moved in front of him, he pulled his pistol and then shot all three of them in the back. Riding up to each fallen man, he placed a second bullet in each head. He kicked his horse into a canter, holstered his still hot pistol and rode to the tracks. Less than three hours later he flagged down a passing train and warned them of a large Sioux attack, of which he was the only survivor.

The end of the tracks was a place called 'Hell Town,' that was filled with Chinamen and Irish, neither of which Crawford had any use for. He intended to take the next train back east, pick up some more money, and then return in the spring with more men. One thing for certain, he'd wait until the Sioux were taken care of before he came back. He suspected Buffalo Watkins would keep working out of Coldcreek and he knew a man like Jeb Patton would stay in the mountains, so it was all a matter of time.

Crawford took a room in what was called a hotel, but it was just a tent with cots in it. The price of two dollars a night was very high, but it was the only sleeping quarters to be had, so he had no choice. The food was terrible and expensive as well. He'd had a plate of tough beans and fatback and the meager meal had cost him another dollar. Finishing the meal, he purchased a ticket to Independence, Missouri, and walked to the nearby saloon.

The structure was a tent with a false wooden front. He bellied up at the bar, which was a wooden plank laid on some empty whiskey casks and ordered a beer. As soon as the big barkeeper brought his drink he stood in front of Crawford with his hand out and said, "That'll be a quarter."

"A quarter for a damned beer? Hell, in Omaha a beer is a nickel."

The big man laughed and replied, "Then get your ass to Omaha and buy a beer. The beer here is a quarter and the whiskey is fifty cents."

"Why so much?" Crawford asked as he pulled the coin from is pocket and dropped it in the big man's hand.

"End of the line here for the track. These Irish you see around here are working their asses off and makin' good money a-doin' it. While most men back east make fifteen a month, these boys are makin' well over thirty to sixty. But, the work is hard and many of them are injured on the job. Hell, you couldn't get a normal white man to take the job, 'cept fer these Irish. Got a hell of a lot of them Chinee heah too, but they cain't come in heah and anyways, they're a clannish group and stay with they own kind."

Crawford nodded in understanding and asked, "Why all the tents. I mean ain't you stayin' here once the line move further west?"

The big bartender laughed, which showed a number of missing teeth, and replied, "Hell no, mister. When this track moves on, so do all of us. See, we're all in tents because that's the lightest way to travel and we supply these railroad men all kinds of things. Not a one of us has any real place to call home right now. We're always at the end of the line, but the money is good."

"If you're getting a quarter a beer I'll bet it is."

The bartender laughed, noticed a customer wanting another beer so he moved off to serve the man.

Crawford had two beers and went back to the tent that served as a hotel. The place was almost empty, but the owner, a small weasel of a man said it would fill up as the saloon closed. Most of the men, like

184

Crawford, had paid for their rooms and then headed to the bar for a few drinks. The fatigue and stress of being out on the plains caught up with Crawford and he pulled his boots off, stretched out on the hard cot, and was instantly asleep.

If the men made any noises as they entered the sleeping area later that night, Crawford never heard them. He slept long and hard, waking just before dawn. He put on is old worn boots, buckled on his gun belt, and walked to the restaurant for breakfast. The eatin' place was almost empty and pulling up a canvas folding chair he sat down at a rough plank table.

"What'll ya have?" A young boy of about fifteen asked Crawford as he rubbed the sleep from his tired eyes.

"Ya got any eggs?"

"Nope," the young man said and then broke out laughing, "all we got is beans or else buffalo."

Crawford laughed and asked, "Then why did you ask what I wanted?"

The kid smiled and said, "Jess wondered what you'd want to eat, not that we have it. You want coffee too?"

"Yep, but how much is all of this gonna cost me?"

"Breakfast is a dollar and the coffee is a quarter a cup."

"Just bring the food. I don't care fer y'alls prices, but hell, a man's gotta eat."

A little after eight that morning, Crawford boarded the train and started his travel's east. As the cars crossed the Missouri River, he felt his tension leave him. He knew he would not fully relax until he arrived in Independence, but he was no longer worried about someone bracing him or shooting him in the back. Most of his enemies were out west and he didn't intend to go back there until the time was right.

In Independence he took a thousand dollars out of a bank, got a nice hotel room for a week, and took a long bath. Since the town had laws against carrying pistols in town, he stuck a small derringer in his coat pocket, and went for a walk. The air was brisk, but not really cold. He stopped one young boy who was screaming the headlines of a local paper and bought a copy. Taking it to a saloon he took a table and began to read. While not a good reader, Crawford was able to understand most of what was printed.

So, he thought, *they found the bodies of Holly, Lee and the rest and blamed it on the Sioux. I'll bet a lot of killings the Injuns had nothing to do with are being blamed on them, but that's one problem I don't have to worry about.*

"It's pretty gory out west right now, huh?" Crawford heard a deep voice ask.

Looking up he met the eyes of a big man standing in front of his table. Not wanting to really talk, but yet not wanting to attract attention to himself he replied, "I just came from out there and it's bad."

"I'm a newspaper reporter and my name is Green, James Green."

"Have a seat." Crawford spoke and then motioned for the bartender to bring two beers to his table.

"Where were you out there?" James asked as he pulled out a small writing tablet and a well worn pencil.

"What're ya doin'?" Crawford asked.

"Why, if it's ok with you, I'd like to interview you for the paper. It's not often I get to speak first hand to someone from out west. You don't mind do you?"

Crawford was a lot of different things and one of those was vain. He suddenly liked the idea of being in the paper. He gave the reporter a big grin and said, "Oh, I see. Well, my name is John Crider and I used to work for the army out west, near Omaha."

"And, what did you do for the army?"

"Delivered dispatches and such for 'em. I quit because the Sioux are fixin' to go to war over the killin' of the buffalo."

"It must have been exciting at times, huh?"

"Ya could call it exciting, but it scared the shit out of me more than just a few times."

James quickly turned his pencil around and erased the comment Crawford had just made and then asked, "Would you give me the details? I think I can get this on the front page. Just imagine, me speaking with an army dispatch rider. I think the readers would eat it up!"

Over the next two hours Crawford filled both the reporter's notebook and his head full of absolute lies about what was going on out west. To listen to him speak, thousands upon thousands of innocent whites had been killed by the Sioux and all over the killing of a few hundred buffalo. Crawford enjoyed being the center of attention and told in great detail of atrocities that had never occurred, people who had been left homeless that he didn't know, and of complete massacres of Federal troops. Lie upon lie was fed to the reporter as beer after beer was ordered. The reporter nodded at times and at others shook his head in sadness of the untrue killings.

By the time the interview was finished, the reporter, still grinning quickly stood and left the table in a big hurry. As he walked from the saloon he yelled back at Crawford, "I'll have this on this evening's front page!"

Little did Crawford realize his interview with James Green and the printing of the Independence Leader later that afternoon was the beginning of his downfall.

CHAPTER
24

Jeb and Night Hawk returned to the others and Ty sent the Sioux back to their village. All the warriors had suffered some sort of injury, so Ty was able to convince them the Great Spirit must not want them in on the revenge against the man without honor. As soon as the braves left, Jarel looked over at Jeb and said, "Okay, now what?"

"Not sure. Many Horses rode out yesterday and came back with some tall tale about a smoking wagon that moved faster than a horse. Now, I ain't rightly sure what in the hell that boy was talkin' about."

Ty and Jarel both broke out in loud laughs and it was many minutes later before Ty said, "Jeb, a smoking wagon is a train. The Injuns have never seen a train, so they compare it to what they do know, and that's a wagon."

Jeb laughed, pulled his hat off and said, "Well, anyway, near the tracks of the smoking wagon, Many Horse found the bodies of three white men. All three of them had been shot in the back and at close range. And, according to him the men had not been scalped or mutilated, which means we can rule out Injuns doin' the killin'. Now, as far as Many Horses and we know, the only group out here that was white was Crawford and his no accounts. So, it looks to me like Crawford most likely killed those men and then boarded a train."

"Shit," Ben spoke and suddenly stood, "we've lost 'em then! Once on a damn train he can go anyplace he wants and a hell of a lot faster than we can on horseback."

"Yep, that about sizes it up in my mind too, but a man filled with as much hate as Crawford has won't stay gone long. He'll be back, but the question is when?" Jarel asked.

Ty had been listening and hadn't commented during the conversation, so he finally spoke, "Well, I don't think he'll come back until the

Sioux and the rest of the plains tribes cool down a little. He's a smart man and he must know that this whole place is about ready to explode. I think he just learned that even with a large group of men the Injuns can cut the numbers down pretty damned quick."

"Okay, I hear all of ya, but what do we do?" Jeb asked out of frustration as he squatted by the fire.

"Go home Jeb, hell, there ain't nothin' we can do now. Look, the man could be anyplace and I'm too old to be runnin' around lookin' fer people. I did enough of that when I was a young coon." Ty spat the words out and was immediately sorry he had spoken so roughly, but it was how he felt. He knew Crawford would return one day.

Jeb met Ben's eyes and said, "In the mornin' I'll leave for the Sioux and take Ben with me, but what about you two?"

Jarel laughed and replied, "We're gonna swing by Butterfield's Trading Post and let 'em know what happened. While we're there we'll pick up a jug or two of whiskey and go visit old Teacher and Zee fer a spell." Then the older man grew serious and added, "Jeb, let it be fer now son. Crawford will be back and when he returns we'll kill his worthless ass."

Two days later, Jarel and Ty pulled up in front of Butterfield's Trading Post and dismounted. The weather during the trip had been dry, but cold enough to freeze water bladders that were not kept next to the fire overnight. Each morning one of the old mountain men had been forced to break ice in a stream or river just to water their riding stock. Neither man minded the cold much, as long as it was dry.

They entered the store, with both men noticing the faint *tinkle-tinkle* of the brass bell on the door, and were instantly overpowered by the intense heat in the small room. A large pot-bellied stove burned in a corner near the window and was glowing red-hot on the sides. Old man Butterfield was sitting behind the counter and had a piece of pine in his left hand and a pocket knife in his right.

As soon as he saw the two mountain men, Butterfield placed the wood and his knife on the counter and said, "Well, now, if it ain't ya two old worthless coons! How ya be boys?"

"Doin' fine Butterfield!" Ty spoke and moved toward the old man.

"Now, don't neither of ya tell my grandson I been whittlin' in the store. He don't like it when I do that inside, but I enjoy cuttin' on some wood when I'm bored."

Jarel and Ty both laughed, and then Jarel said, "Butterfield, give us two of yer big jugs of good whiskey and, oh, let's say about a dozen twists of chewin' tobacco."

Butterfield stood slowly, as if his joints hurt, gave Jarel a big grin and said, "So, yer too good fer trader's whiskey now days, huh?"

Jarel laughed and replied, "Nope, not at all Butterfield, but me and Ty have decided to visit Teacher and Zee, so we thought we'd take some good drinkin' whiskey along fer a change."

As Jarel and Butterfield made small talk, Ty glanced around the store and finally, seeing a newspaper he picked it up to scan the front page. As he read the Independence Leader, he noticed an interview with an army dispatch rider on the front page. After reading most of the story he said, "Bullshit."

Jarel, unsure what Ty was talking about turned and asked, "What's that Ty?"

Butterfield, seeing Ty holding the newspaper said, "We just started gettin' them newspapers in heah couple months back. I don't pay 'em much mind, 'cause they're jess full of foolishness, or so I fig'er."

Ty glanced at his longtime partner and replied, "This here Missouri paper is what I'm talkin' about. They did an interview with some feller that said he was a dispatch rider fer the army out here. He claimed all kinds of folks been killed, including three of his best friends."

"Three?" Jarel asked and then continued, "Ain't that how many men Many Horses saw killed by the train tracks?"

"By damn, it surely was." Ty replied and then asked, "Do ya think this feller who claims he rode for the army, this Crider feller, might be Crawford?"

"Let me read this paper and see what I think. Hell, I don't know what it says yet." Jarel spoke as Ty handed him the paper. Finally, after reading the paper he said, "The paper says this Crider feller is tall and lanky, and from his hair color and the rest he sounds like Crawford, but lots of men could be described like that. What I find interestin' is this feller claims his three partners was killed by the Sioux as they rode beside the train tracks north and west of Omaha."

"Yep, I thought about the description too, but how many other men would talk of the Sioux killin' three men he rode with by the tracks or the terrible massacres he claims to have seen happened out here? Hell, we both know there ain't been very many people killed out here at all, yet. Old Hump's keepin' a tight reign on them braves of his."

"Sound's like Crawford to me, by God." Jarel spoke, grinned, and then asked, "You ever been to Independence Ty?"

"Not since it was called Cold Springs, but I suddenly got me a strong hankerin' to visit there fer a short spell."

Butterfield, who had been listening to the conversation, asked, "Does that mean you don't want the whiskey and chewin' 'baccer now?"

Ty gave a weak grin and said, "Nope, put it all back. But, give us a box of forty-four cartridges and box of Sharps .45/70 cartridges; I suspect we'll be usin' them way before we'll get around to sippin' any whiskey."

Less than three days later the two old men were sitting on a train moving east. For Ty it was his first trip by rail, and Jarel teased him about it endlessly.

"Beats ridin' a hoss all the way to Missouri, don't it Ty?" Jarel asked as he glanced at his friend and could see the apprehension clearly in his eyes.

"Nope, not at all. Too danged fast fer me."

"Fast? Not much faster than a runnin' horse."

Ty shook his head and met Jarel's eyes as he said in a very serious tone, "Jarel, God did not intend for man to travel this fast. It ain't natural like."

Jarel gave a loud laugh and replied, "Relax Ty, it's safe and much quicker than a horse would be on the same trip."

Ty glared at the younger man and said, "I'll agree with ya, it's fast, but I won't relax until we get off this damned thing."

Soot and small burning coals flew past the windows and a few minutes later Jarel heard Ty ask, "How does this thing cross the Missouri River?"

"I ain't seen it yet, but I hear'd tell they have a big bridge that crosses the river and this train rides right over it."

"Excuse me, sir," A fat man in the seat across from them said suddenly, "I have ridden this line often and we're about to come to the river crossing in a few minutes. And, my name is Anderson, Thomas Anderson. I'm selling a new product that perhaps you've heard of, barbed wire."

"Howdy do, I'm Jarel Wade and this old coot is Ty Fisher. Glad to meet you Anderson, but I ain't never hear'd of no bobbed wire, what is it?"

The big man reached under his seat, pulled out a small suitcase and opened it. He reached in with his right hand and pulled out a six inch sample of his product. Holding it up so both of the mountain men could see it, he said, "It won't be the army that settles the west or the gunfighters, it will be this product right here gentlemen, barbed wire."

Ty gave a mighty laugh and asked, "What the hell is it used for? And, how in the world will it settle the west?"

Anderson gave a big grin and replied, "This wire is made of the finest metals, resists rust, and is twice as strong as other comparable products. Why a farm encircled with barb wire, sir, will keep cattle and horses from roaming, as well as mark a man's property boundaries very clearly."

"So?" Ty said and thought about what the man had said.

"Once we start marking our land clearly, the days of the blood thirsty red man will be over my good man. Just imagine farm after farm linked together with countless miles of our product. The days of free range will end and the Indian will no longer be free to roam and kill like he does now. No, gentlemen, Anderson Wire will tame the west way before any other means."

Jarel glanced at Ty, could see the concern in his partner's eyes. Both men knew immediately that once farmers, cattlemen, and others started using barbed wire the old days would be over.

"I don't like it." Ty spoke in a flat voice.

"It's a very good product, sir." Anderson spoke as if he wanted to convince the old mountain man.

"Bullshit and I don't like it. Look, ya start fencing in land, farms and the whole works, hell, ya'll ruin the land I love. How could a man ride fer days on end and not have to cut that damned wire to travel?"

"You'd use roads of course, but . . ."

Ty pulled his pistol, brought the hammer back with a loud click, and then said slowly, "Mister barbed wire salesman, I think ya need to find yer ass a new place to sit. I ain't got no use fer ya, or yer bullshit wire."

The big man's eyes grew large, his face paled, and as he stood he said, "I'll move, but while you may move me, you won't stop me. My wire is a product of the future and your days are over old man."

Ty glared at the man, but didn't kill 'em like he wanted to. He knew, out of the mountains, civilized folks frowned on killings, so he simply watched the fat man waddle to the rear of the car and take another seat. He lowered the hammer on his pistol, placed it back in his holster and said, "Now I'll swear by hook, ain't that somethin'. What do ya think of all of that talk Jarel?"

Jarel thought for a second and then replied, "Fer a farmer or cattleman it might be a good thing. But, fer us mountain men and Injuns it marks the end of our time. If they go stringin' that wire for miles upon miles out on the plains, we'll be hurtin'."

"Waugh, these damned corncrackers are always messin' up a fellers life. Be poor bull if that wire gets out on the plains and ya know it too old son."

The conductor came into the car, looked over at Ty and Jarel and said, "We'll be crossin' the Missouri River in a minute or two. If ya look out yer winders ya'll get a good view of the river below."

Ty gave a loud gulp and said, "Below?"

The conductor was a middle-aged man with wire rimmed glasses and a big friendly smile. He met Ty's eyes and replied, "Yep, I guess we'll be 'bout a hundred feet above the river as we pass over." At that point the train gave a loud whistle, and the man added, "We're at the river now. The engineer always blows the whistle before we cross to warn anyone on the bridge."

Jarel stuck his head out and looked forward. While he could see the river as it meandered across the land, he couldn't make out the bridge coming up. The conductor reached over and pulled him from the window and warned, "Don't lean out like that, sir. A few months back we had a young man on this line lose his head when he struck this very bridge. Ya want to look, stay seated ya'll see 'nough."

As the train started over the bridge there was a noticeable difference in the sound of the wheels on the tracks and the train gave a slight shudder as it started across. Jarel, as full of joy as a young lad would be, grinned, elbowed Ty and said, "Ain't this somethin' old coon? Lordy, that river looks to be a long way down too!"

When Ty didn't answer, Jarel looked over and quickly noticed the older man had grown pale, and his eyes were tightly closed. As he looked closer, Jarel could see Ty's mouth was one thin line and both of his hands had death grips on his knees. In all the battles Jarel had seen Ty fight, this was the first time in his life he'd ever seen the older man really scared, but out of respect for Ty he didn't say a word. Jarel knew all men were frightened of something, but for each man it was different. He knew Ty was scared of no man or beast, because he understood them, but a train was a thing he knew little about. Jarel knew Ty Fisher was scared of the train ride, because he didn't understand trains. *Well,* thought Jarel, *so be it. If Ty don't like trains, it's okay by me. Hell, I think this is great!*

Though their tickets were good for all the way to Independence, the two old mountain men got off the train in Kansas City, Missouri. Jarel had enjoyed the ride, but he suggested to Ty, who'd not relaxed a bit since the bridge crossing, that they ride the rest of the way on their horses. Ty, only too happy to leave the train, agreed immediately and said, "Good idea. I think Crawford might be watchin' the train sta-tion."

Jarel had a light inner chuckle and led his horse down the ramp of the cattle car. Mounting, he noticed Ty was still pale, but his color was slowly returning. *One thing I can say about Ty*, he thought as he placed his hat down lower on his face, *he was scared but still faced that train ride. It takes a man with guts to do what he has to do when he's scared shitless. Ole Ty still has the hair of the bear, he surely does.*

The next day the two mountain men entered the big city of Inde-pendence, Missouri a couple of hours after dawn. The place was filled with folks coming and going, and as far as both old men were con-cerned the people seemed to be moving aimlessly and without a sense of purpose. While each of the men knew the city folks were doing things they needed to do, they both doubted the chores really needed to be done.

"These damned pork eaters are always in a rush. I'll bet ya a dollar to a horse turd, they ain't a one of 'em doin' nothin' important." Ty spoke as he dismounted and quickly tied his horse to a hitching post in front of a restaurant.

Jarel laughed and asked, "Yer feedbag empty old man?"

Ty grinned, met Jarel's eyes and replied, "Been too long since I had me some real taters, grits, and white sop pepper gravy poured over some big thick cat-head biscuits."

Stepping up on the boardwalk Jarel said, "Along with some eggs, country ham, and coffee, right?"

"Sure." Ty laughed as he spoke, opened the door to the place and walked in.

Seating themselves at a table where they could watch the front door, the two mountain men should have felt out of place. After all, both were wearing buckskins, moccasins, old felt hats, and carrying old rifles, but they didn't. Jarel quickly noticed none of the men in the place was armed as far as he could tell, though he suspected one or two might have a pistol in a coat pocket.

Both men ordered a huge breakfast from a small and young woman just barely out of her teens. She was fascinated by the way the two old men were dressed, but didn't question them because she was too busy. Thirty minutes later after the two men finished the meal they sat and sipped their coffee.

Ty suddenly asked, "What now? Want to get a room and then look up that reporter feller? Or do 'er the other way around?"

"Let's get a room first. I need to wash some dust from my dirty carcass, have me a drink of rye, and change my clothes. Iffen ya ain't noticed, we ain't dressed right fer a big city like this."

Ty laughed and replied, "I'll change too. I noticed the look we got from that waitress lady and some of these customers, so we must stand out some. But, I don't take to 'er much. Hell, I ain't worn flatlander clothes in years."

Two hours later they were in the Blue Bird Hotel and they'd both had a bath, changed into jeans and shirts, and sipping on a drink of rye whiskey. They were wearing guns in holsters, but Ty didn't like them much. He claimed he could draw twice as fast from his wide belt than he ever could from a holster. It was only after a long talk that Jarel was able to convince him he'd stand out less if he looked like everyone else.

"So, let's finish these drinks and go to the Independence Leader and see if we can talk to this James Green feller about the man he interviewed."

"Ty, now by God, I want ya to watch yer temper here in town. Every damned time we've been in a town ya've started trouble of some kind or the other." Jarel warned as he looked over the rim of his whiskey glass.

Ty grinned, threw back his drink, and wiped his mouth with the back of his right hand before he replied, "Bullshit. I ain't never in my life started no trouble, but I've sure as all hell ended it a time 'er two." And, then broke out laughing.

Green was sitting at his desk, finishing up a story about a robbery down in southern Missouri, when he heard a slight noise outside his office door, and as he looked up he heard the secretary saying, "You men can't go in there like this."

The door to his office suddenly swung open and two old men stood in front of his desk. Placing his pen on the top of his desk, Green asked, "Franklin, what's the meaning of this? You know very well I am not to be disturbed when I've a deadline to meet."

Nervously, the secretary replied, "I know very well, Mister Green, but these two men just barged in here and demanded to see you."

Green, realizing the situation was out of Franklin's ability to handle, waved the man off, looked up at the two old men and asked, "Now, gentlemen, what's on your minds that's so important you need to interrupt my writing?"

"My name is Wade and I need some information on a jasper named Crider you interviewed for this paper a spell back." Jarel said as he placed his hands on his hips.

"Sir, I'm afraid I cannot divulge personal information pertaining to interviews, because it's against our papers policy."

In less than a heartbeat Ty had the barrel of his forty-four pistol pointed at Green and as the hammer cocked back, he asked, "Is it against this heah papers policy fer me to blow yer ass out of that chair?"

Green paled, batted his eyes a few times, and wisely understood that the old man standing in front of him was not bluffing even a little. He could see it in the man's eyes.

"Son, now I know ya ain't deaf, 'cause ya heard fine jess a minute ago. I asked you a question and, by God, I want an answer."

"I'll give . . . give you what I know, but it isn't much."

"That'll do son. See what ya don't know is Crider is really a man named Crawford and he's a bad sumbitch."

Ten minutes later as Ty and Jarel were leaving the building, Jarel looked over his partner, shook his head, and said, "Well, ya did it again old coon."

Ty grinned and replied, "I ain't made fer this big city livin'. I fig'ered if we went about meeting that Green feller like normal people do here, we'd spend a week before we'd ever see the inside of his office. I got the same information we wanted in jess a few minutes."

"I know, ya did good, but Ty?"

"Yup?"

"Ya really have to stop pullin' that damned pistol all the time. Now, let's go back to the hotel and talk on all of this fer a spell. We know where Crawford is now, so let's figure out how to go and get his scalp lock."

"Sounds good to me, we'll drink a little boldface and then blacken our faces! Waugh, it'll be like old times again son!"

CHAPTER
25

B uffalo Watkins had never been so scared in his life as he was at that second. He'd been riding beside Wilcox when suddenly from a dry stream bed to his right, twenty Sioux warriors had appeared. Leaning slightly in his saddle he spoke just above a whisper, "For God's sake man, don't pull a gun."

Wilcox, who was so scared that he'd peed his trousers, nodded in understanding.

Both men continued to ride and ignored the braves surrounding them. After riding for almost a half of a mile, another large group of Sioux came from a group of oak trees and pulled up in front of Buffalo's path, blocking him. The big man stopped his horse. As he waited to see what would happen next, though the morning was cool, he felt sweat running down his back. *Keep yourself under control here Buffalo and you might still live to see tomorrow*, he thought as he moved his eyes to check on Wilcox, *and don't you start no shit, son or you'll get us both killed.* The younger man sat on his horse unmoving.

"You are the killer of ta'tan'ka!" A warrior screamed as he rode right at Buffalo Watkins.

The sudden command from the chief who was off to the side of the group brought the young brave to an instant stop. Buffalo saw the chief was an older man and on his chest he wore the deep pink scars of the sun dance, which he had circled in red. *He's the leader, by God, that man is*, Buffalo thought as he raised his hand toward the man and said in Sioux, *"Woki'yapi"*

The chief moved his horse up to the white man and replied in thickly accented English, "Peace? There will be no peace for the killer of our sacred buffalo." Turning on the back of his small pony the man spoke quickly in Sioux, *"We will take these two to Buffalo Hump. Let us go now."*

Before Buffalo Watkins or Wilcox could resist, they were pulled roughly from their horses. Weapons were taken from them, hats were thrown to the ground and their hands were tied behind their backs. Watkins, mad at the sudden attack held his head high in defiance as Wilcox mutter prayers in a barely audible voice beside him. Forcefully rawhide ropes were looped around their necks and then the Sioux started back to the village.

Wilcox was so scared that he stumbled and fell frequently as the Sioux led him toward the village. Each time he fell, the rider holding his rope would continue on, as if he had no concerns at all about the man he was pulling. Finally, at a small break, Watkins whispered to the man, "Wilcox, ya need to keep up or these boys will turn mean on ya. Keep walkin' boy or yer a dead man." The big hide hunter had no idea if Wilcox heard him or not, because the younger man sat staring.

A few minute later the group was mounted and moving once more. Wilcox did well for over five miles, and then he collapsed in the dirt on his knees and started crying. "Get up ya dumb sumbitch!" Watkins screamed, but was struck from behind and knocked to his knees. As he watched a warrior approached Wilcox, grasped his hair and pulled his head back. In the bright sunlight Watkins saw the flash of a keen blade and then saw blood spurt from the throat of Wilcox. The brave let go of the young white man's hair and Wilcox fell, thrashing ferociously in the dirt. Watkins continued watching as the dying man's eyes grew large in fear and his feet kicked at the dirt violently. All of a sudden, the brave bent over, ran his knife around the Wilcox's head, and removed the scalp. Buffalo Watkins leaned to the right and puked.

Watkins felt a jerk on the rope to his neck a few short seconds later and heard a command in English, "Walk, white man, or join your friend in his journey to the other side."

Buffalo Watkins slowly stood on weak legs and starting moving once more, wondering if his life would soon to be over. As he walked his mind searched desperately for a way to survive, but he understood fully that the Sioux didn't want him to live. As the killer of the buffalo the best Watkins could even remotely hope for was a quick death, only he knew with the Sioux that was very unlikely. *I just hope they don't give my sorry ass to the women, cause I heard tell they're the meanest bitches this side of hell*, Watkins thought as he glanced madly around for a way to escape, finding none.

Late the next day they arrived at the village of the Sioux and Buffalo Watkins was almost insane with fear, while the need for water and rest had made him a broken man. Though the distance to the Sioux had been short as far as miles go, the hide hunter had fallen and stumbled many times, which had bruised and cut him in many small places. It took all the strength the big man had to stand in front of the Sioux with his head held high in defiance.

"Put the white eyes in a lodge and guard him well. The council will decide tonight what is to happen to him." The leader of the war party ordered as they dismounted their small but sturdy ponies.

As Watkins was led away, the entrance to a lodge opened and Hump appeared in the late afternoon sunlight. Though the temperature was just above freezing, the old warrior stood in nothing but a loincloth. Walking to the leader of the group that found Watkins, he said, *"Come Medicine Bear, we must speak."*

The two warriors entered Buffalo Humps lodge and were soon seated around the flickering flames of a small fire. Many long minutes passed without a word being spoken and then Hump asked, *"Who is this white man you have found?"*

"He is a killer of tatanka and he must pay for the taking of hides with his life."

Once again the lodge grew quiet, and while a long period of silence disturbed most white men, among the Sioux it was of no importance. Each man knew they could speak when they had the desire, but for the moment they thought of words yet to come.

Leaning back on his backrest, Hump said, *"I am thinking many things and I am sure the killing of one man will not stop the taking of the hides. As Proudly Walks and the One Who Speaks have said, the white men are as many as the grasses on the plains. If they speak with one tongue, the killing of a lone white man is nothing but a drop of rain pulled from a lake."*

Medicine Bear thought long over his leader's words and at last replied, *"I see no other way. White men have defiled our land and taken what is not theirs for their own. The killing of tatanka must stop. What will The People eat when tatanka is no more?"*

"I hear you and I know in my heart your words are ones of great wisdom. The leader of the white man's army will speak to me in two suns to do what One Who Speaks calls a treaty. Of this you did not know when you took the white man captive."

"I know of this thing called a treaty. It is the marking of the white man's leaves. It will give The People a place white men cannot come."

Hump gave a light chuckle and replied, *"So the white man says. I have talked long with One Who Speaks and all of the raven men about* this treaty. *Their words were not good words for my ears or for my heart.*"

"*How can that be? If the white eyes will leave The People alone and stop the killing of our buffalo, this treaty must be good.*" As he spoke, Medicine Bear looked deep in his chief's eyes, hoping to see a future for his people.

Hump lowered his eyes and replied, "*The One Who Speaks talked of how the white man will obey the treaty, but only for a few moons. Then, they will come once more.*"

Medicine Bear lowered his head in thought. He could not understand a man giving his word and then not doing this thing he has promised. If the white man could not be trusted to speak with one tongue, what was to become of his people? While the white man had many things the Sioux wanted and needed, they had also brought many things they did not want. Bear considered the spotted illness that had killed so many in this very village, the fire water that drove their braves insane for a short time, and the disease that caused a burning wetness and open sores between the legs of both a squaw and a brave. Finally, the warrior said in deep anger, "*Then we will fight!*"

Hump gave the man a few minutes to regain his composure and then answered, "*No, we will not fight. I have spoken to the council and the elders think fighting the white man is not a good thing. They have asked us to be patient and to wait. And, as we wait we will gather more guns that shoot many times, cartridges, and other things we will need in the future to fight the white man.*"

"*I see no need to wait!*"

"*Medicine Bear, the council has spoken—so we will wait.*" Hump spoke in the same gentle even tone he used when speaking to young boys. It was a voice reserved for those with little patience or no understanding of real issues.

"*I have spoken from my heart Buffalo Hump and I fear for The People.*"

Hump moved a log in the flames, met the younger man's eyes and said, "*It is good to know one's heart and mind. A true warrior must always think of The People first. A real Sioux warrior always thinks of his people before himself. I want you to go and get Moses, the old buffalo man, and the white captive. We must have them speak before the council.*"

Buffalo was brought to the dark lodge and while in pain and suffering greatly from fatigue, he knew something important was being decided. His bonds were quickly cut and he was placed near the fire, across from an old man. Watkins knew just by looking at the ancient

Sioux he was a man of importance, but his face looked as if it'd been carved from stone. Watkins knew little of the Sioux people, except talk he'd heard in saloons and he suspected most of it was pure horse shit. He licked his dry lips and glanced around at the other men sitting near the old man.

"You're in a hep of trouble heah, son." A black voice spoke from across the fire.

"Who who are you?" Watkins asked as he felt his dry lips crack.

"I'm called Moses. Take a drink of this water and then we need to talk." Moses spoke as he handed a bowl filled with water to the buffalo hunter.

Buffalo lifted the wooden bowl and had his first water in over twenty-four hours. As the water entered his belly he wondered how an old black man came to live with the Sioux. He'd heard of many blacks living with the Injuns, but this was the first one he'd ever met.

"Now that you've had some water, I need to ask ya some questions that Buffalo Hump has fer ya. Now, I suggest ya tell the truth, 'cause this old man," Moses rolled his eyes toward Hump and then continued, "ain't playin' no damned games right now. He's one pissed off Injun, too."

"What does he want to know?" Buffalo Watkins asked as he wiped his mouth off with his right hand.

Moses turned to Hump, already knowing the old chief knew what the white man had said. A few seconds of Sioux was spoken and then the old black asked, "Are you a killer of tatanka, or the buffalo as we'd call 'em?"

Watkins raised his head and replied, "Yes, I'm a hide man."

"Why do you do this thing? Do you not know it is wasteful to leave the meat to rot?" Hump was so surprised at the answer Watkins had given he spoke in English.

Buffalo Watkins lowered his head and said in a flat voice, "The money is good."

A long period of silence filled the lodge and then a quick exchange between Moses and Hump. Finally, the old man said, "Hump cain't fig'er out why you'd kill the buffalo fer money. See, Injuns ain't got no use for money. Iffen they need somethin' they trade for it or take it from one of their enemies."

"Tell him I kill the buffalo for money to buy me things that I want and need."

"Hell, he knows that much ya young fool. What he wants to understand is the why part of it all. I mean, he cain't understand why ya'd kill them buffalo fer dollars and let his people starve."

Buffalo Watkins was not only a very brave man, but also a fairly intelligent one. He met the chief's eyes and replied, "I'd not thought of
yer people or the need they have fer the buffalo. I was a foolish man,
thinkin' of only myself."

Once again Hump broke into English, though thickly accented the
hide man understood his words well, "What man does not think of others in all things he does. Only a foolish man would throw a pebble into
a lake and not know it makes the water move. As in life it is with the
water of the lake. The killing of tatanka is more than the taking of
skins, it is an act of war against my people. You, white man, are the
stone and my people are the lake and this must stop."

"Listen Hump," Moses spoke in Sioux and turned to the chief, *"I
think I've a way to make yer treaty go better with the leader of the
white army when ya meet with 'em."*

"What can be done to keep the whites from our lands?"

"You can give this white man to the long knives and show them the
Sioux are not just killers."

"I do not understand the meaning of your words."

*"Mayhap I ain't saying it right. Look, if you give this hide taker to
the army then the army will know you could have killed him, but you
did not. It'll make them understand you do not want to kill, unless you
have to do the job to protect your lands."*

Hump thought on the black man's words for many long minutes
and then he finally said, *"This giving of the white hide man I will do,
because it is a small thing. I will give him to the man with yellow
stripes on his legs, to show I have no anger in my heart. I will give him
the white man as a gift, to show I speak with one tongue."*

Moses gave a light laugh and said, *"I think that's a good idea,
Hump."* Then turning quickly to face Buffalo Watkins he said, "Son,
yer 'bout the luckiest sumbitch my old black hide has ever seen. Looks
like old Buffalo Hump heah is gonna give yer worthless skin over to the
army in two days time when he signs a peace treaty. Now, Iffen I was
ya, why I'd fork me the first hoss I could find and get the hell out of
here as fast as I could. 'Cause I guaran-damn-tee ya, if these Sioux ever
set their sights on ya again yer ass is a dead man."

Watkins felt a sense of instant relief and knew he was lucky. So,
speaking once more to the chief he said, "I thank ya for letting me live.
I will leave the land of the Sioux and never return. I leave not because
I fear the might of the Sioux people, but because I am ashamed of what
I have done."

While Hump said, *"This is good."*

Moses said, "Bullshit."

Two days later Buffalo Watkins was turned over to Colonel James E. Baldwin of the United States Army. The colonel thanked Hump for giving him the man alive and knowing he had to give the chief a gift in return, he ordered five horses and fifty pounds of sugar to be placed in front of the leader of the Sioux. At that point, the hide man forgotten, the army and Sioux sat down by the fire to discuss the details of the treaty.

Watkins lost no time leaving the place and he left with the first available riders returning to Omaha, all of who were returning to report on the progress of the treaty. The group he rode with was a small one, just four others, but they had official business to attend to in the city that couldn't wait for a larger group. The Sioux had returned Buffalo Watkins' pistol, so he would not be traveling unarmed, but they had kept the big far reaching Sharps. The small group, two army dispatch riders and two newspaper men, was just two days of easy riding east of the meeting place when they met two white men camped near a small stream in some willows. Long dark shadows were reaching out and covering the plains as the sun started going down.

It was not until he dismounted that Watkins realized one of the men at the camp had just one leg. Quickly looking the man over, Buffalo thought the one legged man could very well be Jeb Patton; however, he decided to wait and find out. He knew a short introduction would be called for, and it was then he'd make his play.

"Howdy do, I'm Ben and this feller on the log is Jeb. We was jess about to have some bacon and biscuits. If y'all like I can shave off a bit more bacon and ya can join us."

"Yer name Jeb Patton?" Buffalo asked as he neared the small fire.

Jeb looked up and knew right off he'd never seen the man before in his life. And, as far as he knew there were only two men in the world that would ask him a question like that, Crawford or the brother of the man he'd killed at Brown's Trading Post. Jeb had slipped the tong off of his pistol when the men had first rode up, so he stood slowly and replied, "Yep, I'm Jeb Patton, but I don't think I know ya."

Buffalo grinned and spread his legs apart as he said, "My name is Buffalo Watkins, does that name mean anything to you?"

Jeb gave a dry laugh and said, "I killed yer brother Frank a while back after he insulted my wife, but it was a fair fight."

"Maybe it was and maybe it wasn't, but it don't matter much to me. I'm going to kill ya, Patton."

Jeb, suspecting talk would do no good, but not wanting to kill the big man replied, "Buffalo, if ya ain't at least twice as fast as yer brother was, ya'll never do the job. Ya'll find I don't kill easy."

Buffalo's eyes narrowed and his hands moved slowly to his sides. He gave a dry laugh and said, "Ya ready to die, Patton?"

Jeb didn't answer, instead he watched the big man's eyes, knowing when he went for his gun his eyes would betray the act before he ever moved. The one legged man could hear the other men moving away from the coming fight.

Suddenly, Buffalo's eyes squinted and his right hand moved for his pistol. Just as his pistol came up hip level, Buffalo felt one and then two heavy blows to his chest, but because of his enormous strength he remained standing. Looking down he saw bright red blood flowing freely down the front of his shirt. A strong man, he squeezed the trigger to his forty-four and smiled in satisfaction as he watched the one legged man knocked backward to the ground. Buffalo was still smiling as he fired once more and then fell to his knees. After a minute or two, he fell face first to the dirt beside the small fire. The fingers on his left hand opened and closed slowly a few times, and then he lay still.

The impact of Buffalo's bullet had actually caused little injury to Jeb and he had fallen because he'd been caught off balance when the big man shot. The slug had taken him under the right arm, spun him around, and his peg leg had caught in the soil, which caused him to fall. Jeb knew the wound, while bleeding freely, was in the meaty part of his arm, had completely missed the bone. Pulling the sleeve up, he was relieved to see the bullet wound was nothing more than a shallow crease. Jeb slowly stood in the grass and looked around the camp with his pistol ready just in case any of the other men wanted to get involved. He noticed Ben was down.

"We don't want nothin' to do with any of this mister." A soldier with two stripes said as he raised both of his hands. "He was just travelin' with us and I'm army."

"I ain't got nothin' against the army." Then looking at the other two civilians, Jeb asked, "What about yer ass?"

"Hell, I don't even know you mister." One instantly replied.

The other one said, "Nope, me neither, but I suggest you take a look at your partner. From what I could tell that last bullet Buffalo fired struck him."

Jeb stood and slowly made his way to Ben's side. The man was lying on his back and he'd taken a bullet in the center of his chest. As soon as Jeb had knelt beside the young man, he noticed his breathing was irregular and is eyes were open wide in fear. Knowing shock killed many men, Jeb spoke with a gentle voice, "Ya'll be fine in a few days Ben. I'll fix ya up like new."

Ben attempted to reply, but all that came from his mouth were bloody crimson bubbles that resembled foam. His back suddenly arched in pain and his breath became a series of desperate gasps as he attempted to breath. His body gave a mighty tremble, his eyes grew larger, and there came a loud sigh from somewhere deep inside of him. And then, Ben Bacher, the white black man, died.

CHAPTER
26

Neither Cookie nor Jefferson had gone with the Sioux to sign the treaty with the white men. Both of them suspected they would not be received well if seen riding with the Indians, so they remained behind in the Village. Cookie seemed to enjoy living with the Sioux and quickly picked up some of the language, but Jefferson stayed distant and felt more than just a little fear of being round the red men. However, he did enjoy one aspect of being in the village, Faye.

The young black man had taken to spending as much time as possible with the woman and suspected there was little to it, except she was attractive and intelligent. He often fought off a deep sense of guilt as he spoke with Faye, because he would suddenly remember his wife's big smile and gentle laugh. But, Jefferson knew he could never bring his dead wife back and he attempted many times to remind himself that his wife would want him to be happy. Only, no matter how hard he tried to avoid the guilt, his dead wife stayed in his mind.

One evening as he was eating dinner with old Moses, the old man gave him a big toothless grin and asked, "Ya growin' sweet on Faye?"

Jefferson felt himself blush as he replied much too quickly, "I like her, but she's just a good friend."

Moses gave a light laugh and said, "That's the way it usually starts, don't ya know?"

"Moses, we're just friends is all. She's a nice woman and I find her interesting to talk with is all."

"Yup, that's a damn good sign son." Moses replied, leaned back on his elbows on his buffalo robe and continued, "Look, yer both young. Ya lost a wife and some youngsters, and she done lost a man and her baby."

"Well, we do have things in common, I'll agree."

Moses laughed once more and said, "Jefferson, the two of ya need each other, but I 'spect neither of ya will admit that right now. Anyways, that's all fine and dandy. See, out here a man needs a good woman as much as a woman needs a good man. And, I know fer damned sure ya cain't find a woman out heah no better than Faye."

"Well, I'll agree Faye is a good woman, but I don't love her Moses."

The old man leaned forward, brought his legs up and wrapped his arms around his knees as he said, "Maybe ya don't right now. But, it'll come, given time. 'Sides, there is another thing ya gotta think on a spell."

Confused, Jefferson asked, "And what's that?"

"I see where ya have three choices to make in the future 'bout a new wife. First, ya can go and get one in a town someplace, or ya can marry a squaw."

Jefferson chuckled and said, "Moses, that's only two choices."

Moses gave a light chuckle and replied, "I ain't done yet. If ya go to town lookin' fer a woman ya'll have to travel there and back many times, jess so ya can court her proper like. But, hell, the hard part might be ya findin' a black woman. Or, and this is number three, you can latch on to Faye. Now, before ya say no, think on this, some. Faye needs a man, jes like ya need a woman. She's a good woman, and she'd make a good momma fer all of dem young-uns ya got. Talk to her 'bout it son, I know she likes ya a great deal, 'cause she told me so."

Betty had been sitting beside the fire in silence as the two men spoke. She knew Moses as a man with great wisdom and she respected deeply him, as did most of the Sioux. Though in Sioux culture she would be considered extremely rude if she spoke now, she understood with the whites it was not the same, so she said, "What Moses speaks is true, Jefferson. Often in life a man and woman will marry with little love between them at first. Then, as they share life together the love begins to grow. Among the Sioux, love as the white man knows it exists but it's not usually the main reason for a marriage. A woman is wanted among The People for what she is, what she can do for a man, and what she can do for her people. There is more to the joining of a man and woman than love or playing under the robes. They must respect each other and have a desire to please each other in many and all ways too. But, of above it all, they must work together and make an effort to see their life together a good one."

Jefferson was quiet for a moment then said, "Well, it all makes sense when put the way you did, but I'm scared she might turn me down."

Moses chuckled loudly and said, "Hell fire, son, ya won't know unless ya ask her. I 'spect her answer might surprise the stuffin' right out of ya."

Cookie had not said a word during the conversation, but felt a need to speak now, or else his friend might pass up the chance of a lifetime, "Y'all got the right idea, but I see a small problem ain't none of ya thought 'bout. Now, when Faye was married to that Sioux warrior she got married accordin' to Sioux law, so I suspect she thought it was fine in the eyes of the Lord, but iffen she marries ya, Jefferson, she might want a preacher man."

"Your words are wise, Cookie. I think she'll consider the marriage a real marriage if a preacher does the marrying." Betty said and then broke into a big smile.

Moses suddenly gave a serious look and added, "Yup, women is funny 'bout things like that. A preacher mighten be jess what ya need, the problem is, we ain't got no preacher. But, I 'spect old man Butterfield might know of one he can lay his hands on, hell, he knows everybody fer a hundred miles around his place."

"So, go talk to the woman, Jefferson and do 'er now. If I were ya, I surely would." Cookie said with a big grin.

Jefferson gave a sheepish grin and said, "Well, I guess I should, but I ain't sure how to ask her. I mean, I courted my wife for almost a year before I asked her to marry me."

Cookie gave a slight smile and then said, "Look, son, yer a good lookin' feller, big and strong, and yer smart too. A woman would have to be pretty foolish pass up a man like ya. Ya own land, ya'll soon have a big spread, and ya'll make it out heah Jefferson. Ya got sand son."

Jefferson stood, placed his hat on his head and replied, "Okay, I'll give it a try. I mean the worse thing she can say is no, right?"

Moses laughed, slapped his right knee and said, "Well, she could just tell ya to go to hell too, but I doubt it. Go, son, and talk to her right now."

Jefferson found Faye by her lodge, scraping hides as he walked up. Kneeling beside her he said, "Faye, can we talk for a couple of minutes?"

"Okay, go ahead and talk Jeff."

"Not here, let's speak in your lodge, if that's alright with you."

Faye stood, brush her hair back from her eyes and replied, "Sure, let's go in and I'll put on some coffee."

The inside of the lodge was dark and it took Jefferson's eyes a few minutes to adjust to the lack of light. Faye added some small pieces of wood to the fire and as the flames consumed the wood the light in the lodge grew to the point the man could clearly see her face.

Putting a pot with the coffee on the fire, Faye asked, "Now, Jeff, what did ya want to talk 'bout?"

Jefferson, who'd been full of confidence when the left the lodge he shared with Moses and Cookie, suddenly felt a twinge of fear in his gut. While no longer really sure of himself, he knew some things in life had to be done, and he considered his present situation one of those things. Looking deep into Faye's eyes he said, "Faye, I think you know how I feel about you."

Faye smiled and replied, "Yep, ya like me, I think."

"Do you like me?"

"Sure, yer a nice 'nough feller, a hard worker, smart, and I think yer a gentleman too."

"Faye, I came here, today, to ask you to marry me."

The black woman's eyes grew large, her mouth fell open, and she was speechless for a minute. Finally she said, "Jeff, I like ya a lot, but "

Jefferson, fearing she was about to reject him quickly interrupted and said, "I'll take good care of you Faye and treat you like a real lady. I'll buy you things, build you a home you'll be proud of, and even get you to town as often as I can."

Faye laughed and said, "Jeff, I started to say, I ain't got much to offer a real man. Oh, I guess I look good 'nough, but I cain't read, write, or even do my numbers. I ain't got no learnin's and all I know is what my poor momma and daddy taught me. Plus, I ain't got them big manners like you got. See, when I was young girl and still a slave, I don't think my master had much in mind fer my future, 'cept to use me as breedin' stock."

Jefferson reached over and took Faye's hands in his as he said, "Faye, I want you to be my wife. Together we can make a go of it and I don't care about your lack of an education. If you want to learn more, then I will teach you to read, write, or whatever you want. But, understand right now, I would be proud to have you as my wife, even if you never learned another thing."

Faye lowered her eyes and she could feel the hot tears as they ran down her ebony cheeks. Then, she raised her head, met Jefferson's eyes and said, "Uh-huh, I'll marry ya, but we gotta have us a real preacher man. I ain't doin' no Sioux weddin' or jumpin' the broom with ya. If ya want me to be yer wife, ya'll have to find us a bible thumper. I want this marryin' to done up right in the eyes of the Good Lord, or it ain't happenin'."

Jefferson suddenly stood, gave a loud scream of joy and ran from the lodge. As the buckskin entrance flap closed behind him, Faye said with a big grin, "I never 'spected to make no man that happy and he didn't even have his coffee."

Soon the word of the coming marriage was all over the Sioux village and all were glad for the raven woman. Moses and Cookie were happy two lost souls had found each other. But, it was Buffalo Hump who was the happiest and he called Faye and Jefferson to his lodge three days after she'd agreed to marry.

Sitting beside the chief in the dim light of his lodge, Jefferson wondered what the old man was thinking. By looking at his face it was impossible to tell. Hump added some wood to his small fire and said, "I have heard that you will soon be joining into one and that is good. It is not good for the heart of a woman or a man to be alone. The Great Spirit does not intend for us to live alone, or he would not have made both a man and a woman. It fills my heart with happiness to know this thing will happen."

"What you have heard is true, my chief; we will soon leave your village and find us a preacher." Jefferson spoke, but looking closely at Hump he could not tell the man was the least bit happy about the coming marriage.

"This preacher I do not understand. What is a preacher?"

Jefferson quickly replied, "A preacher is a holy man, much like your shaman. The white man will only recognize a marriage done by a preacher man."

Hump thought for a second and then said, "That is good. A shaman can do many things for those who are joined as one. The spirits are needed when a joining takes place."

"Yes, it is good. The preacher man will use our Bible to marry us in the eyes of the Great Spirit."

"And what is this Beeble?" Hump asked, while thinking, *the white eyes may be much smarter people than I have long thought they are, if they too marry with the Great Spirits blessing.*

"The Bible is a book given to the white man and it tells of the way for us to live. It also speaks of what the Great Spirit wants the white man to do and how to do many things."

"A book is the talking leaves of the white man and I have seen it before. I think it is good that the God of the white eyes have given them a book. But it is even better if two are made into one as the Great Spirit watches and the book He has given is used."

"Faye and I feel the same way. That, my chief, is why we will leave in search of a preacher man."

Hump was quiet for a long time once more, but by now Jefferson and of course Faye had grown used to long periods of silence when speaking with the Sioux. Finally, Hump said, "The land you have asked for from the Sioux people is now yours forever. We will take nothing in return for this land. This raven woman is my daughter, in the eyes of The People, so the land is given freely as a wedding gift. But, come, I have more to show you."

Standing and following the old man they were soon standing in a meadow where the young boys stood guard over the huge Sioux horse herd. Hump motioning to one of the youths, turned to Jefferson and said, "The land I have given to you has nothing on it. I do not want a woman of The People to marry without something to call her own."

The young boy soon appeared in front of Hump with fifteen very beautiful horses.

"These horses are my gift to you, so your land will have something on it when you marry. It is not good for a warrior to marry without some wealth."

The young man was speechless, but he finally managed to say, "I thank you and my wife thanks you for these strong horses. But, always remember, in the moon of hunger, the Sioux will be welcome to share with me what food I may have."

Old Hump chuckled lightly and replied, "Of this I know, because the day you marry this buffalo woman, you also marry the Sioux people. Among my people, if one Sioux has food we all have food. If you and your wife grow hungry during the many moons of cold you can come to the Sioux and you will be fed and warmed by our fires. What we have will be yours as well."

Hump said something to the young man with the horses and the animals were driven back to the rest of the herd. Hump said, "I am proud to call you brother." And, as soon as he spoke he turned and walked away.

"My God, now that was a big surprise!" Jefferson exclaimed as he turned to Faye.

"Jeff, these Sioux be good people, if they like ya. If they don't like ya, well, they can turn mean quick like."

"Faye, do you realize he just gave me a large track of land and beautiful herd of horses, and all just because I'm marrying you?"

"Jeff, old Hump, has been like a daddy to me. And, see 'mong the Sioux when a woman in a family marries, the groom usually gives the father of that woman horses. Not so much to buy her, but to show how much he thinks she's worth."

"Now I am confused. Why did Hump give me horses instead of making me give some to him?"

Faye gave a loud unladylike horselaugh and replied, "He knows ya ain't got no hosses to speak of to give 'em, but mostly 'cause he likes us both. I think Hump wants us to be happy and these Sioux hosses are the same as cash money. By givin' us these hosses Hump sees it as givin' us a good start in life. See, we can breed 'em and sell hosses, if we want."

"Well, I'll be damned. I never would have thought an Injun would think like that."

Faye laughed once more and said, "Looks to me like I ain't the onliest one that has some learnin' to do."

Jefferson laughed and responded, "Faye, not all learning comes from a book. I suspect the two of us will teach each other a great deal over the next few years. I'll teach you from books and you can teach me from that wonderful mind of yours."

Faye grinned and said, "Yer a real sweet talkin' man Jefferson Jones, and that means I'll have to keep an eye on you. Man like ya could talk a woman right out of her mind, if she wasn't careful like."

Jefferson, having felt his courage build up the last few days, leaned close to Faye and said in a low but sexy voice, "It's not your mind I'd like you out of, but rather that buckskin dress."

Faye grinned and said, "Jeff, ya ain't never gonna be that sweet of a talker until we meet that preacher man. Once the words are spoken from the Good Book, I don't think the dress will stay on very long. It's been a long time since I was loved, but like I tolt ya the day I first met ya, I ain't that kind of a woman."

"Well, a normal healthy man will always try."

Faye leaned over, kissed Jefferson on his right cheek and said, "I promise ya Jeff, it'll be well worth the wait."

Suddenly Blushing, Jefferson replied, "Of that, my dear, I have little doubt. Now let me walk you to your lodge, because I have to get ready for a hunting trip. I have promised Night Owl to go with him to hunt buffalo and Cookie is going along with us."

CHAPTER
27

Ty and Jarel left their hotel room and slowly walked down the dusty main street of Independence, Missouri, heading straight to Crawford's room. Both of the old mountain men knew it was time start the dance and most likely it would turn ugly as hell. The two of them had agreed back in the room that Crawford had nothing to lose by fighting, and besides, as Ty had pointed out, the man was a known fighter from way back.

They entered the hotel and walked to the door to man's room door. Turning the doorknob slowly, Ty opened the door with his cocked pistol in his hand and entered the room—only to discover it was empty. Quickly looking around, neither man could see the normal things a man living in a hotel room would have out. There were no clothes, no half empty bottle of rye, nor any gear stacked against a wall. Crawford was gone.

"Now, where in the hell is he? Green said yesterday he was here in this hotel and in this room."

"I ain't sure where he's at, but he fer sure ain't here. Let's go down and speak the feller at the front desk, at least he can tell when Crawford left."

The man at the front desk was reading the local paper when the two old mountain men walked up to the desk. Lowering his paper, the balding middle-aged clerk looked over the rims of his reading glasses and said, "Yes?"

"Ya had a tall man in room twelve for 'bout a week. Do ya have any idea when he checked out?" Jarel asked, hoping the man would know something.

Turning his ledger around the clerk quickly said, "That was Mister Crider and he seems he checked out about an hour ago."

"Damn me!" Ty suddenly exploded with anger.

"Is he a friend of yours?" The clerk asked, unsure just how much he should tell the two rough looking old men.

"He's my cousin and we hoped to see 'em before he headed back home."

"Gentlemen, do you live in Omaha by chance?" The clerk asked as he removed his glasses and placed them in his shirt pocket.

"No, we've been out huntin' fer the railroad, but when we passed through Kansas City, his folks said he was heah on business."

The clerk laughed and said, "If he was here on business he must be runnin' a whorehouse, because he had a different soiled dove in his room every night. All I saw him do, and it ain't none of my business really, was drink rye whiskey and sport with the workin' ladies."

Jarel gave a fake laugh and replied, "Yup, that sounds about like my cousin. He didn't say where he was goin' next did he?"

"Well, that's why I asked if you was from Omaha. He said he was headin' out that way and as a matter of fact, he bragged a bit about his dangerous work for the army. And to hear him talk, the army couldn't run without 'em, so he had to get back and ride dispatches for them." The clerk spoke with a grin, scratched his left ear, and continued, "I did see a railroad ticket in his hand this morning as he checked out and it was for Omaha for sure."

Less than four hours later the two mountain men were riding the rails once more. Only, this time, just outside of Independence, Ty pulled a fifth of rye from his possibles bag and gulped about a quarter of it, knowing the bridge was coming up. Jarel gave a chuckle, glanced at Ty and said, "Ya relax some, we're on the boys trail and we'll get 'em. Hell, he's headed back to our country now and there ain't no way he'll get away this time."

Ty gave a weak grin, placed his bottle back in his possibles bag and then replied, "Nope, he'll not get away this time and we know he's in Omaha, so we'll get his ass."

As the train crossed over the river, Ty didn't even glance out of the window, because he had fallen asleep. Jarel let his friend sleep, knowing all the time Ty was growing older and he was not as strong or as alert as he had once been. *He's still one hell of a man though*, Jarel thought as he picked up a newspaper and started reading.

Omaha was still the same busy place it had been when the two old mountain men had been there before. After getting a room, they walked around town asking about Crawford, but experienced little luck in locating the man. Neither of them expected the search to be easy, so they went back to their room to discuss the situation and try to come up with a plan.

"So, what do we know about this man's habits?" Ty asked as he sat on the edge of the bed.

"Well, 'bout all I know is he likes women and whiskey. He ain't a huge man, so it's not likely he'll stand out to most people."

Ty gave the information a little thought and then said, "Now, to me it means he'll be visiting the saloons lookin' fer a woman. He can get his whiskey in a hotel, but he'll have to pick up a soiled dove in a saloon."

"Of course he might jess get one woman and keep 'er for the whole week, ya ever give that a thought?" Jarel said as he put his hat on the dresser and then walked over to look out the window.

"Nope," Ty replied, "I never gave that a thought a-tall, but 'cordin' to that hotel clerk in Independence, Crawford likes to try different women. I think he likes variety in women."

Jarel laughed and said, "Hard to say what the man will do. Ya know as well as I do, we'll have to play all of this by ear and see what happens."

"Well, I think, after dinner, we should hit some saloons and talk to some workin' ladies. Hell, one 'em might know something we can use. I ain't never had much dealin' with working women, but I do know that for a few coins we can get 'em to talk."

Dinner was eaten and the two men were soon moving from saloon to saloon speaking to the soiled doves. Most of the women were still in their twenties, but looked well on the high side of forty. They walked into the Cattlemen's Saloon and took a table near the back wall so they could talk to the women with some privacy. One of the two old men always sat facing the door. No sooner than they had two beers on the table than a very young and attractive woman walked over and asked, "Either of ya fellers a-lookin' fer a good time? Or, mayhap yer both interested."

Ty gave her a big grin and said, "No, we ain't. But, I know how ya can make a dollar and all ya have to do is talk."

The woman gave a big grin, pulled a chair out and as soon as she was seated she asked, "Does that include a drink?"

Jarel gave a loud laugh and as he waved to the bartender to bring her a drink, he said, "Ya drive a hard bargain little woman."

The young whore leaned forward, rested her chin on both of her palms, and asked, "Ya fellers, ain't the law, 'cause yer both too old, so what do ya need to talk about?"

Both of the mountain men waited until the barkeeper left, and as the soiled dove took a drink of her rye, Ty said, "We're lookin' fer a tall, lanky, feller by the name of John Crawford and he's a Missourian by birth."

The young woman actually spilled some of her drink as she slammed the glass down and said, "I know the sumbitch! I had him all lined up so I could make some good money off of him this week and then Laura moved in on me."

Ty and Jarel quickly exchanged looks and both men knew the other wanted to laugh, but dared not.

Ty spoke, "Ya got any idea where he's stayin' or was at. If ya, do," he placed a ten dollar gold coin on the table top and continued, "ya can keep this, plus the dollar. And, ya got a name?"

"My name, not that I want it mentioned outside of this saloon is Kattie. I spent a couple of long afternoons with 'em. But, let me tell ya, this Crawford is a man who uses a woman hard and rough when he's been drinkin'. I spent the first night with 'em, but he turned real mean after a half of bottle of rye, so we had a fight. And, well, he moved on to spend the rest of his time with Laura. Hell, she's jess as big a drunk as he is, so they'll get along fine. But, to answer yer question, he's in room 102 at the Tremble Hotel and I 'spect he'll be there a spell too."

"Ok, how do we find this hotel?" Jarel asked as he ordered another drink for Kattie just by waving at the bartender.

"Two blocks east and one north. Big assed brick building and the inside is all done up nice in red. His room is near the back door, on the right side of the hallway, and it's the last room. Hell, ya cain't miss it."

The two men stood and Ty said, "Ma'am, thank ya for the information. This Crawford man is a killer and yer better off not to be with 'em. It's a rough life ya've chosen, though I 'spect ya know that."

Kattie gave a big grin and replied, "All I got mister is my body. I ain't got no learnin's and no money, but I make do. Ya just make sure ya take care when ya find Crawford, 'cause he don't play around, especially if he's been drinkin'."

Twenty minutes later the two men were right outside of Crawford's room. On the walk to the hotel, they decided to enter the room and to try and take the man alive, if they could. But, they agreed to take no chances with Crawford, if he pulled his shooting iron, they'd shoot to kill.

Ty was surprised to find the door unlocked. He had turned the knob with his left hand as he held his cocked .44 in his right. He quickly swung the door open, and was met with a gunshot, which knocked him back out into the hallway.

Jarel stepped into the room and saw Crawford still in bed, as naked as the day he was born, but holding a smoking pistol in his right hand as he attempted to get out of bed. The old mountain man squeezed the trigger on his horse pistol and actually saw the bullet impact Crawford in the left side of his chest, and he watched as the force of the bullet spun the man around. Moving quickly toward the man, Jarel screamed, "Drop the gun, or the next slug takes ya low."

Crawford let the gun fall from his right hand and both heard it strike the floor. Falling back on the bed face down, Crawford began to moan from the pain. Jarel pulled a short piece rope from his rear pocket and quickly tied the lanky man's arms together behind his back. Glancing over at the whore, who'd passed out from drinking, Jarel pulled the sheet up to cover her big breasts.

At that point the middle-aged hotel clerk ran into the room, after a fearful glance at the wounded Ty, now standing in the hallway, he demanded in an excited voice to know what in the hell was going on.

Ty slowly entered the room and said, "Shut the hell up! Now, make yerself useful and go get us a doctor. And, round up a Sheriff or Marshal if y'all got one. We need to talk."

An hour later, Ty and Crawford had both been treated for their injuries and while neither was life threatening, they were painful. The Sheriff was a man Ty had worked with once in the army, so he listened carefully as the details of Crawford's wrong doings were explained. Sheriff Patrick O'Brien was a big man, well over two hundred pounds, six-six or so, with flaming red hair. Ty had scouted with the man a few times and while not really friends, they'd known and respected each other.

Finally, the big man said, "Ty, I'd love to help you, but there's nothin' I can do lad. I'll have to let him go."

"What! Are you crazy, Pat?"

"Ty, lad, this happened out in the mountains and I don't have the authority to hold 'em. Besides, there is no law against the killing of black folks."

"I'll be damned! He up and kills my friends and ya'll let 'em go free! Pat, what kind of justice is that?" Ty spoke with his voice filled with anger.

O'Brien didn't answer for a few minutes, but finally he pushed his hat back to the rear of his head, grinned and replied, "I just decided I'm goin' down to the saloon and have me a wee drop of the Scotch, or three. Now, I may be there for a while, because I am suddenly a very thirsty man this fine day. If you were to leave town, the three of ya, why I'd never know of it, now would I lad?"

Jarel laughed and said as he handed the Sheriff a dollar, "Have a couple of drinks on us."

O'Brien shook his head and said, "No, that wouldn't be right now, would it? It would look like I took your money as a bribe and momma O'Brien raised her boys to be honest hard working men." And, as soon as he'd spoken the big man turned and left the hotel room.

"W . . . what are you going to do to me?" Crawford asked from the edge of the bed as he glanced at the two old mountain men with deep fear reflecting in his dark eyes.

"We'll take ya back to the mountains and have us a trial, Mister Crawford, and then we'll hang your ass." Ty spoke as he adjusted his gun belt and picked up his rifle.

"For doin' what? Killin' some worthless Niggers?" The tall man asked as he realized he had little to lose by talking big.

"Them worthless Niggers, as ya called 'em," Jarel said as he roughly pulled Crawford to his feet, "were my friends and I don't take their killin's lightly."

Within twenty minutes of O'Brien leaving the hotel, the two old mountain men and Crawford were mounted up and riding at a slow walk from town, heading west. It was late in the day, almost dusk, but they'd agreed to get out of town as fast as they could. They knew the big Sheriff didn't care what they did with Crawford, but they didn't want to cause the lawman any trouble in his town.

The group continued to move through the night and it was only a couple of hours before sunup when they moved into a small grow of trees for a few minutes of rest. The horses were tired and so where the men. While not a rough ride, two of the group had been shot, so Jarel suggested they take a short four hour break. Soon, a small fire was burning and a coffee pot was placed on the hot flames to brew.

Crawford was tied to a large oak tree near the fire and covered roughly with an old worn horse blanket. As soon as the coffee was fin-ished, Jarel shaved off a few pieces of bacon and fried them in his old cast iron skillet. Pulling three biscuits from his saddlebags, he prepared a quick and simple breakfast. Releasing Crawford's right arm from the tree, Jarel sat watching the man eat and drink his coffee. The old mountain man placed his rifle on his knees with the big bore barrel aimed right at the lanky man, kind of hoping he'd try something, but he didn't.

As soon as Crawford was secured to the tree once more, Jarel said, "Ty ya get a few hours of sleep and then ya can relieve me later on. Since ya was shot, ya need the rest more than I do."

"I'll do that," Ty replied and then added with a chuckle, "since a young feller like ya don't need that much rest anyway."

"And, have a cup of whiskey before you sleep too, it'll kill some of the pain."

"By God, I'll do that too!" Ty answered and then gave a loud laugh as he moved toward the supplies.

Six days later the three neared Butterfield's Trading Post early in the morning just as the sun was peeking over the mountains. The trip had been easy, with Crawford not being left alone or untied long enough to cause any problems. As Ty and Jarel secured the three horses to the hitching post, Butterfield walked out and said, "Howdy do John Crawford, it looks like you've had a rough time of it here come late. But, relax old son, 'cause we'll give ya a fair trial, then ya'll stretch some hemp rope. I got a few boys in the store that will lock Crawford up in the storehouse fer ya two. We can give him his day in court in a couple of days."

"Sounds good to me," Ty said as he glanced at the older man, "I took a bullet and while it's healin' it is takin' its sweet time to do so. Ya got any whiskey in yer store Mister Butterfield?"

"Has a dawg got fleas on his balls? Hell yes, come on in boys and the first bottle of rye is on me."

CHAPTER
28

The afternoon passed quickly, with the two old mountain men explaining why they'd been gone so long, searching for Crawford. They learned of Jefferson's pending marriage to Faye, the death of Ben and of Jeb's killing of Buffalo Watkins. They were surprised when, near noon time, Cookie walked from the kitchen and said, "I own me a eatin' place now. I got me a place goin' up beside this tradin' post. The fellers building it tolt me it'll be done in less than a week."

Butterfield gave a loud laugh and explained, "Cookie and Jefferson caught some feller that robbed the army when they was out lookin' fer Crawford, so they got 'em a reward. But, what surprised me was when some other feller rode in heah and handed over three hundred dollars fer me to give to Jefferson. Feller said his name was John Butler and he said that Jefferson would know what it was all about, but hell, he looked like a miner to me. He had a mule he was leading loaded down to hell and back with all kinds of miner's tools and what-not."

Ty laughed and said, "Been a busy place, huh?"

"Yep, last time it was busier was when the Blackfoot attacked back in, oh, I think it was '30 or mayhap '31.

The men all laughed and then Ty asked, "Cookie, tell me 'bout this business ya got now."

"Well," the old man spoke with excitement dancing in his dark eyes, "I own it and Butterfield is gonna tell everyone I'm his favorite cook. Butterfield said he'll make it look like it's part of the tradin' post, so more folks will eat there as they pass through. Startin' to get a lot of movers out this away now days."

"I'm happy for ya Cookie. We need more men like you and Jefferson out here now that folks are moving in. The sad part is some of these movers will be just like Crawford, and that means we'll have to keep the law until we get us some marshals and sheriffs. And, I don't see that happenin' for a long spell yet." Jarel spoke as he pulled the makings of a smoke from his shirt pocket.

Over the next few day's people began to filter into the Trading Post just to witness the trial and eventual hanging of John Crawford. Ty and Jarel had postponed the trial a few days, just to let others arrive. They both knew it was a rare occasion for a court to be held in the mountains, because a man usually took care of business much faster, and with a gun. It was the morning of the third day when Jeb and his group arrived from Hump's Sioux village. What surprised Ty, was at least twenty warriors had come along just to see the white man's justice served.

"By damn, I'm sure glad to see y'all!" Butterfield spoke from his porch as Jeb and his small group dismounted.

"And, why's that Mister Butterfield?" Jeb asked as he walked up to the old man and shook his hand.

"I got me a preacher camped south of here and he's willin' to marry up Faye and Jefferson. And, I got to talking to 'em 'bout you and Betty too, so he'll give ya two a nice Christian marryin' too."

"Does the man know Jefferson and Faye are black folks?"

"Yep, and he said it don't pay no never mind in the eyes of the Lord. He's a damn good man Jeb and his name is James Montana. Big feller, but quiet. Come on in son and let's get some grub into ya folks."

After a meal of deer stew and biscuits, Jeb turned to Ty and asked, "So, when's the trial?"

"Figured we'd have it in the mornin'. We'll let yer two friends marry with that Montana feller later today and we'll do the nasty work tomorrow."

Jeb gave a low sigh and replied, "It's a sad thing with Abe gone. Ya know, I never spent a lot of time with 'em, not really, but I miss 'em like hell now he's gone."

Jarel chuckled and said, "Jeb, it's like that with all people. I guess we take 'em fer granted when they're always around, but once they're gone we miss 'em. Makes a feller stop and think a bit, huh?"

"Yep, it does me." Jeb spoke and then picked up his coffee cup. He was just about to take a drink when he heard a shot, followed by a loud scream, and then sound of a horse leaving the trading post at a gallop. Jumping from his chair he ran outside.

Cookie was lying on his back in the dirt in front of the storehouse where Crawford had been locked up, the door was open, and Jeb knew without looking the man was gone. Moving quickly to the old black man's side, he saw the wound was serious and it looked like the old man's lungs had been hit.

Raising his head slightly, Cookie said, "Sumbitch . . . jumped me . . . when I brought . . . 'em some food."

"Ya rest and don't worry about it. We caught him once and we'll do 'er again." Ty said as he knelt by the man.

Bloody bubbles came from Cookie's lips as he replied, "Won't . . . ma. . . matter to me." And, then he arched his back against a wave of pain.

"Cookie! Ya hang tough old man, we'll take care of ya." Butterfield spoke as he met Ty's eyes and the old mountain man could see the trader crying.

"Ty, come on. Cookie's in good hands right now, so let's go get Crawford. The longer we wait the more distance he's putting behind him." Jarel spoke as he led two horses up, put his foot in the stirrup and continued as he rose into his saddle, "Butterfield, ya take good care of that old man. We'll be back directly."

"Ty, do ya and Jarel want me and the Sioux in on this?" Jeb yelled from the porch of the trading post.

Turning in his saddle, Ty yelled back, "Nope, this has gone on too long Jeb. Me and Jarel will end this on our own. I want ya to stay here and be with Faye, hell, it might be a year before another preacher passes this way. We'll get 'em."

The remainder of the day was spent trailing the fast moving Crawford through the mountain passes. Ty and Jarel stopped every few hours to rest their horses and at one stop Ty said, "He's gonna kill that horse if he don't slow down some and ya know, I can't figure out why he's moving west."

"Could be he's scared and not sure where to head." Jarel replied as he removed his saddle and placed it near the fire. "Man like that gets scared and he don't think right. But, right now ya can bet yer ass he's a dangerous sumbitch, so we got to be careful how we approach 'em."

Toward midnight the snow started to fall and it fell in big lazy flakes the drifted aimlessly in a light wind, so the men stopped for a short rest. Ty always enjoyed watching a good snowfall and he was impressed by the beauty as it slowly covered the land. Jarel, on the other hand, knew the morning would most likely dawn cold and make for a hard day's travel. It was not that the younger mountain man didn't appreciate the beauty, but he had other things on his mind that evening and all of them were ugly.

"Where in the hell is Crawford headed, do ya think?" Jarel asked as he placed a log on the dying fire and then watched it flare up.

"Hell, there ain't nothin' out where he's headed, except the plains, so I 'spect he ain't thinkin' clearly. Only a fool would head out that way with snow a-comin'." Ty replied as he leaned back against a log near the snapping fire.

Jarel thought for a few minutes and then asked, "Ya figure he'll double back on us and head east toward the cities?"

"Now, that's a good question. Right now I'd say if he don't slow down some he'll kill that horse he's ridin'. Then again, if he stops long enough to start thinkin' clearly he might just double back. The key, as far as I see it, is to catch him before he turns, or we'll have to head back east and find 'em again."

"By God, I've had enough time lately with them flatlanders. Let's get a few hours of sleep and then hit the trail. Ya wake me in a couple of hours." Jarel spoke as he moved toward the shelter and his buffalo robe. Within a few minutes he fell asleep while still thinking of catching Crawford before the man turned to the east.

Crawford knew he was in serious trouble. He suspected the men at the trading post were going to hang him anyway, after a phony trial, so he had little to lose by running. What worried him at the moment was the bad weather and the fact his horse was bone tired. He slowly made his way into a small group of oak trees near the base of a big mountain and dismounted. His flight from the trading post had been so quick that all he had was Cookie's gun and the gear on the horse he'd stolen. He pulled the saddlebags off and placed them on the ground near where he intended to build his fire. The men at Butterfield's had allowed him to keep his tobacco and matches, so at least he could have a fire.

I've got to get a fire goin' or I'll freeze to death out here, he thought as he placed the makings of a fire together, *and I'm lucky the wind is light*. Within a few minutes a small fire was burning and he wrapped his horse blanket tightly around his shoulders. *I got to rest this horse a spell, or I'll end up walkin', and if I do that I'll be swingin' from the short end of a long rope in a day or two. I know they're comin', but I wonder which ones? If it's them two old mountain men, well, I'll have to kill 'em both this time. Them two don't play no games. So, I'll rest for four hours or so and then move on.*

Looking through the saddlebags he found some smoking and chewing tobacco, about a pound jerked buffalo meat, a skinning knife, a buckskin shirt, a powder horn filled with powder and about twenty lead balls in a small buckskin bag. Also, wrapped inside the shirt he discovered a box of .44 cartridges that would fit his stolen pistol. From the horse he had the blanket, saddle, a canteen, about thirty feet of rope, and an old Hawken rifle, which he could use with the powder and balls. *Well, it's not the best rifle in the world, it'll do for right now, he thought. A good Sharps would have been better. This horse must have belonged to one of them old mountain men that are always hangin' around the tradin' post. All the gear they own is as old as these mountains.*

Crawford nibbled on a piece of the jerky and dreamed of a steaming cup of coffee, but he understood he was lucky to still be alive. Finally, after he figured four hours had passed, he saddled the horse, mounted, and continued to ride west slowly. As he rode, he considered doubling back once on the plains and moving toward Omaha or perhaps further south to Missouri. He knew one thing for sure, they were coming for him and they wouldn't stop until they found him. He also knew when they met, death would come calling, for one side or the other.

The wind picked up and the weather turned worse as Crawford moved onto the open plains just a little before daylight. He now wore the buckskin shirt over his shirt and he had even pulled the saddle blanket from the horse to wrap around his shoulders, but it was still numbing cold. The snow, which had fallen so gently earlier in the evening, was now falling harder and faster. Finally, after just a few short miles, he realized he couldn't stay alive in the high winds out on the plains, so Crawford doubled back for the shelter offered by the mountains and trees. At least, or so he figured, he'd have firewood and some protection from the wind.

Back at the base of the mountain, Crawford pulled the skinning knife and trimmed enough pine boughs to make a crude shelter from the weather. Within a few moments of completing his shelter he had a small fire burning in the protection of the trees. He sat nibbling on a very small piece of the jerked meat in front of the fire when he suddenly realized the meat from the saddlebags was all he had. *I got to go easy on this jerky, until the weather changes enough so I can hunt*, he thought as he leaned forward and moved a log on his fire. The cold was numbing, even in the protection of the trees surrounding him.

The clouds remained a dark gray and low overhead. Looking up Crawford knew the weather wouldn't break this day and he knew it was not uncommon for bad weather to last four or five days out where he was. He suspected whoever was on his ass, had also been forced to hole up until the weather broke. The fatigue of the last few weeks caught up with the man and he yawned a few times as he sat by the flickering and dancing flames of his small fire. Knowing there was little he could do about the weather he leaned back on the saddle and fell asleep.

If Crawford had been asleep for an hour or for hours he had no idea. He awoke with a start, because something had awakened him, though he was unsure if it was a noise or movement. He pulled the .44 from his belt, cocked the hammer back and noticed the loud snap it made locking into position. His fire had almost gone out and only a few red embers remained in the fire pit. He thought perhaps the cold had awakened him, but no, he realized he had heard something moving nearby.

Finally, after a few seconds, he moved on hands and knees to behind a log. He cursed that he'd placed the rifle in his shelter to keep dry and he was afraid if he went for it he'd be seen. He could see little in the falling snow, but as he squinted his eyes he noticed movement coming toward him. The trail he'd used earlier was now covered with snow, so he was not worried about his tracks being discovered, and his fire was all but dead. If it was them two damned mountain men on his ass, he'd kill 'em and move on. Crawford realized the men following him would have more gear and supplies than he did, and he desperately needed those things to survive as well.

Unexpectedly, he spotted two men on horseback moving down the trail and not fifteen feet away from him they abruptly stopped. *It's that damned Jarel Wade and Ty Fisher,* he thought as he lined the sights of the pistol up on Ty's chest, *I'll end this shit right now.* Just as Crawford started squeezing he trigger, his horse moved on the picket line, nickered, and stomped his feet. Both of the old mountain men instantly dropped from their saddles into the deep snow beside the trail.

Long minutes passed before he heard Fisher call out, "Crawford, give it up son. We know you're behind the log, so we can either do this the easy way or the hard way. It don't pay us no never mind."

"Go to hell Fisher and take Wade with you." Crawford yelled back, figuring the men knew where he was so it didn't make a difference.

A shot shattered the air and a heavy slug slammed into the log near Crawford's face, stinging his right cheek with splinters. He aimed toward a slight movement and returned fire, knowing it was unlikely he'd hit anyone.

The next hour passed slowly with all three men growing cold in the wind and snow continuing to fall. Jarel moved over by Ty and said in a low voice, "I'm going to circle around and try to come up behind 'em.

I want ya to fire a few shots every now and then from different positions so he won't realize I'm movin' in on 'em."

Ty chuckled and replied, "Okay, but watch yer ass. I don't want to shoot ya by mistake. Let's say I give you thirty minutes and then ya move in on 'em."

"Alright, old coon, we'll do 'er yer way. It's too cold out here for us to keep playin' games with this boy. I'm already about froze up, its cold doin's right now."

No sooner had Jarel moved away than Ty rose up and fired a couple of shots from his horse pistol in Crawford's direction. He knew he didn't hit the man, but he wanted Crawford to think they were both still out in front. As soon as he fired, Ty moved to his right and let another shot go. Every five minutes or so he did the same thing, hoping he would keep the trapped man unaware of Jarel's movement. After about a half of an hour had passed, he fired once more and then reloaded his pistol.

All of a sudden there came five or six shots from near Crawford's position and Ty made a mad rush at the man's log. As he neared he saw Jarel standing in the falling snow and he could make out Crawford lying behind the log. He also noticed blood on the snow and realized the man had been hit.

"He dead?" Ty asked as he approached with his pistol ready.

"Nope, but he's hit hard."

"Ya ok?"

"Fine, he fired at me three times, I think, but I must have spooked his ass, 'cause he missed every single time."

Ty kicked the pistol away from Crawford's right hand, bent down and said, "He took a slug in the shoulder again, but on the other side this time and one in the right hand. He'll pull no pistols again for a long while."

"Pisses me off, I was aiming at the center of his chest when he turned and the slug almost missed. Ya bandage his ass real good while I cover ya."

Ten minutes later Crawford was back by his fire, freshly bandaged and tied at his hands and feet. Jarel threw a blanket on him as Ty pulled all of the gear from the horses and moved it all under Crawford's shelter. Placing some squaw wood on the coals of the hunted man's fire, they soon added warmth of the flames.

As the fire ate at the wood like a cancer, Ty gave a grin and said, "I think it's time we put an end to John Crawford running."

"What do ya mean? Ya wanna kill the man, after we bandaged 'em up?"

Pulling his big skinning knife, Ty replied, "Nope, I'm goin' to fix him up Injun style by cutting the tendons on each foot. That way he'll live, but by he'll never run again."

"Ty, I don't cotton to doin' this to a man. I don't mind killin' a man that has to be killed, but torture I don't take to."

Ty leaned over Crawford and with two quick swipes of his razor sharp knife he quickly severed both tendons. The tall lanky man gave a bloodcurdling scream and thrashed violently in the snow. It was a good ten minutes before he quit moving. The snow under Crawford's feet had turned a copper-red with his blood.

Ty took a large piece of cotton cloth, tore it in two and quickly bandaged both tendons. Turning to Jarel he said with a flat voice, "This man has killed too many people and he'll never run from justice again. I don't cotton much what I just did, but now we know he'll run no more and he'll be lucky to even walk. This has to end Jarel."

The storm lasted two more days and it was almost a week since they'd left that they returned to the trading post. Crawford had made no escape attempts and would not have gotten far if he had. He arrived at the trading post tied to his horse and cursing as Ty took his knife and cut his bonds. Since he was unable to walk on his own, Crawford was lifted from the horse and placed in the storehouse, and instructions were given that the door wasn't to be opened, for any reason. He was to be given food and water through a small side window that was too little for a man to use to escape.

Walking into the store, Ty asked as soon as he met Butterfield's eyes, "How's Cookie?"

Butterfield, who'd been sitting at a table sipping a cup of coffee, grinned and said, "I think he'll live, but it's hard to say right now. Usually if they can keep food and water down, they'll make 'er. That preacher man, Montana, had some learnin' as a doctor and he patched ole Cookie up as nice as you please. He claimed the bullet nicked a lung, but it should heal up in a few weeks."

"He been awake?" Jarel asked as he pulled out a chair and sat down.

"Off and on. Hell, he had a bad fever for the first few days and I fig'ered he'd go under then, but he didn't. He's a hard man to kill, Cookie is, he has grit."

"He's a damn fine man and I'd hate to lose him." Ty spoke as he also sat at the table and pulled out his twist of chewing tobacco. He cut off a small piece, put it in his mouth and then added, "That fever of his gone now?"

Butterfield met Ty's eyes and replied, "Most of it. He's still a bit hot, but nothin' like he was the first few days. I've been feedin' 'em some broth and such to keep his strength up. Hell, ya know a shot man always comes down with a fever."

"Well, did that preacher man do the marryin' of Jefferson?"

"Yep, it was right nice too, considerin' what happened to Cookie. As a matter of fact, Jeb and Jefferson are both camped just 'bout a mile from here right now, waitin' fer you two to get back. I'll send Frank out for 'em and in the mornin' we'll have us a trial. This needs to end right now and the sooner the better fer all of us."

CHAPTER
29

The next morning as a false dawn was about to break over the mountains; John Crawford was carried into the trading post and placed in a roughly made wooden chair. In front of his chair was a long wooden table with four men sitting behind it, Jeb Patton, Jarel Wade, Ty Fisher, and Jefferson Jones. A group of about ten other men filled the small room, all interested in seeing justice served.

"Mister John Crawford, ya're accused of causin' the death of three people and seriously injuring a fourth. How do you plead?" Ty asked, because as the oldest he'd been selected as the judge.

Crawford's eyes grew narrow and he spat out, "They were all Niggers, every damned one of 'em. Hell, there ain't no law against killin' 'em!"

"There is out here, and I'll take that as a not guilty plea." Ty replied.

"Kiss my ass, Ty Fisher, and ya can take that the way I just said it, too. I've violated no white man's laws and ya know it too. Hell, this court is a joke!"

"Mister Crawford, we don't have any written laws out here and ya know that as well as we do. But, ya killed or hurt good people who lived among us. Abe, the big black man you hanged, was a good friend of ours and just his death alone demands justice. Not to mention the killing of Abe's wife and Jefferson's child." Jarel spoke as he shook his head.

Suddenly, Crawford asked, "Who in the hell are ya men to think ya can hang me when I've broken no law? Ya've no right to hang me and I'll be damned if I will recognize yer authority. Yer all just a bunch of damned worthless mountain men has-beens!"

"Ya can recognize our authority or not, Mister Crawford, but it don't make a damned bit of difference to us." Jarel spoke in an angry voice, "Because out here we *are* the law."

Turning to look at the three men beside him, Ty asked as he met each man's eyes, "How do y'all see this? Is this man guilty or not guilty?"

"Guilty." Jarel Wade replied and then leaned back in his chair.

"Guilty." Jefferson agreed quickly, thinking of his dead child.

"The same with me," Jeb said and then added quickly, "guilty as hell."

"Mister John Crawford, from the state of Missouri, Phelps County, this mountain man court has found ya guilty of murder. The sentence is death by hangin' and it will be carried out immediately. Now, I heard once I'm supposed to say may God have mercy on yer sorry ass, but I ain't. I personally hope ya burn in the flames of hell forever for what ya did. Ya killed a better man than ya could've ever been. And, by God, there ain't no excuse to kill a woman or a child, none." Ty pronounced judgment, struck the top of the table with his pistol butt and then quickly stood.

"Sit back down Ty," Jeb spoke in soft voice and then continued, "I've some questions for Crawford before we hang 'em."

"Who in the hell are ya?" Crawford asked as he glared at Jeb.

"Jeb Patton, of Missouri, and I want to know why ya were looking for me a while back at Brown's trading post."

Crawford gave a loud insane laugh and replied, "Two reasons, Patton. Ya sonofabitch, ya killed my favorite uncle over a horse in Missouri. Then, I heard tell ya was shacked up with a black bitch out here."

At the word bitch, Jefferson leaped from his chair, and quickly pulled his pistol as he said, "That woman is my wife."

Crawford laughed again and said, "Well, I'm surprised ya'd want her after a white man like Patton done used her for so hard and long."

The sound of the hammer of Jefferson's pistol locking back filled the small room, but Jeb turned and said, "Jefferson, he just wants to piss you off so you'll shoot 'em. That way he won't hang. Let it go. Ya know I had nothin' to do with Faye, she's like my sister, so keep a clear head here."

"Shoot the worthless sumbitch!" Butterfield stood and yelled out. He'd been in the rye way before sunup and was feeling good.

"Butterfield, sit back down and be quiet. Try to remember this is a court of law." Ty commanded as he gave a weak grin, because he knew how the old man felt. Glancing around the room, until he spotted two huge men he knew he said, "Frank, I want ya and Clyde to pick Mister Crawford up and place him on the big bay we have outside the door. Ya'll then lead him to the big oak tree to the south of the trading post. Once there, we'll carry out the sentence. Crawford will hang from that tree for one hour."

Twenty minutes later the group was near the tree, and more than once Ty had to warn folks to stay back. He was afraid when the horse ran out from under the condemned man someone would be hurt. Crawford's hands were quickly tied behind his back and the man began to whimper as he realized his death was near.

"Ya got anything to say?" Ty asked as a rope was thrown over a big limb and a noose was placed around Crawford's neck.

Tears of fear filled his eyes as the lanky man replied, "This makes no sense and yer mostly white men. Please, let me go and I'll leave. I'll never come back."

"You have one minute to pray, then you'll get to meet God in person."

"Please, don't hang me. I'll leave, I promise."

Ty didn't reply, instead he slapped the bay hard on the rump, and as the big horse ran out from under Crawford he said, "Where yer goin' right now I know ya won't be back."

The man's neck snapped instantly, his head instantly moved to an awkward angle, and John Crawford was dead. The small group watched as the body swung from side to side and the body twitched in its death throes. Less than ten minutes later, as the body of Crawford spun slowly from the unwinding rope, the men spoke quietly of justice finally being served.

As the group broke up and the men started back to the trading post for coffee or a shot of rye whiskey, Ty looking over at Jeb said, "Well, Jeb, justice has been served this morning."

Jeb gave a weak grin, noticed the sun rising above the nearby trees, and said, "Uh-huh, and around heah death usually comes at dawn."

The End

About the Author

 **W.R Benton**, a pen name, is a retired U.S. military senior Non-commissioned Officer with over twenty-six years of active duty service. He grew up in the Missouri Ozark Mtns., where hunting, trapping, camping, and other outdoor activities were the norm. Additionally, he spent more than twelve years teaching survival and parachuting procedures to U.S. Air Force personnel as a Life Support instructor. Mister Benton has an Associate's Degree in Search and Rescue, Survival Operations, a Bachelors Degree in Occupational Safety and Health, and a Masters Degree in Psychology near completion.

Mister Benton is a member of the America Authors Association (AAA). You can visit W.R. Benton online at http://www.wrbenton.net or his *War Paint* Site at http://www.warpaint.info.

Visit him on Facebook at
www.facebook.com/wrbenton01

Green River
The Drum Series, Book 3

Available in paperback & for the Kindle at Amazon.com

The Drum series continues:

When Green River confronts a loud-mouthed banker's son in a saloon brawl, it results in a heap of trouble for the old man mountain man. The banker, Perigo, owns over half the town and he has his greedy heart set on owning the other half too. Jeb Patton is in town visiting family when he's drawn into the situation. The cattlemen are watching helplessly as their herd is suspiciously thinned. Jeb's own uncle too has lost many steers, so Jeb agrees to look into it. Before he can find any proof of what's going on several of the white ranchers accuse the Sioux of rustling and the army is called in. Jeb must find proof of his theory or a range war between the Sioux and whites is coming.

Jeb realizes he's kicked over a hornet's nest he can't handle alone. He enlists the help of two aged mountain men, and a runaway slave to help him. If Jeb and his friends can't uncover some solid evidence of the banker's involvement, the town will have a full scale war on it's hands.

Strong characters, suspense, and quick-paced non-stop action add strength to this already exciting series. As you've come to expect from W. R. Benton, this one's another page turner!

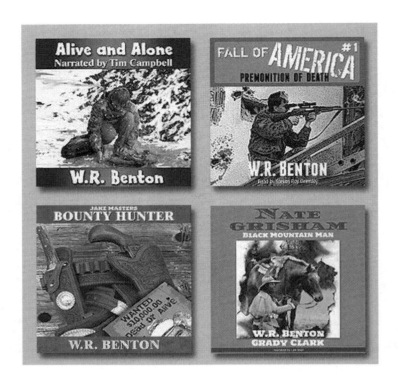

Audiobooks by W.R. Benton

Available now at Audible.com and iTunes

38976678R00132

Made in the USA
San Bernardino, CA
18 September 2016